SEVEN SINS OF SNOW

LOXLEY SAVAGE

This is a Reverse Harem Paranormal Romance and is not suited for those under the age of 18.

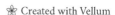 Created with Vellum

COPYRIGHT

SPECIAL THANKS

Huge thank you to my husband and my girls who support me in all that I do.

Special thanks to my alpha readers, Kelly Ryan and Kala Adams. Without your love and support, Snow would have never made it off the ground.

Special thanks to my beta team, Harley Quinn Zaler, Desiree Hayman, Angelique Helmrich, Katie Redmond, and Jordan Simpson. Thank you all for your honesty, your time, and for making me laugh through this process.

DEDICATION

This books is dedicated to my Dad who passed away while I was writing this. I was able to channel my sorrow and poured it into this book. I miss him so damn much. So, though you had no idea what I wrote, this book is for you Daddy. Xo

AUTHORS NOTE

This book is not a children's fairytale. This book is filled with darkness. Snow will suffer, before she gets her happy ending. Some parts of this might not be easy to read, so take heed to my warnings before diving in.

In this book you will find dirty language, torture, explicit sex with multiple partners, m/m relationship, blood play, and various types of kink.

If such material triggers or offends you, please do not read this book.

If you are a dirty, kinky shit like myself, then by all means, dive right in.

PROLOGUE

I have to run faster.

The queen's elite huntsmen are not far behind me, I can hear their footsteps pounding against the damp stone as I escape. My bare feet shred open on the rocky ground, my soles turning into bloody ruins.

But still, I run.

I have to get away.

If they catch me, it will mean my death.

The streets of Riverwood twist and wind, leaving me confused as to where I am. Since my evil stepmother imprisoned me, I haven't been allowed to take walks through the town, banished to my room like a caged animal.

Swollen raindrops crash to the earth, soaking my nightgown and chilling me to the bone. My legs tremble from exertion, my arms shaking as I pump them by my sides.

But still, I run.

The sound of horses grows louder, the huntsmen gaining on me faster than I can get away.

I have to hide.

Then I see it.

Or should I say...him.

A lurker, beckoning me with one pale finger.

Rumors have long spread across my lands. Whispers of monsters disguised in human form. Every sighting tells the same story—they are seen lurking in the dark corners of Riverwood, watching the populace with hidden eyes, lingering far too long under a cloud's shadow. Their descriptions are always the same— tall, cloaked, and hooded, with pale skin and sultry, crimson lips. They lure you with their guise. Beckon you with their smooth words and addictive scent. If you're not careful, they will catch you.

Take you.

Make you one of their own.

I'm drawn to this creature in spite of knowing their proclivity for ensnaring their victims. Veering off course, I run toward him, only for him to vanish when I get close.

"She's down there!" a huntsman calls, blocking the narrow alley I'm racing down. The sound of my feet splashing through puddles echoes off the confining walls as the huntsmen draw nearer.

Lightning cracks, illuminating two more lurkers at the end of the alley. They are just like the others, their hoods lowered over their faces, hiding from sight. And just like the others, they each beckon me with one pale finger. Lure me. I'm helpless not to obey.

I will my legs to move faster as the whinnies of the evil queen's horses grow louder and louder. I reach the lurkers and lunge toward them, only for my fingers to grasp the rain saturated air. Crying out, my heart crashing against my chest, I scurry down the path they were on and smash right into the chest of another.

Jerking back, I observe him standing under an awning with seven slash marks carved into it. His body is hard and cold, like a corpse once rigor mortis has set in. I raise my gaze to his smooth chin, his plump red lips, and his skin that seems to mimic the glowing of the moon.

2

My pulse thumps inside me, hands shaking as I reach up to remove his hood and—

"Snow!"

CHAPTER 1

I jolt awake from my dream to the shrieking of my stepmother, cursing her existence. I almost had him this time. My chest had been pressed against his, my fingers pinching the fabric of his cloak.

"Snow!"

I ignore the screeching, my response to her shouts is needless. Should she want to enter my room, she will, and there's nothing I can do about it.

Lying in bed, I maintain eye contact with the chandelier dangling above me even as the door opens and evil itself stomps to my side.

"Don't ignore me, child, or I'll have you whipped for your insolence."

Her voice crawls over my skin like an invasion of skittering insects. I'm repulsed, wanting to recoil from her harsh words and potent threats while her power infiltrates my room. But I remain still, staring at the crystals as they reflect the candles' flames, causing them to dance across my walls. I remain still as the insults fly from her thin lips.

"You're ugly, worthless, and lazy, a disgrace to your

father's name! It's no wonder you remain unloved and unwed. Who would want to marry you?"

It's nothing I haven't heard before, though when she brings the memory of my father into her harassment, it makes my fingers twitch. She's jealous of me, and in her jealousy she's found solace, drowning in rage. I'm baffled by the fact that she's yet to scar my face permanently, disfiguring my beauty. I hear her at night, her cruel voice carrying through my castle's empty corridors, whispering to her ancient mirror, beseeching it to tell her who is the fairest of them all. In spite of her anti-aging spells, her youthful elixirs, the mirror always responds the same way. *Snow is the fairest, my queen.*

Much to my surprise, during one of my excursions from my castle, I heard the townspeople speaking of my beauty. I had no idea physical appearance was regarded so much, since all I want is for someone to treat me fairly.

Her anger brews when I don't respond, her hot breath fanning my face as she leans down close. Still, I keep my expression stoic. One wrong move and she'll have my back filleted.

I lick my lips, ready to grovel, not wanting another beating today. "I'm sorry, Stepmother—"

"Don't you dare call me that! You're no child of mine!"

A slap lands on my cheek, stinging my skin before she takes a bite of her red apple. I wince in pain, though I'm smiling inside. I call her stepmother to fuck with her. It's the only slipup for which she'll let me go unpunished. Even when my father was still alive, she hated when I referred to her as such. Back then, when I was a young girl, I was instructed to call her mother only. We kept up the facade for years, pretending we were the perfect royal family. My dad eventually succumbed to whatever magic she possesses, becoming almost as cruel as she was until she finally killed him. It's been almost two decades now since my father has passed, and every day that trickles by without him becomes harder and harder.

She takes another bite then shouts, "Get up, child! The servants will be here in moments to get you ready. A suitor has just arrived, and I expect you to accept his proposal."

Of course she does.

The suitors, as the evil bitch likes to call them, come from all walks of life, seeking to use me for their own gain, and all are just as nefarious as she is. The transaction of my life would be mutually beneficial to her and any man whose proposal I accept.

But I never will.

I pull myself up and kneel at her feet, keeping my head low and eyes averted. Catching her gaze for the smallest second is cause to be thrown in the dungeons.

"Yes, moth—my queen."

Her slim fingers wrap around my chin and she pulls my head up, wanting me to slip, to give her a reason to toss me in one of her miserable cells. We've played this game for too long, danced as opposing partners. She won't win, but I won't lose. It's a stalemate.

"See that you do, child. Your back might not survive the talons of my whip should you not." Her threats are not empty promises, she means every fucking word. My blood simmers as she pushes my face away from her and storms from the room, tossing her half-eaten apple behind her.

She's always eating red apples and leaving the cores for me to find. I'll find them in my bath when I thought I was alone. I find them under the lids keeping my food warm. It's like her calling card, letting me know she was there and I wasn't able to see her.

Letting out a sigh, I mentally start preparing for another abysmal night. The servants she's sending aren't just here to do my makeup and bind me in another uncomfortable dress.

No.

They will also be preparing my body in the most embarrassing ways. You'd think I'd be accustomed to it after all these years, but I've never gotten used to the invasion of privacy.

With a sigh, I get up and walk toward the ornately decorated mirror hanging over my vanity. Crystal bottles filled with expensive scents rest on a mirrored tray, ready for use. Drawers line both sides, stocked with makeup from the ends of the world. Priceless colors in embellished cases meticulously spaced in the velvet-lined drawers, but none hold any joy for me. The makeup is another means the queen uses to control me.

Normally, she would select harsh colors that clash with my white skin in order to make me look less appealing when we're seen together in public. But on days when a suitor comes to potentially rid her of me, that changes. Enlarged, unflattering outfits are tossed aside in place of exquisite gowns, woven with threads of gold. Pearl buttons and flowers made from diamonds adorn each one, making me sparkle like the chandelier.

Footsteps rushing down the hall outside my door alert me that the servants have arrived. Turning to face them, I sigh and wait for the process to begin. As usual, a pair of guards flank the team of two women and one man. The queen insists on having guards here to ensure I allow the servants to prepare me exactly to her instructions.

I think she does it as another means to belittle me, to embarrass me, having men look upon my body by her orders. But her shots have backfired.

The portable table is wheeled in, and a servant not much older than myself gestures for me to lie upon it. With shaking hands, I tug at the strings holding my thin nightdress up and allow the fabric to pool at my feet.

The lust-filled stares of the guards make the hairs on my body rise to attention. Try as the queen might to get them to hate me, their desire for my body will always override her dark intentions.

The stone tabletop is cold against my skin, chilling me to the bone as I lay down on my back. "Sorry, princess," a servant named Sherry whispers, so low I almost can't hear her, as she straps my ankles into the buckles at the end. Another servant called Enid grabs my wrists and lifts them over my head, fixing them to another set of leather straps.

I don't resist, knowing if they fail to prepare me to the queen's standards, they will also be tortured. As much as I hate my stepmother, I love my people and I will do anything to protect them. I'd give my life for these servant girls if they needed me to.

And they'd give me theirs.

As their hands whisper along my skin, preparing me for waxing, I see the smallest hint of a snowflake tattoo peek out from their sleeves. My heart warms at the sight—the symbol of the rebellion. My evil bitch of a stepmother doesn't know it yet, but the people are sick and tired of her tyranny and are banding together, ready to take on her armies when I can finally find the nerve to lead them.

But the time isn't right.

Don't ask me how I know that. Call it intuition, but I know in my soul we must continue to wait. To bide our time. The stars will align one day, and when they do, she'd better be ready. Because I'm bringing all the demons in hell with me to take her down once and for all.

Floral scents perfume the air as the wax melts from solid to liquid. My skin prickles with goosebumps as the first layer of hot wax is slathered on my underarms. I grimace as they pull it off without warning, my skin stinging in response. With the male servant watching with his yellow eyes, they must treat me passively, for anyone who shows me a speck of humanity will be reported to the queen. Sherry treats my other side as Enid places a warm cloth on my skin immediately after to help reduce the reddening. Heaven forbid I have reddened armpits when this piece of shit suitor comes to evaluate me for purchase. Everyone knows he will be interested in other things.

The male servant, whose name I don't know, surveys my body with hunger. His eyes trail from my nipples to the place where my legs meet. I want to squirm under his lecherous gaze, but as Sherry smears wax on my lower lips, I hold still, not wanting that wax to touch sensitive places it shouldn't.

I let my mind wander to my dream as Sherry pulls and Enid soothes, repeating the action all over my body.

The lurkers.

I almost had them this time. The legends tell of an ancient species that once inhabited these lands. Creatures who lived underground in vast caves carved into elaborate castles. Seven kings rule their underground kingdom, each one wielding a deadly sin. In the back of my mind, I've always thought the lurkers would be my destiny or my doom, my very existence no more than a bug in their palms, ready to crush should they see fit.

Much to my relief and disappointment, I've yet to see one that wasn't in my dreams, but I hope to someday. And when I face the lurkers, I'll look death in the face with open arms.

When I'm flipped over to my belly, I'm pulled from my daydream and back into the recurring nightmare that is my daily existence. With my arms now crossed above me, someone prods at my ass and spreads my cheeks apart to get any stray hair that might be lingering. It's mortifying, having someone look at the place you shit from, but I do it for the people.

Interesting that the male servant seeks to perform that last task, spreading my cheeks apart and applying the wax. His fingers drift to places they are not allowed as he pretends to be grabbing the wax. Bound, I'm helpless to thwart him, and even if I could move, what good would it do? I don't worry about him penetrating me. The queen insists my virtue remains intact. It works to her benefit. A selling point. Suitors pay well for a virgin princess.

The man continues his searching. The yellow glint in his eye tells me he's under the queen's spell, so I lie here while his fingers wander. Sherry eventually regains control and pulls off the wax, much to his dismay. The girls flip me once more and begin the arduous process of washing my body.

Still tied to the table, the women gather warm cloths doused in expensive soaps and lather my skin. The male grabs one too.

"We've got this, Martin. Why don't you start on her nails?" Sherry suggests.

But Martin will not be swayed. "The queen wanted this bitch clean, and I intend to see her orders fulfilled. Just look how dirty the little wench is. Her tits look like she's been rolling around with the pigs."

That's a lie.

I'm as clean as can be, having not escaped for at least two weeks now. I bite my lip, trying not to give him the satisfaction of knowing he's gotten to me as he scrubs my chest roughly. The women watch me with sad eyes, and I try to tell them with a look that it's okay. I offer them a weak smile as they get to work on my hair and legs.

Thankfully, while Martin thoroughly cleans my breasts and nipples over and over again, Enid is able to sneak between my legs. She's gentle and not overly attentive, washing me as if I was a piece of furniture. For that, I'm grateful.

Sherry scrubs my hair as Enid gets fresh towels and dries my skin. She pats my body dry, knowing if she rubs it will only lead to my skin reddening like my chest has now from Martin's ministrations.

Once my hair is rinsed, the women lower my arms and allow me to sit up before binding my wrists behind me and lowering the table. A robe is draped over my back, giving me the illusion of modesty as the women begin on my hair and makeup. Sherry uses some sweet-scented oil, running it through my wet strands to tame my usually unruly hair, then scrunching them to encourage ringlets to form. The long, black strands respond and curl nicely.

Enid whispers soft orders for me to close my eyes or pucker my lips as she applies makeup. Dark gray tones on my lids bring out the bright blue of my eyes. She brushes red on my cheeks to add some color to my pale face, then finishes with a crimson lip stain.

Martin stands back, watching like some voyeuristic pervert. His fingers twitch like he is going to make a move, but instead, he stands stoically.

Watching. Waiting.

Enid adds more black to my already dark lashes, then takes a step back. She looks at me as if I were an image she painted on a blank canvas, her eyes searching to see if she's left out a stray bird or cloud.

Satisfied, she bustles behind me and helps Sherry pin some of my hair up and out of my face. Without Enid protecting my front, Martin makes his move.

My nipples peak as he "accidentally" knocks the robe off my shoulders, dropping it into the basin of water on the ground. The guards snicker from their position at the door, their not so quiet whispers of naughty things they want to do to me filtering to my ears.

Martin grabs a bottle of body oil and dispenses a generous amount into his palm. He rubs his hands together like a greedy banker hovering over his gold, then places his hands on my body.

At first, he starts like he should, massaging the oil into my neck and shoulders, but as he works his way down to my chest, his fingers become more exploratory, less dutiful.

Enid, seeing what Martin is doing, leaves Sherry and comes to my aid. She scoots him out of the way and finishes oiling up my body.

After they've finished, I'm escorted down from the table and brought over to a slightly raised platform facing a full-length mirror. My feet are once again slipped into leather buckles as they bring over my dress for the night, another way the evil bitch seeks to belittle me, making me less than the servants tending me.

The gaudy ensemble hangs from a hook on the wall, just like all the others. Ivory lace, diamonds, and pearls make up the gauzy gown.

"Arms up, princess," Enid whispers. I oblige and lift my freed wrists into the air. The women gently lower it over my body, and after they do, I'm horrified. It's unlike the other dresses I've worn to greet suitors.

It's barely there.

The base material is practically see-through, and strategically placed pearls and diamonds have been sewn in to hide my pink parts.

Oh, hell.

Now the whole castle will see me. My cheeks heat with frustration. I'm not embarrassed of my body, but it's hard to lead a group of people who've basically seen you naked.

The strapless dress is cinched in the back as the girls

13

button me in. A deep V dips low between my breasts and down past my belly button. Three small, gold chains link the two halves together. I worry they might burst, causing my breasts to spill right out.

The skirt is long and flowy, something a princess would be expected to wear. Enid clasps earrings to my ears as Sherry places my crown upon my head.

I finally look the part. Regal, beautiful, and enslaved. I've always wondered why my stepmother didn't kill me like she did my dad. She clearly has no love for me, so why not dispose of me? But in her greed, she's allowed me to live.

Suitor after suitor come hailing to the castle, seeking my hand, each as smarmy as the next, their pockets filled with gold and jewels to buy my obedience. I'd sooner die than live a life with them. I can see their sinister plans for me by the glint in their eyes, and that's why I refuse each and every one. They don't want me for who I am, but what I am.

Next in line for the Riverwood throne.

Fairest in all the lands.

Princess Snow.

CHAPTER 2

*T*he long walk to the ballroom is most uncomfortable. Heeled shoes squish my feet and force me to waddle like a duck to prevent myself from falling. The guards flank me, each gripping my upper arms as if I'll run for it at any moment. I won't, not today. Fleeing in this flimsy dress in a pair of painful shoes will cause me to get caught sooner rather than later.

Gilded, framed paintings of my long-dead relatives and ancient tapestries illustrating whimsical beasts line the halls. Ornamental tin soldiers stand at attention with their axes and long swords in tow, their armor shining as we walk by. I've wondered why the evil bitch hasn't taken them down. Maybe somewhere in her dark heart she once actually cared for my father.

Unlikely.

The more reasonable option is that it benefits her. Any guest of the castle is always led down this corridor. It's almost as famous as the castle itself. But I find no happiness here under the stern gazes of my ancestors. They can't help me if they're dead.

The guards turn sharply, their grip on my arms tightening painfully. I know I'll have red marks in the shape of finger-prints once they finally release me. The queen will be most unhappy about that.

I laugh to myself, knowing the guards will get a beating for leaving a mark upon me moments before a suitor is set to undress me with his eyes. My feet already ache, my exposed skin chilled in the cool castle. At least a hundred hearths decorated with elaborately carved mantels are scattered throughout the castle. It should feel warm and inviting inside, like it did before she came into my life. But the hearths remain empty and cold, as vacant chambers have taken the place of the roaring fires. It fits the dark person-ality of my evil bitch of a stepmother.

The golden double doors, leading into the ballroom, gleam in the light of a massive chandelier. Guards stationed outside swing the doors wide as we approach, causing us to not even break our stride.

The moment we pass over the threshold, my arms are freed, and I'm once again allowed to control my own move-ments. I stop just beyond the door, my head lowered, and wait for instructions.

My nose itches with the potent scent of some masculine cologne. It's overpowering the space, making me want to sneeze and gag at the same time. The only reason to douse one's self with such an exorbitant amount of perfume would be to hide ailments.

Smelly ones.

My guess is it's his breath. Images of rotten teeth and bleeding gums run through my mind. I've seen it before, particularly in the older suitors who've lost their first wives and want to buy me to improve their status.

Many are old enough to be my grandfather.

Gross.

Even with my head bowed, I can still see the ballroom. White pillars line the outer walls, carved with elaborate floral patterns. The tiled black and gold floor has been meticulously cleaned, leaving not a spot or smudge to be found. Against the far wall rests one of my father's many thrones, but instead of the man I once loved presiding, the evil bitch has taken his place.

I can see her spiked crown resting on her perfectly styled white hair, her harsh makeup, and her velvet dress with a plunging neckline. I see her cape billowing off her back as she stands and stalks over to me, and hear the clicking of her heels against the tile, all without even glancing up.

The tips of her pointed shoes enter my vision. Her breath fans my neck as she leans close to my ear. "Do as I ask and your back may live to see the light of another day." I suppress a shiver, reliving a recent memory of her whip's kiss lashing across my skin. I must not have hidden my body's reaction because she chuckles quietly. "Didn't like your last meeting with the duke, did you?"

The duke.

It's what she calls her whip. No matter what she's wearing, whether it be a classy ballgown or riding gear, the duke is tucked neatly at her side. Some speculate she uses it for protection, but I know better. The menacing weapon is meant to scare others into obedience.

And it works.

One session from the duke will stay with you for the rest of your life. My back can attest to that, having endured at least a dozen sessions. Each time I deny a suitor, she throws me in the dungeons for days, cold and naked, with no food and only rainwater filtering through the stone ceiling to drink.

After I'm weak and frozen to the bone, she allows me out,

ties me to the pole in the center of my father's orchard, and whips me bloody. I usually pass out after the tenth lashing.

I still don't understand the logistics of her requiring me to verbally accept the hand of a suitor. She has the power to give me away, and each suitor has more than enough money to purchase me and my status. There must be some ancient magic that protects me, giving me the final say as to whom I'll spend the rest of my life with.

So far, each suitor has been worse than their predecessor, and I've denied each and every single one. Knowing another stay in the dungeons followed by a whipping is in my near future doesn't help to calm my nerves.

I lick my lips and nod imperceptibly. I can feel her smirk, though I don't look up to see it. "Good girl," she whispers as she turns abruptly, the hem of her cape almost smacking me in the face. I hate it when she calls me a "good girl," just like she hates it when I call her "stepmother." It's another one of those dances we partake in together. Something about the term makes me feel less than the woman I am.

And that's the whole point in using it. To belittle me. To anger me. She does try so hard, the evil bitch, to rile me, giving her an excuse to punish me more often. But after years of becoming an exceptional player at her games, she almost always fails.

"Count Mervin Von Krinklecrumb, may I present my daughter, Princess Snow."

I restrain a snicker at his name. Von Krinklecrumb? Is that even real? And has there ever been a name in history less attractive than Mervin? I don't think so.

My feet begin to move up the aisle, even though my mind doesn't want them to. Each step is a lashing against my back, knowing the consequences I will suffer for my denial of his offering, and I force myself not to jerk recalling the sting.

Inwardly, I cringe when he takes my hand and kisses the

back of it. His lips feel like sandpaper. Swallowing down my revulsion, I manage to respond appropriately. "Pleasure to meet you, sir."

I can feel his lips smile against my hand. "The pleasure is all mine, princess." The decayed scent of a chronic mouth infection wafts over me. I was right. No amount of cologne could hide it.

My nostrils burn when he keeps talking. "Rumors of your beauty have reached my lands, but I never imagined someone as fair as you."

Fair.

That wonderful, awful word.

Fairest of them all...

"Thank you, sir." I tug my hand out of his and clasp both of mine in front of me.

"You may look at me, princess."

Fuck.

I don't want to look. I don't want him or the queen to see the repugnance in my eyes, the disdain, the absolute revulsion.

But I must.

Starting with his well-polished shoes, I allow my eyes to trail up his blue pants which are tucked into bright white stockings. I allow them to appreciate the ornate belt buckle, the fine three-piece suit with gold buttons, and the lace shirt peeking through his coat where it covers his wrists, which matches the ascot around his neck.

Then our eyes connect and I almost vomit. The man must be fifty years older than me, and though I'm not opposed to being with an older man, this one already has one foot in the grave. With hair as white as my skin, a mouthful of decaying teeth, and more age spots from heavy use of cigars and alcohol than healthy skin, the man looks like a corpse.

His neatly cut hair and finely trimmed beard can't

disguise the yellow hue to his skin and eyes, nor can it hide the gullet jiggling under his chin. His expensive suit cannot conceal the giant belly his buttons are straining to hold back. The fancy rings on his fingers are unable to mask the cane he clings to any more than the wicked smile could shield the malevolent intentions in his beady eyes.

The same beady eyes trail over my exposed skin, his gaze penetrating my barely clad body, making the tiny package in his pants twitch.

This man means me harm, and lots of it.

He's no Prince Charming, no prince at all.

He's as evil as my stepmother, only absent of magic. But he won't need magic to have his way with me. All he needs are a few guards to aid him, to subdue me with potions before he takes me.

No.

I choose the duke once more.

I can feel the blood draining from my face, knowing my fate. The evil bitch must sense it, too, as she shifts on her heeled shoes in agitation. "The count is a perfect match for you, dear. His castle is vast, his lands plentiful. You will live in comfort, taken care of with servants at your beck and call all the days of your life. All you need to do is say yes."

Just one simple word and I could be rid of her forever. But in saying yes, I'd not only be forfeiting my own life, but the future of my kingdom. I'm the only one who can over-throw the evil bitch sitting on my throne. Someday, it will all come down to me, and she will rue the day she killed my father when I seize her throat and watch the life leave her eyes.

The ballroom grows silent, the count's wheezing the only noise to accompany my beating heart.

Finding my resolve, I look into the count's squinty, yellow eyes and clearly state, "No."

His smug smile falters, crimson heating his cheeks in his fury, making his yellow skin look bruised. His anger causes him to breathe harder, engulfing me in the nasty stench of his mouth.

I take a step back as the air grows thick with the evil bitch's power. Smoke snakes along my skin and crawls down my throat, choking me. Forgetting my place, I sink to my knees, scratching at my neck for air. My vision blurs as I fall to my back, gasping for a breath.

The chuckling of the guards as they watch me diminishes until it sounds as if they are far away. I almost wish for her to end me now, to pull me from this misery into whatever the afterlife has in store.

But she doesn't.

"Strip her of her crown and tear that gown from her body. Animals don't deserve clothes."

As my vision darkens, the feeling of several hands on my body causes me to curl up on the ground. Hateful hands pull off my crown and rip my earrings out, while others shred my gown into pieces. If I had a breath I'd cry out as the brutal kicks crack already fractured ribs and threaten to break my teeth. But I know something she doesn't. Giving in to the pain brings me to a place of euphoria, a place where I float among the clouds, where nothing and no one can hurt me anymore.

She releases her magic from my body and the beatings stop. Her clicking footsteps falter when she crouches down beside me and puts her fingers around my throat. "You chose wrong, wench. After you spend a few days in the dungeons, the duke will be waiting for you."

Her potent threats ensnare all my thoughts as I pass out into pitch-black darkness.

CHAPTER 3

*G*roaning, I peel my eyes open to see which cell I'm in this time. I'm surprised to find I'm not shackled to the wall in an old pair of rusted manacles. Sometimes, when I'm not bound in here, I wish I was because the ground is damp and frozen. With my wrists bound above my head, the restraints hold me up over the icy liquid and frozen stone, even when I grow tired of standing. I'd sacrifice numb fingers and hands to have my body elevated off the floor.

But today, it seems the evil bitch has other plans.

I shouldn't even say "today," because I have no idea if it's day or night. The cell harbors no windows nor candles to emit light, or even the faintest whisper of warmth. It's only a stone prison.

The queen was always awful, but things didn't go from bad to worse until that dreadful mirror showed up one day shortly after their wedding. She claimed to my father that she found it in a shop on a trip to visit her own mother several days away by horse.

I never believed her lies.

Either she sought out this mirror, wanting to possess its power for her own personal gain, or it was always hers, hidden away until she saw fit to unearth it from concealment. I told my father the truth after catching her speaking to the mirror like an old friend, plotting her course to take over the throne.

But he had quickly fallen under her spell, his blue eyes turning red. That's when everything started to change. The servants I'd considered aunts and uncles, having lost my mother at such a young age, turned against me. I don't hold it against them, they have no control over it. But I hope that one day, when I overthrow the queen bitch, they will remember the love they once had for me.

The windows I would open to let the warm breeze filter through my room were barred. A pair of mated parakeets I kept as pets in a grand cage in my room went missing.

The love from my father's eyes faded.

I try not to dwell on the past, but with nothing else to bide my time, no lessons or books, no conversation, it's all I have to keep my mind from turning insane.

In the darkness of my cell, I can feel the moss growing along the walls and smell the mold lurking in the blackness. Silence is my only companion. Occasionally, a rodent will skitter inside my chamber and attempt to nibble on my fingers. Much to my surprise, when I tell them to leave me alone, they do. I wonder if they'd fetch me some bread if I asked.

"I must be going crazy," I mutter to myself. The idea that a rat would respond to my requests is absurd. Seems the queen's magic has done a wonder on me this time.

My belly rumbles and I lick my parched lips. Dehydration and starvation are two of the many punishments the evil bitch inflicts upon me. But I'm used to not eating. Even when I'm in the castle, the food I'm given is scarce. The armed guards perched outside my room don't allow me to pass to find sustenance when my body needs it.

Instead, I'm forced to wait for one of the servants to bring me something when the evil bitch allows it. A carrot stick, one piece of celery, and leftovers from her own meals filled with half eaten potatoes and cold meat are often my meals. A red apple always accompanies them, usually just the core. I find no happiness in food anymore.

But some days, when a servant still loyal to me feels brave, or when the queen's had too much to drink, foods other than that make their way into my room. The servants have to hide things like desserts from the guards who have all been bespelled by the queen, making sure any aromas from freshly baked items have dissipated before rolling their food cart into my room.

Though I'm grateful to taste something sweet, my body has grown accustomed to the vegetables I'm given, and I'm often left with a stomach ache after consumption.

Shifting, I try to find a more comfortable position on the ground. My bare ass is frozen on the stone, my spine chilled against the walls. I'd give anything for a blanket, or even an elevated bench to get off of this frigid, damp floor.

Part of the torture is not knowing how long I'll be stuck down here and the inability to tell how much time has passed. Sometimes I'll run my hands along the stones and count how many it took to make the walls, ceiling, and floor. I trace my fingers along the scratches embedded in the rock and make up elaborate escape stories for those who made them.

Huddled in the darkness, my mind wanders to the lurkers. Legends claim they are monsters sent to eat us alive, but if they are, why don't we find bodies of the dead? Why aren't our fields strewn with carcasses of deceased citizens? Why are our crops thriving better than ever? Our farms flourishing? Even as the queen's darkness hides the sun from our eyes.

Maybe the lurkers are responsible for some of the goodness in Riverwood. Maybe they are just misunderstood...

If they even exist in places other than my dreams.

A shiver runs through my body, the start of many, the beginning of my delirium. Goosebumps prickle my skin, searching for any morsel of heat. But they'll find none. Deep underground, warmth doesn't exist. There is only cold, dank darkness.

I DON'T KNOW HOW MUCH TIME HAS PASSED WHEN I WAKE UP. All I know is my body aches. Bruises from the punishing kicks I suffered through throb along my ribs, and my fingers and toes feel thick with numbness.

I blink my eyes open and find utter darkness still surrounds me. I try to stand, wanting to move around and get the blood flowing through my limbs, but discover my body is virtually unresponsive. Tremors hard enough to chatter my teeth are constant now, zapping the little energy I have left.

My tongue feels swollen inside my dry mouth, my teeth covered in a fuzzy film that I attempt to scrape off with my nails. It can't be much longer now until my visit with the duke.

Dizziness makes my head swim, even in the depths of the cell's blackness. Slumped against the wall, I grip my head with shaking hands and try to hold it still, but it's no use. The world spins, even in the abyss of the chamber, until I can't hold on anymore and tumble over to sprawl on my back in the arctic, stagnant, and fetid water on the rocky floor.

The back of my head crashes and white blinds my vision,

giving me false hope of light in my prison. But that quickly fades as my brain shuts down, giving me reprieve from this torture as I lose consciousness.

SHE WON'T SEE ME THIS TIME. I'VE MADE MYSELF AS SMALL AS possible after learning a way her into her room with the aid of some helpful mice. Daddy told me to stay away from my stepmother's private suite, but I can't. I'm too curious to see who she whispers to at night, wanting to know who she's hiding in my dead mother's old suite.

She won't find me in here, my small body lodged inside her wardrobe. I've been here for hours now, peeking between the skirts of her long dresses and through the small opening in the wardrobe's doors.

I'm scared. This room is full of objects I'm not familiar with. Skulls rest on shelves along one wall, while another holds severed animals parts in a glowing, green liquid. A large cauldron takes center stage in the room, resting on a substantial wooden table with demons devouring screaming children carved into its legs, like a living nightmare stuck in time. Ingredients in crystal bowls and decanters are scattered about the table.

A sweet but awful stench oozes from this place, like the older women in the castle who wear too much perfume, stinging my nose when they come near me to pinch my cheeks. It's floral with a side of something rotten.

Just like Stepmother.

She likes to pretend she's sweet and lovely, when inside, she's really as dark as a starless night. I've tried to tell Daddy that she's mean to me, but I think she's done something to him. He's not the same anymore, something has changed. And now I'm all alone.

A door creaks and I hold my breath when Stepmother waltzes in. Her white-blonde hair is strategically pinned around her spiked crown and her long, purple gown rustles against the floor as she walks. I keep my hand over my mouth to make sure I don't make any noise.

She can't find me here.

If she does, I know she'll punish me.

Stepmother faces the back wall and pulls on a braided fabric chain that's hanging there. To my surprise, a set of black curtains pull apart, revealing an old mirror. Filigree and words I can't yet read make up the ornate frame surrounding it.

It's hauntingly beautiful.

I wonder why her face is not reflecting back to her when she stands close. And then she starts to speak.

"Mirror, mirror, on the wall. Who is the fairest of them all?"

I can't understand why she's talking to a mirror, but then a face appears inside it, a face that is not her own. I choke on a scream, not believing my eyes. Made up of a swirling mist that constantly changes its shape, the face opens its mouth to speak.

"I FRET, MY QUEEN, THOUGH SHE'S STILL QUITE SMALL,
    Another is fairest of them all.
    She's hiding between your hanging gowns,
    Her destiny is your end, she'll take your crown."

MY BODY BEGINS TO TREMBLE AS STEPMOTHER TURNS TO FACE MY hiding place. Her eyes blaze in anger, her cheeks redden, and a sneer creeps across her face. She prowls toward me, terror spreading to all my limbs. I can't stop shaking. I'm so scared. I look around the wardrobe, but there's nowhere for me to go.

I'm trapped.

"You dare hide from me! Spying from my own wardrobe!" she shrieks, pulling open the doors.

"I'm sorry, Stepmoth—"

27

A slap crashes into my cheek, stopping the words in my mouth.

"Silence! You are no daughter of mine!" Her thin fingers twine around my neck and squeeze. I can't breathe and struggle to inflate my lungs, tugging at her fingers. But she's much bigger than me and I quickly grow tired, the light fading around me. "How dare you sneak in here, you repugnant child." My lungs ache for air and heave against my closed throat. "You're lucky you've been protected this long. But one day that, too, will end, and I promise you now, it will be the day you die."

"GET UP, LAZY CUNT!" FINGERS ENSNARE MY HAIR, WRENCHING my frozen cheek off the ground, pulling me from the memory of the one and only time I saw her precious mirror. My vision is hazy as I squint open one eye, the light from one lantern feeling brighter than a blazing fire to my unadjusted vision. "I said get up!" I see the core of an apple resting near my face as the tension on my hair increases and a guard pulls me to my feet. If not for his grip on my head, I would have fallen.

Everything is numb. My nose and lips, my feet and hands, my breasts... I can't feel anything except the burn from the tugging on the roots of my hair. The pain is the only thing keeping me from blacking out once more.

Metal cuffs are cinched around my wrists, another set securing my ankles. "The queen has had enough of your shit, wench," another guard warns. "Today you're in for more than just a meeting with the duke."

Wondering what that could mean, the first guard yanks on the chain binding my hands, causing me to stumble from the cell. A slap lands on my ass after I've fallen to my knees. Then another. I try to scurry away from his cupped palm and the stinging aftermath of his connection with my frozen cheek, but with my wrists and ankles bound, I can only flop like a fish out of water.

"Get the fuck up, you worthless piece of shit!" Tears sting my eyes at the helplessness I feel. I hate feeling like this— worthless and vulnerable. Clenching my teeth, I pull myself up on wobbly legs.

"Let's go, the queen is waiting." A push on my lower back has me tripping once more, but I catch myself this time. The guard ahead of me looks over his shoulder, and the way he sneers at me could curdle milk. Yellow glints in his eyes, and I know he's under the spell of the evil bitch.

My feet slap against the icy floor, each step painful, my frozen toes not wanting to bend. The guards handle me roughly, tugging me up the winding stairs lit by sconces, and I get my first look at my skin. I'm covered in dirt and grime, my nails blackened from the time spent in my cell.

The guards' legs are so much longer than mine, and I trip on the chain linking my feet, falling hard to my knees. I wince in pain as another hit lands on my ass and I scramble back to my feet. The guard in front lets out a sound of disgust and annoyance before jerking me roughly.

I suppress a groan as we ascend and warmth trickles down from the upper floors. Normally I'm cold even dressed inside the castle, but right now it feels as though a heated blanket is covering me. Burning pain stings through my fingers and toes as feeling tries to restore itself. I wince with every step, but no longer falter.

Keys are taken off the guard's belt and he opens the padlock to the dungeons before tugging me after him. I'm pulled through another set of cells made for royal prisoners and opposing dignitaries, complete with their own bathrooms, beds, and windows. Even in captivity, a person of the upper class is treated well. But not me. Not even in my own fucking castle.

Stewing, anger taking place of the despair drowning me, I hold my head high as I'm led through the hallways. Servants see us coming and duck back into the rooms they were coming from. I don't know if it's to give me a semblance of modesty, a sign of respect, or fear of the guards, but whatever the reason, I'm grateful.

Our pace quickens as we wind through the corridors. My first glimpse outside a window lets me know it's either early morning or late afternoon. I miss the sun's rays shining inside, casting rainbows on the castle walls when its light bounces off the crystal chandeliers.

Heavy gray clouds hang low in the sky, blocking the sun behind them. It's been years since the sun was visible—another way the queen controls our people. It's a wonder how our soil still produces ample food to feed us without it.

Still naked, I'm thrust through the front doors and shoved down the steps. The stairs bite into my tender skin as I roll down them one at a time. My head cracks on a stone edge and my lip catches another. I'm bleeding and confused by the time I stop rolling. Once my head stops spinning, I open my eyes and see our front yard lined with staff. Some hang their heads, others blatantly stare at my body.

I want to cower and hide, protect my nakedness from their eyes, but I won't give the evil bitch the satisfaction. My eyes drift from the servants to a wooden wagon. Strung up inside is a cage, perfect for someone my size. I gulp, wondering what the queen has in store for me now.

"Ahh, I see you've noticed your ride for the morning." I can hear her smirking through her words, and I grit my teeth in response. "Get in, wench. It's time to remind the people of Riverwood who rules these lands."

CHAPTER 4

*T*he guards tug my arms, pulling me up from the ground too fast. My vision swims and I stumble again, only held upright by their fingers digging into my skin. Slowly, they march me toward the wagon. My legs shake from exhaustion. Days stuck in the cell sapped all the energy from my body.

The grounds behind the evil bitch are covered with fog, giving the day an ominous aura. I keep my eyes on the wagon, not wanting to see the look of pity in the eyes of those still loyal to me. I don't want their fucking pity. I want their wrath.

Clydesdale horses are usually used to draw the royal carriages. Dressed up in fancy saddles, their long hair braided and covered in bows, they are as pretty to look at as the carriage itself.

But the queen won't give me a Clydesdale to haul the wagon around. Instead, she seeks to humiliate me further by attaching a pair of mules to it. One turns its head to look at me, flashing a set of giant rectangular teeth. The other brays and paws at the ground.

A guard standing in the wagon opens the door to the cage as I approach. His yellow eyes glimmer with hatred as he pulls me aboard and shoves me inside. My face slams against a wooden pole, bruising my cheek. The guard fiddles with the manacles around my wrists and pulls them above me, cinching the chain onto a hook in the ceiling.

My ankles are also secured to the sides of the cage, keeping my body stretched and spread for all to see.

I swallow down the lump in my throat, the tightening in my chest, and try to keep my anxiety down. This is going to be humiliating.

To add to my misery, a cold rain begins to fall. Each droplet freezes my skin, causing goosebumps to riddle my body and making my nipples bead painfully.

But I grit my teeth and bear it. The evil bitch may strip me of my clothes, deprive me of my dignity, but she can't take away my will to survive. That I hold tight inside me.

My black hair sticks to my face, covering my eyes, giving me a false sense of humility. The queen mounts herself up onto a Clydesdale to lead the misfit parade.

Unhooking the duke from her hip, she lashes the mules who start with a snort. A driver sits between the mules, driving the wagon behind the evil bitch. The wooden wheels bounce along the cobblestone, jostling me in the cage.

My castle sits high up on a hill overlooking Riverwood. A long road winds down from its perch to the town below. The queen uses her magic to fashion herself an invisible umbrella, the water missing her entirely. She wears a sleek set of riding gear complete with knee high boots. Her crown is nestled snugly into her hair, glowing even in the absence of the sun. It must be imbued with her magic as well.

A brisk wind picks up, chilling me even further, and the tremors I just overcame from my time in the cell come back with a vengeance.

I'm so cold.

The arms of Count Von Krinklecrumb even sound good in my delirium. I almost laugh to myself for even considering him as an option for warmth. But my brain is so foggy from lack of sleep, food, and water, I'm not thinking straight.

Brakes are pressed on the wagon as the mules gain too much speed down the hill. The motion jolts me, and once again I'm thrown around the cage. The bindings save me this time. I'm stretched so tight that my face doesn't even come close to smashing into the bars of the cage.

Wooden homes come into view. Thatched roofs offer a smell of wet hay as we draw near. It's almost peaceful watching their tiny homes and the pitter-patter of the rain falling on the ground. If I wasn't strung up and frozen, I might enjoy the view.

"Citizens of Riverwood! I order you to exit your dwellings." I risk a glance and see the bitch fluttering her fingers over her throat, causing her voice to boom over the town. "Come out and see what your precious princess has become!"

We walk slowly past the first few houses. Guards run up to each and every door, knocking to rouse the families inside. "That's an order! Get outside and feast your eyes on your fearless leader."

Shit.

Does she know about the rebellion? We've been so careful to keep all talk of it a quiet, not even wearing emblems of our secret society on our bodies, keeping tattoos hidden below our clothes. Our meetings, though few and far between during the instances when I've managed to escape, have been more invigorating and uniting than I ever thought possible.

Doors begin to open with uncertainty. The angry faces of the men come first, followed by their shocked wives.

"Bring your children with you. All shall see what happens when you disobey your queen."

My heart clenches. Not the children.

Dirty faces of our youngest citizens huddled between the legs of their parents stare at me. It's only under their innocent gazes when I want to cower.

You want to parade me in front of the entire town?

Fine.

But leave the children out of it.

The mere notion should give any who hasn't decided to join our cause yet even more reason to.

"Look at her!" The queen laughs maniacally, pointing toward my cage. "Look at your cherished princess! See what she is below the gowns! She is nothing!" The women shy away from my nakedness, hiding the eyes of their young. The men look on, hard and angry, but I see lust filling their eyes. Not that I can blame them. It's not often a princess is stripped and bared for their viewing.

Fairest of them all.

Fuck me.

We wind through the cobblestone streets, my cage bouncing, tits swaying. The queen manages to parade us down every street, fetching all the citizens.

"I order you, follow your queen. Heed to my words or pay the price." With a crack of the duke, she gallops down the final street to the center of town. Erected in the middle of the town's square, surrounded by rows of wooden benches, is a pole.

A wooden pole.

She must have made this monstrosity while I wasted away in the dungeons. There's only one reason to have a pole built in the center of Riverwood, and my back tingles, knowing the answer.

"Sit down. Sit down, everyone! The lesson is about to begin!"

I expect to be led to the pole, but instead I'm spun to watch as two women are led out from a nearby house, their dresses dirty, hair disheveled. I narrow my eyes, trying to see who they are, and gasp with a start.

Enid and Sherry.

The servants who tend to me, members of the rebellion.

My heart shatters.

"You think you can hide from me? From your queen?" she roars, throwing her head back in crazed laughter. "It's ludicrous! Did you really believe you'd get away with this?"

The women are tugged to a spot in front of the pole and forced to kneel. Their right arms are extended and strapped onto a stone bench I didn't notice before. The queen dismounts her horse and struts forward as the townsfolk sit on wooden benches. Everyone looks haggard with worn faces and wet clothes. Like me, they are careful not to look at the queen directly. To do so would be to forfeit your life.

Not because she'd kill you for looking, although I wouldn't put it past her, but because once you lock onto her gaze willingly, she traps you under her spell. You'll be bound to her forever.

Or until I kill her.

The evil bitch motions to someone beyond my view, beckoning them close. Enid and Sherry scream, their bodies quaking in fear. Only now do I see how their dresses are tattered and torn, with the sleeves ripped clean off. Their cheeks are red from crying, and black and blue marks surround their eyes.

The women's screams grow louder as an object is placed in the queen's outstretched hand.

A branding iron.

Gasps of shock emit from the surrounding crowd. The evil bitch's smile grows as she edges toward the women.

They turn to begging. It won't help them, only serving to fuel the queen's malice. This is why I usually stay silent when she accosts me, try to hold in my cries during my sessions with the duke.

The queen spins toward the women and takes a step closer, then aims the hot poker in their direction. All eyes are on its tip. Heated to a brilliant orangish-yellow is an iron apple.

Of fucking course.

The evil bitch turns to address the crowd, who's watching in horror. "Watch and see what happens to those who rebel!" Then, without warning, she snaps the blazing apple down to the snowflake tattoo on Enid's wrist.

Her wails are deafening.

I wince as she writhes in pain, the queen's smile growing like she gets off on it. Perhaps she does. Though it's hard to watch, I don't avert my eyes. She's being punished because she supports me, supports the movement to overthrow the tyrant leading us.

The queen laughs while retracing the iron. Enid sobs, blowing on her skin to try and quell the burn, but since she's still strapped down, she's unsuccessful. The evil bitch turns to Sherry, her cape billowing out behind her.

Sherry begs. "No. No, please!"

But my stepmother has no soul, no voice of reason. With a grin, she strikes Sherry's wrist. I can hear the sizzle from here, smell the pungent scent of burnt flesh. Sherry's cries echo over the crowd. Someone who can't tolerate the brutality throws up, while mothers hold their children against their chests.

The evil queen tosses the branding iron aside, its tip still blazing, and whirls toward me. I lower my eyes and watch only her lips. "Now for the cherry on top."

Who wants to bet I'm the fucking cherry?

She prowls toward me, crown glowing, cape flapping behind her as the storm rages above us. Raindrops blur my vision, and with my arms bound, I'm unable to wipe them from my lashes. I jerk my head to the left and right, but there's nowhere for me to hide, to make her forget all about me. There's nothing I can do to change her mind. My hands are literally tied.

This is going to happen.

She pats the duke on her side and snickers as she struts to my wooden prison. Her slender fingers wrap around the bars, her perfume invading my nose. She lowers her voice and says, "Time to make the snow bleed."

Then she whirls away and snaps her fingers. A set of guards jump into action. Behind me, the door opens, and I'm unhooked from the cage. Before I can enjoy the relief in my shoulders from having my arms lowered, someone tosses me to the ground and I fall with a thump, the wet cobblestones chilling me, causing me to tremble.

"Tie this traitor to the pole," the evil bitch shouts, as a guard jerks me to my feet. The townsfolk stare with wide eyes as I pass by, naked, bound, and helpless. Some leader I've turned out to be.

But I keep my head held high and stare right back at them. I want them to see the fearlessness in my eyes. I want them to see I haven't given up in spite of this setback. I want them to continue to fight for something better than this.

A kick on the back of my leg sends me to my knees with a grunt as a hand pushes between my shoulder blades, forcing my chest against the pole. My arms are brought forward and tied around the thick wooden post, which has to be a foot in diameter. My shoulders scream when my wrists are yanked up high, pulling me to my feet, and tied to a hook up above my head. I'm forced to stay on my tiptoes unless I want to hang.

The crack of the duke has me flinching, but this one doesn't hit me. It's to grab the attention of the people observing.

"Watch your precious princess. I want all your eyes fixed on her. I hear the rumors spreading across my lands. Lies about her beauty. Let's see how beautiful you find her after this."

The first lashing strikes across my upper back. I jerk at the sting but stifle the cry wanting to pour from my lips. A second lash kisses my lower back, followed quickly by a third.

Heat from the duke's kiss sears down my skin. Her strikes are harder than normal. She's losing control of her anger, and that is a scary thing.

"Look at your leader! See your fate across her back. The next citizen I find even speaking the word rebellion will have a meeting with the duke."

Strike. Strike. Strike.

The duke cracks across my skin three more times and I cry out on the last one, earning a chuckle from the queen. "She is nothing compared to me!"

Whip.

"Where she is weak, I am strong."

Lash.

"Obey my rule and you shall be saved. Rebel against me and you shall be punished."

She strikes me again and my vision goes white, the weightlessness I feel after a beating like this starting to set in. Again and again, the duke fillets my back into shreds. Blood pools around my feet, but I no longer feel the pain. Women and children weep softly, their cries hurting me more than the whip ever could.

Another strike.

I don't even respond anymore, my body numb from her attacks. The weightlessness grows, starting at my feet and moving up my body. My head feels light, like I'm floating on the clouds.

But the queen doesn't know this. She thinks my lack of reaction means she's won, that I've lost consciousness.

"Look at her! Broken and weak! She couldn't possibly take my place!" She whips in a frenzy now, lash after lash. I can hear the people shout as they are bathed in the spattering of my blood.

The children's cries grow muffled as I float higher and higher away. The queen's voice is quieter now, even though I know she's still shouting. "Surrender to me and live, or follow her and die!"

Lightning flashes across the sky and thunder booms in its wake. I open my eyes, not realizing I've even closed them as another strike lands. And that's when I see him

A lurker.

He's hidden in the shadows between two houses. A hood covers his eyes, but his crimson lips purse in interest. His skin is so pale it almost shines like the moon.

So they are real.

The queen's footsteps approach, but I don't react, keeping my eyes fixed on the lurker. I can feel myself fading. The blood loss combined with days in that cell have defeated my body. As the blackness rolls across my vision, blurring the lurker studying me, I hear the queen's final words to the people of Riverwood.

"Even your precious Snow bleeds red."

CHAPTER 5

*T*he familiar scent of my freshly washed bedding lets me know I'm back in my opulent cage—my bedroom. Though vast, it still has bars on the windows and guards at the door. I'm still a prisoner here, held against my will.

I'm lying on my belly with my sheet draped low over my hips, exposing my back. I'm scared to move, knowing the cutting pain that will greet me if I do. The queen has never whipped me that hard or long. Usually, after a dozen strikes, she stops.

But not this time.

This time, it went on and on as she tried to teach the good people of Riverwood a lesson. And that lesson?

Don't fuck with the queen.

If I could just figure out a way to get to that mirror, I know I could take her down. But she guards it with an unknown number of spells and traps that I couldn't even begin to thwart. I'm not that cunning and I have no knowledge of magic to combat her.

I'll need to find some other way. I'd rely on my strength,

my fucking will to survive, but right now I'm in bad shape. As thin as I am, my limbs feel like lead weights. I'm underweight and suffering from malnutrition. Let's not even mention trying to heal the horror disfiguring my back.

I can tell it's about midday when my door opens. I swivel my head to see who's come, praying it's not the evil bitch. I deflate when I see the familiar faces of Sherry and Enid. The urge to apologize for what happened to them rests on the tip of my tongue, but I hold it in. Even speaking the word "rebellion" is now enough implication to suffer the duke's wrath. And with the guards in listening distance, I won't risk it.

They wheel in a basin and glass bowls filled with lotions and salves. My body shudders, knowing they are about to clean me, but in doing so they'll cause me serious pain.

They avoid making eye contact with me though I desperately want it. I want them to see how sorry I am for what they've suffered.

"Hold still, this might sting." The stoic words from Sherry are all I get. I should be grateful she's speaking to me at all.

White rags are dipped into the basin and wrung out before they place them on my back. I grunt in pain, squeezing my mattress as the fabric touches the inner layers of my skin.

"Let me see it," I whisper quietly.

The women pause. "I-I don't think—"

"I don't care. Show me." My words are harsh, but I don't want warmth in my tone. All I want is for them to do as I ask this once. During all the primping, the washing, the hair and makeup, I remain silent and allow them to do their work. Just this once I want something done by my command. I glance back as Sherry and Enid share a look, then they grab a set of mirrors. Enid gives me a hand mirror while Sherry holds up a larger one facing my wounds.

It takes me a minute to orient my mirror, but when I do, I

gasp in shock. My back looks like a piece of raw meat, with more muscle tissue exposed than actual skin. Tears mist my eyes as I hand back the mirror, not wanting to see it for another minute. Enid was right. I shouldn't have looked. Somehow knowing what it looks like makes it hurt worse.

I see the caring in Sherry's face at my reaction, I see the worry still present in her eyes. Though she doesn't comfort me, it's enough.

She's not mad.

My relief takes a huge weight off me. I thought for sure they'd blame me for their suffering. Knowing that's not the case lifts my spirits.

Until the next warm cloth is placed on my back.

Pain works in mysterious ways. Sometimes I find it euphoric, like I did when the queen bound me to that pole. It hurt like fuck, don't get me wrong, but once I got past the pain, I found something so much greater.

But today that is not the case. Euphoria is nowhere to be seen, probably blocked by the bars on my window. This pain is soul sucking. It makes me want to drown in sorrow and give in to my fears. I'd give anything to make it stop. This type of agony makes me want to fall asleep and not wake up.

But I grit my teeth and bear it.

For Enid.

For Sherry.

For Riverwood.

They clean my back with the utmost care, even though my cheeks are stained with tears. Their white rags have turned a sickly pink before their work is done.

Enid lifts a clear lid from a crystal bowl and dips her hands into a white liquid. "This will hurt," she whispers, before swiping the salve across my back.

I scream.

I can't help it.

You'd think I'd be used to the duke by now, but this session was far worse than others I've suffered. The stinging and burning are agonizing. It feels worse than the actual whip did, and I begin to lose consciousness. Enid's hand shakes as she goes in for more. My muscles tense, preparing for the pain, but it's no use.

My wails are probably heard around the castle, my agony traveling on the wind all the way down to the town of Riverwood. I scream and shriek and cry until my voice grows hoarse and my eyes grow heavy.

I won't find my euphoria today.

No.

All I'm left with is the carnage from the torture I've endured.

Painful tremors rack my body. I don't know how much longer I'm going to make it, and I wonder if this is how I'll die—lying here with a mutilated back, thirsty and starving, my life meaningless.

A paper fan is thrust open and the women fan my back. The cold wind feels good on my heated—and in all likelihood, infected—flesh.

Sherry comes around to my head and wipes my tears with a handkerchief tucked inside her pocket. "Drink this." Her voice is soft and tender as she holds a cup up to my lips. The warm broth coats my tongue and makes my taste buds come alive. I wonder how something as simple as broth could possibly taste so good. I nod, letting her know I want more, and drink generously, not caring that some of the liquid is spilling down my chin.

I want it all, and I want it now.

My belly gurgles in opposition. I've been hungry for so long that it doesn't remember what it feels like to be full, as it rumbles in protest. Sherry pulls the drink from my mouth and gently dabs my lips for me. "Thank you," I whisper, before laying my head back down.

My eyes feel heavy and my body is so thoroughly broken. With a sigh, I allow myself to pass out into the blissful realm of dreams.

I WAKE, STILL FEELING GROGGY, AND TURN TO LOOK OUT THE window, finding empty darkness. I must have slept all day long. Even the guards have changed shifts. Looking out my open door, I see new faces I haven't seen before.

Lying here, my mind wanders, wondering why she just won't fucking kill me. If she hasn't realized by now that I won't ever say yes to one of her repulsive suitors, then I don't think she ever will.

Even in my youth, I couldn't understand why she didn't kill me. She hated me as much then as she does now. So why keep me alive?

My young mind brewed up many ideas, imagining a witch cast a spell on me that wouldn't allow her to kill me, or that a warlock made her drink a potion forbidding her from murdering her stepdaughter.

Whatever the reason, I've yet to learn it, in spite of the many hours I've spied on her before she condemned me to my room.

It remains a mystery.

I shift my body, wanting to sit up and use the bathroom, but collapse back down with a cry. The pain from my back sears through me in blinding waves. Even a subtle movement feels like my skin is ripping open again, something I don't think I'll ever get used to even after years of torture. My thoughts go back to the euphoria I felt on the pole while watching the lurker...

The lurker!

44

I'd almost forgotten about him.

Dark and mysterious, cloaked and hooded, just like the legends say they are. He watched me with hidden eyes, stared as I was whipped into unconsciousness. Why did he come for me then? Is he on the same side as the queen and watching under her orders? Was he there in support for me, wanting to join my rebellion perhaps? Or are his reasons more sinister?

My body shudders at the thought. Everything about him was alluring. The manner in which his red tongue licked his crimson lips. The way his pale skin seemed to shine all on its own. His movements, though few, were graceful and fluid, like watching a dancer take the stage. Even though we didn't speak, I want to see him again. I want to pull the hood from his face and gaze into his eyes. I want to hear the timbre of his voice, feel its deep pitch rumble through my body and relish in the touch of his hands on my skin.

This revelation is shocking, even to me.

I've never felt this way about anyone, much less the monsters found in Riverwood lore.

I don't know how to find him, but my heart makes me feel like I won't have to, that he will find me. And when he does, I'll be ready.

I CRY OUT, TRYING TO CRAWL AWAY FROM THE KISS OF THE WHIP AS it sears down my back. No longer am I bound to the pole, but thrown down into a pool of mud, which quickly covers my nakedness. The townspeople laugh at me as I writhe in the muck, all their eyes turned yellow under the spell of the queen.

"You will die!" the evil bitch shouts, as she whips me relentlessly. There's no euphoria, no reprieve from the agony, no lurkers to distract me from her malice. There is only pain. She doesn't leave a

single inch of my body untouched. Guards descend on me, turning me from belly to back, holding me down so she can whip my belly, my breasts.

I can handle the whipping on my back. I've had so many sessions that I've become used to it. She pauses, my blood freezing. "And now for your face. Let's see who's the fairest of them all after I'm through with you."

And then she strikes. The duke slashes across my face, slicing down my eyelid. I scream until my voice grows hoarse, my face mutilated while the queen laughs in utter glee.

I WAKE WITH A START, A SCREAM STILL ERUPTING FROM MY LIPS, my arms and legs thrashing against the grip of guards who no longer hold me. My eyes shoot open and I deflate, realizing I'm still lying in my bed on my belly, my back stiff with dried bandages from Sherry's and Enid's ministrations.

Closing my eyes, I will my heartbeat to slow, taking deep breaths. The ass eating guards outside my door chuckle at my suffering.

Bastards.

I want so badly to hate them, but I know it's not their fault. Once bespelled by the evil bitch, nothing can bring you back.

Except maybe her death.

Or at least, I hope it will.

A soft rain pours outside my windows under the heavy gray clouds covering the sky. In spite of it always raining, I do love the smell of it. Something about it draws on a happy memory, one of only a few from my childhood. Before my father fell under the spell of the evil bitch, we would dance in the rain. He'd come find me, whisk me into his arms, and together we'd run out into the courtyard singing and dancing, splashing in the puddles as our laughter bounced off the walls.

The memory still makes me smile.

My grin falters when the steady clicking of high heeled shoes echoes down the stone hallway and filters into my room. I see the guards outside straighten their postures, tucking their swords tightly against their shoulders in a stance of respect. Then comes the noise that makes me cringe most of all—the sound of a bite into a fresh, crisp, red apple.

"Hello, my sweet, darling daughter."

Sweet? Darling? I want to laugh in her face, though I know she's only taunting me.

"How does your back fare today? Better, I hope? The duke does prefer to inflict his anger on you when you are fully healed." I do my best to school my features, to keep my teeth from grinding, my hands from clenching into fists while her sinister words wash over me.

She doesn't fucking care if I'm healed.

Something is amiss.

I twitch when she sits down next to me on the bed. I have to will myself not to flinch when she reaches down and strokes my hair tenderly before taking another bite of her apple. "The servants will be in here shortly to prepare you," she informs me between bites. "A suitor will arrive tonight, asking for your hand. And should you not accept, I might have to rip your beating heart from your chest as payment."

*M*y heart?

  What in the world is she talking about?

Since I'm unable to look at her, I can't tell what her facial expression is. Like, is she joking? The queen never jokes... which means...

She means every damn word.

Oh, fuck.

"Should you wish to keep your heart, dear daughter, all you have to do is say yes." She takes another bite of her apple and stands elegantly, smoothing her dress with her hands. "I suggest you heed to my words, girl, or tonight may be your last night alive."

With that, she slams her half-eaten apple down by my face and saunters out of my room, laughing all the way down the hall.

I can't think straight, my brain is nothing but a jumbled mess. How does she expect me to see a suitor tonight? Much less get prepared for something like this. My back has barely healed, there's no way I could wear a dress and have the scratchy, diamond encrusted gown rubbing against it. I'd be

SEVEN SINS OF SNOW

bleeding all over the place. What kind of suitor would want me then?

Glancing out the window, I notice it's not quite midday. I still have time to figure this out. The servants don't usually come until an hour or two before I need to get ready. The queen bitch always requests I be freshly bathed and dressed.

Think, Snow, think!

With a sigh, I rest my head back down and come face to face with the bitten apple. I pull my arm up to swipe it off my pillow when something happens. A tiny mouse scurries along my bed and begins to nibble on the fruit. He's adorable, small enough to fit in the palm of my hand. His little round ears twitch in delight, his whiskers covered in apple bits. I smile, watching how he holds a bite in his tiny little hands while sitting on his back feet.

"Hey, little guy," I whisper softly. The mouse pauses, his black eyes watching me with...interest? "Whatcha got there?" He resumes munching, keeping his eyes on me. Slowly, I reach one finger toward him, and to my surprise, he lets me stroke his head between his ears.

A giggle escapes my lips.

A fucking giggle.

I don't giggle. Or at least, I haven't since I was very young. Petting the munching mouse, I forget the horrors of my daily life and just allow myself this brief moment of happiness.

"I wish I could be you for a day, little mouse. Fending for yourself, living off apple scraps. The world at your fingertips. Not a bad way to live if you ask me."

The mouse doesn't respond, but cocks his head at me as if he's listening, which is, of course, absurd.

"I wish you could understand me. Then you could help me get out of here. I can't see another suitor tonight. My refusal will likely end in my death and I'm not ready to die."

That realization hits me hard.

For so long I've pondered whether dying is the better option. My life has no meaning. I don't live, I just exist, like the trees in the orchard or the blades of grass in the garden. They are stuck in the same place day to day, just like me.

But now, when my mortality becomes uncertain, my fate resting in the hands of the evil queen, who loathes the ground I walk on and the air I breathe...I know for sure...

I don't want to die.

I want to live.

I want to be happy.

I want to smile and dance in the rain. I want to sing with the birds and fall in love and eat cake until I grow fat. I want so much more than this.

The mouse drops his apple and moves in my direction. His little paw pats at my face as if to give me comfort. I can feel each one of his tiny nails resting against my cheek. And even though I know he has no idea what he's doing, it feels good. I close my eyes and let a few tears fall. This is the closest I've come to any morsel of affection in the past decade, maybe even longer. Just to have the gentle touch of another, to know that they see you, that you're real too, and that you matter despite what anyone else says or thinks, that's what gets me.

The mouse retracts his little claws and hops back over to the apple, grabbing another juicy bite for himself. Feeling braver, I reach out again and scratch him behind his fluffy ear, grinning like a crazy person as I do. "Now run along and find me some poison or a knife I can kill these guards with like a good little mouse. Can you do that for me?" Wishful thinking can't hurt, right?

His ears twitch and he finishes his bite. I watch with sadness as he hops to the end of my bed and turns back to look at me once more. Then, with a flick of his tail, he's gone.

Immediately, I feel sad and empty.

Alone.

The conversation I just had with that field mouse was the longest one I've had with anyone for as long as I can remember. I'm not allowed to speak, for anything I say is manipulated by the queen and used against me. And in return, no one is allowed to talk to me either, unless it's giving me an order, like the servants when they tell me to stand, close my eyes, or lift my arms.

But that's not real conversation.

Even though my brief chat with the mouse was one-sided, it felt really good to have a friend again.

Groaning, I move my arms and try to lift my body from the bed. My back shudders and I fall down.

How the fuck am I going to do this?

I try to get up again, starting with my legs this time. I let them drop to the side of the bed, allowing my upper half to stay hunched. So far so good. With my feet planted firmly on the ground, I slowly lift my chest. Everything on my back stretches and pulls, like a chain gone too taut before one link snaps. I grit my teeth and inch my way up, my arms shaking from taking the weight of my body, my legs trembling from exhaustion.

But I make it.

I'm standing all on my own.

I look to the door and see the guards deep in conversation, not even glancing back into my room.

Good.

Now to figure a way out of here.

Looking around, I notice there's not much to see. My vanity is filled with makeup and lotions. My wardrobe is stuffed with expensive gowns and not much else. There's the chandelier, but even if I could reach it way up near the ceiling, what would I do with it? Grab a candle and threaten to burn people? The guards would laugh at that.

My eyes drift to the small table near the window. A carafe filled with red wine sits full next to two empty crystal glasses. How could I possibly use that? I don't drink, liking to keep my head clear, but the queen does. That's why the wine is here. She keeps carafes in every room she frequents, in case she has a hankering for the fermented grape drink.

Not wanting to walk around naked in case the queen or the guards do decide to enter my room, I pull the sheet off the bed and tie the ends around my neck, the others around my waist, leaving my back untouched.

It's better than nothing.

I head to my bathroom, gingerly taking each step, not wanting to agitate my healing skin any more than I already am. The mirror is my enemy. I want to go to it, to see the condition my back is in again, but the last time I did, I almost passed out. I need to stay…focused. I need to think.

I pull open the cupboards and drawers, looking for anything, a rogue blade someone left behind during one of my grooming sessions, a hand mirror that I could break into small pieces and use as a weapon.

But again, I come up empty.

Desperation and despair brew like a storm inside me. If I can't figure a way out of this, I might as well dig my own grave. I become slightly frantic, looking around for anything. My bed offers no help, can't hurt someone with fancy blankets and feather pillows.

Shit.

Groaning, I walk over to the table and carefully sit down in the chair, my fingers twisting the stem of the crystal glass. I gaze out my window and through the bars to the bustling grounds below. Servants fill the orchard, selecting ripe apples and fresh grapes. Others dig up potatoes and carrots from the fields, their baskets filling quickly with their bounty.

My eyes drift from the orchards to the stables. Young men tend to the horses, cleaning their stalls and filling them with fresh hay. Others are grooming the stallions, brushing their coats and braiding their manes. Of all the evil the queen does, at least she takes care of her horses. I can give her that.

My gaze wanders further, to the back of the property, behind the stalls and the orchard, past the gardens. And it's there my eyes widen.

A lurker.

No.

Two lurkers.

They stand huddled under the mature trees that line the castle grounds. Their cloaks blend with the tree trunks, making them almost impossible to see if you weren't searching. I wonder if maybe they have magical powers. Maybe they are around us all the time, but we can only see them if they wish it so.

Does that mean they have chosen me?

A horse-drawn wagon carrying bales of hay rolls past them, the driver not so much as even glancing their way.

They stand unmoving, like the statues dancing in the fountain in front of my castle. Their cloaks billow behind them as a gust of wind picks up. I hope that it has enough force to push the hoods from their eyes, but it doesn't.

Their fingers, as pale as the moon, hold their hoods firmly in place. Their full lips remain still as they observe. Are they watching *me*? Or are they here to study the workings of the farm? Maybe they've come for the evil queen. Maybe they wish to kill her. If so, we could work together, if only I could talk to one of them.

A squeak draws my attention. I look down and spot my

little mouse skittering across my floor. I gasp when he climbs up my makeshift dress and plops himself on my table.

In his mouth is a small glass vial. I hold my breath and offer him my palm. The mouse deposits the bottle then scurries back off. My hand shakes as I turn it around to read the label. My breath catches, the word written clear as day.

Poison.

CHAPTER 7

*Q*uickly, I hide the gift in my palm and jerk my head toward the door. The guards are continuing their banter, completely unaware of the power I hold. The bottle warms in my hand, reassuring me that it's real. A sinister plan forms in my mind, a foolproof way to get out of here...

If I'm brave enough to do it.

I have to be.

Looking back out the window, I find the lurkers gone. I'm surprised that I'm sad. Though I've met them in my dreams and once at the whipping post, they are no friends of mine. We haven't so much as exchanged a single word that wasn't me shouting in a dream.

Licking my lips, I struggle to my feet and head back to the bathroom, needing to formulate my plan without the stress of the guards turning to watch. The poison feels like a glowing, lead weight in my hand, and I worry that anyone can see it.

In the safety of my bathroom, I open my palm and pinch the tiny bottle between my pointer finger and thumb. The bottle is old, with a cork as a stopper. I shake it gently and see the liquid inside bubble up in response. Less than half of the poison remains, so I need to use it with care.

The queen said the suitor would be coming tonight, which means I have a few hours left until servants will be here to dress me. I need to devise a plan, and I need to do it now.

First thing I'll need is clothing. I can't run from the castle with a scrap of bedding tied around me.

Feigning nonchalance, I stroll from the bathroom and head to my wardrobe. The guards hear and turn to see what I'm doing before they burst out in laughter.

"Nice dress you've got on there, princess," the taller one teases as he enters my room.

Walking in behind the first guard, the short one chimes in, "Yeah. But it would look a lot better strewn across the floor. Perhaps we could help you with that?"

Anger floods me, reddening my vision. "You lay one of your slimy fingers on me, and the queen will cut off your hands. Mark my words." My voice sounds much braver than I feel, and they retreat from my room with wide eyes and shocked faces.

I don't blame them, I never talk, and they probably didn't think I even had a voice anymore. I'm not a pushover, I'm just not stupid. I remain silent so that I may live to survive another day. But with nothing left to lose and zero fucks to give, I decide to do anything I can to get out of here, using their desire for me to my advantage.

Selecting a gown I've worn once before, but cursing the fact I don't have a set of riding clothes in this bloody closet, I scurry back off to my bathroom. I hang the dress on a golden hook embedded into the wall of white stone. It's simple and elegant, but totally impractical for an escape.

Dammit.

I run my fingers through my hair and wince as the action pulls on my back a little too hard. The top of the dress would work fine, it's the bottom that needs fixing. Full, with layers and layers of fabric, the skirt is heavy and cumbersome.

But what can I use to cut it?

Turning, I look at my vast bathroom. A clawfoot tub rests against the far wall, but that won't do me any good. There's a sink and a mirror, a porcelain toilet...none of these items can help me. The mirror might do the trick, but breaking off a piece would be too loud, alerting the guards that I'm up to no good.

Worry starts to eat away at me. What if I can't pull this off? I'm running out of time. My eyes land on the dress again, then up to the hanger it rests on and the hook in the wall.

The hook!

It's *nailed* in!

If I can just loosen it from the wall, I could use the nail to alter this dress! Grabbing fistfuls of fabric, I yank hard, trying to tug the nail free from the plaster, but stop when I hear a tear somewhere in the dress. Not wanting to rip the parts I want to keep, I unhook the garment and just tug on the hanger, and the nail begins to loosen. My back screams in agony at the movement, but I push that from my mind. Twisting and turning the hanger, I'm almost ready to give up when a small *ping* sounds and the hanger—and hook—are in my hands.

I peek my head out of the bathroom, making sure the tiny noise didn't reach the ears of the guards. Satisfied they haven't heard me, I crouch down and look around for the lost nail. I smile when I find it in the junction where the floor and wall meet.

Now to get to work.

Holding the nail between my knuckles, I lift the skirts of the dress and start to scrape away at the longest layer. It's tedious and my heart slams in my chest the entire time, thinking the guards are going to barge in and catch me.

But I must have scared them with my insinuations, because they don't so much as call for me, much less enter again. By the time I've gotten the first layer off, blisters have formed between my fingers, leaving them raw and bleeding.

Curses fly from my mouth in silent words when I hold up the dress and find it needs to have another layer taken off. So I work furiously, ignoring the bleeding and pain, scratching at the fabric at a rapid pace, pulling the cream skirt off the dress.

I toss the scraps behind me and hold it up once more.

I think I've done it.

My reflection in the mirror agrees. The dress will sit short over my legs, horrifying any royal or noble that would see me. It shows off way too much skin, revealing things only a married woman would show to her husband.

In other words...

It's perfect.

Where I'm going, I don't need to impress the royals or anyone else. Sticking my head out of my bathroom once more, I find the guards unmoved and prepare to dress myself. It has been some time since I've done this on my own.

A hiss escapes my lips when I have to reach around my neck and untie the sheet. It slips from my body, leaving me naked and cold, so I quickly grab the dress, step into it, and shimmy the thing up my frame. But once it's on, I realize there is no way for me to secure it. The back is a corset, just like all the others, but my wounds won't allow me to tighten a fabric against them like that.

Think, Snow, think.

Then I see it. The front also laces up to close in my

breasts. I can take out the longer ribbon from the corset and lace it through the front and tie it around my neck.

Grinning, I get back to work. The back of the dress isn't as easy to manipulate as the skirts. I have to remove the back panels stitch by stitch. I'm thankful most of the remaining dress is black, or it would be covered in bloodstains. Sweat forms on my forehead as I work, but I finally get it done.

My reflection looks much different now with this altered dress. Where I usually see a refined princess, all I see is a village whore. The straps are loose on my arms and hang off my shoulders. I lace up the bodice and tighten it the best I can. Crossing the lace in front of my neck and again behind it, I tie a knot under my hair.

I turn to look at my back. The whip marks are bright red, and the dress no longer covers them with the fabric going no further than my arms. The top of the skirt barely covers my ass, but barely will have to do.

Turning back to the front, I fix my breasts, making sure they are tucked into the severed corset top as best as they can be. The hem of the skirt reaches my knees, then gathers in the center, pulling up into a red bow. Normally it would have looked beautiful with the layers of fabric hanging below it, but now all you see are the tops of my thighs.

There's nothing I can do about my unruly curls, I don't have the oils needed to tame them, so I fluff my hair the best I can, wincing at the pull on my back. Maybe I should take a drink of that wine to take the edge off.

The wine...

That's it!

I can use the wine to slip the poison to the guards!

"You can do this," I whisper to my reflection. I give my cheeks a pinch for some color and take a deep breath. It's now or never.

The poison seems to pulse in my hand, like it's a living,

breathing thing as I exit the bathroom. I struggle to keep my composure, knowing what I'm about to do. The guards are still standing idly when I enter my room again. With a shaking hand, I pour equal amounts of poison into the crystal glasses, using the entire bottle. Then, I unstopper the wine and fill a quarter of the glass, before turning to my door.

"Guards. Would you entertain me for a moment? I need help with something." Their voices quickly stop and they exchange a glance before stepping into my room. Their eyes, though tinted with yellow, telling of the queen's spell, still aren't dead. I watch as they undress me with their eyes, the bulges in their pants confirming my suspicions.

Even though they are the queen's minions, they still want me.

Just like all the others do.

I've never tried to be sultry or sexy, always trying to stay invisible, but right now I need to entice these men. Like I was taught in my youth, I assume the posture of a princess, lifting my chin, pushing my shoulders back, and sticking out my chest.

"You see, I feel awful for having yelled at you earlier, and I want to make it up to you. So I've poured you each a glass of wine as an act of contrition. It's all I have to show you how sorry I am. Please, won't you accept my apology?"

I hold the glasses out and blink up at them with pouty lips. For a moment they act as if they won't indulge me. But with a shrug of their shoulders they each take a glass and sip, drinking until it's gone. My blood surges inside me and I feel like I might explode as I wait for something to happen.

With the wine drank, they round on me. "Well, there is another way you could show us how sorry you are."

Shit.

"Oh? Would you like more wine?"

The tall one snickers and reaches for me, his hand surrounding my upper arms as the small one steps behind me. "I've never fucked a virgin before."

My throat closes.

No.

This can't be happening.

"Y-You can't—"

A hand covers my mouth. "We can and we will." I cry against his fingers when his chest pushes into my wounded back. I start to thrash in their hands while they fumble with my dress, my back feeling like it's ripping apart.

Then, as quickly as it started, it all stops.

The hands once gripping me drop, and I look up to see foam pouring from the tall guard's mouth. His face turns red as he grips his throat and falls to his knees. Blood coats his hands as he tears at his neck with his fingers, falling to his back. Behind me, I hear a thump and turn to see the other guard has also collapsed, his eyes bulging from their sockets. They gurgle and gag and I cover my mouth in shock.

It's working

It's fucking working.

Their bodies slacken, eyes rolling back into their heads, and then they still. At first I'm in disbelief. I just killed two men.

Me!

Then the terror sets in. What if I'm caught? I never even thought about how I was going to get out of the castle. My head starts to spin.

Oh my God!

I'm a murderer!

I'm no better than the queen!

Tears mist my vision and I fall to my knees next to the men I just killed. Something glints in the light, catching my attention, and I look to my right. A set of keys dangle from the guard's belt.

This is my way out.

I hold in a scream and lunge for the keys, then step carefully over the dead. I say a quick prayer to the gods, bidding them safe passage into the afterlife, and head to my door.

Before I stick my head out, I listen. No clicking of shoes. No biting of apples.

Blissful silence.

Cautiously, I peek out the door and look down the hall to my left and find empty halls. The right is the same.

Here goes nothing.

Slipping out of my room, I turn right and run as fast as I can while on my tiptoes, trying to make no noise and stay invisible. Nothing exists inside the rooms I pass. Not since my father died. They used to be filled with extended family, visitors, and guests. Now the rooms lie vacant and empty, save for the dust coating the furniture.

I quicken my pace, heading for the back staircase at the end. No one ever uses it anymore, my room being the only one occupied in this wing. Using the guard's keys, I unlock the large, wooden door and enter a darkened spiral staircase. The only lights come from the arrow slits in the turret, leaving me virtually in shadow.

The air grows colder as I descend, and though the chill feels good on my back, I wish I had left the sleeves on my dress attached. Goosebumps rise on my skin and my toes begin to grow numb as I reach the bottom of the stairs and face another large, wooden door. I fumble with the keys, my hands shaking as I try and fail to unlock the door over and over. I curse the need for fifty keys on this damn keyring until, finally, the lock clicks open. Switching the keys to my other hand, I reach up and grasp the handle, ready to make a break for it out of the back door.

But I hesitate.

Instead of ripping it open and running for my freedom, I slowly inch it ajar enough for one eye to see out of. With the rainstorm brewing into something much more substantial than the daily precipitation we're used to, the grounds are empty. Thunder crashes overhead and the raindrops increase their pace, falling heavily to the ground.

Keeping hold of the guard's keys, I heave the door open and run for it. The wet grass squishes under my feet and the raindrops pelt me. My back simultaneously hates and loves the cold liquid descending on us.

A wicked wind picks up, blowing my hair, whipping my dress around my legs. This storm is going to get worse and fast. Not wanting to get lost in the vast lands outside the view of my bedroom window, I head toward the town. There once was a time when I knew every tree, every animal-made pathway in the woods, but after years of captivity, my memories are fleeting, and they would be as unfamiliar to me as another kingdom across the world.

I look over my shoulder as I run down the hill toward Riverwood and see no huntsmen chasing me, no horses ridden by angry riders, and no evil queen.

Grinning, I pump my legs faster and make it to the town in no time as lightning cracks overhead. Surely there is an empty home or a dilapidated shed I can hide in for the night. I won't survive long out here in the storm, which has only begun to show its rage. Thunder rumbles, shaking the ground as I hurry through the vacant streets. It's eerie being here with no one else.

I pass the square and risk a glance. The whipping post stands proudly, taunting me with memories of the duke still as fresh as the wounds on my back. I surge past it, pushing away the memories, and see the spot where I saw the lurker. I wonder if I had imagined him as I run down a narrow alleyway.

That's when I hear the trumpets sound in the distance. Soon, people will be peeking their heads out of their doors and windows to see what all the fuss is about. I need to find a place to hide, and I need it now.

The alley turns sharply, and I push my legs harder, my feet slapping into puddles on the cobblestone. Lightning strikes overhead, illuminating the alley and an almost invisible footpath I would have missed without the help from the storm.

I veer down it as the trumpets sound again, and stop dead in my tracks. Above me is an awning with seven slashes carved into it, shielding a wooden door.

My blood runs cold.

The lurkers.

My dream.

They're real, and I've found them.

CHAPTER 8

*H*oly shit.
They are real, and I've found them.

Or maybe they found me. Somehow, they were able to infiltrate my dreams and plant this image in my mind, almost as if they knew this moment would happen.

The trumpets blare, ever closer, accompanied by shouting of the queen's many huntsmen. I don't have long to decide what to do. Do I enter through the door in front of my eyes, knowing the deadly creatures of legend may prowl just behind them ready to devour me? Or do I keep running, knowing that I will inevitably be caught and dragged back to my castle prison?

Either way, I could die, but I'd rather end my life surrounded by the monsters of legend draining my life than by the hands of the evil bitch slashing the duke across my flesh or tearing my heart from my chest.

A howl from a hunting dog spurs me into action, and I reach for the rusted iron handle only for the door to open all on its own. "Hello?" I call into the darkness beyond, stepping through the threshold, only for the door to close behind me, seemingly by itself. Empty blackness greets me, and for a moment I consider running out.

I turn my head sharply when a sconce ignites, its fire blazing along a red wall. I walk toward it, almost drawn to the flame. Just as I near it, another comes to light a few feet ahead. I look over my shoulder at the way I entered, but find the door is now absent, only a solid black wall exists. I'm trapped, but I've never felt more alive, even though I'm a bit apprehensive.

I take another step and another as candles in their glass houses spark to life down the corridor. Then I hear a haunting sound.

Is that music?

My bare feet quicken along the wooden floor as I pass under the flicker of candle flames, until a door morphs from the darkness. Elegant carvings depicting lovers are embossed in the dark wood. A man has a woman bent in a low dip as if they just ended an elaborate dance. The woman's head is dropped back, her chest pushed out, arms draped pliantly over the ground. The man holds her up with one strong arm under her back, his mouth pressed against her neck, teeth sunk into her skin.

My eyes dart back to the woman, expecting her expression to be one of pain, but instead she looks woozy with lust, her eyes hooded, mouth open in an O.

She's...enjoying this bite?

The revelation shocks me. My whole life I've only heard rumors of how inhumane and barbaric the lurkers are. But this? This isn't a depiction of a beast taking what isn't his, rather, it's a piece of art illustrating two willing participants.

The background draws my attention. Six more lurkers huddle in the darkness. Watching. Waiting. Even in the shadows, I can't mistake the crowns on their heads or the erections in their pants.

Seven kings to wield the seven deadly sins...just like the legend says.

Shaking my head, I look for a handle, needing to see where the music is coming from, but I don't find one. Frustrated, I raise my hand and knock, grunting in frustration when I get no response. I begin slamming my hands against it, but then a prick stings my palm and I jerk my hand away, looking at my hand for inspection. In the middle of my palm is a drop of blood. Intuition takes over and I wipe my blood on the door. It groans as if it's sentient and enjoyed the taste, then swings inward.

The music blares, disturbing and beautiful, just like the scene before me. Four large, candlelit chandeliers hang low from the ceiling, illuminating a gathering of gorgeous people. Each face I look at is as beautiful as the one before. Immaculately dressed men and women mingle, adorned in fine dresses and suits. The women have their hair pinned up in elaborate styles, laughing as they drink from crystal goblets. The men are impeccable, with shined shoes and ironed jackets.

On my left are vacant tables and chairs with half-drunk glasses of what looks like wine. To my right, a couple are deep in a sensual kiss, sitting in front of a long table with elevated seating. A fierce-looking man who appears to be taking requests from those gathered, stands behind the table and fills up their glasses with one of the hundreds of bottles lining the wooden shelves behind him.

The majority of this party's guests are in the middle of a sparkling, tiled floor, dancing and swaying to the eerie music. But the most interesting sight is in the far back of the room. Above the musicians who are playing a variety of instruments—from the piano to the violin—are cages suspended from the ceiling. Inside them are scantily clad women dancing to the music.

I watch in awe as the music moves to a crescendo and the cages are lowered. Hungry hands reach inside and tug at the fabric covering the women, baring them to the sultry eyes of all who look. Seeking fingers scratch at the women's flesh, causing their blood to trickle down, but the women don't look pained, they look excited. Their eyes flash and they moan as the onlookers swipe at the fresh blood and suck it off their fingers.

They…drink…blood.

Suddenly, I feel faint.

This is too much to handle and completely overwhelming. I shouldn't be here. As I turn to retreat, my fingers slip off the door and it shuts with a bang. The melancholic song abruptly halts, and all eyes turn to me.

Oh, shit.

Everyone here looks similar, like some fucked up army. Dark hair, bright eyes, crimson lips. Someone hisses, another snarls. I back up with my hands raised in surrender until I thump into the door. My back reminds me of the fresh wounds scored into it and I wince in pain.

The loud snap of someone's fingers echoes off the walls, which feel like they are closing in on me. Faces once tearing into me with only their eyes turn to a raised seating area in the far left corner, one I somehow missed before.

Standing, no, *lurking* in the shadows are seven figures. The top halves of their faces are covered in darkness, leaving only their mouths unveiled in the candlelight.

The lurkers!

Their lips move in unison, but I hear no words, no voices to command such respect. The haunting music picks back up and the guests return to what they were doing before I interrupted, my presence no longer of concern. The seven stay huddled in the shadows through the chaos, their posture emitting an air of royalty. Even squinting hard, I can't make out the top of their heads, unable to discern anything that would mimic a crown.

"Thirsty, dear?" a voice croons. I look sharply toward its origin and see the fierce man twirling a bottle in his pale, practiced hand, his eyes flashing.

I swallow hard. "No! I, uhh…"

He smiles. "Of course you are." He pours a drink for an equally fierce-looking woman with her hair pulled back into a tight bun. "Come closer. I have a gift for you."

A gift? Why would this man have a gift for me?

"Don't be shy. I don't bite." He laughs, and so do all the people sitting at the table before him. Each person looks like they are in on some sick joke that I'm not privy to but am the brunt of.

My feet move even though I don't want them to, and a moment later I hoist myself onto the raised chair. "I am Vincent," he says, strutting over with a goblet filled with red liquid. When he stops in front of me, his eyes widen, and his face morphs from a refined man to one of something feral, more beast than man. He sniffs the air around me, and a growl releases from deep in his throat.

My fingers turn white as I grip the table in fear, the hair on the back of my neck standing on end.

I've got to get out of here.

I move to push off the chair and make a run for it when the snapping of fingers captures his attention. Vincent tears his eyes from me and looks behind me to the corner where I saw the seven. I watch in terror as the ferocity marring his expression softens, his dilated pupils shrink, and fangs I didn't notice before retract into his gums.

What the fuck?

Is this proof that the legends telling of monsters are real? This man became something other *right before my eyes...*

Vincent, now back to normal, turns to me. "Sorry, Miss..." He rolls his hand, the gesture implying he wants me to tell him my name.

"S—" I clear my throat to delay responding. I almost told him my name. I can't be that stupid again. If these people are under the queen's orders, they would snatch me up and send me back to my castle in chains. "Sofi. My name is Sofi."

"Sofiiiii." He elongates the last sound as he tries out my alias on his tongue, making it sound like a dark promise.

"Yes. That's me." I force my fingers release the table, seeing he's no longer a threat. Whatever he saw behind my back was persuasive enough to tame the beast within him.

Vincent smirks and pushes the goblet toward me. "Here. For you." Unsure, I reach for the glass in spite of how unsettled he makes me. Our fingers touch and I snatch mine back. His skin felt cold.

Dead.

Reminding me of how my father's body felt when I threw myself onto his corpse at his funeral, screaming for him not to leave me.

I immediately regret my response when he looks at me more like I'm prey than a woman. "I said I won't bite, dear, unless you ask me to."

I swallow hard and lick my lips as he takes a step back, and gestures to the glass before looking behind me once more. "Drink. This is a gift from the seven."

So he calls them the seven too?

My fingers curl around the crystal stem, and I pull the drink in front of me, but instead of taking a sip I just spin the glass, watching how the candlelight makes it sparkle.

"I would drink that if I were you." I raise my gaze to

Vincent, who nods at the glass. "A gift from the seven is one you should not waste."

I raise the drink and stare into the blushed liquid as if it would give me the answers I seek. Even that subtle movement is enough to make my back scream in pain. I've tugged on the fresh lashings far too much tonight, and now the burn won't quench.

I narrow my eyes in suspicion before responding, "But why would they give me a gift? I'm no one."

Vincent sighs, then leans down, resting his elbows on the table. "Apparently you are not no one, *Sofi*." He knows my name is a lie, but indulges me. I wonder if he's figured out who I really am. He turns his attention to my cleavage. "That is some dress you are wearing this evening. May I ask who the designer is?"

Designer?

"Uhh. It…was…a custom job. Yes. She was an, er…traveling seamstress."

"You don't say." Vincent acts more interested than he should be, resting his chin in his palm. "Go on, dear. Take a drink." When I don't, he implores, "Please? You don't want to feel *wrath* tonight. Instead, be *gluttonous*, and enjoy what lies in front of you."

I open my mouth to ask exactly what type of wrath he means, but he stops me with a quick jerk of his head, his eyes darting behind me and back to the drink. Not wanting to cause a scene, I raise my glass and sniff. The aroma is most pleasant, reminding me of fresh strawberries I haven't had since I was a child. There's something underlying in it too. Cinnamon maybe? Something spicy?

"Do it." Vincent's voice is a step above a whisper, and I can see the utter desperation in his face. The glass feels heavy in my hand as I move it to my lips. The moment the drink spills into my mouth, I'm thrust into overwhelming emotion.

71

I'm angry, so very angry that I want to rip out the hearts of any who looks at me, yet I'm completely turned on, my body coming to life like never before. I want to consume all the wine on the shelves, but take my time doing it, making sure everyone watches in jealousy. I want to wear my crown with pride, be the envy of anyone who stares, looking regal and royal, yet I want to strip off all my clothes and feel mouths licking me, hands touching me, a cock thrusting inside me…

And then I feel it.

My back begins to tingle and itch. I look at Vincent with wide eyes as he watches with a knowing smile on his face. "Take another drink, dear." This time I listen, letting a huge gulp slip down my throat. It's more like a juice, an odd combination of all my favorite flavors. I taste sweet and salty, spicy and sour. There's a smoothness to it and a bitterness, rich and savory.

It's addicting.

My back feels tight, like tiny strings are tugging on my skin, and I know my body is healing itself, stitching its broken pieces back together. The process only takes a few minutes. By the time I finish off the last of my "gift," my back is repaired and reconstructed. I laugh like a crazy person, swinging my arms around in the absence of pain.

"Can you thank them for me?" I ask Vincent, sliding the empty glass toward him. "Also, do you think I can purchase a bottle of whatever that was?"

Now it's Vincent's turn to laugh. "What you just drank, money cannot buy." He steps back to help others wanting their glasses filled while I ponder what that means. Of course money could buy that. Any royal or upper-class citizen would pay pounds of gold to have an elixir that can cure.

My skin tingles with unused energy. I feel like I could run around my kingdom three or four times without becoming winded. It's like the drink gave me liquid courage, took away all my worries and cleared my mind, so I can just enjoy myself for once.

Vincent slides me another glass with a wink before heading back into the masses. The music changes from a sad melody to an upbeat tune. With a smile on my face, I slip from my seat and waltz into the crowd of beautiful people. I know I don't belong here in this "custom dress," but right now I don't fucking care.

My body moves all on its own. My hips sway to the music and my feet dance to the beat. I take a sip of my new drink and almost spit it out. Unlike the decadent one I had before, this one has only one flavor. And that flavor is gross.

But still, I drink it, letting the alcohol go to my head. The giddy feeling that puts a silly smile on your face when you've had too much wine takes over inside my head. I feel unstoppable. Invincible. Like magic itself is coursing through my veins.

The moment my glass empties, I find Vincent running to me with another filled and ready for consumption. I drink to my heart's content, letting the flowy, happy sensation course through my body, warming my blood.

I can see now why so many turn to alcohol when they have no reason for staying alert. With so many stressors and problems to face every single moment of my life, it feels so good to just not give a fuck for once.

As I move my body to the music, a handsome man comes up to me and smiles. He's quite attractive, with dark brown hair and bright eyes, a young face that would put him about my age, but I feel nothing for him.

Where my body was alight with heat only moments ago, I feel only icy toward this man. But I let him dance with me anyway, since it's not as fun to dance by yourself. His hands begin to wander my body, sliding up and down my spine, slipping below my dress to cup my bare ass.

I look up into his hooded eyes and take a breath to tell him to fuck off, when his eyes widen in fear and he takes a step back. I'm almost proud of myself, thinking I was able to persuade him with my gaze when I feel a body behind me.

A hard body.

Cold fingers snake around my neck possessively as he leans down to sniff my hair. I freeze to the spot, excited and terrified at the same time. His scent washes over me, sweet and spicy, like a freshly baked spice cake that tingles your tongue after you eat it.

Parts of my body I didn't even know worked spring into life. My nipples tighten behind my dress and something aches between my legs, making me want to rub my thighs together.

But I don't move.

A finger trails up and down my back slowly, tracing every single vertebra. When the finger becomes a hand that slips inside my dress, snaking over my stomach, my body ignites, even though the hand touching me is ice cold.

My skin buzzes with magic, every nerve ending firing, and I wonder for a moment if it could be the wine causing my body to react this way, even though I know that's not true. My breathing becomes labored. Then something odd happens and I think I've peed myself as wetness gushes from between my legs.

What is happening to me?

I want to pull away from this man, but I can't, or I won't, I'm not sure which is the real truth. Then he chuckles as if he can sense the turmoil happening inside me. His voice washes over me like a warm blanket. I want to get lost in the richness.

"Time to go, pet. The sun will soon rise, and before it does you must be gone from this place."

Who is this man?

I move to turn my head, wanting to see him with my own eyes, when he warns, "Don't," with absolute authority, and I obey like a good little pet would. The hand around my neck tightens before letting go. A moment later, I feel something pressed into my hand. "Another gift," he whispers into my ear, causing goosebumps to erupt on my skin. "Use it only when you have a great need."

Fingers tug at my hair, but as the pressure decreases, my hair slipping through his hands, he vanishes. I turn quickly when I no longer feel his body pressed to mine, but it looks as if he was never there. People act none the wiser, drinking and dancing to the music. I wonder if I could have imagined his presence, then I feel the skin prickling sensation of someone watching me.

Many someones.

My gaze drifts to the seven. Seven noses, seven pairs of lips. I let my eyes settle on each one, looking for any differences. Two have beards but it's the one with a cleft chin who draws my attention. He licks his lips and nods almost imperceptibly when my eyes land on him. His supple lips form the word, "Go."

I've lingered here for too long.

Backing up, I bump into a couple who tries to pull me between them for a dance while they tell me how good I smell. I tug myself out of their arms and stumble right into the hands of another who wants me to dance. I excuse myself, my words slurring, when someone grabs my hand and spins me into a dip. The world keeps spinning even when my body stops, and I curse, almost dropping the bottle before I'm able to tug my hand free and jog to the door.

My bare feet slip on a spilled drink and I stagger to the door, but again, find no handle. I become frantic, feeling another stalking up behind me, and just before I cry out for help I hear a snap and the door opens by itself.

I hurry through, past the sconces scattered along the red walls as the door slams. Dizzy, I run over to the blackened wall I came through and feel for something, anything that will let me out. With a shout, I bang on the wall hard, the wine numbing the pain in my hands, until something creaks. Feeling the urgency, I thrust the door open just as the gray clouds above begin to lighten, still hiding the sun behind its gloomy, skyward blanket.

CHAPTER 9

I lean against the door and catch my breath, reliving what happened inside. My head is still fuzzy from the alcohol and whatever was in my gift.

The gift.

Looking down, I open my clenched hand and stare at the small glass vial. My breath catches when I see it's virtually the same as the one filled with poison brought to me by the mouse.

How is this possible?

The same tarnished white label, the same handwriting as before, only this time instead of *poison* it says *nectar.*

How perfect. If this is indeed the same stuff that healed my back, then I suppose it is a nectar—the food and drink of the gods, making normal people immortal.

I laugh to myself.

Immortal.

How silly.

Everything dies. The grass, the flowers, even the ancient trees in the forest will someday perish. Every animal I've ever seen, every person I've ever met, they all have an expiration date. I wish the evil bitch would meet hers sooner rather than later. But that woman hasn't aged a day since I've known her. She has the same white-blonde hair and smooth skin as she did the day my father brought her to the castle for the first time when I was only three or four years old.

I know I should be worried about being captured, but I feel too good to hide away, even though I'm being foolish. Instead, I let the wine take over and, after taking a quick peek to make sure no one is around, I walk out into the streets, wishing it was a bright, sunny day. I miss the feeling of the sun's rays warming my skin, even if I did ripen like a tomato when I stayed out too long.

With thoughts of capture banging at the back of my mind, I tie my nectar into the bodice of my dress and retrace my steps down the cobblestone path. I stroll through the narrow alley smooshed between the too close buildings and find myself back in the town square. The whipping pole still taunts me, looming over my head like a storm cloud.

Anger surges within me. How dare someone think they have the fucking right to strip a human and whip them to shreds, in front of her own kingdom no less! That will never happen again.

Seething, with red smattering across my vision, I stomp between the meager homes, trudging through the backyards until I find the item I'm looking for.

An axe.

The wooden handle feels powerful in my hands, and I give it a few good swings before stalking back to the post. Before my evil stepmother took away everything I loved, my father taught me how to use tools. He used to say that even a princess should be able to take care of herself. So I learned how to chop wood, how to saddle and take care of my horse, and the proper way to change the wheel on a wagon should I be stranded.

Smiling, I send a grateful prayer up to my father and take aim. Pulling the head of the axe back over my shoulder, I swing hard and strike the pole. My muscles surge with adrenaline, reminding me how energized I feel as I assault the wooden monstrosity. Again and again, the blade of my borrowed axe bites at its enemy until a great notch forms.

My muscles are only slightly fatigued, so I continue my siege, obscenities flying from my lips. I chop ruthlessly until blisters form on my hands and blood seeps between my fingers. Lowering my axe to catch my breath, I wipe my brow and see that the citizens of Riverwood have exited their homes. Families are standing on their doorsteps, watching me with rapt attention.

I see the look in their eyes, it's one of loyalty, of anger, but their wrath is not aimed at me. It's for the oppression we all are facing.

My eyes widen in surprise when several men come toward me with their own axes in tow.

"May we help you, princess?" a large man asks.

"It would be an honor," another says. My heart warms at the support, and I take a step back and allow them to assist me. There must be twenty men, and some even brought their older sons to come to my aid, each one taking a strike at the pole. The gesture feels monumental. During my hours of confinement, I have often questioned if the people would still support me after so long. Even though I see the tattoos, notice the quick glances and firm nods to assure me of their loyalty, anxiety sometimes lies to me, telling me the opposite is true.

The queen is nothing if not terrifying, and I've thought, perhaps, it was easier for them to give in to her demands rather than fight alongside me.

Now I see that's not the case.

Tears mist my vision when the final blow strikes and the men push the post to the ground, cheering in celebration.

I fall to my knees with emotion, cradling my head in my hands. Life is so damn hard, every day is torture, and I struggle to find the will to keep surviving. But seeing this support from the people, *my people,* gives me a reason to keep fighting, to live.

I'll do it for them.

For the husbands protecting their families, for the mothers caring for their children, for the babies who have their entire life ahead of them, and for the elderly who have so much knowledge and wisdom to share.

Every day, until I can find a way to free myself from the tyrant restraining us all, I'll fight for them.

Caring hands cradle my shoulders and I jerk my head up to see a woman's warm face smiling down on me. "You bow to no one," she whispers softly, pulling me up from the wet ground. And I let her. She lifts me with ease then takes a step back into the crowd. I think all of Riverwood is now here in the town square, and once again, I am the center of attention. But then they do something I did not expect.

They kneel.

Every man kneels, removing his hat in respect. Every woman kneels, placing her hand on her heart. Every child bows their head in respect.

My heart feels like it might burst. I feel so undeserving of their support. Then they begin to speak as tears blur my vision, dripping down my cheeks.

"We're with you, Princess Snow."

"Keep fighting for us."

"We admire your strength."

"Don't let her wickedness ever make you doubt us."

"We will always stand by your side."

I choke back a sob, my chest squeezing with love for these

people. I will never doubt them again, no matter what convincing lies the queen whispers to me.

I wipe the tears from my eyes and try to make eye contact with each and every person, letting them know that I see them. That they matter. I wish I had the words to tell them what this means to me, to have their support, but they are lost in my burning throat.

And that's when I feel the rumbling under my feet. The others feel it too and look to each other with wide eyes. There is only one thing that could cause the ground to shake in the absence of a storm.

Horses.

And lots of them.

"Run!" I yell, urging people to hide in their homes. Men shout orders to their families, and the women scoop up their children before bustling back to where they came from. But I don't run. Instead, I pick up my axe and stand in front of the downed pole. It's not often I can say I'm proud of something I've done, but I am proud of this.

So I stand, axe in hand, as the huntsmen come tearing through the square riding their great steeds. Each set of yellow eyes stares down on me in hunger, though I can't tell if it's a desire for lust or pain.

One man dismounts and stalks over to the pole, kicking the chopped timber before turning his gaze on me. "You'll pay for this," he promises.

I raise my chin defiantly, a retort ready on my tongue. "And so will you, in this life or the next."

He bursts out in laughter and pulls a length of rope from his side. "That may be true, wench, but you have more to account for than just a broken pole."

What the hell is he talking about?

The huntsman prowls closer as two more dismount. One rips the axe from my hand while the other holds my wrists tight behind my back. "Don't you remember, *princess*? Or have you forgotten about the two dead men found in your room?"

Oh fuck.

The guards.

My bravado falters, and despair settles deep in the pit of my stomach. In the craziness since my escape from the castle, during my alcohol induced haze, I'd forgotten all about the fact that I became a murderer.

Twice.

My head swims, and this time it isn't from the wine as a huntsman tightly binds my wrists with coarse rope. He might as well have secured it around my neck because after pulling off an escape, yet again, the queen won't let me get off unpunished.

I cringe, thinking about the duke's kiss, but then I remember my little secret—the bottle tied snugly inside my dress—and pray that they don't strip me of my clothes as they often do.

Strong hands surround my waist and toss me, face down, over the front of a horse. The huntsman riding it chuckles deeply as his hands slide over my bare ass.

It's mortifying.

I kick at the huntsmen trying to spread my legs with his rough fingers when I connect with something and hear a crunch, my heel smashing into someone's nose.

"Get her back to the castle before the queen castrates you for touching her prized possession," someone shouts.

The huntsman behind me grunts in disappointment, then kicks his heels into his horse. With a whinny, we're off. My stomach is crushed during each and every stride of the horse, and the huntsman continues to rub my ass with his coarse palm.

He murmurs about the things he'd like to do to me, about

the items he'd like to stick inside me and fuck me with if he ever gets the chance.

My stomach lurches in disgust, and I try to distract myself by counting the houses we pass.

I gasp sharply, and not because of what the huntsman is doing, but because of what I see.

A lurker.

Hiding in the shadows between the homes, hood covering his head. Then another, backed into a cluster of trees. Two more conceal themselves in the cemetery, their still forms could easily be mistaken as morbid statues.

Instead of counting homes, I'm now counting lurkers. When I reach the seventh one, concealed against a stone wall stroking a dark beard, I stop counting. I wonder why they chose this moment to allow me to see them.

Is it to show their loyalty like the people? Is it a warning? Or a reminder of the gift warming against my chest.

Whatever the reason, seeing them, knowing they are here, gives me strength.

I keep my eyes locked on the seventh lurker, even as the horse under me gallops up the hill to my castle. Once at the stables, I'm pulled off my mount and thrown over the shoulder of another huntsmen. He snickers and gives my ass a pat before storming inside the castle. I expect to see the evil bitch waiting for me, a smile on her thin lips, the handle of the duke warming in the palm of her hand.

Instead, I'm met with silence. Keys jingle as the gates to the dungeons are unlocked and we begin the descent into hell. I accept my fate and stiffen my resolve for what's coming. After the week I've had, I expect to be punished cruelly and severely. Let's just hope I make it through this alive.

CHAPTER 10

*M*oaning fills my ears, lust coating the breathy voice. By its high pitch, I'd guess it belongs to a woman. She sounds like she's in utter bliss, her voice cracking and breaking, gasping seductively.

Fingers and mouths assault my body and my eyes fly open to see seven heads of hair moving along my skin. Lips suckle me, teeth bite gently, and fingers explore places I've never had them before.

The moaning starts again, and I realize I'm the one doing it. Lying on a bed of white, we are surrounded by a glowing, white room. Nothing exists except them and me. No windows or walls, no doors or guards, just bright white space, seven men, and me.

My eyes close as a mouth kisses me between my legs while hands tug my thighs apart. Another set of lips suckles on my nipple and my back arches, wanting more of the decadent sensation. The mouth between my legs extends his tongue, licking the length of me.

I gasp and writhe, my hips thrusting, wanting more contact. Someone chuckles, deep and sexy, the sound smoldering over my skin. Teeth nip at the crook of my neck, sucking on the vein I can feel throbbing there. Next go my wrists as two men hold them down, licking at my veins. One more sucks on the tender skin along *my inner thigh, while another pair latch their mouths around my nipples.*

The sensation is too much. I cry out, needing more, desperate for something as a heat builds inside me, and just when I think my body might explode from pleasure, they bite.

I AWAKE WITH A START, MY EYES FLYING OPEN. SWEAT COATS my skin, heating me in the usually frigid dungeon. Pulling my chest off the ground, I sit up and rest my back against the stones.

Who were those men?

The memory of their lips and tongues tasting my body is still fresh in my mind. Seven. There were seven men touching and licking, making my body ignite in ways I didn't know were possible. But it was all a dream, a figment of my imagination.

Wasn't it?

But if it was only a dream, then why is my skin still tender where they bit? Why are my thighs still damp from their wandering fingers, their soft kisses on the forbidden places of my body?

My core aches, and I almost snake my fingers between my legs to soothe it. And I might have, if I wasn't filthy on a cell floor. Remembering my gift, I slam my hand to my chest and deflate when I feel the bottle still snug between my breasts.

Not wanting to draw attention to my secret, I lower my hands just in case a guard or the fucking queen takes this moment to come hassle me.

I don't think I've been here long, maybe a day or so. The hunger pains aren't too bad yet, and my bones don't feel frozen. But the real question isn't how long I've been here, but how long will I be?

Long enough to sap me of all my energy and thin my body to a point of weakness, just in time for another suitor to come to claim me.

What will the queen say when she sees my back is healed? Will she whip me harder, make the wounds deeper to ensure they take longer to mend? Will she hold true to her dark words, and rip my heart from my chest?

Or will she lower her standards to something even more cruel, more permanent?

So many questions without any answers. All I know is after one of my best days, I'm once again alone, my only companion a memory of the seven.

THE SOUND OF MY CELL DOOR SLIDING OPEN WAKES ME, AND I squint against the light of the lantern.

"Get up." The guard's gruff voice does nothing to encourage me, but I still hoist myself off the floor. "Turn around." Before I can move, his rough hands spin me and tug my arms behind my back. I don't fight when a rope is woven around my wrists, knowing my disobedience will only cause me more pain. Sometimes, I have to pick my battles.

I'm yanked from the cell and have to catch myself from falling, then the guard shoves me ahead of him and sticks the point of a blade in my back. "Move."

My feet patter on the wet ground as I wind my way down the hallway and to the stairs, once again finding the other cells empty. The ascent is the same as always, and feelings of dread become all-consuming as I wonder what horrors await me as my body warms, my fingers and toes tingling painfully as they thaw.

The weapon's sharp tip prods at my shoulder blade harshly, encouraging me to move faster or pay the price. I'm still not entirely sure why no one has mentioned that my back is healed, and I worry about the disregard for such a slight. Surely the queen would have been told by now, her anger severe at my lack of pain.

Another guard waits for us at the top of the dungeon stairs and grins at me creepily as he swings the iron door open. I step out into the light and try to give him a wide berth. He has one of those faces where you can't quite tell if someone is completely with it or not, and I'm not just referring to the fact that he's under the queen's spell. His expression reminds me of one of those court jesters my father used to have come and entertain us, with their faces painted white and red, wearing jingle bells on their hats as they pranced around. I never liked those jesters, and when my father finally realized how much they scared me, he banished them from the castle.

Now I'd give anything for the distraction, for another to humiliate themselves so all eyes were on someone other than me.

The second guard flanks me, and the two of them grip my upper arms and march me toward the grounds behind my castle. By the gloom outside, I'd say it's midafternoon. How many days have passed since I destroyed the post, I cannot say.

I hear her high-pitched laughter before I see her and avert my eyes to the ground. A select few staff stand somberly in front of the orchard, their gazes cast to the ground. I see Sherry and Enid, and cringe when Martin's face smiles at me darkly. There are about a dozen guards too, all looking at me with bloodthirsty faces.

"There she is! Our little murderous escapee!" The queen's voice sounds even worse when she croons, "How was your little trip into the city, daughter, after you murdered those poor men in cold blood? Do anything...stupid? Like knock down my freshly built whipping post?" She ends the last sentence in a growl and gathers her skirts to march over to me. "What the hell did you think you'd gain by such an act? It's treasonous! Why, if anyone other than you had committed such a crime, they'd be hanged for their betrayal of the crown."

She takes a bite of a fresh, red apple and prowls back and forth in front of me. "Now what to do with our little stray?" My head twitches as her teeth sink into the apple's flesh once more. "Should we tie you up? Slaughter you as a menace to society and feed you to the pigs? No. You'd be getting off too easy that way." She chews obnoxiously, every bite feeling like someone is smacking me in the head with a piece of lumber, every crunch causing my blood to boil with fury, with *wrath* so potent, I haven't experienced anything like it.

"I would whip you again, but I see that type of pain has had no effect on your fucked up mind. So we will try a different kind today, one that offers pain *and* humiliation." She presses her lips to my ear, sliding her fingers around my neck. "And since you insist on dressing like a village whore, you are ordered to wear this and only this until I say otherwise. But for now..." She digs her nails into my throat before walking back to the others. With a swish of her cape, she spins to face me again.

"Guards, tie her up to the picket line like the beast she is. She wants to act like a rabid animal, then it's time we treat her like one."

A boot lands on my back and I stumble toward the row of horses on my way to the picket line. I see a spot has already been readied on the far end, away from the horses who have yet to be put away for the day.

Just like before, my hands are untied and rebound in front of me. But this time, I'm not stripped. I guess there really is no need since this dress I fabricated covers almost nothing.

"Good," the queen praises her sniveling men. "Now, everyone to the orchards. Time to pick your switch."

Switch?

Oh no…

Everyone gathered except the queen lumbers into the rows of fruit trees and my skin shudders, knowing what's coming. Once they are out of earshot, she speaks to me. "I don't know how you did it, whore, but I won't let you undermine me again. Whatever magic you came in contact with, I can promise you it won't stand a chance against mine. I—"

A guard exits the trees and the queen staunches her accosting. She would never want another to think she has less power than someone else, so she doesn't finish her thought. The others quickly follow, and soon there are twenty people lined up with switches in various sizes.

The evil bitch turns to address those gathered, and points a slender finger at me. "Now! As penalty for murdering two of your own, men who you'd call your close friends, I offer you the gift of revenge. You may all strike this guilty woman twice, one blow for each fallen guard, in a place of your choosing. Should I find your punishment insufficient, then I will switch her for you."

Murmurs whisper through the people, no doubt they were not expecting this. I can't even bear to look at Sherry or Enid, not wanting to see the pity on their faces.

"Who wishes to cast the first act of retribution?"

"I would, your majesty." I look and see the sniveling asshole Martin stepping forward.

The queen moves to examine his switch. "Martin, is it?"

"Yes, my queen." She returns his switch to his hands as he turns his yellow eyes on me.

"You may proceed."

And so it begins...

Martin stalks over to me like a man who has a carrot shoved deep in his asshole, and I almost laugh in spite of myself. But then he holds out the switch for me to see and any humor I once had dies immediately.

"Now, where to strike you, whore? Should I choose your pretty face? Your breasts? Hmm." He prowls around me, his eyes drinking in my skin as he ponders the best place. His face lightens and his smug grin returns. "Your ass. Bend over and prepare for your punishment."

When I don't move, he kicks at the back of my knee and I fall to the grass. Before I can scurry back up, I feel the back of my dress lifted, then a searing pain assaults me. I hiss through clenched teeth when he lands his second strike.

Chuckling, he walks back to his place.

"Very good, Martin," the evil bitch praises. "Who would like to go next?"

A guard whom I do not recognize steps forward with a rather thick switch. The queen doesn't even try to inspect his weapon as he stalks over. My legs shake as I stand, my ass burning in pain. "I will take her ass too. Bend over, slut, and take your beating. It was my brother you killed. And for that, I mean to hurt you." His voice is filled with dark promise. The hardest part of this punishment isn't the pain, though I know it will become unbearable, it's the humiliation. I have to present the part of my body my abuser wants to harm. "Move now, or I'll strike your face, pretty girl."

I wince as I sink to my knees once again and allow this wretched man access to my ass. I hear the switch hiss through the air a second before it lands. This time I can't hold in my cry, and I scream out at the blistering pain, my cheeks clenching in response. I try to relax my muscles, knowing it hurts more when I'm tense, but I fail to do so in time and he lands his second strike. I howl, the supple skin of my ass not used to such torment. I won't be able to sit for weeks.

"Well done, Thurmond, well done. Who's next?"

And so this routine goes on and on for what feels like hours, each man taking his time in choosing the spot on my body he wishes to mark. One guard pulls down my bodice, and another holds me down while he whips my breasts. His second attempt lands right on my nipple. I think the entire town of Riverwood was able to hear my howls. I just pray that my bottle of nectar doesn't become discovered or dislodged from where I tied it.

Not an inch of my body is spared. Greedy arms push and pull my dress to expose what they want to whip. My breasts, my belly, my thighs... Every part of my body blazes from the lacerations, every single inch...besides my face.

My chest heaves in exhaustion, my entire body coated in sweat. The tremors are uncontrollable now, each part of me quaking involuntarily. Euphoria escapes me tonight and I know it's because the pain has been staggered. I can hear the smile on the queen's face when she calls the next person forward.

Enid.

Her quiet whimpers reach my ears as she stumbles over to me. I can't look at her, the sadness in her face will cause me to break. I simply nod and present my back to her.

"Remember, Enid, strike her hard enough to mark her, or I will hit her for you." The queen's promise hangs over me like a rain cloud. Enid sniffs and pulls her arm back. I close my eyes and wait. Enid screams then brings her arm down, her switch searing into my back two times in rapid succession.

"Good job, Enid. Now you, Sherry."

This is it, the last person. I can do this.

"I can't—" Sherry sobs, but the queen cuts her off.

"You can and you will, or you, too, will feel the switch on your skin."

Crying, Sherry waddles over. I can see her reddened face from the corner of my eye, but I won't look at her.

"Just do it," I whisper so low, I'm not sure she could even hear me.

Sherry tries to gather her resolve, bringing her arm back twice before letting it fall.

"Fine! I'll do it!" The evil bitch stomps over and pulls the switch from Sherry's grasp, then strikes her across the cheek. Sherry falls to the ground shrieking, holding her face in her hand while I feel the fury of the queen as she strikes my back.

I scream as she lands her second one and collapse to the ground. My head gets woozy from the pain and my vision falters, my hearing growing muffled.

"Animals like you don't belong in the castle, little beast, so from now on you'll stay in the stables, sleeping next to the heaping piles of horse shit." Before her words even register, I'm thrown into a stall with a massive Clydesdale.

As the stable doors are shut and locked behind me, I curl up into a ball and cry. I usually have much more control over my emotions, but this is just too overwhelming. I cry because I'm in pain from the abuse done to my body. I cry because I'm sad for my friends, Sherry and Enid, who were forced to hurt me for the queen's own revenge. I cry because I'm angry about having my freedom and my pride stripped from me. I cry because, for just a few hours inside the hidden party, I knew what happiness felt like. I cry hard for anyone who needs to hear it. Because tears don't make you weak. No. Tears are the manifestation of emotion, evidence of accepting who you are, that you're dealing with your suffering, proof that you have faced your fears and survived. They are a way for the mind to heal, to let out the excess anger, pain, and sorrow. And right now I'm letting it all pour down my face to heal my mind from torment and cleanse my soul of deep despair.

As my tears dry up, I feel a moment of clarity. Someday, I will become the thing the queen most fears, and when she faces me for the final moments of her life, I vow to make her weep tears of blood.

CHAPTER 11

I wake to something soft and cold, rubbing against my cheek. I push it away, but it comes back, poking at me with interest. My eyes shoot open when I remember I'm in the stables, and I come face-to-face with a pink muzzle. The horse nudges me again and I realize he wants me to pet him. I smile for the first time since I was at the secret party and stroke his head between his eyes. His big ears twitch and his tail swishes behind him.

"Hey there," I rasp, my voice still broken from yesterday's cries, bringing my fingers behind his ears for a good scratch. "Aren't you a pretty boy." He snorts and pushes his head into my hands harder. I laugh, but the happiness falls short when the wounds on my body remind me of what happened yesterday.

I fiddle with the ribbon wound through my bodice and slip my fingers around the tiny bottle of nectar. I haven't used it yet for several reasons. One, I'm scared to. What if the nectar isn't the same stuff as yesterday, just a ruse to fuck with me? Two, what will the queen think when she sees my wounds healed yet again? Will she punish me harder?

Longer? Will she take it a step too far and do something to me I can never fully heal from? Maybe keep her promise to steal my heart.

Maybe I'll just take a small whiff.

As I watch the red liquid swimming in my hand, I feel almost drawn to it, like it needs me as much as I need it. It's an odd sort of feeling, and I can't quite understand what to make of it. Gently, I pull the tiny cork from the bottle and sniff.

I'm immediately blanketed in warmth and power. The drink calls to me, begs me to consume it, my body craving it. It smells just like it did yesterday, sweet and salty, spicy and savory...all the things I used to love. Not wanting it to make me drunk like it did yesterday, but unable to place the cork back in without tasting it, I place my finger over the opening and tip it quickly upside down. When I right the bottle, I lift my finger and a tiny drop of nectar waits for me. Extending my tongue, I lick the juice. My taste buds awaken, my mouth watering at the decadence.

Before I know what's happening, my lips pucker around the vial and I let the luscious liquid cover my tongue. Reluctantly, I pull my mouth off after the first swallow and hold up the glass, almost half gone already.

Then the euphoria sets in, my muscles become strong once again, and the wounds on my body heal with a pleasant tingle. My stomach no longer growls, it's as if this liquid also substitutes as food. In other words, I feel amazing.

I take a deep breath and let it out slowly before corking the vial and tying it back inside my bodice. I wish there was another place to hide it other than on me. Should I be stripped of my dress, the nectar would be lost.

But for now, this will have to do.

The horse nudges me again and shakes his black mane. I pet his smooth, bay-colored hide. "It's okay, Cupcake, I'm okay." I know Cupcake isn't the best name for this noble steed, but he's just so damn sweet. Pulling myself to my feet, I check out my skin. The marks along my body are still present, but instead of being fresh wounds, bright red and angry, they are a soft pink and no longer hurt like they are moments old.

Satisfied with the results, I reach up and hook my fingers over the edge of the stable door, then hoist myself higher. I see the orchard bustling with people. Servants walk through, loading their baskets with berries, apples, and other fruits while the stable hands bring horses to the picket line for grooming.

If I didn't know any better, I'd say these people are happy. Maybe they are. Out here there is a freedom. The queen seldom leaves the castle, so being outside does offer a reprieve from her oppressive presence.

I drop back down before anyone has a chance to see me peeking out. I don't want to give the queen a reason to come check on me. But my respite is soon over as the lock on the stable door clicks open and a pair of guards greet me with malicious smiles.

"Time to go, beast."

"Get your ass up, we have orders to bring you to the queen."

Groaning, I stroke the side of Cupcake and walk out of the stable. As usual, the guards' hands grip my arms to guide me. After consuming the nectar, I feel as though I could shrug them off and outrun them, but with only half a bottle left and a magical evil queen threatening my death, I don't.

A stern-looking guard with a white mustache opens the door to allow us entrance. Usually, I'm led upstairs to my room, but with that taken away, I have no idea where we are going. We pass through the kitchens to the servants' quarters. I think I'm going to be given a new room amongst them when I'm stopped next to a small door.

I can hear the rustle of her cape as she flutters down the hallway and avert my eyes accordingly. "Ah, here is our little beast. Come to see what I've had stocked inside your new cupboard?"

My new cupboard?

I almost ask her what the fuck she means, but catch myself before the words slip past my lips.

"Go on, show her." One guard releases me and pulls open the door by my side. "Take a look," she says, laughing like a crazy person. I turn my head and see nothing of real interest. A broom, some buckets, and rags. "Well, go on! The castle won't clean itself! I expect you to start on the top floor and work your way down. Wash every floor—*by hand*—and shine every set of armor. Once that's complete, you must wash all the windows then help the servants with the laundry. And should you complete all of that, you can clean out the stables, also by hand."

I can feel that surge of anger brewing in the pit of my stomach. I would give anything in the world to punch this bitch right in her snarky fucking face. My fury rages because I can't. I *have* to obey her...for now.

"Go on, beast. Grab your pail and get scrubbing!" I flinch when she reaches for me and pulls on my hair, tossing me to the ground with a strength I didn't know she had. "Don't test me, beast! I have had enough of your disobedience! I will not tolerate it another second!"

Spittle flies from her mouth and sprays me in the face, and I have to force my hands to stay clenched by my sides.

"Now," she growls, straightening back up. Swallowing down my anger, I crawl to the pail already filled with water and throw in a few rags. "Carry that upstairs and get out of my sight. Gerard, follow her and make sure she doesn't get in trouble."

As her heels click on the floor, growing farther and farther away, I pick up my pail and head for the nearest staircase when the evil bitch's shrill voice shrieks at me from down the hall. "On second thought, clean your old room first." Then she laughs as she walks away.

Grumbling to myself with Gerard behind me, I start to climb the stairs. The pail weighs a fucking ton, giving me a whole new respect for servants required to do this. My thighs are shaking when I get to the top floor—the same level my room is on.

Using two hands, I basically have to waddle down the long corridor while escaped water sloshes over my feet. The air becomes thick with a wretched, putrid odor as we near my room. It churns my stomach, burns my nostrils, and makes me want to puke.

"Keep moving, beast," Gerard orders, encouraging me with a push between the shoulder blades. As I turn into my room and the rancid smell grows stronger, I know it can only mean one thing.

The evil bitch left the guards.

Lying in pools of their own blood and urine are the two guards I murdered. Their eyeballs are missing, the tips of their fingers gnawed on by rats or mice or worse. Insects cluster around their mouths, and maggots and other creepy crawly things enter between rotten teeth and exit through gaping nostrils.

I can't fucking do this.

Gerard gags behind me as I take a few steps back, only to bump into his chest. "You're not getting out of this one, beast. Get to cleaning or else."

I want to ask him, *or else what*, but I'm too afraid of opening my mouth and actually tasting the air in the room.

But I'm at a loss for what to do. The bodies need to be moved before anyone could clean up, and I'm too small to carry them by myself. I could chop up the bodies into pieces, but that would require a blade, and I'm sure Gerard would not be willing to lend me one.

Even the bottle of poison still lies strewn between the guards. I must have dropped it in my frenzy to escape. Seeing that one makes me think of the other one strapped to my body, snuggled between my breasts. Maybe I was hasty in using the nectar so soon. Maybe if I had let the queen see my wounds still fresh, she wouldn't have sent me up here.

Of course, that's foolish. The only reason she would have left the bodies rotting in *her* castle is for me to find them.

The buzzing of the insects makes me feel dizzy. I can't stand bugs, never could, and freak out when the smallest of spiders makes its home in the corner of my room. Now I have to watch in horror as they skitter about in the goopy fluid like a fucked up insect feast.

Bile rises in my throat. I try to swallow it down, but end up turning past the guard and dry heaving in the hallway. I haven't eaten for the past several days other than wine and nectar, so nothing comes up but acidic waste from my belly.

"You better get back in there, beast, or the queen will find something worse than switches to punish you with."

"Nothing can be worse than this," I grumble to myself, turning back to the room. Just as I'm about to ask Gerard for a blade, another set of guards show up, equipped with a gurney. They shove me aside and tug the two corpses onto it without so much as a single word. The movement of the bodies stirs the decomposing scent and we all gag. Even the sound of another gagging makes me gag even harder, so right now I'm totally fucked.

With a grunt, the guards carry the bodies out of the room and down the hall. One stiff hand hangs off the gurney, its finger pointed, a yellow liquid dripping off like a trail of breadcrumbs.

With the bodies gone, I can try to clear up the sludge left behind. I start to accept this penance. I did kill them, so it seems only fair that I should have to clean up the mess I've caused.

Looking around for the best way to attack this, I head to my bed and strip the sheets, throwing them over the putrid pool. The white linen quickly becomes an unappealing brown, but works to soak up the fluids. Knowing I can't prolong this next step any longer, I hold my breath and scoop up the soaked sheets, quivering as the trapped bugs skitter around underneath it.

I cringe when the wetness seeps through to my skin, even though I'm holding them as far away from my body as possible, and hurry out to the hall with the load. Gerard steps out of my way, not wanting to touch it himself, I'm sure.

I grab a spare set of linens from my wardrobe and repeat the process, soaking up the last of the body fluids before tossing them into the hall. With the hard part done, I grab the pail filled with soapy water and get to scrubbing. I try to keep my body sideways so Gerard doesn't get a full view of my ass, tits, or the nectar still tied to my bodice.

It takes a while, and by the time I'm done, my fingers are pruned and the backs of my hands are cracked from the harsh soap.

But it's done.

Sweat trickles down my forehead and I swipe at it with the back of my hand, feeling proud that I actually finished. Gerard seems impressed too, and I think, just for a second, his lips quirked in a smile.

CHAPTER 12

*A*fter successfully cleaning the dead from my room, I have to make the long trek down to the well outside the castle, dragging the putrid sheets behind me. Guards shout at me, calling me every foul name they can think of as I pass.

"Ignorant wench."

"Foul beast."

"I've got a place you can clean."

Each snide remark is fouler than the last. Some spit at me as I walk by, while others think my punishment is an open invitation to touch me. Hands slap against my ass, others tug at my unruly hair, and some grab at my dress, trying to bare parts of me they want to see.

Ignoring them as best as I can, knowing they just want a reaction from me, I head to the well with Gerard close behind. The well is deep and it takes several minutes for the empty bucket to reach the water below. My arms shake as I tug on the rope, pulling the pail back up before I dump it into my awaiting, unfilled bucket.

I have to repeat the process several times before my pail is filled to the top. Then comes the long walk back through the castle and up two flights of stairs. My back aches by the time I get there. Staring down the long hallway, I almost cry. My body won't be able to finish this job in one day, and the queen knows that. I'm sure that's why she's tasked me with the impossible, so she can inflict her wicked punishments on me once more.

Sighing, I carry the bucket to the end of the hall and begin to wash the floor in front of the staircase I escaped down only two days ago. Thoughts of making another break for it begin to fill my mind as I scrub mindlessly. Gerard takes up a post, sitting with his back against the wall, giving him a perfect view of my ass and other more private places on my body. And he's not shy about staring either. His hand grips his gross dick through his pants, and he grunts, displaying yellow teeth behind his blistered lips. But what can I do besides get this over with as fast as possible?

"Yeah, spread those thighs, beast, show Gerard that pretty cunt."

Fucking gag.

Yeah, that really makes me want to just spread myself for him. What an idiot.

My ass cheeks clench in response to his shitshow of failed encouragements, and for the remainder of the hallway, I keep my thighs pressed tightly together. Gerard isn't dissuaded, however, and pulls his dirty dick from his pants, and I'm immediately assaulted by the pungent stench of moldy cheese. Unable to stop myself, I mistakenly look at it. A huge bush of hair surrounds the base, making it look like a baby ostrich poking its fleshy neck from a fluffy bundle of feathers. Gerard catches me looking, and his smile grows wider, making me wonder how someone can eat when all their back teeth are broken or missing.

I wonder if all dicks look like that. Small, stinky, and

hairy... If so, why would a woman want one anywhere inside her? No fucking thanks. I'll keep my holes empty, thank you very much.

Speaking of empty holes, Gerard looks like he's lost in the sight of my vagina. His eyes are vacant as he stares at my butt, his jaw slackened as his hand works furiously on his tiny dick.

I wonder if I should make a break for it now? I'm not far from the stairs. I glance up toward the window and find the gray clouds are bright. It's still daytime. There's no way I'd make it without someone seeing me. And as exhausted as I am, I won't be able to run very far. I consider using the rest of the nectar, but quickly squash that idea. The mysterious member of the seven who gave it to me told me to only use it in times of great need. So far, though I *want* it, I don't actually *need* it.

Damn moral compass.

If I were the queen, I'd say fuck the rules and drink it. But even though the seven wouldn't know I drank it out of plain desire, I don't want to disobey them. That revelation surprises me, making me determined to see them again, even if it's just their crimson lips.

A disgusting moan has me looking at Gerard once again as he comes all over the floor between his legs.

Great.

Now I have to scrub up cum.

Add that to the list of bodily fluids I've had to clean up today. Should be some kind of record for the grossest day ever.

The water has morphed from clear to brown, and I know I'll need to make another trip down to the well. Once Gerard has put his cheesy, stinky, flaccid wiener back in its hiding place, I quickly wipe up his mess and begin the long walk back to the well.

My fingers cramp from carrying the heavy pail and my legs shake even going down the stairs. By the time I get to the well, I'm feeling dizzy. Sweat covers my skin and my belly rumbles with hunger. I crumble, falling to my knees. My tongue feels swollen and thick, my throat dry. I desperately need something to eat and some water.

"There you are!" The voice of the evil bitch carries to me from across the grounds. "Hungry, are you, beast? Well, I have just the thing." With a snap of her fingers, a guard brings over a pair of bowls, and she takes a bite of a fresh red apple. Usually, I'd contemplate the queen's motives before taking anything offered by her or her minions, but in my exhausted delirium, I greedily reach for the bowls.

"Not so fast," she barks, apple flying from her mouth as she stops the guard with a snap of her fingers. "Beasts don't eat with their hands, so neither shall you. Gerard, bind her wrists."

No.

I want to scream and yell, I want to cry and roar and kick and beat the ever-loving fuck out of this woman. How can someone be this evil? This...this heartless, insensitive, and indifferent about another person?

I try to keep my face devoid of emotion as my arms are wrenched behind me and quickly secured. My *pride* is long gone, my dignity tossed away after my father's demise.

You need to eat, Snow. Get on the damn grass and just do it.

I swallow hard and lick my chapped lips, then fall to my knees. The water calls to me, the liquid clear and sparkling.

Fuck it.

I spread my knees and bend down, stretching my tongue to reach the water. I'm so delirious that I don't even realize the smell is all wrong. I lap like a fucking dog and immediately spit out the contents. It's not water.

It's vinegar.

My lips curl in anger and I almost make eye contact with the queen, wanting her to see the *wrath* in my gaze, but catch myself at her nose.

"What's wrong, *dear*?" she sneers, chewing loudly on her fruit. "Something wrong with your water? Take another drink, I wouldn't want you to go thirsty, not when there's so much of the castle yet to clean." She laughs and squats down next to me, fisting the back of my hair in her hand, then shoves my face in the vinegar. My eyes sting, my nose burning. The sour liquid fills my mouth as I gasp for air, and I swallow a mouthful down my throat.

My stomach churns, my tongue turning to ash in my mouth before she pulls me back out. I suck in deep breaths while she laughs maniacally, shoving my head away from her. "So *refreshing*, isn't it, dear? Perhaps you'd like to try the food next? I had it specifically made for you by my chef."

Pathetically, I try to hop away on my knees while the queen and the guards laugh at my expense. I fall to my back, completely out of breath, sapped of energy. The world becomes fuzzy and I squint, trying to make things less blurry. That's when I feel something hot crash into my cheek. It's putrid and gooey, reminding me of the leftovers from the dead guards.

"Won't you try some?" she requests happily. "I think you'll find it almost as delicious as the water." Another drop lands on my face, and with my arms bound below me, I just have to lie here with it dripping down my cheek. "It's haggis, you know, specially ordered." I almost gag then. I've never been picky when it comes to food, but haggis is one I could never stomach, no pun intended. Knowing it's something's intestines boiled in its stomach always made me want to throw up. "The chef went above and beyond for you, beast, don't you like the seasonings?"

Seasonings?

It smells like asshole and death.

Another splash lands on me, this time right on my lips. I gag hard when some of the mixture passes into my mouth and I spit it back out as hard as I can. The repugnant flavor still lingers, causing my gag reflex to work overtime, but I can't figure out what it is.

"Since you're not worthy of haggis made from a sheep or calf, I had to improvise," she continues. "This one was a custom order, made from the meatiest parts of the guards you killed."

Bile rises in my throat, burning through the tissue already seared by the vinegar.

The queen laughs at my distress, giggling while I heave the meager contents of my belly.

"You know I had him boil it in one of their stomachs too, for that extra little kick. Here, take a bite." Hands attack my face, covering my eyes, pinching my nose. I fight them, but I'm at a total disadvantage and have to open my mouth for air. The moment I do, the miserable meat pie is shoved past my lips as another hand holds my mouth closed.

I choke and gag, trying to open my mouth and expel the rotten meat of a corpse, but the strong hands keep hold of my nose and jaw, not allowing me to chew or breathe, much less open my mouth. I kick my feet, trying to connect with anyone, anything, but then firm hands hold them down. The bite in my mouth is too big to swallow, and my throat begins to close, burning for an entirely different reason now. Helpless, my limbs become unresponsive as oxygen evacuates my brain, until, finally, I pass out into the welcome hands of unconsciousness. The last sound I hear is the queen's demented laughter.

CHAPTER 13

J'm not sure I've ever felt this bad or this low. I'm not even sure where I am until the same velvety muzzle greets me from yesterday. Though Cupcake's tenderness makes me happy, I can't even form a smile. I'm lying in a puddle of sadness, my body broken, my mind worn. My dress is sticky and smells of blood, sweat, and death. My hair has more knots than I think a comb could remove at this point.

But my eyes, mouth, hands, and stomach...they are in agony. I've lived days without food, but not having had any water is literally killing me. I would have drunk from Cupcake's trough if they had left it in here. My eyes have dried up, with no more tears to cry, still burning from the vinegar. I feel as though death is knocking at my door. My head pounds as if the huntsmen are laying into me with their axes. My gums are sore, and my tongue is so dry and thick, it burns, yet also feels foreign, like it's an object in my mouth and not part of my body.

Even my jaw aches from having that human haggis shoved inside, then from fighting the hands holding my mouth closed. I think about the nectar hiding in my dress and frantically feel for the bottle, only to find it missing. I look down and see the ribbon that held the sides of my dress closed across my chest is gone, probably removed for some sick fuck to grope me while I was unconscious.

Despair threatens to consume me. How much longer can I survive this? I mean, really? My body grows weaker by the second. Every moment spent here is another foot my grave has been dug deeper.

I've got to get out of here.

Cupcake nudges me again, and I reach up a shaky hand to pet him. He blows at me. "Such a good boy, aren't you, Cupcake? Thank you for sharing your stall with me, and for not pooping on me." He shakes his mane and turns so I can scratch his ear.

Then an idea pops into my head…

It worked once, maybe it will work again.

I lift my head and hold him under his fuzzy chin. "Cupcake, could you do me a favor? Could you kick at the door to open it for me please?" Cupcake looks at me, I mean *really* looks at me, his brown eyes staring into my soul. "Please?" My voice cracks this time. "If I don't get out of here, I'll die."

That realization hurts.

I'm probably a few days from death, and I sure as fuck smell like it. Cupcake shakes his mane and my head falls back to the hay strewn floor, defeated.

Then a miracle happens.

Cupcake kicks at the door. My eyes widen in half excitement, half fear. It's sometime in the middle of the night, so the castle is sleeping, but his assault on the door is so loud that I'm sure someone might hear it and catch me.

"That's a good boy!" I croak, falling to a coughing fit. The final crash sends the stable door hanging off its iron hinge. Then something surprising happens, Cupcake lowers himself to the ground and snorts at me. "D-Do you want me to ride you?" His head bobs and my heart surges. I do my best to move my exhausted body, using his hair as handles, and I half tug, half crawl onto him. Just that slight movement is exhausting, and I pant harshly while lying across him.

Cupcake heaves himself to his feet and heads out of the stables. "To Riverwood. Go!" The ride is bumpy as Cupcake takes off, his hooves clomping hard on the stone road. I haven't ridden a horse in so long, I forgot how exhilarating it was, how much I liked it.

Using all my remaining strength, I hoist my upper body off Cupcake and ride him like a horse was meant to be ridden. I try not to think about the fact that I'm riding him bareback and his horsey hair is gonna get all up in my business. Or how bad my breasts hurt thumping up and down with no support. All my thoughts come down to one...

The seven.

Get to them and get help.

They helped me once, they've watched me. They will help me again... I hope.

But who would want me like this? I'm in the same exact clothes they last saw me in before and haven't had a bath in days.

But what choice do I have?

I try to steer Cupcake as best as I can with no reins, encouraging him to move with soft pats to his sides. He obeys me, like he shares my mind, almost moving before I've even directed him where to go. Before I can risk a glance back, we are barreling through Riverwood's quiet streets and down the narrow alley taking me to the lair of the seven.

Thunder booms overhead, and a steady rain begins to fall. I welcome it with open arms. Tilting my head back and opening my mouth, I let the rain fill me. The cold liquid seeps into my desert-like mouth, bringing my soft tissues back to life. I could cry as I swallow down more and more. Then I wash my arms, my face, and dig into my scalp with my unclipped fingernails.

It feels so good, I almost miss the entrance. "Stop here, Cupcake," I coo, patting his side gently. My horse slows and prances before coming to a halt right in front of the slashed awning. My legs feel like lead weights, and I have to hoist my thigh up with my hands to move it over Cupcake's back before sliding off.

That was the wrong move, because I crash hard into the wet ground, cracking my head on the stone before collapsing onto my back. The rain washes over me, cleansing me of the funk caked onto my body from the past few days, even as it chills my skin. My vision swims as rain sticks to my eyelashes. I can't even lift my hand to swipe at them. Cupcake is anxious, snorting and nosing at me, but I can't move. "Go back to the castle, my good boy," I whisper, before my eyes close and the world no longer exists.

"WAKE UP, SOFI. ONE MUSTN'T NAP ON THE TABLE FOR TOO long. People might think you are drunk and force me to kick you out." I groan, lifting my head from my folded arms, and look straight into the eyes of—

"Vincent?"

He smiles and bows. "At your service. Tell me, what can I bring you to drink?"

How the fuck do I ask him for nectar? "Umm, may I have a water please?"

He frowns. "Water is so boring. Perhaps I can entice you with something more intoxicating?"

I rub my temples. "Listen, Vincent, you have no idea what I've been through in the past two days. My head is pounding and my stomach is empty... I just need some water to start. Please."

He nods deeply then heads off. I turn in my chair, realizing I have no idea how I got here. The party seems like it never ended. The same beautiful people dance to the same mournful music played by the same band. I wonder if it was all a dream last time and has only now become reality.

I move my gaze to the platform where the seven once stood, but find the dais empty. I try not to let disappointment settle in. I knew it was a risk coming here, but to not have any of them present is upsetting.

Vincent returns with a tall glass of ice water and a plate with bread and cheese. "Thank you," I say with gratitude, before diving in. I grip the bread first and tear a huge chunk out of it, then devour the cheese, eating it so fast I don't even taste it. The bread is soft and fresh and oh so yummy. If Vincent wasn't watching me, I would have licked the plate clean too. Picking up the glass, I guzzle the water, not caring that half of it leaks from the corners of my mouth.

Finished, I swipe at my mouth with the back of my hand and lock eyes with an awestruck Vincent. "Feeling better?"

"Much." I push the empty glass and plate toward him, then rest my elbows on the table, clasping my hands. "So...do you know how I got in here? My brain is a bit fuzzy."

He looks at me with a raised eyebrow. "One of them found you," he says cryptically.

"Them? Them who?"

He glances at his nails as if they are very interesting. "You know...one of the seven." My heart thuds rapidly. "There was a commotion out front. Seems one of the queen's horses escaped and found you first. He was most concerned about you. His cries were heard and Kin—one...of the seven, went to investigate. You were found, he brought you in, and here we are."

"And the horse?" My concern for Cupcake makes my voice squeak.

"Unknown. He ran off after you were taken care of." I nod in understanding and take a deep breath, already feeling better. "Who are you really, Sofi?" His question catches me off guard and I freeze on the spot.

"No one of importance," I mutter. It's not an entire lie. My life once held great value, but now? Now I'm treated worse than the scum of the Earth, even if the throne is actually mine.

"You're lying." I can feel the color drain from my already pale face. "I can smell it in the air around you."

My jaw drops…is he a lurker too? The memory of him smelling the air, of his face morphing to more beast than man, plays in my mind. He is something other…

"What are you?" I ask, womaning up.

Now it's Vincent's turn to stiffen. "I don't know what you mean."

I grin. "I think you do. I saw you that first day when I came in, and I've seen other lurkers—"

"Lurkers? Is that what you call them these days?"

Shit.

"Umm…"

Vincent laughs and takes a step back. "They left something for you, you know. Another gift…" Vincent slips back to the bottles along the shelf and pulls out a pre-poured glass. My mouth waters in anticipation, hoping it has more nectar inside. I'm not disappointed when he slides the glass down the table with practiced hands. The crystal goblet stops precisely in front of me without spilling a drop. I don't even have to taste it to know what it is, because the smell assaults me immediately.

I lick my lips and wrap my fingers around the cold stem before bringing the nectar to my mouth. Decadent, smooth, and delicious, the nectar slides down my throat and I swallow greedily. I'm much more careful than I was with the water and don't waste a single drop. But I've become too *greedy*, and don't stop consuming the luscious drink until every single morsel is gone.

I set the glass back down and sit back in my chair, eyes closed, just letting the feeling it causes consume me. Emotions of all varieties assault me again, my body almost tremoring at its ferocity. Anger and desire, pride and envy, and the need for more, but wanting others to do things for me are mixed tumultuously with lust filled thoughts. I'm reminded of my dream of the seven men whose experienced lips tasted my body...

Fuck.

Skin tingling sensations run over and through me. My burned throat repairs itself, my dry eyes healing. Smooth and flawless once again, my pale skin is no longer marred with remnants of the switches once lashed across me.

Now all I need is a bath to contain this hair.

The frenzy of emotions soon settles, and I'm left feeling drunk.

A smile replaces the scowl on my face as the alcohol makes me feel happy, and silly, my body loose and relaxed. Vincent replaces my empty goblet with a fresh glass, and even though I know nectar won't be greeting my lips this time, I still drink with voracious desire.

The music shifts from one of sadness to something unfamiliar yet more upbeat. Slipping off the chair, I pad to the center of the party on my bare feet and move my body to the music. The people cheer in excitement, and I look to see what all the commotion is about. High over the crowd, the cages containing the scantily clad dancers lowered.

I finish my wine and leave the empty glass on a nearby table before wading my way through the people to see what

113

all the fuss is about. Just like before, the guests extend their hands inside the cages, pricking the skin of the women with their claw-like fingernails. Blood is consumed, clothes are torn off, and the women end up naked with trails of their blood trickling down their bodies.

The women wear their naked skin with pride, dancing sensually, moving their hips seductively, their breasts pushed out proudly. I'm in awe, wanting to be like them. I've been naked in front of an audience more times than I can count, but it's never been with my consent, always forced by the evil bitch.

As the wine and nectar flow through my body, I realize I want to feel like those caged women. Lusted after and desired, because I chose to expose myself, not because I was forced to. My eyes raise to the ceiling where I see a third cage, an empty one. My skin prickles and I look over my shoulder to see Vincent staring at me. He flicks his eyes to the cage, then back to me. I answer with a slow but obvious nod. He inclines his head in return and moves down the table and out of sight. A moment later, the empty cage descends on the gathering.

Vincent joins me. "You sure this is what you want, Sofi?"

"Yes," I reply without hesitation.

Vincent guides the cage to the floor and opens the door for me. I slip inside while the guests watch with interest. "Be careful up there. You can get lost in your mind, even though you are encased behind bars."

Contemplating his words, the enclosure begins to rise. My fingers slip around the wooden bars and I watch as the people below grow smaller. I feel my foot bump into something, and I look down to find a glass filled with wine, ready for me.

I'm starting to like Vincent more and more.

When the cage stops its ascent, I grab my glass and raise it up to the sky. The crowd goes wild below me. I smile and take a long drink, letting the wine flood my veins.

My hips begin to sway to the music, and I hold onto the bars and move with the beat. I shut my eyes and forget everything else in the world. Right here, behind these wooden bars, I'm free. I let loose, spinning and twisting, undulating my body. I don't hear the crowd below me, I don't feel the many eyes staring at me, wanting to tear off my dress, I don't remember that I have no panties on or that I'm flashing everyone under me. All I know is this moment, this one sliver of happiness in my dismal life.

I raise my arms high in the air and twirl, bobbing my head, my hair flying crazily around. It's not until the tiny hairs on the back of my neck prickle that I open my eyes and really see what's happening around me. They are back...

The seven.

Lined up just like before, stoic and cast in shadows. I turn to face them, still rolling my hips, letting myself get lost in the music. I can't even tell if they are watching me, but I desperately want them to see me. So I decide to do something I never thought I'd be brave enough to do.

Still staring at the seven mysterious men, I finish off my wine and bring my hands to my shoulders. Slowly, I peel my dress down inch by inch. The crowd roars when I free my breasts, my nipples peaking in the air. I keep moving, keep dancing, my breasts bouncing to the beat along with me as I shimmy the dress over my ass to pool at my feet.

Stark naked, the crowd cheers and begins to chant, "Lower the cage!" I feel powerful in this moment, knowing they all want me, desire me, and are desperate to touch me through the bars. My hips sway, my chest pumping, and I turn my back to the seven, shaking my ass in their direction. Then in a brave and maybe stupid move, I spread my legs and bend over, running one finger down my ass to my slit.

I don't see their reaction, but I can almost *feel* it. A wave of lust cascades over me, making my insides clench in desire and a gush of wetness expel from inside me. I'm beginning to learn my body better now, and understand I get wet when I'm sexually excited. It's an odd sensation, but one I'm learning to like.

As I stand back up, the cage begins to descend, and I grip the bars for stability, still dancing to the fast-paced song. Greedy arms reach up for me, desperate fingers stretching toward the enclosure.

The moment my feet are available to their groping, I'm surrounded. I keep my body pliant, waiting for the sting of many nails poking into my body, eager to feel their touch, ready to donate my blood to them. I close my eyes and raise my hands to the top of the cage, offering myself to the crowd when something odd happens.

No one touches me.

My eyes fly open and I gasp in shock.

The party is empty.

Not a single soul remains. Not at the high table, not at the small tables and chairs, not even one person is left to dance. I close my eyes and will my heart to stop racing. Surely this must be just a dream like the others have been and I'm still asleep next to Cupcake.

But when I open my eyes, I find that's not the case. Six men, hooded and cloaked, hover about fifteen feet from me, eyes hidden from sight. I wonder where the seventh one is when a deep, sultry voice speaks from behind me.

"Snowwwwww," he purrs, my name sounding like a desperate lover's promise, and my whole body shudders in response. Yet I can't move to look at him. "We have been watching you, waiting for the right time to take you."

Take me?

"There is a better way, a better drug. Wine is beneath a princess such as yourself."

So he does know who I am.

I lower my arms from the cage bars and suddenly feel embarrassed about what I've done and move to cover myself.

"Don't!" His voice is sharp and stern. The unfamiliar accent gives him more authority, that one word sounding like an order. I freeze in response. "Do not cover what we so desperately want to see, what rightfully belongs to us. You were meant to be ours, Snow, and one way or another, we shall have you when the time is right."

I want to ask him what that means, why he can't take me now, but my words shatter in my throat when I feel an icy finger trail down my spine. My back arches, breasts pressing to the bars, nipples tightening as a wave of desire sends goosebumps rising across me.

The six in front of me stay motionless, minus the clenching of their fists and the flaring of their nostrils. I wonder why their chests don't move... Don't they breathe?

I'm breathing hard enough for all of us, my chest rising and falling rapidly.

"I know you feel it coursing through your veins, our *lust* flooding you. I can smell it leaking from you, Snow. It will not be long now until I taste it, until I devour you."

Another wave of desire blasts through me and something inside me aches, a place between my lower lips throbbing. My fingers twitch, wanting to rub it, but I'm still frozen in place.

"You want this as much as we do. You crave us. We can feel your body calling to us, your mind desperate. We can feel the fierceness building inside of you to feel things you've not felt before. We can give it all to you after you beg for it, pet, but it will come with a cost."

117

I want to tell him that I'd do anything but allow the queen to keep her reign.

"When it's time, when you take what you need from yourself, I will feel it, and we will come for you. You'd do best to be ready when we do."

So many questions lodge in my throat, but I've been conditioned not to ask them. Why do they want me? Will they help me kill the queen? How long must I wait? Where do I go in the meantime?

One of the seven jerks his head slightly, and I feel a cold wind whip around me. I close my eyes against the force. When I open them again, I'm all alone and locked in this cage. The tables and chairs are gone, the shelves once filled with wine are vacant. This place is entirely deserted, as if no one has set foot here for years. I turn around and find the musicians disbanded, vanished with their instruments.

Before I can scream for the seven to come back and help me, the large wooden door opens, and in walks several guards with Gerard in the lead.

"Hello, beast. Escaped again, have you? Well, we've come to reclaim our dog. I see you've already found yourself a cage. How fitting." As he stalks closer, I recoil against the back side of the cage, trying to tug on the remnants of my forgotten dress. "I much prefer you naked, beast. Now, won't you be a good girl and come home to your owner? Her Majesty has been quite...distraught by your absence."

"No." The desperate cry escapes my lips as they descend on the cage. The door is hacked off with an axe while I scream in terror behind it. Wood chips pelt my body, nicking my skin before rough hands grab me and haul me from the cage.

I kick and scream and fight, but none of it matters. Then something hard crashes into the back of my head, and the world goes black.

CHAPTER 14

*N*aked and cold, I wake up frozen on the bottom of a cell…again. How stupid am I? Living more days in the dungeon than above ground doesn't do me any good. I can't escape while I'm down here. Hell, I can barely survive.

The seven said they'd be coming for me when the time is right, but what the fuck does that even mean? How can I take something from myself when I have nothing to give? And how can I prepare for them when I have no frame of reference? Could they have been any more vague?

I suppose they could have…

In the darkness of my cell, I relive the moment he touched me, the feeling of his finger sliding down my back, the waves of lust, so erotic I thought I might explode, pulsing through my body.

And that was only with the tip of one finger. If what he claims comes true, and he does come for me, *and* the queen allows him to take me, which I highly doubt, what will he do to me? What will they do to me? One thing I know for sure, anything is better than this. The way he spoke, as if I

119

belonged to them, as if it was their right to own me...it did something to me. My body shuddered at the thought of them possessing me, so different from how I feel when the queen exerts her control over me. Her actions infuriate me, where the seven's insinuations made me desperate to belong to them, caused something inside me to throb and clench. How could someone actually *want* to be owned by another? What the fuck is wrong with me?

The heavy stomping of footsteps clomping down the dungeon's stone stairs has me turning my head toward the noise. The light from a lantern grows brighter as the footfalls draw near. Along with the light is the stench of dirty men. That's one thing I have to give the seven credit for... All the men in this castle reek of something foul and disgusting, but the seven? At first I didn't notice the enticing aroma, as my other senses were overloaded. But once they vanished and I was alone for that brief, terrifying, and glorious moment, their scents lingered. Sweet and spicy, decadent, rich and luscious. I can't really find the right words to describe them, but every smell I noted instantly became my favorite scent. Now that I think about it, their combined fragrance reminds me of the nectar's seductive bouquet.

The cell's door slides open and I squint to see the foulsmelling man standing proudly in the door. Like being one of the queen's minions is something to strive for. How pathetic.

"Get your ass up, beast. The queen has orders for you." I feel around on the floor, hoping my dirty dress is lying somewhere near me, but all I feel is cold sludge and wet, frozen moss.

Fuck.

Wincing when my pounding head reminds me how hard I was struck, I heave myself to stand and turn backwards when the guard indicates I should. Heavy iron manacles are closed

SEVEN SINS OF SNOW

around my wrists and tightened far too much. My fingers will lose feeling soon.

The guard guides me out of the cell and urges me down the damp corridor. That's odd. Usually I'm thrown to the ground, maybe kicked while I'm down. Even the usual slaps that land on my ass to get me to move are absent.

Something is up.

I remain alert, trying hard to pay attention to anything said or done. The queen must be up to no good, there's no other reason for her to instruct for me to be handled less roughly. She gets off on my mistreatment. I can hear the happiness oozing from her in the pitch of her screeching voice, the way she laughs like a lunatic when something pleases her.

The sconces along the stairwell flicker as the warm breeze from the floors aboveground filters down here. I'm anxious to be out of the dark cell, but also apprehensive. I hate when I'm forced to parade around the castle naked, feeling the sinister eyes of the guards watching my breasts as they sway when I walk, or watching the space between my legs for a glimpse of what lies between my lower lips.

If it were up to them, I'd be bound and spread so they could use me as they saw fit. I guess I do have something to be grateful to the queen for after all. She has seen to it that I remain untouched, virginal. And so far, I remain pure.

A guard stationed at the top of the dungeon's stairs opens the iron door when we approach. His lips curl in a sick sneer as his gaze runs up and down my body. I fucking hate this.

It's incredible how different it was yesterday. Choosing to bare myself before the seven was invigorating, freeing. I felt wild and alive. But having that choice literally stripped from me is as depressing and embarrassing as it is upsetting.

When the seven looked at my nakedness, even though I couldn't see their eyes, I could feel my body responding to them. My core ached and leaked, my nipples tingled and tightened, my breasts felt heavy under their hidden gaze.

The guards' malicious stares are nothing in comparison. They make me feel dirty and disgusting, they make me hate my body.

Sometimes it's hard to compartmentalize the fact that the guards were not always like this, that the queen's bespelling of them has actually changed them into something they haven't always been.

Someday, when I bathe in the blood of the queen, I will give them a chance to repent, a chance to earn my forgiveness, for they know not what they do.

We pass the guard and my body tenses, ready for him to spank my ass or slap my breasts, but he doesn't. All I'm met with is a low groan, and that I can handle.

I'm led to the stairs and up both flights, surprised when my destination is my old room. My bed is freshly made with fluffy pillows and plush blankets, the table near the windows has a decanter filled with red wine and a plate filled with breads, meats, and cheeses—I'm ignoring the glaring red apple—and a basin filled with warm water and floral soaps is waiting for me with steam rising enticingly from its surface.

What. The. Fuck.

I'm still staring in awe when the manacles are removed from my hands. Without another word, the guard exits behind me and I hear the click of my door shutting.

I turn around and rub my eyes.

My door is shut...

For the first time in a decade, I have privacy.

None of this makes sense. I just escaped for the second time in one week, yet I'm not beaten or chastised. Instead, I'm...rewarded?

Fuck it.

Throwing caution to the wind, I walk to the table and

122

pour a generous amount of wine into a crystal glass then slip inside the basin. I groan loudly as my body sinks into the heated water. It's been so long since I've been allowed to wash myself, much less given a bath to do so. I'm usually cleaned by the hands of others with sponges while bound to a hard table.

This? This is luxury.

My muscles relax and my mind heals while I soak. I try to cleanse my head as much as my body, leaving my mind blank, thinking about nothing but blue skies and the warmth of the sun's rays caressing my skin. Of course I struggle not to question everything, this is all too good to be true.

I drink my wine in peace, letting the alcohol heat my body and decompress my overloaded brain. I fail to control my thoughts as they wander from the queen's motives and my newly given privacy, to my curiosity regarding the seven. But no matter how consuming my thoughts might be, the end result is the same. I can't do anything to change, well, anything.

After drinking my glass of wine, I scrub my body with soap and wash my very dirty hair. The water around me turns from clear to murky, signaling it's time to get out. For once, I can stand in my own room, stark naked and wet, without an audience ogling me. It feels amazing.

I wrap myself in a crimson robe laid out for me on my bed and sit in front of the large windows taking up an entire wall in my room. I've never just sat here to relax before. Ignoring the apple, I fill my cup and take in the food spread out before me. Could this be another trick of the queen's? Is the cheese made from some piece of the dead guards? The meat, a cured, decayed muscle? Maybe she's poisoned the food, wanting me to die the same horrible death...

I pick up a piece of cheese and meat and sniff. They smell so delicious. My mouth waters and my stomach rumbles in appreciation. Taking a tentative bite, I swirl the flavor around my mouth. When I notice nothing awry, my body not responding to some unknown contaminant, I feast.

It's so odd to feel happy in my castle. Most of the time I try to hide away in my mind, remembering times in my childhood when my father was still alive and not yet a victim of the queen's magic.

But as I stare out the window, watching the castle bustling with life, I begin to envision my future. Our future. A world where we all live in absence of fear, a place where evil no longer exists and people are kind to one another. I dream of a utopia where everyone shares their goods to help sustain each other, where smiles are met with warm expressions, and the town becomes a community again, not just a place to exist, but to thrive.

And someday, I will make my dreams come true. But for now I'll wait... I'll bide my time, contemplating the cryptic words of the seven and remain on high alert at all times.

I survey the grounds, hoping to see a lurker hiding in the shadows, but find none. Sighing, my food finished, I walk toward my wardrobe and pull out a white, velvet nightgown. Yawning, I draw back the fresh covers of my very inviting bed and crawl inside, tugging the covers up over my shoulders.

With my worries forgotten for one glorious moment, I fall into the most restful sleep I've had in many years.

THE NEXT FEW DAYS COME AND GO WITHOUT ANYTHING OF substance transpiring. Servants clean my room and bring me two meals a day, every day. My privacy is sustained and I begin to feel like my old self, but remain cautious. In the stories I've read, all hell breaks loose the moment the main character feels like everything is going as it should.

Lying in my bed, I watch the gray clouds brighten with the rising sun hidden behind them, and wonder if this is the calm before the storm.

The prelude to my epic demise.

Have I been foolish to partake in wine and food and comfort, forgetting the only thing that keeps me living— envisioning murdering the evil bitch?

Who can be sure, really...

My mind drifts to memories of the seven as they have much of the most recent days. I think of how they smelled, how plump their red lips looked, how badly I wanted to press my mouth against theirs.

Then I take myself back to only a few days ago, when I met them a second time. How I bared myself before them, spreading my legs for their viewing pleasure as I soared high above in that cage. I remember how my nipples tightened with their hidden stares, how my core ached and leaked when one cold finger trailed down my spine...

I moan...out loud, like some sex fiend. That place between my pussy lips aches, making me rub my thighs together to quench the desire. I glance toward my door and find it still closed.

Turning back, I relax my body and close my eyes, then trail my hands down my body, pretending it's one of them... or several of them. I squeeze my breasts and play with my nipples until they harden into twin peaks. Then I slide one hand down my body and slip a finger between my lower lips. I find I'm wet down there already.

Exploring, I glide my finger lower, finding my virginal hole. But that's not where the throbbing is. I pull my finger back up and find a tiny button at the top of my pussy. When I touch it, I gasp. This is it. This is the spot one of the seven sucked on during my dreams of them.

I slide over it, slowly at first, feeling the little nub hardening under my touch. I quicken my movements, gliding faster until a heat grows low in my belly. My chest feels tight, my breaths coming out swiftly as something inside me intensifies. My finger rubs rapidly, sliding all over the button. My hips undulate, fucking the air, my pussy clenching as wetness leaks from inside me.

I feel like I'm at the top of a waterfall looking down, just waiting to take the leap. I remember my dream with the seven men sucking me, tasting me, pretending my finger is one of theirs.

Then they bit me.

And something glorious happens. I jump off the waterfall, my body coming to life. My vision goes white and my room no longer exists as a pair of ice-blue eyes flashes in my mind.

"We are coming," a sensual voice croons, as I keep rubbing myself through the feeling of elation, pure ecstasy washing through me, tingling every nerve like a bolt of lightning.

The feeling starts to fade, and I rub lighter and lighter until it's gone, the nub too sensitive to touch anymore. I wonder if I had imagined the eyes, conjured up the voice, but I can't be sure of anything anymore.

My body is pliant and immobile as I bask in the aftermath of overwhelming sensation. I don't know what that was, but it was incredible. To think I've had the ability to do this to myself all these years and have never been able to is astounding. All I needed was a memory and one little finger...

Lying in a pool of my own wetness, I decide to sleep away this afternoon's boredom, and fall asleep with a smile on my face and the seven on my mind.

CHAPTER 15

a knock on my door wakes me, surprising me once again. No one knocks, they simply enter if they are so inclined.

Wondering how long I've slept, I smile when I see Sherry and Enid, looking healthy and well. They curtsey to me—actually fucking curtsey—and my jaw drops.

"Evening, princess," Sherry greets softly as I sit up. "We've come to prepare you for a suitor."

My smile falters and I groan, throwing myself back down onto my pillows.

"I'm so sorry, princess." Enid's apology is irrelevant. I'm not upset with her by any means, I just don't want to face all of this again.

The half dead suitor, my refusal of his proposal, and the inevitable punishment I'll suffer afterward.

Looks like the storm is here after all.

"No need to apologize. None of this is your fault." Slipping from the bed, I pad over to the table I've only just realized they brought in with them. The smell of melting wax assaults me. I'm so angry with myself. I promised I'd stay more aware, more vigilant, knowing the queen is up to something, and here I falter when I see a friendly face.

I should know better than this.

Not wanting to hear the pain in their voices for asking such a dehumanizing thing, I strip before the question leaves their lips. From the corner of my eyes, I can see how they gaze upon me in awe, wondering how I've healed from the wrath of their switches lashed across my skin. But I won't tell them, as much as sharing my secret would bring me joy. No. This secret will stay with me and the seven.

The arduous process of getting my body ready begins. Since I've already bathed earlier today, hot cloths are laid upon my skin in preparation for the waxing. I'm not bound, instead urged when to lift my arms, move my legs, or turn over. It's much more pleasant this way, even if they are ripping the hairs out of my body. I notice the absence of Martin but do not ask about his whereabouts. I don't really fucking care as long as he's not here.

The women wax me, then apply a soft smelling lotion that reminds me of the lilac trees in front of the castle. With my mood turning sour, I don't even glance at the dress hanging from the velvet hanger as they slip it over my head. I get lost in my thoughts, wondering what horrible man has come for my hand this time.

I don't look as shoes are slipped over my feet. I don't move a muscle when I'm led over to my vanity to have my hair and makeup done. I don't watch as the hair oils are pulled through my dark strands. Sherry works hard on my hair, twisting and pinning while Enid applies harsh black makeup to my eyes and red stain on my lips.

With my eyes still unfocused, I'm walked back to the mirrors, and my crown is placed on my head.

"Take a look, princess." Enid's voice jostles me, and I glance up at the mirrors. I don't recognize my reflection.

Someone regal stares back at me, a woman with poise and confidence. The dress is unlike anything I've ever worn. Colored in a deep crimson, the strapless dress hugs my curves like a second skin. While the skirts are usually made of many layers, this only has one. A slit cut into the skirt rides high up my right leg, past my hip bone, even though the hem is long enough to cover my shoes.

The bodice is a corset, tied tight up to my shoulder blades, and the top holding my breasts cups them just enough to cover my nipples, leaving the tops and swell of my chest exposed.

I look sexy yet refined, a perfect royal. Too bad there's no Prince Charming for me.

"We finished early, princess. Would you like to sit at your vanity until the time is right?" Sherry's comment startles me.

I turn to her. "Why wouldn't we go now?" There is never extra time between preparation and meeting the abominable men. They are always waiting on me as if they've been here for hours in anticipation.

Sherry and Enid share a look. "There have been, umm... special orders," Enid starts.

"Such as?" I motion for them to continue.

Sherry sighs and clasps her hands. "The queen has requested that you not be brought until the sun has set."

"Really?" How interesting. I lower my voice. "So, how are you two really? Have you heard anything from the rebellion?" I know I'm reaching here, but I'm desperate for any news of advancement for our cause. Since they were branded by the queen, all whispers of the rebellion have failed to reach my ears.

Sherry pales and glances to the door. "We can't discuss such things anymore, princess. I'm sorry."

"But know that things are in the works. Please be patient," Enid adds quietly.

I nod in understanding and don't bring it up again. Instead, I walk to the windows and gaze outside, my heart thudding in my chest as I search all the dark spaces. Disappointment has my heart sinking to my feet. The ones I wish to see are absent. Maybe they have forgotten about me.

Sherry and Enid huddle near the door, whispering in hushed voices. I wonder if they are trying to hide their conversation from me or from the guards... Perhaps it's both.

The skies turn dark and the servants once tending to the orchards and fields walk back to the castle with baskets filled with ripe fruits and vegetables. The horses are led back into their stalls, their coats brushed and stables filled with fresh hay. I watch Cupcake as he's brought to his stall, his tail swishing behind him.

The dress grows tight around my chest, making breathing difficult. I could never understand why this is the fashion for women. Surely something that allows you to breathe properly could also be in style.

Once the grounds are no longer discernible, other than the torchlit pathways, Sherry and Enid come to retrieve me. This time, they've elicited the help of the guards stationed outside, as I'm sure they were instructed to do.

"It is time," Sherry says, gesturing for me to follow them. With a sigh I stand, smoothing my hands down my gown, ready to face yet another disaster. I wish I had more wine to calm me down, because my heart is racing.

My heels click on the floor, reminding me of the evil bitch's shoes. I shudder with bad memories. The women walk ahead of me, unspeaking, while the guards flank me on either side, but do not touch me.

I still can't understand the reason for the newest treatment. Maybe I'll get some answers tonight, but I have to be prepared that I might not like what I learn.

My palms turn clammy as I grip the railing tightly, willing myself not to trip down the stairs. I lick my lips nervously. Why am I so anxious? Sure, I'm leery of these meetings, but this one feels different. The whole aura of the castle is off. Usually, the stone walls feel stark and oppressive, but tonight they feel grand and beautifully detailed. The paintings of my ancestors, typically so stoic as they stare down upon me, *look* different, as if a smile is tugging at their painted lips.

The doom I feel has been replaced with something else. I can't quite put my finger on what it is, but it feels monumental. I can feel my pulse thumping in my ears as we round the corridor and face the double doors, behind which sits the old ballroom.

Sherry and Enid incline their heads and scurry off, but glance at me over their shoulders with wide eyes.

What do they know that I don't?

Trumpets sound, startling me, and the doors are swung open. I keep my eyes low, not wanting to connect my gaze with the queen's, not wanting to see the deplorable man standing there wanting me.

But then I hear it, something odd.

A hand presses gently on my back, encouraging me to move my feet. The queen's voice floats to me as I slowly make my way down the long aisle. She giggles, her voice pitched higher than normal. Is...is she flirting? I double my efforts to keep my head lowered, feeling like I'm interrupting a moment I'm not privy to.

Her cheerful laughter makes my heart beat faster, my nerves catching on fire. This is the thing she's been hiding from me. Whoever has come for me tonight is part of her wicked plan to hurt me, maybe even kill me.

The clicking of my shoes echoes in my ears, each step feeling like another shovel of dirt digging my grave. I stop moving when the hem of her skirt and her pointed shoes come into my vision.

"Ahh, there she is. Come here, daughter, and meet the one who has come for your hand."

I take a step closer, not foolish enough to be in close proximity to the queen. Her false politeness doesn't fool me.

"I said come here, bea—beautiful daughter of mine." She almost slipped up there and called me beast, showing her true colors. Why hide what she is now? Why him? "Forgive my daughter. The tragic death of her father, my beloved husband, still haunts her. She's not spoken more than a few words in years. Come now, child, speak up. He's traveled a long way to meet you."

Rage builds within me. How dare she bring up my father. Tragic death, my pale ass.

You fucking killed him, you bitch!

My fists clench and my nostrils flare, but then I smell the man so close to me. Sweet and spicy...

My pulse spikes, the muscle thrashing against my chest. I inhale deeply and let the scent wash over me. I recognize it, having smelled it twice before...

"Snowwww," he purrs, my name a sweet, dark promise, causing my insides to clench, my nipples to harden.

Holy fuck.

"Look at me." His deep voice rolls through me like melted chocolate seduction, and I lick my lips in anticipation.

Just raise your eyes, Snow!

I start with his polished shoes and slide my gaze up his pressed pants that hug muscular legs. I see the outline of a cock straining against the dark fabric and my mouth fucking waters in response. His belt comes into view next, his buckle a beautifully carved golden snowflake.

His blue shirt is tucked into his pants and a black jacket covers it. I reach his chest, finding his muscles bulging beneath the fabric, testing the strength of the buttons holding it closed. The top buttons of his shirt are gaping, leaving the pale hollow between his collarbones visible. I see the tie around his neck, indicating he wears a cape like the evil queen. Perhaps he's a royal too...

Unable to put it off any longer, I raise my eyes to his and gasp.

Ice-blue eyes meet mine, deeply set in the most handsome face a woman could possibly dream up, and my insides explode. They're the same eyes that flashed in my mind when I brought myself to climax. Feverish desire and desperate need have me panting, my chest rising rapidly. A mess of thick, black hair covers his forehead, making him look rugged and sexy, making my core clench with want. His pointed nose fits his face perfectly, with his high cheekbones and plump red lips, lips I want to taste with my own. But it's the dimple on his chin that gives him away.

He's one of the seven.

A lurker, demons of the night.

A fabled king with the power of the seven sins.

The golden crown he bears sits proudly upon his lush hair, bejeweled with dark blue gems that sparkle in the light. He looks royal, regal, everything a king should be like and more.

My knees grow weak and I almost fall as the room around me grows silent. Then he reaches for me, catching me in his arms before my legs give out. He pulls me into his hard, cold chest, and I melt into his embrace.

"I told you we'd come." His words make me weaker. He lived up to his promise like no one has done for me since my father was alive.

"What did you say?" The queen's frigid question hangs in the air like a nocked arrow ready to strike.

The man holding me, whose name I don't even know,

turns to her and meets her gaze, but doesn't fall under her spell. "It is none of your business what we talk about."

What magic is this? How have his eyes not fallen yellow?

Energy builds up in the ballroom, power threatening to suffocate everyone inside. It feels like two storm fronts merging, each wanting to strike first with their lightning bolts, battling to see whose thunder is the loudest.

"She is my business," the queen growls. "She does nothing without my permission. Now, I'll ask you one more time, what did you say?" It's more of a statement than a question. The queen demands answers, never earning them.

The man removes me from his grasp and steps in front of me. "Perhaps you did not hear me the first time, so I will repeat myself for the first and last time. It is none of your business."

I stare hard at the floor, not believing what I'm hearing. No one stands up to the queen and lives to tell the tale. Her rage brews as thick, black smoke swathes the floor, winding up my legs. It won't be long now before it chokes me.

"Snow, do you accept my proposal?" he inquires, turning to face me, concern lacing his exotic eyes.

I take a breath to say yes when my throat closes. My hands jerk to my neck as my access to air is denied. I fall to my knees, gagging and struggling, scratching at my neck but finding nothing I can pull to free myself.

It's her magic that's crushing me.

"Fuck this," the man snarls, bending down to scoop me up. "Snow is mine!"

"She will never be yours!" Smoke billows and my throat tightens, feeling like she's actually collapsed my airway as my vision swims. "Leave now and never return! You are forthwith banished from my grounds forever!"

No! This can't be happening.

Through the haze of my wavering vision, I see the man's

face grow shocked in surprise. Like an invisible rope has been tied around him, he's yanked through the ballroom and out the double doors, his arms stretched out, reaching for me as he shouts my name. The sound of his voice grows farther and farther away, and darkness covers my eyes. This is it, the moment the queen will kill me. And then I'm rendered unconscious.

CHAPTER 16

"Wake up, you stupid wench!" A slap lands hard on my cheek and the queen's spittle sprays my face. "Who the fuck do you think you are, meeting men outside the suitors I choose for you!" Another slap connects, this time jerking my head to the side with the force, my brain still fuzzy from its lack of oxygen. "And to think I listened to his propositions, giving you comfort by his demands, keeping your body free from punishments. Well, not anymore. Your reprieve from me is over."

Before I can open my eyes, I'm assaulted on all sides as feet, fists, and magic hammer into me. I can feel her black smog invading my throat while others pummel my ribs, smash into my stomach. An onslaught of punches bash into my skull, cracking the side of my jaw, ripping my hair from my scalp. I scream and cry and thrash, but it makes no difference. Large hands hold me down, opening up my body. Nothing is left unhurt.

Tears trail down my face and I scream until my voice grows hoarse as my will to survive falters, until my muscles give way and I can no longer struggle. My body goes limp under their assault. I don't even know who is attacking me with the queen. I feel her magic twisting my insides, restricting my air over and over again, never letting me catch my breath. And I feel the sharp kicks of a toed boot, the hard jab from a clenched fist.

Blood pools in my mouth and trickles from my ears. I can't take this any longer, my body won't survive. The queen orders a full stop just as I'm about to pass out, and I cry, wanting to have a moment in the quiet blackness.

"There will be nothing more for you to live for, wench. No man will save you this time. All that's left for you is pain and suffering, and I mean to make you smother in it."

I screech in pain as her magic slithers inside me, filling me to capacity with as much rage and torment as she can muster. My head pounds, every muscle in my body contracting painfully, and my blood feels like it's boiling as it sears through my veins.

My eyes ache like they might pop out of my head from the pressure, or my throat may explode from my howls. The evil bitch laughs at my anguish, her high-pitched, shrieking voice adding to my torture. I beg internally for mercy to any god that might be listening.

Please end this now, end my suffering. I can't withstand this any longer, no one can save me now.

As my eyes glaze over in pain, my throat now hoarse from screaming, my limbs tangled into unnatural positions, something happens. Through my pulse pounding in my ears, I can hear the frantic voice of a guard. The queen responds to him, anger lacing her tone. Then I feel her magic pulling from inside me. It's excruciating. Like a giant snake was lodged down my throat and has finally slithered out. I choke and gag, my entire body quaking. Red coats my vision, and something warm leaks from my ears.

Then it stops as quickly as it started.

137

I lie in a pool of warm liquid, unsure if I've wet myself or if I'm bleeding to death. Maybe both.

"Where are they?" the queen's seethes, her anger brewing.

"The worst fires are in the back orchards," a guard responds quickly, his voice trembling under her questioning.

"Gerard, detain the beast, get her down to the dungeons while I deal with this."

The click of her footsteps scurrying off down the ballroom floor grows quieter.

Fires?

Who would dare set fires to anything the queen says belongs to her?

"Get up, beast. It's the cells for you." Gerard plants a kick in my ribs, but I'm so depleted of energy that my body doesn't even jerk at the contact. It's a strange feeling. Like I'm inside my body, but I'm not at the same time. My mind is trying to separate from the pain, disassociating my thoughts from my feelings.

He kicks me again, but he might as well be assaulting a bag of grains. Can't he understand? Can't he see how broken I am?

"Stupid fucking cunt," he growls, as his hand snags around my ankle and begins to drag me down the long hall. I'm grateful for the lack of furniture and the well-polished floors, because I don't think I could avoid any obstructions on my own. Gerard struggles to open the double doors by himself. They are heavy and wooden, and he grunts as he pushes into one with his shoulder while keeping my ankle locked in his grip.

I wonder for a moment where the guards, who are usually stationed outside this door, are, but remember about the fires in the orchards. The queen has likely pulled all the guards to help combat it. As Gerard pulls me through the threshold and into the hallway, the shutting door slams against my head and I almost blackout, my vision swimming.

Then the pounding starts, and at first, I think it's my swollen head, but as the noise grows louder, I realize it's the sound of many feet running through the castle.

"What the..." Gerard starts, but his words get lost in the onslaught of noise—shouting and stampeding feet bombarding us at the same time.

"There she is!"

"Save the princess!"

"Kill the guard!"

I can't understand who wants to help me. Mustering the very last ounce of strength I have, I turn my head and force my tired lids open. Through my blurry eyes, I can see the outlines of men holding axes and torches hurtling toward me.

Gerard's screams play like music to my ears as he's attacked next to me.

I want to ask how and why as I'm carefully picked up by a strong man. "There, there, princess. We've got you now. You're almost safe. Just hang on." Through the haze, I see it's one of the men from Riverwood who helped me chop down the whipping post. Emotion constricts my chest at his kind gesture. My vision leaps from one face to the next, seeing all the men from my village have come to rescue me.

There are old men with gray hair and white beards, and adolescent boys only a few years younger than me fighting alongside their fathers, with pride beaming on their faces.

Gratitude chokes me, to know someone cares enough about me to storm the castle under the rule of the evil queen just to save me... It's too much.

The dam holding back my tears releases and I cry, gripping onto the shirt of the man holding me as he runs through the castle. Candlelit chandeliers pass over my head, and when the extra large one that dangles over the foyer comes into my vision, I know we're almost out.

The cool breeze coats my heated skin, soothing my aching body. The man doesn't stop. Instead, he picks up speed as he hurries down the hill toward Riverwood. Over his shoulder I see the bright light of the blazing fire roaring behind the castle. I also see men engaged with guards, fighting and shouting. Men from both parties fall as battle cries and howls of agony become a cacophony around us. My heart swells, knowing they did all this just to rescue me.

"Almost there, princess," the man promises. Our pace slows and we turn the corner, jogging through the houses of the townspeople. The path he's on leads to the village square, and that must be our destination. The women are all gathered, surrounding a raging fire where the whipping post once stood. The stronger women are wielding weapons of all types—axes, knives, and pitchforks. Wheelbarrows full of fist-sized stones are spread out in equal distances around the square.

They came ready to fight.

The starless sky gives the night an ominous feeling as I'm brought to the square and placed on some patched-up quilt.

"Princess. Princess." The muffled voice of someone draws my attention. I roll my head slowly toward the sound and see Enid's smiling face. I try hard to return a grin. "I told you things were in play." I can't hear her well and read her lips instead. I try to thank her, but all that comes out is a low groan. "Shh, princess, don't try to talk."

"I'm so glad you're finally out of there." Sherry falls next to me with tears leaking down her face. "Just look at you." Her hands hover over my broken body, wanting to touch me, but unsure if she'll hurt me more.

The sound of a man shouting pulls our attention. "They are coming! The queen and her huntsmen! Everyone, prepare!" Worried voices, hushed whispers, and the raised tones of men barking orders grow louder around me. Men returning from the castle appear bloodied and exhausted, their chests heaving below ripped shirts.

Then comes the inauspicious sounds of the huntsmen's trumpets, causing everyone to fall silent. This is really happening, a battle for the ages set to commence.

And here I am, battered and broken, unable to help, unable to fight.

It won't take long for them to get here on their massive steeds, hunting dogs on their heels, the evil bitch bringing up the rear. I applaud the villagers and their bravery, but we don't stand a chance against her.

The quiet square quickly turns into chaos as everyone rallies to prepare in any way they can. I turn my head toward the fire behind us and squint my eyes, looking through the flames.

My heart stutters, my whole body flooding with relief at the sight.

Seven lurkers stand just on the edge of the square, each holding a shiny weapon. One carries a longsword, the next a bow and arrow. One holds twin axes in his hands, while the next effortlessly clutches a pair of short swords. A shiny war hammer with a wooden handle rests in the hands of another lurker, while a terrifying looking flail weapon, its ball filled with spikes, dangles from the grip of the next. The final lurker carries a tall spear with a sharpened point.

Did they come to fight with us?

Movement behind them draws my attention as the pale, yet beautiful faces of men and women gaze across the fires toward my castle, eyes blazing. I recognize some of them from the party room.

Before I can question the rationale of the lurkers, the

eerie trumpets sound again and the ground shakes with the clomping of the huntsmen's horses. It won't be long now.

Sherry and Enid leave my side to join the forces, but I'm not alone for very long.

"Snowwww." That voice. That decadent, sensual voice belonging to the messy-haired suitor removed from the castle by some invisible rope.

It can't be.

"We will not allow her to take you from us again. She has no power beneath the sky." Strong arms heave my battered, lifeless body. Every inch of me pulses in excruciating agony, but my screams are muffled against a strong, hard chest. I want to cry when he turns away from the fight, carrying me off somewhere where I might finally feel safe. But I also want to order him to put me down so I can stand and fight with my people, though I know I'm too broken to help.

"Fear not, Snow, for the evil queen is about to enter a fight she is not prepared for. She cannot win, nor can she lose. The battle will end as soon as it has begun, while we prepare to defeat her in the final fight. The war will be ours. We shall taste triumph in the form of blood, celebrating our victory as the queen's head watches over us, skewered to a stake."

How can such awful things turn me into mush?

With my tongue still thick inside my blood-filled mouth, my voice remains lost. I can only offer him a single nod as he takes me back through the town toward the party house I've now crashed twice.

He seems to float instead of walk, gliding over the cobblestones and grass as if he were a low-hanging cloud. I don't question reality anymore. My broken brain doesn't have the energy to debate semantics. Because regardless if I believe it can happen or not, the fact of the matter remains—it *is* happening.

I want to ask him why...why me? What makes me so special?

The buildings become a blur as he flies toward our destination. My eyes close and I feel consciousness become more and more difficult to hang onto, until the last sliver slips through my grasp as the sounds of a battle ring out in the distance.

CHAPTER 17

The huntsmen are gaining on me. I should have never run away. The sound of their hunting dogs, the clomping of their horse's hooves, the eerie trumpets wailing in the night draws closer.

My bare feet crash against the stones, the skin peeling off my torn soles. But still, I run. She can't get me this time, I won't survive it. Her maniacal laughter chases after me too, chilling the blood in my veins. It won't be long now before I've run out of energy and into the hands of my soon to be murderer.

"We're coming to get you, beast!" Her shrill cackle rustles the leaves in the trees overhead as I whip around their trunks, trying not to slam into one in the pitch-black dark.

Behind me, the hounds yelp, the horses grunt, and the huntsmen shout. Every noise makes my body flinch and jerk. I'm so tired. Tired from running, tired of being afraid, tired of fighting for a life not worth living.

But still, I run.

Faces of the townsfolk pass through my mind, the old and the young, the fire in the eyes of the young men and women who want to overthrow the tyrant as much as I do. And that is what keeps me moving.

My legs tremble as I push myself well past the limits of exhaustion, my body completely depleted. Yet my arms pump at my sides, and my feet slam into the ground. Thunder booms overhead and raindrops begin to fall, the cool water pelting me through the canopy of trees.

Then I feel it, crying out as something wraps around my ankle, and I crumple to the ground.

"We've got her!" a huntsmen hollers, dismounting his steed. His large fingers encircle my neck and squeeze. "You're dead, beast."

Unable to fight him off, my chest heaving for air, I can only dangle helplessly over his wide shoulder as he carries me to my doom. My heart races as we emerge into a clearing I didn't know existed, as if the trees parted from their roots just for this moment.

Standing in the middle of a dozen fires is my fate, my death. Her crown sits wickedly upon her pale blonde hair, which whips around her face. A bolt of lightning shoots across the sky, followed by rumbles of booming thunder.

Two poles have been erected for me this time, and the evil queen stands proud between them. "Bring her here!" Her arms rise and the fires roar around her as the huntsman holding me hauls me to my end. "String her up! I want everyone to see this!"

A second man helps the first, and soon, I'm hanging between the two poles, my arms stretched over my head and out to my sides. My legs are bound the same way, forcing all my weight to pull on my small wrists.

I cry out as my feeble nightgown is ripped down the center, exposing my nakedness to the gathered huntsmen. They shout and cheer as the raindrops drizzle down my skin, making my flesh erupt in goosebumps.

"What do you think of your precious princess now? She is nothing compared to me. Nothing! No longer will I suffer your presence, sharing my castle, my air with you. Tonight, I will end *your pathetic existence, and in your death, I will find my immortality."*

The queen circles me as I tremble in fear, every muscle shuddering uncontrollably. I just pray she makes it quick.

"And after I kill this miserable excuse for a princess, I'll let you fuck her dead body."

Tears trickle down my face, mixing with the raindrops. I'm grateful for my blurred vision, because I can't watch this anymore.

"Come closer, huntsmen. Touch her, taste her, use her for the first and last time. She's no beast, she's worse than that. Useless. Expendable. Forgettable." She turns from them to me, shrieking, *"There won't be a soul on this Earth who will mourn your loss. You are scum, you are a waste. You. Are. Nothing!"*

"No," I cry out, as the huntsmen draw near, their blurred outlines growing larger in the pouring rain.

"Yes!" The queen answers my cry by pumping her fists into the air in victory. *"Gather! Watch! See how soft and weak she is, feel how easily I will crush her."*

As the huntsmen swarm me, I try to retreat into my mind, find a dark place to hide until my life leaves my body. But with dozens of hands groping me, fingers pinching me, and teeth biting into my skin, I'm unable to. With my body spread and completely exposed, every inch of me is touched, fondled, spread, groped, penetrated...

I think about that last dream I had of the seven men, and how different I felt with their hard bodies pressed against mine, how dissimilar my own response was, even if it was just a dream.

I want to throw up at the sensations forced upon me, my stomach churning in fear and disgust.

"Enough!" Every hand leaves me abruptly, and I'm almost grateful to the cause of my suffering for the moment's respite. Then she laughs, the sound sinister, evil, foreboding. *"Now it's my turn to play with you, beast."* Extending her arm, she reaches toward me and places the pad of one finger in the hollow of my collarbones. I flinch, her touch burning my skin as she trails a line between my

breasts. Up and down, up and down, her finger searing a pathway on my chest as my howls of pain become one with the rolling thunder.

Then she stops and presses, her nails piercing my tender skin. I scream in terror while she cheers with joy, her thin lips spread in a wild and demented smile. With a roar, she pulls her arm back then jabs it straight through my chest. My screams become unending howls as she cups my heart in her hand. "I told you I'd take your heart, beast." Then, she rips my heart from my chest and—

"WAKE UP, SNOW." MY EYES FLY OPEN, BUT I DON'T EVEN SEE what's in front of me. Instead, my hands shoot to my chest, patting myself to make sure I'm whole as memories of my heart being ripped from my body replay in my mind. My cheeks feel sticky with tears and my throat is sore from screaming.

"Snow, it's okay. You are safe."

That voice…

It can't be.

"Come back to me, Snow."

Above me, I can see distorted candles, seeming to hang all by themselves in the darkness.

"Snow. Look at me." The voice deepens, ordering me, and I obey, turning my head toward the sound.

"It's you," I rasp, licking my lips, my eyes darting between his arctic blue ones, then over his handsome face. He's too handsome to be human, too perfect. He's so beautiful it makes my chest squeeze tight. "You're real, it wasn't a dream."

The man—king?—strokes the side of my face, and I shudder in response. "I am the nightmare you wish to come true, pet. Soon you will learn exactly what that means."

147

"We're ready," a voice calls in the distance before I can ask a single question.

The man—lurker?—nods toward the voice and turns back to me, still strumming the backs of his fingers along my jawline. "Who are you?" I ask, unable to stop myself from placing my palm on his cheek, the movement causing a wave of agony to stream through me.

His eyes flash at the contact, and a low growl leaves his lips, making me jerk my hand back. "I am no one and everyone. I am the darkness in the night, the voice that tempts you. I am pure seduction, the choice you shouldn't make. I am the *sin* you can't help but commit." He stands, smoothing his hands down his regal suit, the one he was wearing in my castle, making me realize he's been kneeling at my side where I lie on the ground. He extends his hand to me, but I hesitate before accepting it.

He basically said he's everything sinful and wrong, so then why does my body completely reject that idea? Nothing could be worse than my fate should the queen capture me again. After this night, things will change. Lines have been drawn and people have been killed. I look back to the gorgeous man standing before me, offering me a choice.

"Make your choice, pet. But know this—your decision is permanent. Once made, you may not take it back. It will affect everything as you know it for generations to come. Choose wisely, choose for the lives of the many that are hanging in the precarious balance between one outcome and the next. Their lives are in your delicate hands at this very moment."

Reaching up, I slip my fingers into his, and his hand curls around mine. His lips twitch as he pulls me to stand. "Wise choice."

"There was only ever one option for me," I murmur softly. "I don't want to die."

He chuckles deeply. "But you must die if you are to be reborn."

I take a breath to respond, but before I can get a word out, he crushes his lips to mine. And I let him. Oh God, do I let him. His hands run up and down my back possessively as he tugs me hard against his chest. His velvet tongue slides against mine, tasting me. I savor this moment, the sweet and spiciness of his tongue, his seductive scent, the coppery tang accompanying his lips reminding me of the nectar I've come to crave.

The blood inside my veins surges, boils, and cools all at once, and I feel every broken part of me healing like I did the two times I had the nectar. The ache in my ribs dissipates, my burning throat now back to normal.

The kiss deepens, and he slides one hand between us to run his fingers across my peaked nipple, poking at the fabric of my dress. It's such a subtle touch, but it lights me on fire, and soon I'm moaning into his mouth. He growls in response, and I feel his dick grow hard against my stomach. Instead of being repulsed like I would usually be, knowing I make him hard makes my core dampen.

He growls against my lips and pinches my nipple, making me pull away from his mouth with a gasp. For a long moment, we just stare at each other. I wonder what he sees when he looks at me, covered in blood from the beating, my dress in tatters, hair wild, and makeup smudged.

Gazing at him, I see a royal from an old family. I see a man who is impeccably dressed, oozing confidence and dominance. I see a man who is used to getting what he wants when he wants it, a man who has not experienced rejection. Before me stands the most hauntingly beautiful man I've ever laid eyes on, and he's just kissed me as if I hung the stars for him.

Without a word, he tugs my arm and guides me across the

floor. I'm surprised to find myself inside the secret party room, but we are the only ones inside. He pulls me up a short set of stairs to the shadowy corner where the seven once stood watching me while I stripped and danced in a suspended cage.

In the darkness, a door forms, seemingly out of thin air. Like the one I used to enter the party, it's old and ornate. Carved into it is a sprawling castle, unlike anything I've ever seen. I marvel at the creation, wondering how someone could ever imagine such a thing.

The man places his hand on the door and it hums in response. "Are you ready?" he inquires, pulling his hand away.

"R-Ready for what?" I stammer, my heart thrashing inside me.

"For the end to your beginning and the start of your transformation." With that cryptic response, he pushes the door open.

CHAPTER 18

*A*long, torchlit tunnel carved out of stone extends before us. Tunnel seems like too small a word for how grand this is. Though you can see marks in the walls from the tools used to cut it out, it doesn't feel like we're underground. Huge flames, blazing in iron sconces, are fitted to the arched walls. The fires flicker and dance as a cool breeze filters toward us.

"This is amazing," I mumble stupidly, as I let my fingers trail along the walls.

The man smirks. "This is nothing. Just ahead of us is a sight that will captivate your eyes."

With a squeeze of my hand, he pulls me along. I'm surprised to feel shoes still on my feet, and hear my heels click down the massive corridor. Scented wax perfumes the space, making it feel warm and inviting. Rich, red stone makes up the walls, floors, and ceiling, and I wonder if this is a natural rock formation or if it has been dyed somehow.

Up ahead, I can see the end to our short but incredible journey, and of course, it stops with another door. This one is almost nondescript, except for some words written in a language I haven't spoken nor seen before. The man utters a sentence which sounds like a promise that lovers might whisper to each other in the heat of passion, and then the door lifts, rising into the ceiling to allow us passage.

He wraps my hand around his bicep—his extremely hard and muscled bicep—and steps through the threshold alongside me. I gasp and rub my eyes, not believing what I'm seeing. This can only be described as something that was made from drug induced dreams.

Someone greets us, but I don't even spare him a glance. "Good evening, King Lucian, welcome home." The fact that the man whose arm I'm clinging to was just addressed as "king" should strike some feeling in me, but I'm too overwhelmed and awestruck to even care.

Sprawled out in front of us is a massive spread of underground castles, each easily the size of my own, maybe even larger. Carved right into the red rock are dozens of towers with exposed parapets connecting them all. Spires rise from the rock, gothic and beautiful. Corbels decorate each tower and chiseled ramparts surround the entire thing. Massive torches blaze mightily on either side of each pair of doors. It must equate seven of my castle.

Wait a second...

It *is* seven castles, all connected.

Holy fuck.

Looking harder, it's clear that only the very front of each castle is embossed on the outside of the cave's gargantuan wall, which means the rest of them must lie deep inside the rock.

It's a wonder of the world, an unimaginable feat. I mean, the sheer manpower it would take to create something like this, and to do it underground...it's unfathomable.

Shivering from the chill in the underground air, I take in the sight before me. We stand atop a grand flight of stairs that have us about midway up the face of the castles. Down below, people walk about. Some speak in groups as they stroll, while others talk or sit on stone benches overlooking an underground river. I look for the obvious signs of a kingdom—storefronts, little stands perched on the road to purchase food, and homes for the lower class—but see nothing even remotely close.

How do these people eat?

Right now, I don't fucking care.

"This way." The lurker king and I—how fucking crazy is that to say—begin to descend the tall flight of stairs. As we walk, I notice what I can only assume are guards are stationed every twenty yards or so. Meanwhile, half naked women line up between them, baring their chests to us, exposing the plains of their necks...

I can't tell if they just want to be fucked by a king or if there is some ulterior motive I haven't been told yet. The women sneer at me, their eyes no doubt darting from my tangled hair to my bloodstained dress, then to where King Lucian and I are joined. To my surprise, he ignores them, as if this is just a daily annoyance he intends to avoid.

I'm shocked.

If a woman—or women, as in this case—lined themselves up and flashed their tits to a passing man in my castle, they'd find guards who'd shove one of their tiny, stinky cocks in all their holes faster than they could blink. But yet, that's not happening.

Is this some weird lurker normalcy? I guess I'll have to wait and find out. But if someone tells me I have to perch along these stairs, disrobe, and offer my body to any who might wander by, I'll punch them right in the nose. I'm done being forced to do things I don't want to.

Paying no attention to the guards, or the naked women, I focus on the seven castles, wondering which one I'll be taken to. After reaching the bottom of the massive staircase, we venture straight and right into the center set of doors.

Nervous, my pulse thumping in my ears, I follow Lucian's lead and step up to the huge, arched doors. Like the others, this one has a carving. This time it's a pair of lovers fucking. The woman is lying on her back, her large breasts gripped in the hands of the man—or a king, rather, if we can judge by the crown on his head—who is buried between her spread legs.

I want to take a closer look, to see if the man depicted is, in fact, the one I'm holding on to, but the guards quickly open the doors for us. Beyond the threshold, the air changes, becoming warmer. Incense burns, the tendrils of smoke perfuming the air.

Statues of carved, white stone are placed along the corridor. Each one is intricately detailed, and all of them depict naked men and women doing sexual things. A bulky man holds his massive cock while his mouth gapes open in pleasure. A woman sits on a pedestal, her legs spread wide, her finger dipping between her pussy lips, while another woman stands with her back turned to us, her arms holding up her hair, exposing her perfect ass.

I could go on and on.

The fact that nudity is so natural here is…unusual. Things like this would not be permitted under the queen's reign. Men are always covered, the women even more so. But not here…

As we travel deeper down the long corridor, farther into the subterranean castle, the halls become more crowded. I wonder if these lurkers have a sixth sense, because they part for their king well before we even get to them. Is it me? Do I smell?

I have to resist the urge to lift my arm and sniff my pit. Something in the king's kiss may have healed me, but it didn't clean me, and my poor body has been through the wringer since I last bathed.

So many questions filter through my mind, but my voice locks up. Years of forcing myself to remain quiet has made me habitually unable to ask things, even simple things, in fear I'll be punished for it.

King Lucian guides me past the statues, through glamourous halls filled with more gorgeous people, and up a swirling set of stairs. Those gathered have a mix of reactions. Some bow to the king with reverence. Others extend their necks in some kind of fucked up offering. A few hiss at me while others reach to touch me with claw-like extensions on their fingertips. The king keeps me close, growling at any who linger too close, and hurries me along. At the top lies a set of ivory doors, gilded in gold filigree. The king nods to the men stationed at the top and they pull the doors open.

I gasp when guided inside. The room before us is massive. Resting under an arched ceiling, painted to mimic the sky at sunset, is a plush sitting area. Oversized, opulent couches and intricately carved chairs with overstuffed cushions greet us. Heat blazes from a giant hearth, casting warmth and shadows around the room. Luxurious tapestries hang from the ceiling all the way to the floor, making the space feel warm and cozy, even though it's in the middle of an underground cavern.

Looking around, I realize one could easily get lost in the details of this space. Every nook and cranny has a carving or a painting, each one more erotic than the last. I almost feel uncomfortable looking at the profound nakedness surrounding me, even if the subjects are inanimate pieces of art.

The king drops my arm and walks farther into the room before turning to face me, his cape billowing out behind him. He takes my breath away.

Everything about him oozes seduction and dominance, from the way he wears his crown to the swagger in his step when he walks. His eyes are brighter than the sky on a cloudless day and the dimple in his chin enhances his stern jawline.

He's regal.

He's pure seduction.

"Come in, pet. I will not hurt you unless you ask it of me." Even his voice is luscious, his dulcet tone smooth and sensual like melted chocolate, distracting me from even considering why I'd ever want him to hurt me. With my heart racing, I take a step deeper into the room. It's so perfect that I feel like a smudge on the floor that needs to be scoured away. Still in my dirty clothes, I don't even think of sitting on the furniture, though I'd love to be able to relax for a bit.

"This way." He turns swiftly, elegantly, and strides through a door I didn't even see on the back wall. Unsure, scared, and very curious, I follow. The dense fabric on the walls mutes my clicking heels, and for that, I'm grateful, since the noise reminds me of she-who-must-not-be-named.

Beyond the sitting room is...a bedroom.

His bedroom.

Lush silk drapes over a lavish bed, big enough to sleep six or seven people. A canopy hovers above the massive sleeping area, carved in the likeness of a tree complete with branches and leaves. You'd think the silk would be out of place, but they complement the bed perfectly.

Speaking of the bed...

Dark blue sheets and blankets are thrown across in a strategically messy way, showing off the many layers of comfort. Plush furs and velvety silk make the bed opulent and inviting. My feet walk toward the bed without my brain even telling them to do so. The rest of the space is much like the first room, with fabrics covering the stone walls. Paintings are hung around the room, each portraying lovers performing sexual acts. They are quite erotic, and something low within me clenches while looking at them.

The king removes his crown, runs his fingers through his messy, black hair, and places the jeweled number on a bureau in front of a large, ornamental mirror that must be taller than he is. His eyes bore into mine as he unbuttons his cape next and hangs it on a golden hook. Next go his shoes, then his jacket, until he's only wearing his unbuttoned pants and an untucked shirt.

My mouth waters and I lick my lips, just watching the show with absolutely no shame. Observing him undress does something to my body. My nipples tighten and the little nub between my legs flares to life, tingling, aching, and I desperately want to soothe it, to make myself feel good.

King Lucian arches one dark eyebrow at me and heads through another door behind him. Like a good pet, I follow on shaky legs. What could possibly be through this door? I consider that it could be the kitchen, but that would be silly. No one has a kitchen off their bedroom. My hungry belly is just too hopeful for some food.

"Come, pet." The king's voice washes over me, pulling me toward its origin. I cross through the archway and find myself inside a room I've only read about in epic fantasies. Dark stone is exposed inside this room, unlike the others, and unlike the red rock I've seen so far, this space is onyx. Stacks of lit pillar candles are placed in nooks and crannies around the small space, and incense burns, creating a pleasant aroma. And even though all of this is incredible, it doesn't hold a candle to the huge pool in the floor.

Steam rises from the still liquid, misting the room. I lower my hand to the water and dip my fingers inside, finding it warm and inviting.

"It's a hot spring," King Lucian informs me before I can

even ask. "Out of all seven castles, I'm the only king who has one. It isn't sexy to bathe in a tub or basin like a commoner. No, I prefer to soak in heated pools."

"Underground spring, how about that," I mutter to myself.

"Come, let us get clean before the unveiling." I glance back up to the king who begins to unbutton his shirt. The process is painstakingly slow, as I long to see his body underneath the clothes. Button by infuriating button, he moves down the shirt until it gapes open like a broken door. As the sleeves slip off his shoulders, his muscled torso is revealed.

Pale like me, but with a moonlit glow to his skin, the king is pure male perfection. Smooth and hairless, his body is all toned, hard muscle, not too big or small. His chest is strong, his pectorals thick and defined. My gaze trails lower to his rows of chiseled abs that flex as he moves. My tongue longs to lick over each and every one of them.

Lower still, I watch as he slips his thumbs under his waistband and begins to lower his pants. I can't help it. My eyes are fixated on his crotch. With a deep chuckle, he drops his pants to the floor.

CHAPTER 19

With a groan, my hands fly to my mouth and my cheeks heat as red as the evil queen's precious apples.

Wow.

I thought his body was perfection, but I was completely unprepared for how immaculate his dick is. Unlike the hairy, tiny, gross, and stinky dicks I've had the misfortune to see, his is an artist's masterpiece. It stands proud and thick, protruding from his hairless figure like a statue. Symmetrical and erect, a shade darker than his own skin, just the sight makes me ache with some deep desire. I want to touch it, taste it, and feel it buried deep inside me.

But I also have no idea what to do with it.

The head of his dick is engorged beautifully, and his flesh looks so silky and smooth. I can't stop staring.

Another deep chuckle has me remembering he can see me brazenly ogling. He looks amused, his eyes sparkling as he watches me gape at him.

Remembering myself, I lower my hands from my mouth and avert my gaze.

"You can look, pet, for you can be sure I will be feasting on your body in only a moment." His promise makes me shiver. Not moving to cover himself, he folds his arms across his chest and nods at me. "Your turn. Remove your clothes so I may look upon you."

Suddenly feeling shy and totally insecure, I freeze. My body is nothing compared to his. He's impeccable, flawless, *inhuman.* I'm just some undernourished, fallen royal with knotted hair. I'm too thin, too pale, and my boobs are too big for my small frame.

"Now, Snow." His voice has become a growl, a command. "You are *mine*, and I intend to see every inch of your body." He takes a step closer. "Strip for your king, pet. Show me what I wish to see."

His possessiveness does something to my insides. It makes my eyes unfocus and my breasts feel heavy. It makes my stomach twist with desire and my core clench with need.

I close my eyes and take a deep breath, trying to find a sliver of bravery. Funny thing, bravery... I could stand up to the huntsmen with an axe in my hand, I could face the queen and deny every suitor who came to claim me, yet simply baring myself to a man who means me no harm, one who is bare himself, seems almost insurmountable.

"My patience grows thin, pet. Do as I ask, or I'll have your clothes removed for you." I'm so scared. I don't know this man... this, this lurker king. But he saved me. How could I not trust him, or at least repay him? My body has been flaunted by the queen, used against me. In this moment, right now, I can use it for my own choosing. Because despite my apprehension, I want to show him, I wish for him to desire me, but at the same time, I feel super embarrassed.

Licking my lips, I open my eyes and find he's moved, sunk deep within the black depths of the pool. King Lucian leans back with his arms stretched out to his sides, resting on the ledge of the pool as he sips a red liquid—probably wine—from a crystal chalice.

The water hits him just below his chest, leaving the rest of his muscled physique submerged and out of view. I almost pout, but then something I can't explain happens. Faster than my eyes can track, King Lucian jumps from the water and rushes to me. His delectable scent renders me helpless while a ripping sound echoes as if fabric is tearing, then he's back in the pool. This all happens in a matter of a single second, and before I know it, my dress puddles at my feet.

I look down, shocked, and instinctively move to cover myself. "Don't, pet. You are mine, *ours*, and I will look at you if I wish." He cocks his head to the side as his unnaturally light eyes peruse me. I feel like a caged animal, like he's shopping for a new pig or cow, looking for imperfections. "Turn," he orders, making a tiny circle with his finger. My fists clench at my sides and I chew on my lower lip. His bright eyes flash, and his eyebrows arch. "Do it."

I stifle a groan and spin. Come to think of it, I'd rather he look at my ass than my breasts or nipples...or my slit too. Because an ass is just an ass, right?

He growls, literally fucking growls, and goosebumps prickle at the sound. It's low, deep, and rumbling, like a giant cat sending out a warning, except I don't know if he's hunting me or wanting to remove me from his territory.

Perhaps both?

"You have lower back dimples."

I turn to look at him over my shoulder, having no fucking clue what he's talking about.

"Just there, above your supple ass. My, my, pet. You are just full of *sexy* surprises." I stand there like an idiot wondering what ass dimples are and why someone would like them. "So spankable, *fuckable*. I can't wait to watch you submit to my sin, Snow."

His sin...

"So it's true then?" I question, finding my voice now that I don't have to look at him.

"Depends on what you are referring to. But before we suffer through chitchat, I wish for you to join me in the hot spring. I want you near me." I hear him take a drink and let out a long exhale and I release one of my own.

Should I walk backward? That way I don't have to pretend he's not staring at the way my breasts sway when I walk. No, don't be silly. What would he think of the backward walking princess? I know he wants me, I felt it in every aspect of our kiss. I need to own this.

I turn toward him and take a few steps toward the pool. I don't look to see what part of me he's watching, instead focusing on how to get in. But it doesn't matter that I don't watch him, I can literally *feel* his eyes on me. It's like hot wax drizzling on my skin. First, he starts at my breasts, then lingers on my nipples and trails his gaze down my stomach to my slit, before focusing on my nipples again.

Trying not to panic, I look into the water but find no stairs. I don't think I should just jump in. I'd cause a mighty splash which would surely piss him off.

"Just get in already." He chuckles, finding my compromising position amusing. "Just sit your pretty ass down and slip inside."

Of course, why didn't I think of that?

Keeping my legs pressed firmly together, I sit, dip my legs into the heated water, and slide in. I let out a groan as the hot liquid kisses my skin. I've never felt anything so glorious. The hot spring is true to its name, its temperature just below the point where I couldn't stand to be in it without boiling.

I sink in up to my neck and tip my head back to wet the rest of my hair, groaning again.

"If you insist on making that damn noise, then I'll be

forced to make sure the next time it leaves your lips it is because of something I'm doing to you."

I stiffen at his words, his promise. I almost feel bold as the words *do it* perch on the tip of my tongue, but I refrain. I need to figure out this situation first, make sure he's not an enemy in disguise.

I've been fooled before.

I won't be fooled again.

Instead, I clench my lips shut and push myself to the opposite end of the pool, at least ten feet away.

"Care for a drink?"

I nod, thinking how great a glass of wine would be to help me relax. King Lucian grins and snaps his fingers. A servant appears, seemingly out of thin air, holding a chalice in her extended hands. I take it, careful not to touch her as she vanishes back into the wall she just stood in front of.

With a shaking hand, I take a long drink and tell myself to relax.

"I know you have questions, Snow. I will permit you one, so choose carefully."

"Just one?"

"Mm-hmm. You will have to earn another. You can't get something for nothing these days."

I take another sip, swirling the sweet wine around my mouth, letting the burn settle my nervous belly. I want to ask so many questions. How do I pick just one? And when I do want another, what will he require in return?

"Are you a lurker?" I mentally slap myself. Not only is that not the most pressing question I should have asked, but it also might be condescending.

"I have been called many things, pet. *Lurker* is one of a hundred names given to us since the beginning of time."

The beginning of time? My eyes narrow. "How old are you then?"

"You've not earned the answer to that yet." King Lucian rests his glass on the ledge and dips below the surface. I can see his pale outline slinking toward me below. Fingers wrap around my knees and spread them apart, only then does he surface between my thighs, his fingers still digging into my skin.

He stands, the water resting just below his hips, and shakes the liquid from his hair. Droplets coast down his skin, sinking into every dip and valley on his body. Fucking yum.

"This is much better," he says, lowering himself to my eye level. "Now, where were we? Oh yes. Another question. I suppose you've earned it." He rises a little, his head now slightly above mine, then he bends down and runs his nose along the crook of my neck, making me shiver. "I am older than most, younger than some. I've lived long enough to watch your great grandfather's reign, witness the trees in the forests grow from saplings, and observe the fall of your house."

His lips press against the pulsing vein in my neck, but he doesn't kiss me or even lick me, just feels. I almost wish he'd bite, but that would be silly. A man like him—or whatever he is—wouldn't do something like that. His breath fans my ear, his fingers sliding up my legs to hold my thighs. "Now it's my turn to ask questions."

My core aches. And he's barely even touching me. What would it feel like to be under this king as he thrusts inside me? My voice is breathy when I respond. "What do you want to know?"

"Answer truthfully, for if you lie, I will know it." He pulls his head away and takes a step closer, my pussy resting above his length, which I can feel pressed against me. His hands slide up my sides and I find myself leaning into his touch. "How badly do you want me to fuck you, pet? How painful is that ache between your legs growing?" I'm startled by his question, my breath catching when his forehead rests against mine, so close to his perfect lips. "What would you do if I impaled you on my cock right now? Would you scream? Cry? Would you shriek my name for all of my coven to hear?"

"That's five questions," I whisper against his lips, moving my hands to cup his ass. "So fucking badly. Throbbing. I'm not sure, but I'd like to find out. Probably. Maybe. Yes," I answer, and he pulls away in surprise, a smile tugging at his lips. "My turn again."

He swims back to his drink and takes a long sip. Even the way his throat works when he swallows is sexy. I need to make this question count, but his sexual approach has me all flustered, unable to think of anything but his hard body, his perfect dick. "Umm…"

"Yes?" He sounds amused.

"Why did you help me? Why save me over and over? What's in it for you?"

His face darkens. Clearly, I've struck a nerve. "Those questions will be answered at the unveiling."

"The unveiling?" I repeat. "I don't understand."

"You will soon."

That doesn't leave me feeling very comforted. Something tells me I might not like what I have to hear.

My eyes are drawn behind him where the black wall appears to be moving again. It's another servant, male this time. He wears the token cloak I've seen the lurkers don, and bends down to whisper into the king's ear. King Lucian's gaze flickers to me before he dismisses the servant with a small wave of his hand. "It is time."

"Umm. Time for what?"

He smiles, but it is not kind. It's dark and filled with mystery and secrets. "For your unveiling."

CHAPTER 20

"My unveiling?" I hate how weak I sound, how scared.

"Yes. We've been summoned." The king pulls himself from the pool, displaying his delicious body with beads of water running down him. Fuck, he's so hot. I can't even comprehend how someone could be this good-looking. That in itself is a sin.

"Keep looking, pet, for soon you'll be doing more than fucking me with your eyes." With that profound statement, he walks off to his bedroom, his dick bobbing proudly. As he passes me, and I get a look at his ass, and I have to disagree with my earlier thoughts... Not all asses are created equal.

"What about me?" Here I am, still soaking in the hot spring with no idea what the fuck is about to happen.

He turns and snaps his fingers, and I can't help but flinch, the sound reminding me of the evil bitch. More servants melt from the walls, but he stops them with one raised hand and lowers himself next to me, his finger lifting my chin. "Do not cower before me, Snow. I'm not like her. *We* are not like her. You are a princess. Though you've been dethroned, the kingdom still belongs to you. The people are loyal to you. So hold your head high, pet, as we give you the power to take back what is rightfully yours."

King Lucian nods to someone behind me and releases my chin. I sit in the pool, dumbfounded. He just praised me, scolded me, and put me in my place. And you know what? He's right. If I want to take back my kingdom, then I need to stop flinching, stop cowering, and keep my head held high and own who I am—Princess Snow of Riverwood.

Several cold hands wrap around my arms, and before I can protest, I'm hoisted from the pool like a child. A red robe is placed around my shoulders and I cinch it tight around my waist.

"Come." A beautiful woman beckons me to follow her. As we move toward the back wall, I see that it's not really a wall like I thought before, but a dark cavern. The woman grabs a nearby candle and heads inside. I follow, my bare feet padding on the stone, and when two more people flank me, I suddenly feel anxious.

I'm half naked and in some secret, underground fortress with creatures that shouldn't even exist. And I'm to be unveiled—whatever the fuck that means.

The tunnel twists then rises, and soon we're climbing a winding staircase. My thighs are rubber by the time we reach the top, and I feel like I need to bathe all over again.

"We're here," she calls over her shoulder, not even slightly out of breath. She looks just like the other people I've seen here—pale with light eyes and red lips. I wonder why they all look so similar. Perhaps they are related? One big fucking lurker family. But if they are all family, then how do they procreate? Come to think of it, I haven't seen a single child here.

The room off the top stair is bright and cheerful, unlike the lower levels of this place. The white walls are decorated with pictures of beautiful women and gorgeous dresses hanging inside gold picture frames. Vases holding red roses are scattered through the room, and the smell reminds me of my garden when it blooms after the spring rains cease. A vanity, much like my own, sits near an empty frame, and next to that is a dress—a white dress.

I almost groan.

Must the virginal white dress card be played again?

Déjà vu strikes, making me feel like I've done this before, been here before. Maybe it's the stark white room, maybe it's the dress, or maybe it's something more profound, I just haven't figured it out yet.

A second woman, wearing a revealing gown of her own, motions for me to sit at the vanity. She reminds me of Sherry with a round face and lifeless brown hair. She tugs my wet tresses out of my robe and gets to work. She hums as she combs and pins, the tune melodic and haunting, reminding me of a song played at the party I crashed. The other women —lurkers, I suspect—busy themselves by rushing around the room, but seemingly getting nothing accomplished.

Fake Sherry pulls her brown hair behind her head and ties a ribbon around it, the movement exposing her neck. Two red wounds, crusted over with scabs, stare right at me like a pair of red eyes.

"What happened to you?" I ask quietly, anger building inside me. If this girl needs aid, then I intend to help her. I won't allow people to suffer if I can help it.

"I'm a donor," she replies happily, like I should know what the fuck that is.

"What exactly do you donate?" As she moves in front of me, I can see similar marks on the tops of her breasts, though these are pink scars which are totally healed.

She laughs and points to her neck. "Really? Isn't it obvious?"

I lower my voice, not wanting the other two to hear me. "The only thing obvious to me is you've been hurt, repeatedly. If you need assistance, please tell me. I'll help get you out of here."

"I donate freely, miss. And in return I get to live here in this immense castle with everything I could ever want."

"So…no one is forcing you?" I'm so confused. Why would she happily submit herself to that kind of pain?

"Of course not. And if someone did, the seven would rip their heads off faster than they could touch me."

That statement is surprising. The seven seem like the kind of men who take first and ask later, or maybe that's only with things that pertain to me. I guess I really can't judge all of them yet, having only met one.

"Do you know what is going to happen tonight?" I try to seem calm and cool, when really, my insides are twisted in anxiousness.

"Dunno. I was just ordered to get you ready. But everyone seems a bit on edge, don't they? Whatever is going on, you can bet your pretty ass it's important. I've never seen the kings in such a tizzy before."

The woman continues working on my hair, crimping and pinning while one of the lurker females begins to apply makeup to my face. This feels an awful lot like the process I was put through to prepare for a suitor's arrival. I try not to dwell on the similarities as my mind drifts to the faces of Sherry and Enid.

Suddenly, my stomach drops and my nerves surge. How selfish have I been? I've forgotten all about my friends, the people of the kingdom. I fled in the arms of a lurker king and abandoned them just as the huntsmen were arriving. Tears mist my vision and the woman working on my eye makeup pauses. "What's the matter, dear?"

I sniff, trying to hold the tears back. "I-I just left my

people for slaughter! I'm not worthy of their loyalty. What a shitty princess I've turned out to be."

The woman cups my cheek and I glance up at her, my nostrils flaring. I prepare myself for her to look upon me with disdain, but it's understanding I see in her eyes. "No, you didn't. The kings were prepared for a fight and brought soldiers with them to aid your people. The battle was over as quickly as it began. Fear not, young Snow."

The battle was over as quickly as it began...

Those were the same words the king had told me.

"But why? Why put his people on the line for mine? What's in it for him? For them?"

"I'm not the one to give you those answers. But I promise, if you have patience, you will find the answers you seek."

I groan in frustration and cross my arms. Why won't anyone fucking tell me anything? It's infuriating! Maybe I should just escape from this place and never return. Just flee Riverwood altogether, find a new area to live, and create a new life for myself. But then the evil bitch would win, and I can't allow that to happen. I owe that much to my father's legacy and to the people of Riverwood.

I take a deep breath, let it out, then close my eyes and allow her to finish. By the time my hair and makeup are complete, I've calmed down. Knowing the people of River-wood had assistance puts me at ease. But as the robe is slipped off my body and the white gown is placed over my head, I can't help but feel like a sacrificial lamb being led to my doom, where a great dragon waits to eat me whole in order to save my people.

Pushing those thoughts aside, I glance at myself in the mirror with appreciation. The gown is simple yet beautiful. Swaths of gathered cloth reach up from my waist on opposite sides of my belly button. They cover my breasts, leaving the swell of my chest exposed, then plunge down my back, connecting to the skirt just above my ass. The skirt is light and flowy, with several layers of fabric offset at different lengths, causing the skirt to look like waves cascading up onto a sandy beach.

The material is soft yet gauzy, making my rosy nipples visible beneath it. Part of me is super self-conscious about that, and part of me is totally turned on. King Lucian was proud of his body and didn't hide it from me. I should take a note from his book and do the same. For we are all just the same really, a shell of flesh, filled with blood, muscle, and bone. Some of us are bigger than others, some smaller. There are tall people and tiny ones, dark ones and light ones, but at the end of the day, we all bleed the same, we all feel the same...so why shouldn't we be proud of our bodies? Each of us is perfectly imperfect, and I'd have it no other way.

With a newly found appreciation for myself, I slip on the proffered shoes as the women wrap the connecting ribbons around my calves, binding them just below my knees, then I practice walking in them. Like I was taught, I hold my chin high, shoulders back, and chest out. I let my arms lie loose at my sides, my fingers neither clenched nor straight. The shoes, though heeled, feel good on my feet while giving me that extra bit of height I need.

I look every bit the princess my dad raised me to be when he was alive. All that is missing is my crown. Instead of the heavy, silver diadem resting on my head, a single red rose is tucked into my hair near my left ear. Ruby earrings are eased through my ears and I can feel the heaviness of them. It's been so long since I was allowed to wear jewelry, I'd forgotten how much I like it.

Two necklaces are slipped around my neck. The first is tight about my throat, a line of diamond cut rubies that look like blood dripping from my skin. The other has a long chain which dangles between my breasts. The pendant on this one is stunning. A single, round, red, strategically cut ruby, the various edges catching the light and making it sparkle as I move, is surrounded by seven smaller ones. The rubies make my nipples seem more prominent somehow, their colors matching, drawing attention to my chest.

To finish, ruby bracelets are secured around my wrists, the gemstones embedded in a thick bangle, making them look more like restraints than jewelry.

"You look beautiful," Fake Sherry compliments behind me. "We best not be late."

I turn and see Fake Sherry smiling kindly at me. She's been so nice to me, I hate calling her Fake Sherry in my head. "What is your name?"

"Katie."

"Nice to meet you, Katie."

She grins and gestures to the exit. "Follow me."

We leave just as we came, with Katie in front and the two lurker women behind me. Descending the stairs, I begin to feel anxious, not knowing what awaits me or where I'm going.

Everything back at the castle was predictable, even the punishments. But this is a new experience. It feels like something monumental is about to happen, a once in a lifetime opportunity. A boulder rests snugly in the pit of my stomach, not helping my apprehension or my hunger.

The stairs end and I expect to exit into King Lucian's hot spring room, but I find myself atop a long, open bridge of sorts. Elevated above some type of hall, the pathway hovers at least fifty to sixty feet in the air. I lean against a golden balustrade, looking down below.

Beneath the tall ceiling of the cave, rows and rows of people are gathered, dressed in fancy clothes, while haunting music floats quietly through the room. Enormous candlelit, crystal chandeliers dangle from the ceiling, casting their yellow light across the crowd. The guests mingle, most carrying a goblet filled with red wine. Some have taken their seats and face a raised stage on which seven ornate thrones are perched.

The thrones are similar, yet different. Each chair glitters and shines, their freshly polished golden arms and legs ending in clawed feet. The backrests rise up ten feet in the air, making them appear grand. And that's where the similarities end.

The fabric upholstered on each seat is different. One is green, while another is orange. Crimson, yellow, violet, and two shades of blue adorn the others. I try to think of a reasoning for this, reflecting back on my history lessons of ancient royals, but I come up with nothing.

Glancing around the hall, I see the decor also varies in color. Lining the outer walls are silken fabrics, which hang from floor to ceiling like giant curtains, following in the same color pattern as the chairs. I know it must be a symbol for each king, but what they stand for, I cannot say.

I take a breath to ask Katie what it all means when a whoosh of cold air courses through the cavern, and all the candles flicker out.

CHAPTER 21

I grip onto Katie's arm and squeeze. Surely this is the work of the evil queen. She's found me and has come to release her power on us all.

"It's okay," Katie whispers. "Nothing can hurt you in here."

I loosen my fingers and take a deep breath, but being surrounded by total darkness isn't helping. What's going on? And why aren't the guests gathered below freaking out like I am?

Silence blankets the hall. I don't hear any normal sounds one might hear in a crowded room. No coughing, sneezing, clearing of throats. No friendly banter, no laughing, not even the clink of a glass.

It's like everyone but Katie and I have turned into statues. I don't even want to shift on my feet in fear of being the first to break the absence of noise. Is this some kind of fucked up game? To see who bursts into tears, their fears getting to them first?

Flames shoot up from below, erupting from two massive torches I didn't see before, and the crowd gasps in response.

A silhouette stands in an archway between the blazing fires. From his outline—flowing robes and a pointed crown—I know he's one of the kings.

As I'm wondering which one, a dramatic voice begins to speak. Even though I haven't known him long, I recognize it as Vincent's. "Before time began, before civilizations came to be, there were only humans. Those people fell into sin, killing each other at will, unbound to morality, unchained from humanity, and the world fell into chaos." As Vincent continues to speak, the king begins to move, slowly walking to the farthest throne on the right while another king waits between the torches.

Then, Vincent continues, "As the people become more driven by greed, tempted by lust, angered by wrath, careless by sloth, blinded by pride, consumed by gluttony, and fueled by envy, humanity began to change. It evolved."

I watch with rapt attention, listening to the story as the second king heads to his throne and the third takes his place between the flames.

"People grew into something other," Vincent says ominously. "Something that took those sins and created a new society, a new culture. One that embraced depravity, fell deep into it, yet thrived in the process. Food, as we knew it, became unnecessary as other needs persevered. Sunlight became a distant memory, as our penance was to live in the dark."

The third king sits and the fourth takes up his stance.

Vincent's voice deepens. "We were reborn in the night, keepers of chaos, wielders of sins. We accepted all that is dark and demented, we became the creatures of legend, the monsters in the stories, the almighty power in the world."

The fourth king sits, and the fifth stands in the archway, each moving with elegance and grace like a well choreographed dance.

"Together, the first seven gave us life," Vincent announces proudly. "They accepted our darkness, our deviant needs. They sucked the sin right out of our very blood, leaving their victims cleansed and ignorant to our ministrations, and together, our coven grew. Then, a new evil spread across the lands, one we'd heard whispers of long ago. But we ignored the evidence, thinking it couldn't hurt us down here in the deep, but we were wrong."

The fifth king sits and the sixth stands at the ready.

"The first seven died because they would not listen, would not see reason. They didn't evolve as we once had, and so they fell to the evil that holds our world in its powerful hands, an evil that once aided in our very creation."

The sixth king walks to his throne and the final king enters the archway as Vincent continues the story. "The first seven fell because they failed to unite, failed to come together, each wanting to lead instead of ruling together. Because of their distrust, they collapsed into ruin and despair, either dying by the ever present evil, subjecting themselves to the sun, or being impaled by the sharp end of a wooden stake... And so, the second seven came to be. For a century, they've been watching, waiting, and biding their time, ready when opportunity strikes. Then, during a winter storm over two decades ago, there was a sign."

The final king sits as the story carries on.

"The snow fell in heaps from the skies, leaving the world trapped under its thick, white blanket. But through the winds, the hail, and the ice covering our lands in its frozen grip, a new life began, one that will change our world as we know it. She is drawn to them as much as they are to her. They are fated, destined, and once she's fallen into sin, she will rise as the ultimate ruler, the Queen of the Vampires."

I gulp, my throat suddenly dry. He can't possibly mean—

"Would you like to meet her?" Vincent asks. "I know the

kings certainly would." The crowd erupts with cheer from below, and I take a step back from the balustrade, searching for an escape, but I'm still surrounded by utter blackness.

"Where are you, Snow?"

I look around anxiously so I can tell Vincent to shut the fuck up. I'm nothing special, certainly not a vampire queen. Don't you have to be dead to be a vampire? Are vampires even real, or are these people some part of a sick fucking cult?

Then I feel it... Magic. Power. It grows thick in the hall, choking me, caressing me. I feel it swirling inside me, flowing through my veins, in every stuttered breath I take.

How are they doing this?

A concentrated beam of light shines down from the roof above and it's aimed directly at me. The light is blinding, and I throw my hands up to shield my eyes.

"Snowwwww." I freeze as the voice of King Lucian washes over me, heating my skin. "The stage is yours, become who you were meant to be. Save your people, save your kingdom, save yourself."

Fuck.

I let out a breath I didn't know I was holding and lower my arms. I can do this. I have to do this. It's the only way. I take a tentative step toward the bannister and gasp when I see it's no longer there. In its place is a set of stairs, leading right down into the middle of the hall.

"You can do this," Katie whispers from behind me, giving my back a gentle push.

I can't see the faces in the crowd, or the kings on the stage. The glaring light makes everything else cease to exist, leaving just me and the stairs.

I take a step down, then another, trying not to fall in the heels I'm not used to wearing. The jewelry on my body suddenly feels heavy and restricting. The necklace is choking me, and the pendant feels like it's burning through my skin. The bracelets are restrictive like the manacles in the queen's dungeons. But still, I walk. I take another step, and another, wondering how many fucking steps there are.

I keep my head held high, my shoulders back, my chest lifted, even though I'm terrified. My fate is unknown, and I have a feeling I might die before it all ends, but I'm going to fight the anxiety building within me and be who I was born to be.

The steps finally end and the light continues to guide me, showing the way. The guests remain quiet, stoic, motionless. I don't hear the rustling of someone adjusting their position or the shuffling of feet. It's as if I'm totally alone.

I follow the light, forcing one foot to move in front of the other along the long aisle, until I come to the bottom of an additional set of stairs. I know from before that these lead up to the stage, to the kings. The light moves away and I'm left alone in shadow. Looking toward the elevated stage, I see the kings, their faces obscured by the relit torches blazing behind them.

My heart thrashes inside me and my legs feel like lead as I lift them. One stair at a time, I keep moving, climbing to my destiny, to my doom. As I reach the last stair, something incredible happens. From the floor between the fourth and fifth king, another throne rises, an eighth throne.

Unlike the kings', this one is all white marble with streaks of silver sparkling through it. Gemstones create a mosaic on the top of the backrest in the shape of a crown, and giant wings spread out behind it, making it look like it could take flight at any moment…or consume me whole.

Realizing this chair is meant for me, I walk toward it, then I turn and sit down as elegantly as I can, crossing my legs. The arms feel smooth under my palms and the silver cushions hug my body. If I closed my eyes, I could forget where I was and sleep here until someone woke me.

But that's not my destiny.

The king to my left rises and comes to my side. I know it's King Lucian without even looking. His scent washes over me, sweet and spicy, and my body ignites, reacting to his closeness. I have to wrap my fingers around the armrests to keep myself from reaching for him.

"Stand, pet," he whispers. "You are about to become ours in every way possible by completing the very first step of your transformation."

Another king comes close, smelling of leather and expensive wine. "You will be touched," he says, running a finger down my arm.

"Tasted," a third king adds, whispering in my ear.

Another scent permeates my senses, belonging to another king I can't see. He smells fresh, like crisp morning air. "Stripped bare and exposed," he promises, his deep voice rolling through me.

King Lucian speaks again. "By doing this, you will allow us to unveil you to our coven as a sign of your loyalty to us, a sign that you accept your destiny to become not just the queen of our coven, but the queen of the world."

I shiver when a baritone voice whispers to me. "You still have a choice, Princess Snow. Leave now and forget all that has transpired here, or submit to your kings by giving us control of your life. In return, we shall bestow upon you your salvation, an eternity of utter bliss."

"Stand and decide," King Lucian orders. "Walk out of here unharmed, all memories of us erased from your mind, or submit to the unveiling. The choice is yours."

The choice is mine? For once in my life, I'm given the right to choose my fate, but the pathway I want to take seems dark and dangerous. If I walk away, leave this place forever,

I'll end up back in the hands of the evil queen with no memory of the lurkers, or their…coven, I think they called it. She won't tolerate my presence much longer, and without help, I have no means with which to defeat her.

The other option is to stay. If I do so, I must submit to yet another person, seven persons actually, but in doing so, they have promised me the world in exchange for my submission and my life. That's much more than I could ever hope for from the queen.

Determined to change the course of my fate, I grip the armrests tight and rise with as much grace as I can muster. The tenacious light shines bright in my eyes, keeping those gathered, the silent ones, shrouded in darkness.

Time feels like it pauses, the very fate of the world holding its breath to see what I might decide. I close my eyes and open myself up to the powers that be. My arms hang loose at my sides, my head held high. I remain poised on the outside, even though inside I'm a raging storm.

I can feel the kings surrounding me without even seeing them. Just their presence is enough to make my heart race and my nerves fire, as if every part of me is being caressed even though no one is touching me.

"For wrath, you will suffer," the leathery smelling king pledges, as his fingers slip under the right strap of my dress, his cool digits kneading my shoulder.

To my left, another hand caresses me, his touch sliding under my dress on his side. "For greed, you will become insatiable," he vows.

"For gluttony, you will become voracious," another croons, as the straps of my dress are pulled off my shoulders.

"For envy, you will constantly want more." Large hands cup my breasts, thumbs toying with my nipples.

Hands move to untie my skirt, deft fingers skating below my waistband to rub the tender skin below. "For pride, you will become superior in every way imaginable." The ribbon is unraveled, and my dress is shimmied over my hips before pooling at my feet, leaving me bare before all.

Then I'm lifted in the air and laid down on something soft. "For sloth, you will ignore all duties, and indulge in that which you crave."

"For lust, you will be pleasured beyond human comprehension," King Lucian promises, making it clear which sin is his to wield.

Only then, after the last king has spoken, do I open my eyes. All I see is white, blinded by the spotlight as seven crowned heads descend on my body where I lie on a bed of white.

Just like my dream...

Lips, teeth, and tongues taste me. The sensations are overwhelming. My legs are parted as a tongue glides up my pussy, while another pair of hot mouths suckle on my nipples.

My wrists are kissed, tongues flickering against the tender skin, as two more nip and bite my neck. My body begins to tremble as something deep inside me starts to stir, to grow. A heat builds within me, turning my blood into molten lava. My core aches and the nub between my legs pulses, throbs, my hips thrusting to find a tongue to touch me there.

My breaths become shallow and sultry moans escape my lips. Every nerve in my body ignites as the waterfall I've fallen down once before appears again in my mind. Pleasure unlike I've ever known is forced upon my body and I revel in the sensations.

"Yes!" I cry out, my back arching, breasts pressed tighter into the mouths teasing my nipples.

And then, they bite.

All seven.

Teeth pierce my skin, the coppery scent of my blood filling the air, and I explode.

My eyes close, sounds become muffled, and my vision turns white, but not from the spotlight this time. My body feels like it's floating as I plunge over the waterfall. Waves of pleasure flood me, my pussy gushing, dampening my thighs as the kings continue to suck on me relentlessly.

It's not until the last rumble of pleasure shakes me, until I almost pass out from the sensations, they finally let up.

I can't yet open my eyes as the world darkens beneath my exhausted lids, but before I fall into unconsciousness, I hear King Lucian proclaim, "Coven of Sin, before you lies your future, your queen. Her blood runs through our veins now, and by extension, yours. The time for hiding is over, her transformation has begun."

Then, all I know is darkness.

CHAPTER 22

I wake up not wanting to open my eyes. I can't remember the last time I slept so well. I'm sure the guards are watching, waiting for me to stir so they can report me to the queen, let her know I've awakened, and get me ready for my punishment.

"I know you're awake, Sofi. The cadence of your breathing has changed. You may open your eyes so we may have a chat."

"Vincent?" I peel my eyelids back and find myself in a luxurious bed, surrounded by soft pillows and a plush blanket. The canopy overhead is layered in white fabrics, making the bed feel very ethereal.

"Miss me?" Turning toward his voice, I watch him rise from a nearby chair and walk over to where I lie, a grin plastered on his face. I smile at his brashness. "Of course, we all know your name isn't Sofi, is it?"

My cheeks heat. "No."

"Why did you hide who you are, Princess Snow?" Vincent perches on the foot of the bed, making sure not to touch me.

"I was afraid," I respond honestly. "I was afraid you might have been working for the queen."

"*You* are the queen, my dear." Why do his words fill me with excitement and terror?

"Did you know? Did you know who I was when I first came into your party?"

Vincent laughs. "Of course I knew. Everyone knew. It took everything I had in me not to taste you right then and there. So much sin inside your blood. You ooze it. If the seven hadn't been there to stop us all, you may not have survived the night."

I gulp. "So...you're drawn to sinners? Then why am I here? I could hardly commit a sin stuck inside my castle prison."

Vincent stands and ambles up next to me. He reaches for me and I flinch reflexively. Ignoring my cowardice, he tugs on a rogue curl hanging near my cheek. "Oh, but you have, princess. There is so much wrath inside you, so much in fact that it feels like you might explode. The air around you is thick with it, even after the kings fed off you."

They bit me...

I look down at my wrists, seeing the two red circles neatly pressed into my skin. Then I reach for my neck, feeling two more. I don't search for the other three bites, remembering they were in places I don't wish to show Vincent at this time.

"You came so prettily for them, princess. It's a wonder how they held back and didn't fuck you right then. Though I suppose they've learned a thing or two over the centuries."

Centuries?

I glance away, finding his crass words embarrassing. Knowing all those people—lurkers—vampires...all watched how easily I allowed the kings to strip me, expose me, drink from me...

184

Groaning, I cover my face with my hands, shaking my head. "They probably all think I'm some fucking whore," I mutter, mortified.

"On the contrary, they were quite impressed. You see, there are many covens around the world, and each revolves around a particular set of rules. Ours is the Coven of Sin. We survive on sin and we'd die without it. We need it as much as you need oxygen. It is our food, our drink. Without sin, we'd perish."

"So...you don't, like, eat food?"

Vincent laughs again. "Oh, princess, there is so much you don't know. Vampires—"

"So you're a vampire?" I interrupt, already knowing the answer, but I need to hear him say it.

Vincent responds by lunging toward me and exposing a set of bright, white, sharp fangs. I recoil and press my back against the headboard of the bed, my heart racing. The movement causes the blankets to slip down my body and Vincent jerks his head toward my chest, his eyes flashing. The cool air puckers my exposed nipples, and I hurry to cover myself back up. Mentally, I'm smacking myself for not realizing I was naked. No need to test his control.

Vincent, realizing his actions, moves away and rolls his shoulders like he's trying to regain command of his senses.

My head spins.

So all these years, the legends, the lurkers...they were vampires the entire time. "And t-the kings need me to become one of you?" I hate how I stammer, how weak I sound.

"Yes and no." Vincent, impeccably dressed, strolls around the room, his hands clasped behind his back. "*You* need you to become one. It is the only way to earn your crown."

Could he be any more vague? What's with these vampires and speaking in riddles? "What do you mean?"

Vincent spins to face me. "It means...that to become a vampire of the Coven of Sin, you must actually *become* the sin. Each sin actually. Most of us have only drunk from one particular king whose sin calls to us. But you, my dear, you will drink from them all. You will submit to each king, falling into their sin. And by doing so, you will acquire power the likes of which none living have ever experienced before. You will be the ultimate weapon, wielder of the seven, an imposing force. And behind you will be the kings and your coven."

My skin tingles.

The ultimate weapon...

"Then I can defeat the queen," I say, more to myself than to Vincent.

"Exactly," he responds. "But it will come with a cost, as do all things worth having."

I don't want to know what I'll have to pay for this gift, but I'm more than willing to give it everything I've got. I have obeyed for as long as I've been alive, but it will be different submitting to the kings. Because this time, I'll get something in return, something other than a day free from punishment.

My people need me, and I'll do anything to protect them. "When do I begin?"

"Such an eager little thing," Vincent croons with a grin. "Soon, I expect. After that display you put on last night, the kings won't be able to keep their hands off you. They can sense you now."

My face scrunches up in confusion. "What do you mean sense me?"

"Sense you. I don't know another way to put it. They've drank from you, therefore your blood courses through their veins. They will always know where you are, they will sense your emotion when you feel strongly about something, your desires...that sort of thing."

SEVEN SINS OF SNOW

So much for privacy.

"Once I drink from them, will I sense them too? Do all the lurkers—I mean vampires drink from a king? Are there any humans in the coven? I met one when I was getting ready for the unveiling. Katie was her name, she said she was a donor."

"Whoa!" Vincent says, putting his hands up. "One question at a time, my dear." He struts around the room again, and I let my eyes wander. The walls are a soft gray, the decor white with splashes of pink. Vases filled with flowers are displayed from hanging planters. A rather large bouquet sits in the middle of a side table, and on either side are two plush chairs, both in white. An archway leads off to my left with no door, which I expect has a bathroom beyond. Behind Vincent is a large, heavy-looking wooden door and I wonder if that's the exit.

"Don't even think about it," Vincent warns, following my gaze. "Though the coven is controlled by the kings, there are still some who would feast on you faster than you could blink. You call to something deep inside us, princess. Every vampire here wants a piece of you, you make us regress to the side of ourselves that is more beast than human. Some of the younger ones won't be able to control it."

"Like when I first met you?" I question, remembering how Vincent's face changed, how he lunged at me.

"Yes," he replies rather poignantly. "Kings Marcel and Thorin felt me change and stopped me before I could hurt you."

I lick my lips. "What would you have done to me if—"

"If I'd gotten to you? Not sure really. Once the change takes over, our minds are no longer our own. I would have drank from you, fucked you, whatever I would have wanted."

"Wow." My head is reeling from all this information.

"To answer your other questions, yes, all vampires

consume the blood of a king, but not directly from the vein. And yes, there are humans among us, donors who allow vampires in need of a meal to drink from them in exchange for the pleasure we bestow. Some linger here in servitude, hoping one of us might turn them into a vampire."

"But the nectar…was that king's blood?"

Vincent nods. "It was indeed, but less potent than drunk directly from the kings themselves."

"Which king was it?"

"All, of course." My eyes widen in shock. "Don't be foolish, dear princess, do you really think one of them would stand by idly while their future queen drank from the others? Come on. You, of all people, understand the minds of those in power. You should know better than that."

"But I don't *feel* them, Vincent."

He grins. "Because your dose was controlled, a single drop from each king mixed with honeyed mead. It was enough for you to heal, to taste a morsel of each sin, allowing it to course through you, start the cravings. No more, no less."

That explains the sex dream.

"So when I drink from each king, I will become their sin?"

"Things don't work that easily, I'm afraid. They will require your submission sexually. That, in combination with their blood, will give you their sin, their power."

My stomach drops. "You mean, I have to have sex with them?"

He nods, his eyes hooded. "All seven of the kings will fuck you, dominate you, bring you immense pleasure. We are the Coven of Sin, princess. Everything we do revolves around sex. We like to feel good and make others feel good. It is our way."

We remain silent for a while. Vincent assumes his position on the chair next to the table, while I huddle under the blankets, chewing on my lip.

A vampire queen...

Throughout my life, I've envisioned my future. As a child, it was filled with moments found in the fairy tales I read. A gorgeous prince would find me, we'd fall madly in love, marry, and have children. Growing up changed my perceptions, took my head out of the clouds and threatened to snuff out any light I kept inside me.

No longer did I wish for a prince to find me, but for someone to rescue me. Parenting became an idea I tossed aside, for who would want to raise a child in a corrupted world like mine? I pictured the evil queen's death, every day, since I was a teenager. I'd kill her in my mind, brutally, strategically, wanting to make her suffer as much as I had.

Then the suitors started, and again I foolishly thought a prince might find me, but I quickly learned I couldn't have been more wrong. As the ancient men vied for my hand, as I felt the wrath of the duke, as I fell deeper into despair, I knew a prince would never come for me.

But never in my wildest dreams did I even imagine it would be a king who saved me. Not one king, but *seven.* Now look at me, swept off my feet to an underground network of castles run by vampire kings. My future may not have been the one I'd wished for as a child, or one I've hoped for as a woman, but it's the one I need to fulfill my vow to the people of Riverwood.

But sex with seven men—vampires—kings...

Will they take me all at once or one at a time?

Can I handle that?

What if my lack of experience disappoints them? Vincent did allude to the fact that they are centuries old...

I groan, once again cradling my head in my hands. After

taking a moment to calm myself, I look up to ask Vincent yet another question, but find him gone.

I'm all alone in a strange castle filled with legendary monsters who crave my blood, kings who can sense what I'm feeling and know where I am. I should be scared, terrified, but right now, all I feel is excitement.

Prepare to die, evil bitch, because I'm coming for you.

CHAPTER 23

*L*iving in the castle of the Coven of Sin is somewhat similar to the dungeons belonging to the evil bitch, in the essence that I have no sense of time. There are no windows to watch the bloated, gray clouds grow brighter or darker. There are no changes in shifts of the guards to notify me that half the day has gone.

Meals are odd too.

The vampire servants are sneaky things, slipping in and out of my room—or the room I'm staying in—when I'm not looking. Boredom becomes the norm in my stark chamber. The bathroom is sparse, with an empty tub and toilet. I don't have a wardrobe or a bureau filled with clothes to rummage through, forcing me to remain naked. There is no vanity to practice makeup, no mirror to help me tame my crazy curls.

It's just me.

And this bed.

And that's about it.

But I've begun to change…

My hearing feels more acute, or I've just become hyper-aware of any noise from being locked in this room. My vision seems more defined, colors brighter, definition clearer. Even my body is doing odd things. I never thought I could become paler than I was, but my skin is altering. I'm becoming brighter. I know that's an odd way to describe yourself, but my skin seems to have a slight glow to it.

Then there are my teeth. Pain pricks at my palate, making me remember what it felt like as a child to lose teeth and grow new ones. But who grows new teeth as an adult? The idea is preposterous. Yet, I feel something changing near my canines...

Other senses are also developing. Smell, for one. I can sniff out when someone has passed by my door, but the one scent I yearn to inhale again has not returned to me. There's also a deep-seated craving for something, a taste that has my mouth watering, but what I desire escapes me.

A knock on my door has me scurrying over to my bed, ensuring my blanket cape is wrapped tightly around me. "Come in." A familiar head of muted brown hair peeks in through the door, a huge smile on her face. "Katie!" She laughs and opens the door, bringing a covered tray with her.

I pat the side of my bed eagerly. "Please come join me. It's so nice to see you again." And it really is. I'm lonely. After my conversation with Vincent, I had expected the, umm... sinning to begin shortly. But so far, there's been no word from the kings, and with no way to tell time, I have no idea if it's been days or hours since I've been here.

"You look so good!" she compliments before sitting next to me. I wonder if she can see the changes in my body. "So! How are you?" she asks, removing the lid from the tray. My mouth waters at the sight. Fresh beef covered in gravy, mashed potatoes, and warm bread with a slab of butter.

I take a bite of potatoes and moan like a hussy. "I'm good. Bored, but good."

Katie slices off a huge chunk of beef, places it on her

plate, and cuts off a huge bite. Her eyes close in pleasure as she slips the meat into her mouth. "Mmm, that's so good."

"Surprisingly so, considering vampires don't eat regular food."

She quirks a brown brow at me. "And how do you know that?"

"Vincent."

"Ahh." Seems she needs no other explanation. With a personality like his, I'm not surprised he's known.

Katie shows off her newest selection of bite marks along her inner thigh. She simply beams while displaying them, like a father who's just watched his daughter hit her first bullseye in archery.

"So, who was the vamp?" I inquire, eyeing the red wounds and thinking back to my own.

"Shh!" she scolds, glancing around. "Don't call them that. They hate that."

"What? Vamp?"

"Yes! King Thorin's wrath could become uncontrollable for saying such a thing." Katie takes a scoop of potatoes and groans at the flavor. "It was a younger vampire. His name is Julian. And fuck was he good. Sucked the sin right out of me and then some."

"Sounds hot," I offer, feeling awkward talking to someone about sex.

She smirks. "You would know. Not only did you have seven kings bite you, but they are some of the oldest vampires in the coven *and* they bit you all at once. It had to be breathtaking."

I can feel my cheeks heating. "Well…it was pretty amazing. But I'm so fucking embarrassed. Having that done to me in front of a whole coven—"

"And all the servants and donors too," she cuts in, making me redden even more.

"Yes. Them too."

"What was it like?" I think at this point I might explode, and I cover my face with my hands. "Oh, come on! You can't be that bashful about sex!"

I peek at her through two of my fingers before releasing my hot cheeks. "Okay, fine. It was like nothing I'd ever experienced before. I thought I was going to burst from the sensations. It was too much and not enough at the same time. Does that make sense?"

"Completely." We finish our meal, then Katie surprises me by grabbing a bottle of wine she'd left just outside my door. She pours us each a generous glass and I sip eagerly, letting the heat infect my brain, calming me down.

"That's delicious," I comment after exhaling loudly. Katie smiles at me sheepishly and glances toward the door for what has to be the tenth time. I narrow my eyes. "Are you expecting someone?"

"Err. Kinda?"

"It's a yes or no question, Katie."

She frowns. "It's just that, well, I've been told that someone will be summoning you shortly."

A flood of adrenaline rushes through my veins. "One of the kings?"

She looks at me with apologetic eyes. "All of the kings."

"That's a good thing, right?"

Katie licks her lips nervously. "Well, once word is given, you are to enter their private throne room."

I can feel my excitement building, mixed with trepidation, wondering why they want me. I slide off the bed but stop short, turning back to Katie. "I don't have anything to wear. Will someone be coming to get me ready?"

"That's the thing, princess—"

"Please just call me Snow."

She smiles. "Snow. Well…you won't be getting ready in

the normal sense." She fiddles with the blanket, blushing furiously. What's she hiding?

"I'm not surprised that things around here would be unusual. But to tell you the truth, my life has been anything but normal. I wouldn't even know what 'usual' would be like." I'm surprised by my admission. Usually, I keep things to myself, but conversation with Katie just seems so easy. She's my first real friend.

"Well—"

I groan in frustration. "Out with it already, Katie! What won't you tell me?"

She chews her lip and looks at the door again. "Umm. You won't be getting ready per se." She glances at me and continues, "Water for a bath will arrive shortly, and I'll do your makeup while Renee does your hair but...there won't be a gown this time."

That strikes me as odd. "No gown? That's okay, I find them restricting anyway. What will I wear instead?" Now it's Katie's turn to look like her face might burst into flames. My stomach plummets. "Don't tell me..." I can't even finish the sentence, but Katie nods emphatically. "Fuck."

"Yeah... I didn't know how to tell you."

I take a deep breath and let it out. "I just wonder why though. You would think most men wouldn't want the eyes of others seeing their future partner naked."

Katie's eyes flash. "They aren't men though." I give her the side-eye. "No, seriously. They are vampires, they are kings, they are sin personified. And soon, you will be too."

With that cryptic comment, my door swings open and in walks Renee, pulling a basin of hot water behind her. "I'll get your bath prepped. Give me a few minutes."

"Thank you." I sound defeated.

"It will be okay, Snow." Katie slips from the bed and

wraps her arm around my shoulders. "Just think of it as your second test. You've already done it once, right?"

"I guess." I get what she's saying, but it doesn't make me feel any better.

"Plus, you're fucking gorgeous! Why hide this hotness under clothes anyway? It would be a shame."

I can't help but smile. "Thanks, Katie."

Renee huffs from the bathroom. "This is all so cute and all, but can we get this over with? The seven don't like to be kept waiting."

"Sorry." Quickly, I follow her inside and allow the blanket to fall from my shoulders before stepping into the tub. I groan as the hot water hugs me. If I had it my way, I'd take two baths every day. Hell, maybe I will once I become queen.

If I can survive...

Katie and Renee get to work on my body. Renee scrubs me though I try to get her to let me do it myself, while Katie grabs a pitcher and pours water on my hair. I'm reminded of my time back at my castle with Sherry and Enid doing the same thing. Gosh, I miss them, even though our conversations were virtually nonexistent. But in our quiet moments, the silence gave me strength, just their mere presence was profound.

Renee and Katie work as a well-oiled machine, making me wonder if they've done this for other women the kings might have shared. But that's not a question I'm prepared to ask in fear of the answer. Because of course they've had other women! I mean, they are hundreds of years old! Who has heard of a virgin man past the age of fifteen? A hundred-year-old virgin is unimaginable. I feel stupid for even considering such a thing.

The bath is over much too quickly, and though a robe is wrapped around my shoulders as the women fuss over my hair and makeup, I couldn't feel any more naked. My stomach turns into bubble guts, and my belly threatens to expel its contents.

I stare blankly at the wall as my hair is oiled and the top half is pinned out of my face, allowing my longer curls to cascade down my back. I follow Renee's orders to close my eyes or pucker my lips. But my mind is elsewhere, already suffering the humiliating journey through the castles to meet with the kings.

Fuck.

I wish I didn't have to do this. Could there be anything more demeaning? Having strangers look upon the very thing you've always hidden since you were small...it's undignified. And yes, I understand Katie's point—they are not men. But regardless of that, I'm still a woman, a *human* woman. After hundreds of years of life experiences, you would think they've learned a thing or two about what women like.

This?

This is not one of them.

But then again, this is not about what I like. Perhaps Katie is right. I should look at this as another test to pass. Hell, it might be.

"It is time, princess." Renee's voice pulls me from my thoughts, and I open my eyes. With no mirror, I have no idea what they've done to me. I can only guess.

I lick my lips, close my eyes, and give myself an internal pep talk.

You can do this, Snow. You've been paraded around naked before, right? It's only skin. Everyone has skin. You can do this. Think of the end result. The ultimate weapon... Kill the fucking queen.

When my eyes open again, I slip off the chair and stand, willing my legs to move.

This is it.

How did Katie put it? Sin personified?

197

Renee pulls the warm robe off my body and goosebumps immediately rise on my skin. "Just the final touches," she coos. The cool metal of a heavy necklace wraps around my neck, almost chokingly tight. Several more gold chains are layered down my chest, while another is wrapped around my narrow waist. Cuff bracelets are secured over my wrists and biceps, while seven rings are slipped on my fingers. Heavy earrings pull at my ears while my feet are encased a flat shoes. The laces wind up my calves and tie behind my knee in a bow. Finally, a red rose is slipped behind my ear again.

A knock jars me, and I jerk my head toward the door. "Come in." I try hard to steady my voice, but it trembles in spite of my attempt to remain calm.

The door swings open, and in walk two of the largest lurkers—I mean, vampires, that I have ever seen. Twins who are around seven feet tall. Armor covers their pale skin, their bright eyes terrifying and inhuman. Armed with swords and daggers tucked into their belts, they seem ready to take on an army. The twins look down upon me with hunger in their eyes, shamelessly feasting on my body as if I'm their last meal.

I gulp.

"We are Cerino and Jovie, here to escort you to your destination," one of them growls, but I don't know which. It doesn't matter. I can't even respond, my voice lodged in my throat. I didn't even think that I'd have an escort, but seeing these huge vampires makes me wonder why such extreme measures are necessary just to walk to the kings. Is my life in danger? Why couldn't Katie just take me? I'm sure she knows the way.

"This way, follow Cerino." Jovie holds the door open with his giant hand and gestures out into the hall where the other waits for me.

"You got this," Katie whispers in my ear, squeezing my

shoulder. Remembering what I was taught, I assume the posture of a princess. Head up, shoulders back, chest out, hands loose at my sides. If I'm going to be queen, I need to act like one. I can't allow a little public nudity to rattle me. I've done it before, I can do it again.

My feet begin to move without me telling them to. I turn right as suggested by Jovie and begin the walk of shame. Thankfully, wherever I've been kept is isolated, as the hallways are vacant. I can feel the large vampires hovering just behind each of my shoulders, their presence making me uneasy.

I'm guided down a flight of stairs that swirls down the outside of a huge tower. How quickly I forgot while in my dark room that I'm literally in an underground castle. But with seven castles to choose from, and me having no idea where I am, I realize it could take hours to get to my destination.

That means hours of walking, a feat I'm not used to in my castle prison, and hours of my body freezing in the cool air deep below the Earth's surface.

The sconces blazing off the walls offer me little respite to the cold. I'm desperate for a coat or a blanket, even a thin sheet. My nipples tighten painfully, shivers chattering my teeth as well as my body. And the lower we descend, the colder it feels.

I flex and clench my fingers, making sure I don't lose feeling, and I scrunch my toes for the same reason. Finally, I can see the bottom of the tower, and to my horror, it's filled with people. Vampire or not, this is a distressing sight.

Some hold torches, some drink red liquid from goblets, but all eyes are fixed on me. As I get closer the sneers begin. Vampires of both sexes lunge at me, fangs exposed. I jolt in reaction, trying to save myself from a bite or scratch. Jovie and Cerino take up guard, using weapons to command the group.

Comments about my body flit through my ears.

"I'd like to take a bite out of her."

"Behave, this could be your future queen."

"I'd sink my teeth and my cock inside her."

"She's just so fucking erotic. I want her."

"Fairest of them all..."

I jerk my head toward the last comment, but in the sea of faces I can't identify the owner.

I make eye contact with a rather lustful-looking man. That was a mistake. His fangs descend and he hisses at me, battling the guards to get to me. But Cerino and Jovie persist, slashing at anyone who attempts to touch me. They can't fight them all, though, and random hands slap at my ass, stroke my arms, tug at my hair, and grope my breasts.

As the guards swipe at the onslaught of lurkers, blood spatters all over me. I wipe at the blood, fucking hating the kings for allowing this to happen, to force this upon me, but all I end up doing is smearing it on my skin. I mean, what the fuck? This serves no purpose but to demean me.

After I make it through the crowd, I walk under an arch-way, panting to catch my breath, and find myself on a battle-ment raised above the exterior wall of a castle. More guards are stationed here, but unlike the creeps at my castle, these ones don't even look my way. Instead, they face down, watching the vampires below. Hundreds are gathered at the base, their faces contorted into something vicious and feral, just like those I just passed. To my surprise, some of them leap up to try and reach me, causing me to jump back right into Jovie's chest. Or is it Cerino's?

"Don't worry, princess. They will not reach you." His words do little to comfort me as more and more spring from the ground like mutant frogs. I can hear their hissing and growling, and their nails or maybe even claws digging into the stone for grip. I scurry along the battlement and enter a turret. The stairs here wind down again, but they are narrow, only large enough for us to pass one at a time.

I'm surprised no one leads me, my guards both behind me. At the bottom, I'm met with a large, wooden door which rattles loudly, as if someone is crashing into it over and over again.

"Stand back," Jovie orders. He pushes in front of me, sword drawn, and opens the door. Vampires reach in to get me and I shriek as a dozen arms stretch through the opening, grasping at me. Their faces remind me of Vincent's the first day I met him, when he lost control. Snarling half beasts bite at me, sniffing the air, their bright eyes haunting.

I'm so fucking scared.

All I have to fight with is some fucking jewelry and a rose.

I cower between my massive guards, spinning my body out of the way. Cerino and Jovie prove to be outstanding defenders and slice off limbs before they can touch me. I see now that we are outside the castles, and I'm escorted to a lowered drawbridge I didn't notice before. Below it is a moat that surrounds one of the castles, but it's not filled with water.

A silver liquid swirls around the basin, like molten metals. I've never seen such a wonder before. My guards hurry me over the bridge and under a partially lowered portcullis, which is also coated in the same silver color. It closes behind us with a bang and the drawbridge is drawn up.

As the bridge closes us off from the mass of vampires, it becomes eerily silent. I'm shaking, my eyes darting around as I wait for the next monster to attack me.

"You should be safe here," Cerino assures me.

Should be?

Well, that doesn't fucking help.

"This way." Jovie gently presses on my lower back, his fingertips grazing my ass, and I jump. "Sorry, princess." He pulls his hand away and I move. A torchlit corridor extends before me. Heavy drapery line the sides, mimicking windows. Between the curtains are paintings of various landscapes. One has a canopy of trees in the fall, their leaves a plethora of warm colors. Another is a winter scene, snow falling on a pine tree.

Farther down, there's a painting of an orchard. Rows and rows of trees bursting with apples, oranges, and bananas. I narrow my eyes as it looks oddly familiar, like my own orchard.

A massive mountain makes up the last picture, its peaks covered in snow, but below the trees are green and plush grass surrounds a calm lake, home to a family of swans.

Another door looms ahead of me. Before it even opens, I know the kings are on the other side. The air here grows thick with magic. Tantalizing scents assault me, each one reminding me of that sweet nectar I drank not so long ago.

Power swirls around me, caressing my skin like a gentle lover, and I shudder in response. One of my guards says something, but his words are lost on me as the door lifts into the ceiling and I'm drawn inside by some unseen force.

As the door lowers behind me and I find myself all alone in a dark space, I can't help but wonder...is this the end to my beginning, or the beginning to my end?

CHAPTER 24

*M*y breaths saw in and out of me, the only noise in the blanketing blackness. Nothing moves, no sounds to distract me. It's like I've walked into a void.

But I can *feel* them in here, their overwhelming power consuming me. Like a drug addict, I ache for more. My body hums in appreciation of the magic invading my every cell. It makes my mind swim, my limbs feel light and airy, even though I stare into a seemingly empty abyss.

I take a tentative step forward, my arms outstretched ahead of me. A whooshing has me jumping back, my heart thrashing inside me, as huge braziers erupt with roaring fires. "Wow," I murmur, awestruck at the sight before my eyes.

An imposing, massive cathedral-like room greets me. High, arched ceilings rise above me with wooden beams crisscrossing elegantly. Candlelit chandeliers hang from the beams, illuminating the immaculate space. Stained glass windows twenty feet tall line the exterior wall and candles glimmer behind them, casting a rainbow of flickering shadows throughout the space. Statues of regal kings in full armor stand proudly in niches between the windows. There must be a dozen of them, each more noble than the one before.

Rows and rows of benches flank the aisle on which I stand. It looks like there must be enough seating for a thousand people. My gaze follows the walkway to where a raised altar sits at the end of the room. Perched upon the altar are seven thrones shrouded in shadow, and sitting on them are the kings who have summoned me. Behind them, hundreds of candles burn brightly, illuminating a strange depiction on the back wall. Written in a language of which I have no knowledge are seven symbols in seven distinct colors.

Red, orange, green, violet, light blue, dark blue, and yellow.

The seven sins...

My heart stutters as I move down the aisle. Each step feels like I'm immersing myself in frigid water, and the light feeling that once consumed me now feels like a pit in my stomach.

They're here, and they're waiting.

My legs tremble and my mouth feels dry. The seven sit stoically, unmoving, and I wonder if they are statues as well. Fear begins to weave its way through my insides, icy fingers gripping me, twisting my stomach into tight knots. I feel like I've walked into a lion's den and they are just about to notice me.

A growl rumbles, and I jump, stalling my steps. They must still be fifty feet away from me.

"Come closer, pet, let your kings look upon you once more." King Lucian's smooth voice has my nipples hardening into tight buds, and the nerves in my body ignite from just the sound of him speaking.

I take another step, and another, remembering how a princess should present herself. I take deep breaths, raise my chin, shoulders back, puff out my chest, let my hands hang loose. The jewelry surrounding me feels cold and heavy, like restraints weighing me down, even though I'm naked.

Slowly, one king rises, his every movement graceful. His long blond hair glistens in the candlelight, and his crown glimmers with purple jewels. He unbinds a cape from around his neck and tosses it onto his throne before descending down the five stairs leading from the altar to the aisle.

With his face still in shadow, he prowls toward me like a big cat stalking its prey. I freeze, unable to move or blink or breathe as he closes the gap between us. Then, finally, I see him, his masculine features highlighted by the flickering fires.

Deep set eyes in a sparkling shade of ice green graze my body, his gaze burning my skin. His nose is strong and sharp, leading to pouty, crimson lips. Dimples adorn his cheeks, accentuating his strong, square jaw. He's beautiful, a fallen angel, recently cast from the heavens above.

And his eyes are eating me alive.

If I could put a name on his scent, I'd call it expensive. It swirls around him, reminding me of freshly laundered bedding, or a spring breeze after a storm. It's soothing, yet dominating.

"Hello, *Regina*. It is nice to see you again." His accent is thicker than King Lucian's. He begins to circle me, taking in my body. "I am King Strix, and pride is my sin." He stops behind me, leans his face into the crook of my neck, and inhales. I have to stifle a moan. He makes my head feel foggy and he's not even touching me yet.

"You have passed my first test, *Regina*. Pride can be a tricky sin, but here you are in spite of the difficult task set upon you." He trails a finger from one shoulder to the other, his touch sparking immense desire and confidence. "You obey orders so sweetly, submitting to your kings like a good girl. Tell me, how did it feel to be stripped and flaunted in a frenzy of rabid wrath vampires who so badly wanted to touch you, taste you, *fuck* you?"

He stops in front of me, his eyes piercing into my very soul. Suddenly, I feel embarrassed. I can feel my cheeks heating, the redness creeping down my chest. I can't hold his gaze any longer, it's just too intense. Averting my eyes, I move to wrap my arms around myself for warmth, for comfort, for privacy, but a growl has me pausing.

"Don't."

It's like invisible hands hold my body in their grasp, making me pause. Or am I unable to disobey a single command from them? Is that the price I paid for allowing them to drink from me? They can now control my body as they see fit?

King Strix reaches for me and I can only watch helplessly as his hands sweep my long hair off my chest, pushing the curly tendrils behind my shoulders. "So beautiful, *Regina*. I could get lost pleasuring your body for days and never tire." My insides clench at his admission as his hands trace around my neck from back to front, then tickle down my collarbones. I shiver when his fingers continue lower, until he's circling my nipples.

My rosy buds tighten painfully, aching for him to touch them, but he ignores my need. Still, he traces my areolas with the pad of his finger and I'm unable to move, unable to stop him, unable to ask for more. I become wet between my legs, coating my inner thighs, and my breaths become shallow, shaky, as simmering heat slowly builds deep in my core.

"Look at me." I hadn't realized I was enraptured with his lips, so I raise my gaze to his as demanded. Sparkling, icy green jewels stare back at me, mischief and desire searing through me with just one glance. "Fall to your knees."

Moaning, I obey, the chilled floor cooling my heated

body. I can feel my hips wanting to thrust, desperate for friction, my abandoned breasts craving more contact. Chest heaving, he stalks behind me and lowers himself to the ground. His breath fans over my ear as he whispers, "I am going to spread your legs for your kings. Allow their eyes to penetrate your pussy while I make you come for them."

"Fuck," I rasp, the nub between my legs throbbing with need. I've never been so achy, so wet before. My knees part on their own, but it's not enough for King Strix. His hands slide along my waist and under my legs. He lifts me with ease, settling me into his lap with his legs stretched out before us. I can sense how much larger he is than me, his feet must be over a foot away from my own. I want to glance back, to see his beautiful face, but instead, I wait for him to tell me what to do.

Slipping his hands under my knees, he lifts my legs and places my feet outside of his thighs, my knees bent. The muscle inside my chest pumps at a maddening speed, it's so loud in my ears that I think the kings can hear it.

King Strix's large hand snakes under my arm and fondles my breast. My head lolls back to his chest. I had no idea that could feel so fucking good.

My core clenches when a wave of lust washes over me, the sweet and spicy scent of King Lucian accompanying it. King Strix's cock pushes against my bare ass, so close yet so far away. So badly I want to feel him buried inside me.

He chuckles deeply, the sound vibrating my nipples. "Do you want me to fuck you, *Regina*? Do you want to feel my thick cock plunging inside your tight cunt?"

I can only moan in response as his free hand trails down my stomach and slips across my wet pussy lips. King Strix growls, then begins to move his legs outwards, taking my legs with him until my core is spread wide.

I'm so fucking turned on right now with a gorgeous king

touching my body, another showering me in his magic, while knowing seven pair of eyes belonging to very old and powerful vampire kings watch me, waiting for me to explode.

King Strix's finger dips between my swollen lips and finds that pleasure nub I've only recently discovered. My hips move, trying to get his finger to that aching place I desperately need him to touch for me.

I gasp when he spanks my drenched pussy, but my legs only open farther, inviting him to do it again, the pain fueling my desire. He chuckles again. "Seems our princess likes a little *bite* with her pleasure. Don't you, *Regina?*"

"Yes," I moan, managing to find my voice. But I don't sound like me, I sound like a desperate woman on the verge of losing it. "Please," I whisper, my legs trembling, my pussy hyperaware of the loss of his touch.

"Oh!" I cry out, when his finger swipes over my sensitive nub.

"You like that don't you? You like when your king plays with your clit."

So that's what it's called.

He abandons my breast and uses one hand to spread my pussy lips, and with the other he spanks me again, directly on my clit. I moan and jerk at the contact, my pussy leaking juices all over his lap. Fuck, it feels so good.

I gasp when he dips a finger inside me, but only just. I can feel him circling my entrance before attacking my clit. His finger slides across it with ease, back and forth, back and forth, with my pussy spread wide.

Pleasure bubbles inside me, causing my legs to tremble and my breath to leave my lungs.

"Come for me, *Regina.*"

The next second I explode, my screams echoing off the cathedral walls as the fires around me ignite, blazing hotter and brighter than before. King Strix strums my clit with his practiced hands until I'm nothing but a puddle on the ground.

My eyes close, I'm out of breath, unable to move my arms or my legs. The King of Pride must know I'm useless because he scoops me up into his arms, his hard body pressing against mine. When I open them again, we're standing before the other six, their faces still cloaked in shadow.

"Give her to me," a stern voice orders.

"Getting antsy, are you, Thorin?" another king jests, but I can't see who. "Wanting to play with our new toy?"

"Just give her to me." I turn my head to the king I now know is Thorin and see he's the largest of the kings, his arms outstretched toward King Strix and I.

King Strix plants a kiss on my forehead before handing me over. "You are so beautiful when you come, *Regina*," he coos, before his hands leave my body.

"And so responsive," King Lucian adds, strutting over to me.

"Her cunt opens like a newly blossomed flower," a king with long, red, luscious hair comments. I'm grateful for the dark as my cheeks are surely flaming. Who talks about a cu— pussy like that?

"You will pay for the effect you have on us, little one." I look up at the giant holding me. He's everything the story-books warned me not to trust. Tall and handsome with piercing gray eyes and short, spiked brown hair. King Thorin is muscle upon muscle. He has a stern jaw with a full, thick beard and mustache, making him look more feral, more angry. His face seems to be in a permanent scowl, even as he scrutinizes me.

Just then, I feel a cold finger slide along my pussy, and I jolt in King Thorin's arms, looking toward the source. The rest of the kings have crowded around us, so big and tall, making me feel even smaller in the large king's arms.

"Mmm," a king with sandy blond hair and roguish good looks hums, sucking his finger.

Did he just...

"Yes, I did, sweetheart. And may I just say, you are as delicious as the pet name I've chosen for you." He smirks at me, flashing a gorgeous smile, his full lips framing a set of white teeth. He flicks his head to get his bangs out of his bright green eyes. "Yum."

"Must you be so crass, Killian?" King Thorin holds me firmly against his chest as he scowls at the talking king, but I'm now fully aware my pussy is flashing everyone. "We all want a piece of the new princess." The king who compared me to a flower smiles at me, but it doesn't meet his eyes. His narrow face compliments his sharp nose. A head full of hair as dark as blood cascades down his shoulders. Bright green eyes compliment his hair, making him look noble, regal, just as gorgeous as the others. "King Ramsey is my name, and envy is my game. When it's my turn to play with you, flower, I will leave you shaking, wet, and wanting."

I recoil from him slightly. Something about him doesn't sit right with me. Even the massive King Thorin puts me at ease more than this one does. King Ramsey's eyes trail over my exposed skin and lock onto my pussy. "Soon," he promises, before returning to his throne.

"My turn. You've had her long enough, Thorin." A stocky king prowls toward me. Unlike the others, his eyes are dark, demonic. He reminds me of the demons I've read about in books, monsters risen from hell, friends of the devil himself. He has neatly trimmed black hair and his lower face is covered in short coarse hair. His beard and mustache are shaved in sharp, angular lines, making him look very put together.

"Back off, Marcel," King Thorin growls, his chest vibrating against me. "Don't fuck with me tonight."

"Or what?" King Marcel taunts. "Are you going to release your wrath on me? Have you forgotten how much I feed off your anger, Thorin, how much I like it? Our last time together still plays in my mind. I remember how your cock tasted in my mouth, how it felt when you sheathed yourself inside me, how hard I made you fucking come."

King Thorin growls and my eyes go wide. King Thorin and King Marcel...are lovers? Why does the thought of them together make my pussy fucking clench?

"Ahh. Seems our precious princess likes the thought of us together, Thorin," King Marcel coos, glancing at me. "Perhaps we can share her in the future." King Marcel turns to me, his dark eyes studying my body, his pink tongue darting out to lick his thick lips. "Would you like that, precious girl? Do you want to be shared by two of your kings, hmm?"

Absently, I rub my thighs together, forgetting the kings can sense my thoughts, my desires. King Marcel laughs, flashing a very sharp set of fangs at me. I'm simultaneously turned on and terrified. His dark eyes flash with even darker promises. "It seems that you do." With that, he turns sharply, his hair flying out behind him wildly, and sits back on his throne. I see now that King Marcel is also covered with gold jewelry. Necklaces, bracelets, and rings sparkle as he moves.

"Can we just fucking get this over with? I have a donor waiting back in my quarters for me." I lift my head off King Thorin's massive chest and look to my left.

"Eloquent as always, aren't you, Dante?" King Marcel scolds. A scowl forms on the face of the king sitting in the last throne, one I've not met yet. He's sprawled in his throne, his posture thrown to the wolves. Slumped down with his hands clasped behind his head, one foot propped up on the opposite knee, he's been absent from all the conversations so far, while he sits carefree on his light blue throne.

Even his hair has not been tamed. Soft brown waves reach his shoulders, which he runs his fingers through after removing his crown, then replacing it on his head. He's thinner than the others, as if he doesn't partake in food and drink as much as he should. His eyes are haunting, though, the lightest shade of brown. His cheekbones are prominent, maybe because he's so thin, and dark brown stubble covers his cheeks and chin, accentuating his cheeks. I don't need someone to tell me that this king—Dante, going by King Marcel's lax introduction—is the King of Sloth. It's written all over him, and his nonchalance is over the top, as if he wants me to see that he doesn't care to meet me. He strikes me as the type of man—err...vampire, who does things out of necessity rather than desire.

"Snow will stay with me tonight." King Lucian's seductive voice washes over me and I find myself nodding eagerly.

"You've already had a night with her, Lucian," King Strix argues. "The girl stays with me. It was my task she completed to get here tonight. Therefore, I should get to keep her."

His task? What is he talking about?

"No, I should take her!" King Thorin shouts, standing up. He sets me on his throne before stomping toward Kings Lucian and Strix.

King Killian scoffs, "You? Why? So she can run away from us screaming her first night here?"

"You're right, Killian," King Marcel agrees, joining the battle. "Thorin has no place in keeping our sweet princess, but neither do you. It will be me who takes her tonight."

I watch in horror as five kings scream and shout at each other, unable to decide who gets me.

Me!

I can't even wrap my brain around it. I'm nothing special, yet the kings are drawn to me as much as I am to them.

"Be quiet, flower." I startle, following the voice to find King Ramsey crouching next to King Thorin's throne. "I've set a bit of envy on the others. It will keep them occupied while I whisk you away to my suite. I am envy personified, and tonight, I won't fucking share you. No. Tonight, you will be mine."

CHAPTER 25

*K*ing Ramsey pulls me from King Thorin's throne while the others shout at each other. All the while, King Dante watches us leave with indifference.

I shiver in the cold, missing the warmth from the throne, the heat I felt when King Strix's hands were on my body. King Ramsey deftly unties his cape and whips it around my shoulders. "Thank you," I mutter, as I huddle beneath it.

"You won't be thanking me for long, flower." I wonder what he means as we practically run through the dark tunnels that make up the castles. Scarcely lit, I stumble through the black corridors, my flimsy sandals barely staying on my feet. "Enough of this," King Ramsey grumbles. In one swift move, he swirls around me, and in the blink of an eye, I'm thrown over his shoulder.

His pace quickens while my mind races. What did he mean when he said I won't be thanking him for long? Does he mean to punish me? Spank me like King Strix did?

That thought has my blood heating. How could someone like being spanked? Yet I-I did. What is wrong with me?

Have years of punishment at the evil bitch's hands warped my mind?

I think I already know the answer to that. The euphoria I've experienced during the worst of my whippings, the ones that have brought me to within an inch of my death, it's during those times I've found fleeting moments of bliss.

Maybe I'll find that again at the hands of the kings...

King Ramsey's deep chuckle has me blushing. I need to remember that they can sense what I'm feeling. But for so long the only person I've had to talk to is myself, so I've become accustomed to having in-depth conversations with my mind.

"Almost there, flower." King Ramsey's grip around my body tightens, and I lift my head off his back to see where we are, but find nothing even remotely familiar. Not that I thought I would. "I have everything set, having planned this little excursion earlier. I knew I had to be the first one from whom you drank. The thought of it being one of the others had me consumed with jealousy."

Drank?

That's right. Didn't Vincent mention something about that? Or am I completely losing my mind?

The thought of his blood coating my tongue, swirling around my mouth, mixing with my own has me panting. I want it. No. I-I *need* it. That craving, that one I couldn't put my finger on, begins to consume me and my canines start to ache. It was blood all along.

King Ramsey turns sharply and glides up a staircase. Though I'm looking backwards, I can appreciate its beauty. Candelabras blaze in niches carved into the walls, lighting our surroundings. Paintings surrounded by gilded frames pass by, but we're moving too quickly for me to appreciate the artist's work.

We stop at the top of the massive flight of stairs, only now realizing just how high we've climbed. King Ramsey sets me down but isn't even slightly out of breath. In fact, I don't think he's breathing at all. Why isn't he breathing?

The king's bright green eyes pierce my baby blues, and he has a knowing look on his face. I find myself becoming lost, mesmerized by the way his eyebrows arch so elegantly, how his pointed nose fits so perfectly on his narrow face. He looks like one of the paintings hanging in my father's castle. King Ramsey has the features of a noble, with his slightly upturned nose and a callousness to his gaze. He has an arrogance about him that even the evil bitch would appreciate.

"Behind this door is my personal suite. I think you'll find what I've prepared for you quite...enticing. Should you allow yourself to be consumed by my sin, you'll earn my blood as your reward and be one step closer to your complete transformation. Any questions, flower?"

I shake my head, unable to form words. My stomach is churning with anxiety, and my limbs are shaking beneath King Ramsey's green cape.

"Well, if you're sure..." The King of Envy waves his hand elegantly in front of the ornate door and it swishes inward. Immediately, I'm bombarded with fragrances of expensive perfumes, rich leather, and a coppery tang. At first, my vision blurs as we walk through a thick wall of smoke pouring from a nearby hearth, but as the smoke clears and I see what lies beyond, I gape in shock.

There are people everywhere. Gorgeous women dangle from the dark ceiling, suspended in shackles with their naked bodies on display, while others, both male and female, feast on them. One woman has two men and one woman tasting her body, her head thrown back in ecstasy. Another has her back turned toward me while a naked man strikes her ass with a whip as she hisses in delight, wiggling her striped cheeks for another lashing.

In the corner are two men, almost as beautiful as the kings. Pale and naked, their bodies chiseled to perfection, they devour each other's mouths. Their large hands explore delineated muscles while they pump each other's hard cocks.

Next to them, lying on a bed of emerald green silken sheets, is a woman writhing in pleasure. Between her legs, a tanned woman licks and sucks her pussy, while a man wearing a mask attaches something metal to her nipples. A third man—a lurker, by his pale skin—is nibbling on her arched neck. A moment later, he bites, and the woman screams, thrusting her hips and pushing her pussy into the mouth of the hungry woman devouring her.

Desire floods me, my body igniting with need. "You may look, but you cannot touch, flower." King Ramsey's voice angers me and I glare up at him. He chuckles. "Don't look at your king like that. This is envy at its finest." He sweeps his hand across the room, as if presenting the most erotic scene I've ever witnessed. "Before you are several of the most beautiful members of the Coven of Sin. Some are vampires, some are donors, all are enchanting."

King Ramsey walks to a nearby woman, naked and strung from the ceiling. She eyes him with absolute desire and my blood begins to burn. How dare she fucking look at him like that. The king stands behind her, staring at me over her shoulders, then reaches around to skim her belly with his fingers. "How does it feel, flower, to see me touching another woman? Does it make you...jealous?"

Jealous?

How about enraged?

Red mists my vision, my hands clenching, teeth gnashing against each other. Anger consumes me, turning me into someone I almost don't recognize. My chest feels heavy with envy, wanting his hands on me, but also with a side of wrath.

Even though he's the one touching her, I want to tear her fucking face off.

"How does it feel to watch me pleasure another?" He slides his hands up to her heavy breasts, cupping them before twisting her nipples between his fingers. She groans, rubbing her thighs together as her nipples harden into pointed beads.

King Ramsey laughs, deep and sexy, so arrogant I want to slap him across the face. "You don't like it, do you?" His hands slide lower, hovering over her pussy. "Is it the idea of me touching another, or do you wish to taste her yourself?"

That thought intrigues me. I've never considered being with another woman. But seeing her gorgeous, naked body on display, her plump nipples peaked, noticing how her thighs glisten with her own excitement, her desperate desire evident as she arches her back and bites her lip... It-it does make me want her.

King Ramsey smiles maliciously, then slinks over to the two men devouring each other, striding up behind one. He slithers one hand around the man's neck, pulling the man to his chest. The man releases his lover's mouth and melts into the king's hold. The king lowers his head to the man's neck and inhales deeply, then he maneuvers them both so they are facing me.

The king squeezes the man's neck with one hand and trails his other down his prey's torso. Starting between his collarbones, he traces his fingers around the man's nipples, then over his rock-hard abs. I watch in awe as the man's proud cock seems to grow thicker, longer, as the king's hand gets closer to it.

I gasp as loud as the man when King Ramsey's hand encircles the naked man's cock and pumps it slowly. "Is this better, flower? Are you less angry, less jealous when I give a male my attention?"

No.

Fuck no.

Now all I can think about is sinking down on that man's hardness, letting it fill me completely, while King Ramsey uses his talented hands on my body.

The king's eyes flash and he pushes the man back to his forlorn lover. Then, he takes a step closer to me, pausing in the middle of the room. Sounds and scents of sex assault me as he reaches for the top button of his dark green shirt and undoes it.

I can feel my core clenching as he loosens button after button, his pale skin glowing under his dark shirt. My mouth waters when he shrugs off the top, displaying his gorgeous body.

Lean and fit, King Ramsey is lithe but well built, each muscle defined as if painted on his body. His red hair flows around his shoulders, making me desperate to either run my hands through it or pull it hard. I watch in rapt attention as a male and female vampire strut toward him. He stares at me, his gaze dark and inviting as, together, they fall to their knees and begin to remove the king's pants.

My fingers curl into tight fists, my nails digging into my palms as they touch him. Those should be my fingers, my hands, not theirs. Who the fuck do they think they are? The king laughs deeply, sensually, and tilts his head. "Is this better, flower? Would you prefer others touching me instead of me touching them?"

Fuck.

I want him so badly, but I also want everyone else in this room. My pussy leaks with need, my breasts hanging heavily on my chest. Even my skin feels neglected, desperate to have another's hands groping me.

The couple frees the king's cock from its fabric prison. It's not hard, though I have no idea how it isn't considering our erotic surroundings, and hangs seductively between his legs. My mouth longs for it, to suck him between my lips and feel him grow hard along my tongue.

"Do you want my cock, flower? Do you want to taste me inside your mouth, or feel me thrust deep inside your cunt?"

He pushes the couple away and prowls toward the woman on the bed. He stands behind her head, his cock dangling mere inches from her face as she stretches her tongue out to lick him.

Envy and wrath swirl inside me like a gargantuan storm, and I'm ready to explode.

Fuck this.

Two can play at this game.

I tear my eyes away from the king, unwilling to watch another female press her mouth to his cock.

My cock.

When I became so possessive of this vampire I've only just met, I couldn't say, yet the feeling persists nonetheless.

I scan the room, looking for my own victim, and settle on the first woman King Ramsey played with. Her gaze locks on me and she mewls—fuck if the sound doesn't make my pussy clench.

With the king's cape still surrounding me, I stride over to her, head held high, shoulders back, and chest pushed out, though my posture is likely hidden beneath this cloak. The woman's breasts are at my eye level from where she hangs, so supple. So enticing.

My movements are tentative at first as I reach through the gap in my cape and squeeze her breast. I'm surprised by how soft it is, having never really paid attention to my own other than wanting to hide them. But hers? I could play with them for days.

I thread my other hand through the cape and fondle her breasts, loving the sensual moans escaping her lips. I run my finger across her nipples and watch the buds flick back into place. I moisten my lips, then press my mouth against her breast. So soft and silken, I kiss my way over to her tight bud, then suck it into my mouth.

The sensations are so fucking hot. The woman moans, her back arching as I bite on her hardened tip. She hisses as her nipple slides through my teeth, making me desperate to touch more of her. My own nipples bead painfully, and I burn with desire.

As I suck her nipple back into my mouth, I glance out of the corner of my eye and find the King of Envy staring hard, his bright green gaze flashing, his sharp teeth glinting. I can't tell if he's jealous or turned on or pissed, and right now I don't fucking care.

The cape suddenly feels suffocating, so I tug at the tie around my neck, needing it off my body. I moan around the woman's nipple when the cape slips down my back. The cool air caresses my skin like a lover and I press myself against the woman.

"Yes," she groans, as a new scent assaults me. It's familiar yet different, and when my hands travel down her body and rub between her legs, I realize what it is.

The woman is aroused.

Her pussy is slick with it.

As I wonder what she would taste like, a growl reverberates through the room. I turn to see that King Ramsey has slinked his way closer, his gaze feral and menacing.

I smile wickedly. "Oh, my king, do you not like it when I touch another woman?" His look could curdle milk and cause a rose to wilt.

Not this flower.

I take a handful of the woman's breast and squeeze hard, then tug at her nipple as I walk away, the tight bud slipping through my fingers. I circle the king like a predator, sliding my fingertips around his waist. I can feel him shudder at my touch.

Smirking to myself, I prowl behind him and strut over to the two naked men, then turn back to face the jealous king. His gaze follows me like a shadow. I flash him a smile and take a step back, pressing myself in between the kissing men. Keeping my eyes locked on King Ramsey, I reach up and trail my fingers down the men, from their jaws to their necks, down their chests and abs. Lower still, I run my hands until my fingers find their cocks.

They groan simultaneously, their moans causing my insides to grow molten. I love how soft yet hard they feel, so big in my small hands. I feel empowered, stroking them, knowing I'm the cause of their moans, their pleasure.

But King Ramsey?

He doesn't like it.

"Is this better, my king?" I taunt. "Watching me squeezed between two men, their hard cocks in my hands?" When did I learn to talk so dirty?

The men touch me in response, running their hands along my back, caressing my breasts until I'm moaning right along with them.

"Fuck, they feel so good, Ramsey." His eyes flash at my omission of his title. "Do you wish it was your cock in my hands? Your touch making my pussy ache, your caress causing my blood to heat and liquify?"

He growls, "You are crossing the line, flower."

"Why?" I ask, as I pump their cocks harder. "Are you envious, my king? That's what this was, after all, right? A test of your sin? What are my grades, sir? Did I pass? Or have you failed?"

The men begin to tremble in my grasp, their grips growing hard on my breasts, causing heat to pool between my legs. But before they can climax, I release them and saunter over to the gorgeous woman splayed on the bed. She's being serviced by three people still, her whole body trembling with unending climaxes. A sheen of sweat coats her skin and her voice has grown hoarse from screaming in pleasure.

"Perhaps I need a drink. I'm feeling quite parched." I turn to the vampire drinking from the woman, fisting his hair in my hand before pulling him off her body. Blood drips from his mouth, a stark contrast to his white fangs, and drizzles down his hard chest. "Or maybe I need to be drank from?" I sweep my hair back in one hand and expose my neck, offering myself to the vampire.

The vampire growls and sniffs hard in my direction, his light eyes more beast than human. His mouth opens wide as he lunges for my neck, but just before his fangs sink into me, I'm scooped up into the arms of King Ramsey.

"No one drinks what is mine," he growls, slicing the vampire in half with a single, extended claw before storming out of the room and into another. I'm tossed onto an opulent bed encased in sparkling jewels. The king pounces on me, caging me with his arms and legs. He brings his face down to mine, his minty breath fanning my skin. "If you ever offer yourself to another vampire again, I'll fuck you so hard, you won't walk right for a week."

"Promise?" I challenge, lifting my eyebrow.

Faster than my eyes can follow, he sits up and plunges his cock inside me. I shriek at the sensation, so full, so huge within me. I thought my first time would be painful, excruciating even. But because I'm so aroused, so fucking wet, he entered me with ease. And though there is a deep ache, it feels incredible. It's like he simultaneously broke me and put me back together.

King Ramsey's fingers dig into my knees, which he shoves apart as he starts moving. My core throbs from the intrusion, but also with the impending climax. I'm so fucking turned on as he moves in and out of me.

"Mine," he growls, his crimson hair as wild as his eyes while his length slides in and out of me.

I fucking groan, my pussy literally clenching down on him.

"You feel so good, flower. I could fuck your cunt all day, every day, and never tire."

"I'll hold you to that, King Ramsey," I croon, and his eyes roll back. His movements grow faster as he thrusts inside me harder and harder. My tits bounce with the movement, and he trades my knees for my breasts, holding them as he fucks me.

The heat inside me builds like a raging inferno, and soon I'm panting like a bitch in heat, the image of a waterfall coming into my mind.

The king changes positions, lowering himself over me, his lips pressed against my neck.

"Oh God!" I scream, then he bites, and I explode. The world becomes a tornado of colors and sounds, as if I can see everything and nothing at the same time. King Ramsey moans against my neck, then I feel his hot cum spurting inside me.

The orgasm goes on and on as pleasure cascades over me, until I'm trembling and shaking, almost numb from the force of it. Then, something happens that I did not expect. The place where the king bites me begins to burn and I cry out, but I'm unable to fight him off. My blood boils, scorching through my body. I feel as if my very soul is on fire.

King Ramsey pulls away from my neck and flips us so I'm on top of him, his cock still hard inside me. I begin to move, feeling a new strength surging through my body. My tits sway as I roll my hips. "Yes, my flower, take what you need from me. Fuck me with that tight cunt of yours."

"Fuck," I moan, loving his dirty talk. It's only now that I realize we're surrounded. All the men and women, human and vampire alike, from the previous room encircle the bed. Their eyes are hungry as they watch my tits bounce, as they watch me rise and fall on their king's hard cock.

My mouth tingles and something sharp pokes my lip. The taste of my blood coats my tongue, bringing forth a new desire. I flash the king a smile, his eyes locking onto my new fangs.

He grins roguishly and offers me his neck. "My sin is yours, take it."

I bounce on his cock, needing to take more from him. His hands grip my hips firmly as he lifts me up and down. My moans are interrupted by the bouncing, my wetness drenching the place where we're joined. And just before another orgasm consumes me, I lower my head to the king's neck and bite.

We climax together.

He roars as I suck, his blood coating my tongue like fresh honey, his hands fisted into my hair. I growl against his skin, drinking as much of him as I can as my cunt clenches on his hardness buried deep within me.

Power begins to swirl inside me, my muscles growing stronger, my senses more acute. I continue to draw on his vein long after our orgasms have stopped, until he grows soft inside me and the mixture of our cum becomes sticky against my thighs.

It's like a drug. I can't fucking stop, even if I wanted to.

"Enough, flower," he rasps, tugging on my hair. "Let go."

My body shudders, desperately wanting to disobey, but I'm completely unable to. My fangs retract into my mouth as I sit up and I swallow a mouthful of his honeyed blood. Glancing around, I find that we're alone again, and wonder if I'd just imagined everyone else watching.

King Ramsey reaches for me and pulls me into his arms. "You performed beautifully, flower, just like I knew you would."

I look up at him. "How did you know?"

He smiles down at me and plants a kiss on my forehead. "From the first moment I saw you bound to that whipping post, I knew in that moment that you were made for me. You were so strong, so beautiful, naked and gorgeous, regal and poised though the queen brought you to within an inch of your life. You had me then, and you have me now, I will always be yours."

"Mine?"

"Forever. Until the sun disintegrates me or a stake pierces my chest. Until the end of time."

CHAPTER 26

J woke up alone in my room feeling happy and refreshed, albeit a little sore, after sleeping for what felt like days. When Katie stopped by to bring me food and water, I asked her to send word to the kings, wanting to speak with them this afternoon about the future of Riverwood. I need to round up the rebellion and aid my people in fighting off the evil queen and her army of guards and huntsmen.

I've even dressed for the occasion, wearing a white gown similar to the one I wore during the unveiling. It doesn't leave much to the imagination. The barely there number accentuates my newly grown muscles, hugs my curves in all the right places, and is semi-sheer across my breasts. If I can't talk my way into getting what I want, I'm hoping to use the power of persuasion as a backup plan.

Once again, I find myself surrounded by the seven where they sit on their massive thrones, perched on the altar in the throne room. I'm standing five steps down from them as they leer at me.

I remember my posture and hold myself with pride. King Strix beams at me.

Taking a deep breath, I exhale slowly and declare, "I need to see my people."

King Marcel scoffs at my proclamation. "Now? You haven't even completed all seven sins and you want to run off, outside of the coven? This is a shit idea."

"I think it's a good idea." King Strix, looking gorgeous, leans forward on his throne, his elbows perched on his knees and his chin resting on steepled fingers. "Why not let her leave? What harm could it do?"

"She could be caught," King Thorin interjects. "I don't know about the rest of you, but I'm not willing to lose our future queen to that imposter queen once more. Lucian almost blew it once. I'm not willing to risk it again."

"Since when did my choices reside in your laps?" I challenge confidently, causing their banter to cease. "I'm not asking for permission. I'm telling you what I'm going to do." My voice sounds more assertive than I feel. "My people need me. I've abandoned them to fend for themselves. You've seen the power of the evil queen. They can't fight her alone."

"They won't be alone," King Lucian proclaims, pushing himself off his throne. "Our little pet here wishes to guide them, so I suggest we let her."

"Seconded," King Strix agrees, rising from his throne. The two kings descend the short flight and walk my way. Fire licks along my skin from the gazes of the seductive kings prowling toward me.

King Thorin growls, "What is the purpose of this dangerous quest?"

"The people need to see me, to be reassured I haven't abandoned them or worse." I fiddle with the ribbon around my waist, now hating myself for wearing something so revealing. Currently, King Thorin isn't taking me seriously.

"The last they saw of me, I was broken and beaten, my life hanging in the balance while some rogue lurker took my body back to an unknown place."

"But the *lurkers* are the ones who, in fact, changed the tide of that battle. It was over before it even started," King Marcel interjects.

"That's not the point," I counter, placing my hands on my hips. "People need a leader, right? Someone to follow. If you were ensnared by some creature of legend and gone for days, how would your coven feel? Insecure? Scared? Would they act rashly out of concern for their king?" King Marcel exchanges a look with King Thorin and the two deflate, leaning back against their thrones. "I'm not asking if I can build a house and live there with them."

King Ramsey's emotions are clear on his face. "Absolutely out of the question, flower. I need you near me now."

I huff. "I'm not actually going to do that, *Ramsey*. They just...they need to know I'm safe. And in return, I need to know they are okay."

King Ramsey narrows his eyes, unhappy with me not acknowledging him as king, before standing. "Then I'm coming too." He uses his crazy vampire speed to rush toward me in a blur, and before I know it, he has me lowered in a dip, his mouth crushed against mine.

I kiss him eagerly, my body igniting, remembering our last time together.

"Let our little pet go, or I may end up fucking her right here on the floor," Lucian growls.

King Ramsey grins against my lips but pulls me back to standing. "Noted. As much as I'd love to see my flower freshly blossomed for me, I have no desire to see your tiny dick, Lucian."

"Tiny! Why, you cock sucking—" King Lucian lunges for his foe. The two men twirl and snarl around each other. King

Ramsey's red hair flies about his head as King Lucian's blue eyes flash in malice.

"Stop!" I shout, stomping my foot like a child. "This isn't about you two. This is about me."

"Which means it's about all of us, sweetheart." I turn to see King Killian striding down the stairs, a swagger in his step. "You are ours now, you've pledged your life to us. Your blood runs within our veins. If you hurt, then we hurt. You must understand the enormity of what you are asking of us."

I guess I hadn't thought of that.

"So if it were up to you, I'd hide here in your vast castles until I become like you? Is that what you'd do if you could have it your way?"

"If it were up to me, I'd lock you in my room, bound and gagged, and keep you in a cage until the bond was complete," King Thorin states.

"B-Bound and gagged?" I stutter.

King Thorin grins, but there's no happiness in his gaze. "That mouth of yours could sweet talk a bear into a spot of tea, and a single touch from you can bring the most formidable vampire to his knees. So, yes. Bound and fucking gagged."

I gulp as Killian stands before me, his soft hands cupping my face. "Don't listen to the big bad vampire over there, sweetheart. My princess gets what she wants and then some. If you want to go into town, I'm okay with it, as long as I can also come with you."

"Y-You would come too?"

He nods. "All four of us will accompany you."

Suddenly, I feel quite small as Kings Lucian, Killian, Strix, and Ramsey stand around me in a circle. They are so much larger than I am, it's like being at the bottom of a well looking up. Except instead of sunlight, my field of vision is filled with beautiful kings.

My kings.

"Don't you wish to share an opinion, Dante?" King Marcel inquires, looking down at the seventh king. He's so quiet that I forgot he was even there.

King Dante waves his hand dismissively from where he slouches in the farthest throne. "I don't really fucking care what she does. Keep her here and cage her or set her fucking free. Doesn't matter to me."

"It should matter you. Your indifference could mean a matter of life and death," King Marcel seethes. "Take a side for once in your life, dammit. Stand for something. Make one fucking choice."

King Dante rubs his prickly chin, feigning deep thought. "I choose...not to choose. You can fucking deal with this shit. I have better things to do." With that, he pushes off his throne, tall and lean, and struts from the room without so much as a glance back.

How the hell am I going to win him over?

"Don't worry about him, pet. He'll come around." King Lucian's comforting words have no effect on me. That vampire is going to be trouble.

"Well, what are we waiting for?" King Killian grabs my hand and tugs me toward the exit. As I almost jog to keep up with him, he looks down at me and smiles his roguish smile. I literally almost swoon. Like, if swooning was a competition, right then I would have won the prize. "Ramsey told me how well you performed in his envy test. Might I say that I cannot fucking wait to see how you handle gluttony."

He pulls my hand to his mouth and lays a chaste kiss on the back, causing my belly to tumble. A goofy smile stretches my lips and he grins in return, showing off his perfect teeth behind a crimson pair of plump lips...lips I can imagine kissing, lips I can imagine tasting me—

"Stop it, my sweet, or the four of us will have you stripped and your holes filled in a matter of seconds," he whispers. That thought scares me and turns me on. What would it be like to be with four of them at once?

"One day you'll find out, pet," King Lucian promises, striding up to my vacant side. "Just how many kings can one tiny princess handle in a single night?"

I don't respond as some questions don't require answers. But it hangs over my head like a bloated rain cloud.

How many could I handle? Four? Five? Something tells me I'll have the hands of all seven kings exploring me before my transformation is complete. And you know what? I want it. Bring. It. On.

THE KINGS WOULDN'T ALLOW ME TO CHANGE MY CLOTHES, insisting I looked every bit the queen the people would want to follow. They described me as stunning and vulnerable, innocent and regal. But all I feel is anxiety. My stomach buzzes as if a nest of hornets is living inside me.

What will the people of Riverwood think of me now... descending into the arms of fabled monsters...abandoning them...

They probably hate me.

Leaving the castle—ermm...castles for the first time in days makes me nervous. I'm jumpy, waiting for a huntsman to charge out of every corner. The kings have come prepared, though, adorned in gilded armor, their weapons donned, and polished crowns sitting on top of their heads... I can't even begin to describe the feeling of walking between them.

Pride swells inside me as these powerful vampire kings flank me. If the evil queen could see me now, her blood would curdle. She always told me how ugly and worthless I am, in spite of knowing her magic mirror tells the truth...

Fairest of them all...

Envy already surges inside me from my night with King Ramsey. I've grown more powerful but still thirst for more. It won't be long until I can take back my castle and pull the queen's black heart from her fucking chest.

Kings Killian and Lucian grip my hands as we exit the narrow alleyway and emerge into town square under the darkness of the night sky. My heart stutters and almost fucking stops at what I see.

First thing I notice are the patrols—lurker patrols. Hooded men and women march through the streets wearing cloaks the same color as their sin. I see mostly red, and know that color is more than likely Wrath, which I think is King Thorin's sin. How interesting that he was the most opposed for me coming here, yet he's sent more of his followers than the others.

The next thing that catches my eye is a massive wall being erected outside the perimeter of the city. Torches blaze around the top, illuminating the spiked structure.

"How is this possible?" I whisper to myself.

King Lucian squeezes my right hand. "I told you they wouldn't be alone."

"And we have more tricks up our sleeves, Princess Snow, that will change the tide of this war," King Killian promises.

This is news to me. "What tricks?"

"A power I can bestow on you when you take gluttony for your own."

While I contemplate his cryptic response, King Strix wanders ahead, his long, blond hair whipping around him, his purple cape billowing.

Fuck, he's so sexy.

As if he could hear my thoughts, he glances at me over his shoulder and winks.

Ah shit...he *can* hear me.

A grunt sounds behind me and I whirl around, expecting to see huntsmen with their swords raised and manacles swinging from their belts. I gasp in surprise when I see King Thorin carrying a massive boulder on his muscled shoulder.

His grunts grab the attention of all those in the square— lurker and human alike—as he stomps over to where the whipping post once stood and drops the massive rock to the ground.

I'm perplexed. "What are you doing here?"

King Thorin angles his giant body toward me, his muscles bulging, and his pointed crown glinting with crimson jewels. "You are mine, little one, and I'll be damned if I'm not here to protect you."

The giant king struts over to me, so tall and handsome, his short beard accentuating the squareness of his jaw. His gray eyes flash with an emotion I cannot decipher. He reaches for me, his large hands encasing my small ones. "If you want to take over the world, fine, but you're not doing it without me by your side. Besides, I need reasons to punish your hot little ass."

My pussy clenches at his admission. Why do I want to be punished by him? My mind wanders to King Ramsey's suite, where I watched a naked woman being pleasured by the kiss of the whip, her round ass bouncing with each lashing.

"I'll make it good for you, little one, when it's my turn. But until then..." King Thorin slides his hands around my waist and carries me over to the boulder. I realize now that the townsfolk have gathered, and I'm suddenly very unsure of myself. I know they will be expecting me to say something profound and meaningful, but my mouth turns to ash as all their hopeful eyes descend on me and the kings proudly standing behind me.

I take a deep breath, lick my lips, and begin. "People of Riverwood, let me start off by saying how proud I am of you. You've taken a dire situation and have come together as a community, uniting against the evil oppressing us. I'm in awe of your resilience, of your bravery. You make me feel honored to be among you here today."

Power swirls around me, infusing with my blood. It's pride, the magic of King Strix, giving me the will to find the words I so desperately seek.

"Don't be afraid of the lurkers in our town. They are friends and allies. They will stand by our side and fight with us to dethrone the evil bitch and take back my throne."

The crowd begins to cheer, raising their fists or weapons, pumping them into the air.

"The time will soon come when we must face our true enemy. I'm preparing for the final battle, knowing that, in the end, either the evil queen or myself must die. We cannot both exist in this world any longer."

The people murmur amongst themselves, whispering to their neighbors.

"The legends are true about the seven kings who wield the seven sins. They have claimed me for their own, and in return, I've pledged my life to them. By doing so, I will not only become their queen as well as yours, but I will also have their powerful army by our side to fight for us, to defend our elderly and our young, and to help create a new world where we live amongst each other in peace and harmony."

The people are not sure how to react to this declaration, and I have to admit, it's even hard for me to believe.

"My people, know that you've not been abandoned, nor have you been forgotten. I am freely giving my life for you, one piece at a time, to save you all from tyranny and give you the freedom you so desperately deserve. Have patience as I earn the power to defend your lives. For with that power, together, we will create a new future. One where our children play freely in the streets without fear, one where everyone relishes the bounty of the harvest. A future where we can celebrate life instead of worrying about its end, where friendly greetings are met with smiles, where the clouds part from the skies and sunlight shines down upon us once more. Together, united in our common goal, we will take back our lands and destroy the evil prowling within it!"

The gathered crowd shouts and cheers. People whoop and holler. Chants rise up, shouting, "Kill the queen," while others cry out for me. "Queen Snow. Queen Snow. Queen Snow."

"To Queen Snow!" a man shouts from somewhere in the crowd. Then, one by one, my people and lurkers alike fall to their knees, heads bowed in reverence. I'm moved to tears as a hand snakes around my waist. I look over into the sparkling ice green eyes of King Ramsey. "You've done it, flower. The people here no longer rebel for an imprisoned princess, instead they follow a queen reborn. This" —he gestures to the crowd— "is who you were born to be."

Pride swells within me as I look at every man, woman, and child. They are devoting their lives to me, and in return, I'll sacrifice mine for them. I'll die a princess and rise a queen, then I'll tear this world apart.

CHAPTER 27

I feel amazing, curled up against King Thorin's chest. The large vampire king has insisted on carrying me back to the castle. Considering that I like being taken care of for once in my life, I'm allowing it. Not that he would have taken no for an answer.

Smiling, I wave goodbye to the people of Riverwood as the five kings and I head back to the cavern castles. My impromptu speech really rallied them as well as the lurkers present.

You need to stop calling them lurkers, Snow, and refer to them by their real name.

Vampires.

Even thinking about the word sends shivers of desire through me, which is followed by a wave of embarrassment as I recall how insane I became with envy during King Ramsey's test. I can't believe I touched all those people like that—people I didn't even know. And I let them touch me!

My fingers ghost across my lips, remembering how my fangs descended, how hot it was to sink them deep inside King Ramsey's neck, and how satisfied I felt as his sweet

237

blood coursed through me. I was consumed by envy, needing the king all to myself.

And boy did I get him.

I really thought my first time sleeping with someone would be painful or at least uncomfortable, and maybe it was because I was so fucking wet, but he just slipped right inside me. I was so gloriously filled, every inch of me sizzling with sensation.

I can't wait to do it again and wonder which king will be the next to take me.

I yelp when a spank lands on my ass and glare up at King Thorin. "What was that for?"

His gray eyes rove over my face. "For thinking the thoughts that you are. My cock is rock-hard right now, little one, and it is taking all my effort not to impale you on it and fuck you while we walk." He chuckles at my sharp inhale. "Fear not. I know you're not ready to handle me just yet. You'll take one of the other kings second. But maybe I'll watch the test this time."

Fuck.

The thought of him watching me fuck another of the kings has my pussy clenching in need. Another spank lands on my ass, but this time I moan in response.

King Thorin growls, "Strix, take her. I can't handle her thoughts right now. I'm about to lose control."

Without another word, he tosses me to King Strix as if I was a feather pillow, then rushes off into the surrounding woods. King Strix catches me with sure hands and wide eyes.

"What was that about?" I ask the king, glancing back to where King Thorin ran off, but all I see is a large, black tail disappearing into the trees where he once stood.

King Strix pulls me tightly against him, his hard body enticing me as his long hair fans around my face. He lowers his head, running his nose along my neck, his lips grazing the tender skin. My head grows cloudy with desire and the urge to rip his clothes off tingles my fingertips.

"Because, *Regina*," he starts before placing tender kisses along my jaw, speaking between pecks, "his need for you—" *Kiss*. "Calls upon his—" *Kiss*. "Animalistic instincts." His mouth hovers over my ear, his tongue darting out to lick the shell. "His desire for you consumes him and his beast."

"Beast?" I choke out. What the fuck does that mean?

"Yes," he responds, pulling away and leaving me aching. "Some of us not only personify our sins, but become something other, or have additional powers." When I look at him in confusion, he explains, "Like Thorin. Those afflicted with Wrath sometimes not only have deep anger, but they can shift into another form. A beast."

My mind drifts back to something Vincent told me, that he had both Kings Marcel and Thorin in him. I remember the first time I entered the secret party room, which I now know is the entrance to the underground castles... Vincent lunged at me after smelling me. I recall how his face changed, how a snout formed, and his teeth became sharp like a wolf's.

King Strix nods. "Exactly."

I frown. "So, can you actually read my mind?"

He chews on his lip. "No. It's more like feelings. When you're mad, I can feel your anger. When you are happy, I can feel your elation. When you are filled with desire, I can—"

"I get the picture," I interrupt.

"But there are pictures too. Paintings in my mind when you feel strongly about something. Like just a moment ago, I saw you with Ramsey through your eyes."

My cheeks heat, knowing the kings are privy to my most intimate moments. I need to school my emotions from now on in order to save myself from embarrassment.

"Don't be shy, *Regina*. I liked it. Wish I could've seen you through Ramsey's eyes though. I bet you looked spectacular."

"I can assure you, she did," King Ramsey cuts in, as I wriggle out of King Strix's arms. "Pale skin flushed with desire." His finger trails under the strap of my dress. "Cunt wrapped around me so tight and perfect."

"Okay, enough," I growl.

"No, please continue," King Lucian urges. "How sexy did she look when she came?"

King Killian joins in on the onslaught. "Did she scream in pleasure? Beg you for more?"

"Were her nipples all tight and plump, breasts heavy with desire?" King Strix adds.

King Lucian's eyes flash as he looks at me, his eyes focused on my mouth. "Was her cum as sweet as her lips?"

"I can't hear you!" I shout. Jogging ahead of them, I cover my ears with my hands and make incoherent noises to drown out their taunting.

The weathered, wooden entrance to the coven comes into view, and I dash inside, not waiting for the kings to follow. The once dark room is now lighter to my eyes. I wonder if that's part of the enhancements I've acquired from drinking King Ramsey's blood.

Candles flicker as I rush past, anxious to get back inside. A firm hand surrounds my upper arm, jerking me to a halt. "What's the rush, sweetheart? Got an important meeting to attend?"

I glare up at King Killian. "No. Well, maybe." I square my shoulders. "I have questions."

"Yes, you can take off your clothes. I won't be mad."

I narrow my eyes. "That's not what I was going to ask."

He grins. "Could have fooled me. I could smell your arousal the entire journey back. It coated the air like mist, I could taste it on my tongue."

I throw my hands up. "Ugh. You lot are infuriating."

"And you are so cute when you're angry," King Killian

retorts, booping my nose. Turning away from him, I stomp toward the door, but King Lucian is already there donating his blood. I startle, wondering how the fuck he snuck past me in the hallway. Damn vamp speed.

Lucian licks his plump, crimson lips. "I'd be happy to suffer your questions, pet. Won't you join me in my suite? I would love to soak in my pool with you once more."

"The hell she will," King Strix growls. "It's my turn with the princess."

"We can just share her, you know. I have a feeling our future queen would like that very much." I turn to glare at King Ramsey who has snuck up behind me. "Don't deny it. Your desire was pouring off of you in waves back there. It's a wonder we made it back without fucking you."

King Lucian flicks his cape behind his shoulders, revealing his broad chest and tapered waist. His eyebrow arches, and he has a knowing look in his eyes. He knows what he does to me.

"H-Have you, umm…Have you shared…umm…" I can't even bring myself to ask.

King Lucian's eyes darken. "Yes and no."

"You and your damn riddles," I growl, shoving my way past him and through the open door, but King Lucian is back in front of me in the blink of an eye.

"Are you…envious, pet?"

"I'm not responding to any more of your questions. Not until I get some answers of my own."

King Strix glides up next to me. "I say we indulge the princess. Over a glass of wine perhaps?"

"Here, here," King Killian agrees. "Now, where to have such a meeting? There's a space inside my pants that's vacant."

King Ramsey scoffs. "Our girl needs satisfaction, Killian, not a journey to find a needle in a haystack."

Our girl? Why does the sound of that cause something low inside me to clench?

"I'll show you a fucking needle," King Killian counters, laughing and swatting at King Ramsey's crown. King Ramsey twirls out of the way and lands right behind me. I still when his talented fingers grip my hips, pulling me toward him. He presses his hardness against me, and memories of our night together flit through my mind.

No.

He won't do this to me again.

I pull away from him and reach for King Strix. "Since he will give me answers, I'll go with him. Come on." He grins at the others as I pull him toward the hidden entrance to the castles.

"If you want to get me alone, all you need to do is ask, *Regina*." Before I can groan again, he covers my mouth with his lips. My groan turns into a whimper, a desperate need for more. The King of Pride takes his time, tasting me delicately and gently nipping my lips. His hands cup my ass as he hauls me closer, deepening the kiss.

I open my mouth when his velvet tongue seeks entrance, and moan as our tongues clash. The intricate dance of languid massages has my body igniting with want for this vampire king. I grip his hard bicep in one hand and run my fingers through his long, blond hair. The strands feel like silk against my skin.

Behind me, someone shifts my hair away from my neck and a hot mouth descends on my skin. I groan into King Strix's mouth, needing more, my thoughts consumed by trying to get the pleasure I crave.

Another king plays with the hem of my dress and I feel my panties sliding down my legs. My grip on King Strix's arm tightens when one of my legs is lifted and a mouth descends on my pussy.

Fuck, it feels so good.

A tongue slips between my pussy lips, licking me, tasting me, and my hips thrust against the unknown king's face, needing more. King Strix's hands tighten in my hair, pulling just on the edge of pain as my dress is shifted off my breasts. Fingers tweak and tug on my nipples as the tongue between my legs flicks my clit.

I moan into King Strix's mouth, my body beginning to tremble. My breathing becomes shallow and my body heats. A warm mouth replaces the fingers on my breasts, grazing my nipple with sharp teeth as plump lips surround my clit and suck the sensitive nub.

I come undone.

King Strix holds me to his mouth, forcing his tongue deeper into mine, as the king on my neck bites.

I explode. A myriad of colors passes over my eyes as waves of pleasure course through me. My pussy gushes, coating the king between my thighs, and I take great satisfaction in that.

They are mine. All of them.

By the time I'm done claiming each vampire king, there won't be a member of the coven left who doesn't know my name. Maybe I'm more like the evil bitch than I care to admit as envy surges through my veins at the thought of the kings drinking from another, *fucking* them. The price of approaching my kings for sex or blood will be their lives. Because after years of having nothing, no one will touch what's mine.

No one.

CHAPTER 28

"So, what was it you wanted to ask?" King Killian pulls my hand to his lips and plants a soft kiss on the back as we walk down the huge staircase to the cavern castles.

Did I have questions?

"Oh, umm. Yes. For one, why did you guys choose me? In his speech, Vincent said you knew from the moment I was born that I would have a part to play in your world, but I don't understand how."

"Ah, yes. We should probably get the seven together for this." King Killian snaps his fingers, and the nearest guard turns, asking the king how he could be of service. The king whispers in his ear, then the guard nods and speeds off.

I allow the gorgeous king to guide me down the stairs, trying my best to ignore the naked women with perfect breasts seeking their attention. "Don't worry about them, sweetheart. Trust me, they have nothing on you."

I harrumph in response, scowling down the steps. I know I should believe him. The way the kings are drawn to me should be proof enough. But even as we descend, I look back at Kings Ramsey, Lucian, and Strix, however, none of them pay the women any attention. All their focus is on me, or rather, my ass.

King Lucian licks his luscious lips and flicks his tongue at me, causing my face to heat. It was him who feasted between my legs, and fuck, I can't wait to do that again.

We turn left at the bottom of the stairs, and King Killian pulls me through the throngs of vampires, donors, and servants. I stiffen at the slightest gesture, thinking back to when I was forced to walk through them naked and vulnerable. I keep waiting for one of them to slash at me, growl with bared teeth, or grab hold of me.

"Nothing will happen to you, princess, not while we're around," King Killian assures me. But I'm not convinced. I see the way they look at me. The women sneer down their noses, jealousy flashing in their gaze. The men undress me with their stares, lust gleaming in their unnaturally bright eyes.

"Really? Because I don't remember seeing you there when you lot forced me to walk naked through the hordes of vampires with only the protection of two guards."

King Killian deflates. "Yeah. Sorry about that. It was a stupid idea."

I growl, making a mental note to berate them about that, then push that thought into the back of my mind. The king keeps his arm wrapped around my shoulders, as King Strix strolls on my other side. Envy himself has walked ahead of me, which means my lusty vampire is behind me. Figures. I think King Lucian is an ass man.

King Killian ushers me to the third castle on the left. King Ramsey enters first as the guards open the doors and we follow in quickly behind him.

"Wow," I say in awe, looking around. Talk about over the top. Everything is excessive, almost borderline eccentric.

Double staircases wind up to an open second floor, and a gorgeous chandelier blazes above our heads. There must be hundreds of candles lit inside it. Thick, fur rugs cascade over the tiled floors, each more plush than the last. Paintings in ornate, gilded frames decorate every inch of available wall space.

Servants rush to us as we enter, holding trays of filled goblets. King Killian picks one up and sniffs, puts it down, then grabs another. He continues this odd behavior until he finds a scent he likes and the other kings follow suit.

"I want one," I tell him, reaching for a glass.

King Killian smacks my hand as if I were a child reaching into a bowl of candy. "What is in these glasses is an... acquired taste, one you've not learned yet."

The king nods to another servant who brings me a glass of my own. I take a deep drink, letting the wine burn my throat before exhaling. "Ah. So good."

"Indeed," King Lucian agrees, taking a sip from his own cup.

An impeccably dressed servant hurries toward us, his black hair slicked back, his suit pressed and shoes polished. "This way, my king. The others are already here."

"Others?" I ask.

"You know, Marcel, Thorin, and Dante," King Killian jests. "Perhaps you've not met them yet. Not that they are good company, are they, Ramsey?"

The King of Envy laughs. "Depends on who you're asking and what your kinks are."

Kinks? Ugh, I have so much to learn.

We follow the servant through an arched corridor. Here, the ceiling is covered in golden leaves making the whole thing glitter. It's breathtaking. We enter an orange door on the right and walk into a sitting room.

"Wow," I say again. If I thought the foyer was opulent,

then I don't even know what to call this. Everything in here is exorbitant. Chairs upon chairs fill the space, leaving hardly any room to walk. Plush cushions rest on each chair, and huge baskets filled with pillows and blankets are sporadically placed throughout the room.

Three of the four walls have fireplaces with flames blazing inside. Thick curtains hang from the vaulted ceiling down to the floor, making the room look even larger than it already is.

There is just so much of everything, then it dawns on me...

"King Killian, is your sin gluttony, perhaps?" The gorgeous king tosses his head, getting his sandy blond bangs out of his eyes, and smirks.

"Is it that obvious?"

I laugh. "Just a little."

He smiles and guides me farther into the room. There's so much to see that I didn't even notice Kings Marcel and Thorin already sitting.

"Where's Dante?" Strix growls, his ice green eyes searching the vacant chairs.

"I'm coming, I'm coming. Didn't want to arrive early for something I don't wish to be a part of." King Dante, the King of Sloth, arrives. His lean form weaves through the mess of cushy chairs as he meanders over.

King Dante doesn't even glance my way and I find myself completely irritated. The other six can't take their eyes, or hands, off of me. Even King Marcel, who doesn't seem quite sure what to make of me yet, still talks to me.

King Thorin's eyes are wide as he stares at me. I can see from here that he's a bit untidy. His clothes look like he's thrown them on in a dark room. His buttons are undone, and wrinkles and dirt are scattered along the fabric. Then I remember what King Strix—or was it King Ramsey—had said about King Thorin having another form. I shiver at the thought of the beast caged inside him.

King Marcel stands as we approach, and fuck if he doesn't look amazing. His dark hair is neat and trimmed, his beard and mustache well manicured. He wears a gold necklace around his neck and similar chains around his wrists. Rings surround eight of his fingers, leaving his thumbs bare. He oozes nobility.

His dark eyes subdue me, and I walk toward him as if driven by a silent call. He holds his hand out to me and I reach for him, allowing him to take me to his side. It's not until I'm sitting when I realize I'm on a soft couch between Kings Thorin and Marcel.

Kings Strix and Ramsey move to create a circular seating area, where all the chairs are facing each other. King Dante sits next to King Marcel and uncaringly picks at his fingernails. Directly across from me is King Lucian, to his left are Kings Ramsey and Killian, and between Kings Marcel and Lucian is King Strix.

All seven.

All for me.

I glance at King Dante, and when I see he's ignoring me again, I search deep within myself and find my envy. I wrap the green magic up into a tight ball and throw it at the sloth king.

I can tell the moment it embeds into him, because he glares at King Ramsey who just smirks and shakes his head before jutting his chin toward me. King Dante turns to stare at me with wide eyes. I toss him a wink and flutter my fingers in a small wave.

There.

Much better.

"Why does she smell like arousal?" King Thorin growls

from beside me. His gray gaze caresses my skin as if it was his fingers.

"It's decadent, isn't it, Thorin?" King Killian says with a grin. "Of course, you'd have to ask Lucian how delicious she tastes. He's the lucky bastard who got to try her."

"I've tried her too, you know," King Ramsey jumps in. "Speaking from experience, she's divine. She's—"

"Enough," King Thorin rumbles, causing me to jump, inching closer to King Marcel. The large vampire closes his eyes and takes a few deep breaths, his massive hands gripping his knees.

I glance to King Ramsey with wide eyes, wondering what I did to piss him off. Then something weird happens. A vision flashes in my head, one in which I'm naked and strapped down to a bed while King Thorin hovers above me.

He wants me.

King Ramsey nods and whispers to King Lucian.

He's trying to restrain himself, and the scent of my orgasm still sticky between my legs is driving him mad. I wonder if I should move seats.

"Stay," King Thorin growls, just as I move to stand. "I'm under control now."

I nod and try to relax, not wanting to piss him off even more.

"Can we get this moving along? I have other things I wish to be doing." King Dante tries to keep his voice casual, but I see the way he's looking at me now, the way his nostrils flare in my direction. Seems my envy magic did the trick.

Fiddling with the skirt of my dress, I take a deep breath. All eyes are on me. "I have questions, things I need to understand."

"Like what, flower?" King Ramsey inquires, concern in his eyes.

I fold my hands in my lap and lick my lips. "Like...why

me? Vincent said during his speech that you knew the moment I was born that I was destined for you or something. What does that even mean?"

"You want this one?" King Killian looks to King Strix, who settles his green gaze on me.

"Well, *Regina*, that is an astute question. But to answer it, we must go further back in time, when evil first made itself known in the lands. Back then, when the vampires were a new species and coming into their own, humans believed it was our doing, that we were the darkness, that we stoked the fires of hatred across once peaceful lands."

"I don't understand. What evil?"

King Strix smirks. "The one who invaded your home, stole your throne, and killed your father."

My heart stops. "The evil queen? What does she have to do with this? With you?"

"Everything and nothing," King Lucian answers. "As we kings are the embodiment of our sins, she is evil personified. The queen is as old as we are. She has ancient magic, strong and powerful."

King Killian nods. "Back when the first seven ruled and our kind were beginning to gain strength, the evil queen saw an opportunity. Of course she wasn't a queen back then, but a sorceress coming into her own dark powers. She sought to exploit us, to use our power for her own."

"When the first seven, who had no use for her, refused to submit to her reign, all hell broke loose," King Marcel adds, rubbing his hands up and down my arm. "She was desperate, greedy, even more so than I. Unable to persuade the first seven into submission, she instead cursed our kind, banishing us to walk in the darkness."

"That kind of magic almost killed her," King Ramsey interjects. "Pity it didn't, though we wouldn't be here if it wasn't for that selfish act. For years, nothing was heard from the sorceress, and the vampires gained ranks and power in our underground castles."

"Then, shortly before you were born, she resurfaced," King Lucian explains. "We surmised she would be back to find us, and try again to take us and force us under her rule. But we—the second seven—are not as pompous, or as arrogant, as the seven that came before us."

"Hard to believe, I know," King Killian teases with a smile. "But instead of seeking out the vampires she'd banished so long ago, she sought a new reign, a new set of victims...your parents." My heart drops like a lead weight into my stomach and I suddenly feel sick. "And so her reign of tyranny began. Disguised as a traveling midwife, she propositioned the king and queen, your parents, to care for your mother who was then pregnant with their first and only heir."

King Thorin's grip tightens on his legs. "She could sense you even then, little one. She was drawn to your pure soul, as we all were. Something about your purity calls to those who live in the shadows."

"It became her goal to corrupt you." My head jerks as King Dante adds to the conversation. "To take your pure heart and blacken it for her own wicked desires."

King Lucian nods. "But, Princess Snow, even though your inner spirit shines blindingly bright, you have become both the darkness we crave and the light we seek."

"Our rage and hate have morphed into passion and devotion," King Thorin proclaims, turning to grab my hand. "This will be hard to hear, little one, but on the day of your birth, with a poisoned red apple, she killed your mother."

Tears blur my vision and I hang my head in my hands as sobs rack my body. I always knew she killed my father, though I haven't been able to prove it, but never did I consider that she was responsible for my mother's death as well. My sadness quickly turns to rage, flowing inside me through King Thorin's touch. His hand vibrates on my leg, his anger, his wrath pouring through him and into me.

I've always hated the queen, even as an innocent young girl. But that hatred has morphed into something deeper, darker. Not only do I want to kill that cunt bitch, but I want her to fucking suffer. She's stolen my life from me, killed both my parents, condemned me to servitude in my own fucking castle...

Tears dry on my face and I feel power brewing inside me. I turn to King Thorin and watch his dark eyes shift to red. But it doesn't scare me. If anything, I'm envious of his power and want it desperately for my own. "Soon, little one," he promises darkly.

I nod and turn back to face the others, my hands clenching King Marcel's and King Thorin's tightly.

"Are you okay, flower?" King Ramsey questions. I dip my head, unable to form words. He nods, running his hand through his long, crimson hair. "But her plight to snuff your light, to invade your pure spirit, has failed time and time again."

"Her enslavement of you didn't make you wicked or evil as she'd hoped," King Strix says. "If anything, you've become more radiant, graceful even through your punishments. The people of Riverwood are more loyal to you than they ever have been before."

"The moment you came into the world, ripped from the body of your dead mother, we knew you'd one day be ours," King Lucian purrs. "Because only someone pure could take the power of the deadly sins and use them for good."

King Marcel's eyes blaze proudly as he squeezes my hand. "It's you, Snow. It's always been you."

I nod slowly, taking all this information in and digesting it. I guess in a way I always knew they would be my destiny. From the time I was small, I'd dreamed about the creatures hiding in the dark. Come to think of it, the lurkers invaded my dreams long before I learned the legends passed down about them. I've always thought they'd be my destiny, that they'd be the deciding factor in choosing the path of my life. But never did I conceive how profound their impact would be on me. With them I have grown confident, earned power, and amassed a small army. Slowly, I'm becoming one of them, but still holding true to what I hold dear—my morals and virtues. My end goal has never changed—kill the queen and free my people.

"You are so special, pet, born among the brightest snowfalls in the history of man. Haven't you ever realized you could do things others couldn't?"

Things others couldn't?

The first thing that comes to mind is that sometimes, I could get animals to respond to me. I thought it was just a fluke, but after the last two situations with Cupcake and that little mouse, and the fact that the queen's whippings should have killed me...

"Yes, flower," King Ramsey croons. "Those are just two of the many reasons you are so special, so cherished."

"Have we answered all your questions?" King Dante asks on a sigh, his usual, carefree posture and tone back. The sloth king stares at me with his light brown eyes and an annoyed look on his face.

"No." I turn to King Lucian. "Why was it you who came for me?"

He glances at King Ramsey before explaining, "There are several reasons, pet. The first is that given my sin and knowing how arrogant the queen is, we thought I would be able to use my power to persuade the evil cunt to allow me to take your hand. A little flirting, a little push of lust, and she'd forget how much she hated you and allow you to leave."

"But that didn't happen..."

King Lucian shakes his head somberly. "No. I had her trapped, under my spell, but once she heard you say we'd met before, I lost her. Her anger was too great for me to contain alone and she banished me from the castle."

The memory of that moment flits through my head, the pure agony during his excision and even more when I was beaten to a pulp. "It was so odd. It looked as though an invisible rope was removing you from the castle."

"That's basically what it was." King Lucian leans forward in his chair, his hands folded across his knees. "As vampires, we cannot enter a dwelling without invitation, and we also cannot linger once prohibited. The queen got lucky. We don't think she knows she can rescind an invitation, but she did so by mistake. Unfortunately, the old magic remembered, and it removed me from the castle."

"But…the castle is mine. Not hers. Shouldn't it be by my order?"

King Killian shakes his head, his blond hair falling into his eyes. "She was canonized as queen when your father married her. And until she either gives up her rule or dies, all that was your father's is hers."

"Well, shit." I chew on my lips and consider their words, then remember something King Lucian said. "Wait. You said there were several reasons you came to free me. What was the other?"

The lust king smirks. "I could sense you more than the others, pet. When you first came to our gathering, I stole a droplet of blood from you. My reasons were selfish, I just had to taste you, even the smallest morsel. But in doing so, I was able to sense you. I told you something the second time you came, before you were stolen by the huntsmen and forced back to the queen's castle. Do you remember what I said?"

I think back on our conversation, remembering how I felt

facing the kings, naked and vulnerable as King Lucian stood behind me, whispering in my ear. "Y-You said that once I took what I needed from myself that you would come."

He grins and bites his lip. "And you did, like a good little pet."

I scrunch my nose. "I don't understand."

"It was your first test, pet. A riddle for you to solve. As the king of lust, it's my sin to make you feel good. And you, my dear princess, were very pent-up. I wanted to empower you to take pleasure from yourself, and you did."

My cheeks heat. Oh, God! Does he mean...

"Yes." King Lucian's gaze darkens. "I felt it when you came and knew you were ready for us. You'd finally succumbed to sin."

"I heard you in my mind, I-I saw your eyes in my head."

"You drank the nectar," King Lucian croons. "It started our joining, began your transformation."

My life has been nothing but turmoil, a series of failures and punishments. I've never known happiness, never felt a sliver of power. Looking at the seven surrounding me, I know this is my destiny. It's time to become whom I was born to be, the one to vanquish the evil bitch from the face of the Earth forever.

"So," I begin, locking eyes with the kings. "Who wants to share their power with me next?"

CHAPTER 29

"*I'm coming for you, Snow!*"

The dark corridors of my castle are closing around me as my bare feet pound the tiled floor. Vacant hearths offer no heat as I run past the menacing eyes of my deceased relatives.

"Get back here, wench! Give me what's mine!"

No. I have to keep running. I can't let her catch me. If I fall into her hands again, it will surely be my end.

The dark halls of the castle morph into the quiet, shadowed alleys in Riverwood. I recognize the narrow path as the one that leads to the secret entrance to the Coven of Sin. Knowing safety is close, I push myself harder, pumping my arms by my sides, my legs burning from exertion.

The beaten, wooden door comes into view and I burst inside. But instead of a darkened room, I come face-to-face with King Lucian.

"Oh, thank God," I cry out, rushing to him.

The lust king turns to face me, but the desire once filling his eyes is absent, disdain replacing any emotion they once held. "Do not touch me, wench. You are not worthy of my presence."

"No," I sob, shaking my head. "This can't be happening." I push around King Lucian and rush down the hallway to the door guarding the party room. The door hangs off its hinge as I run past it. Behind it, the party is going full force. Vampires and donors alike are dancing and singing. Goblets filled with wine or blood are raised in a toast.

"To the queen!" someone shouts.

My heart swells. Are they speaking about me?

"To the evil queen! May she succeed in her conquest to vanquish that traitor Snow from our lands!"

Traitor? Me?

Tears misting my vision, I keep to the shadows and scurry to the entrance of the castles. No guards protect the doorway, an odd occurrence, putting me on high alert. Cautious, I continue forward. At the top of the stairs, I'm met with an eerie sight. Not a soul is here. No guards flank the stairs. No donors to tempt the kings with their blood. No vampires leer or sniff at me.

It's vacant.

My heart pounds in fear and I rush down the stairs, desperate to find someone, anyone. I spot the lowered bridge leading to the kings' throne room and dash toward it. The silvery liquid once floating in the moat has been replaced by putrid, black water.

I screech when the portcullis almost slices me in two as it comes crashing down when I pass below it, and I run. I run so hard my vision blurs and my head becomes dizzy, but I don't stop until I breach the throne room.

I jog down the aisle, the braziers flaring with bright flames until I reach the end. Any hope I had sinks into the floor and a lead weight drops into my stomach from the sight before me.

Surrounding a bed of white, the seven kings—wearing only their crowns—lean down over a slender woman. Their lips caress her naked skin. Her lithe body writhes under their touch, her moans echoing around me.

Betrayal and hurt have my chest clenching. I thought they

wanted me. They told me I was born to be with them. They-they lied to me, just like I've been lied to my entire life.

Brazenly, I take a step closer, my jaw dropping open. "You..."

The evil queen lifts her head, her malicious eyes boring into me, her thin lips curling in disgust. "Did you really think they'd want you when they could have me?" she sneers. My heart plummets and the evil bitch sits up, holding Kings Killian and Ramsey to her bare tits like suckling babes. Her legs spread wide as Kings Thorin and Marcel play with her pussy, their massive cocks erect and bobbing. Behind her, King Dante massages her shoulders, while Kings Marcel and Lucian rub her feet.

I can't handle this.

"Why? How?" The words tumble from my mouth.

"They want a woman with power, a creature of magic, just like them. No one wants you." Her fingers curl into King Ramsey's long hair and she rubs the soft strands against her face. "Why would they want an inexperienced girl, a shit-eating slave, when they could be with the queen, ruler of all the lands?"

Tears drip from my eyes, my lips trembling as I hold back my cries. The evil bitch cackles, every sound feeling like daggers stabbing me. "Stupid girl. Your time is almost up. You'll be with your dead parents soon." The evil bitch tips her head back, capturing the mouth of King Dante, then she screams into his mouth, her body convulsing in climax.

I want to scream. I want to cry. I want to tear this place to the fucking ground.

"T-This can't be hap-happening," I stutter out.

As one, the kings remove their mouths from the evil bitch and turn to me. My chest squeezes painfully as their yellow eyes assault me.

Yellow eyes...

I knew it was too good to be true. They've finally fallen under the queen's spell.

"You are nothing," King Killian growls.

"You are weak where she is strong," King Thorin rumbles.

"She is sexy and experienced, where you are pathetic and ugly," King Lucian ridicules.

"You could never truly please us, silly girl," King Ramsey adds. "Why would we want a wilted flower when we could have a blooming garden?"

Tears fall from my eyes as I drop to my knees, my legs no longer able to hold me, and I cup my face in my hands. Acute despair and profound hopelessness threaten to drown me.

Bare feet enter my vision and I still. My gaze travels up thin legs to glistening thighs and a bare pussy. Higher still, I lift my eyes past her tits to her face.

Where the kings encompass their sins, so too, does the queen— she's evil personified. I shiver at her look of disdain. "You can't hide from me, beast," she growls. "There is nowhere in this world that will keep you safe, no one who can protect you from my plans." She leans down and captures my chin, and I can't help but flinch, hating how weak I am.

"I'm coming for you, Snow, and when I do, I'll have you on your knees, begging for mercy, beseeching me to take your heart. Once that beating organ is pumping in my fingers, I'll watch with utter bliss as the light leaves your eyes."

She drops my chin to stand back up, reaching for two of the kings' hands. "You are weak, miserable, and undignified...more beast than human. How could you possibly hope to save your people when you can't even save yourself?"

The room shifts and I find myself in the middle of the woods. I recognize this place. It's the same spot she let the huntsmen have me, the place where she almost took my heart.

Bound between two wooden poles, I'm helpless. She's right. I can't protect the people of Riverwood. I'm not worthy of their loyalty.

Surrounding the wood platform are the seven. Their enchanting eyes, once filled with wonder and intrigue, now stare at me as if I was a stain on their boots. Dressed in battle attire, complete with armor, the kings draw their weapons and advance.

I pull on the ropes holding me, but it's no use.

I know this is the end for me.

There is no escape, no future existence in absence of the evil queen.

My cries lodge in my burning throat as they surround me, weapons poised to attack. I watch in horror as blood pours from their eyes and mouths, dripping down their faces, coating their armor.

"Now!" I hear the evil queen yell.

I close my eyes and accept my fate just as the first sword impales my chest.

"Regina, wake up!"

Something grips my arm like a vise and shakes me vigorously, but I can't bring myself to open my eyes, even as King Strix's nickname for me warms my chest.

"*Regina*," he whispers softly. "You're safe. It was just a dream. Open your eyes."

His voice is soothing but commanding. I can't help but obey the demand. My lids slip open and I see the concern flashing in the king's pale green eyes. His long, blond hair is pulled back and bound with a length of leather revealing just how beautiful he is. Even frowning, his dimples are prominent, enhancing his square jaw.

He's gorgeous, so much so that just looking at him has my chest squeezing. Tearing my gaze away from him, I see that I'm in my room, but I have fallen off the bed and onto the floor. White sheets are tangled around my body, ensnaring me like an insect in a spider's web.

King Strix reaches down to cup my face. "What happened?"

I look back at the King of Pride and gulp. "It-it was her."

His face scrunches. "Her who?"

"The evil queen. You were there too. You all were."

His thumbs slide across my cheeks, wiping the tears away. "Then why does your face look so sad, *Regina*?"

I close my eyes as more salty liquid leaks from them. "Because you chose her over me."

The concern on his face morphs to one of anger, his green eyes flashing. "Enough of this." The king pulls himself to standing and hauls me to my feet. I clutch at the sheet, trying to keep it wrapped around me, realizing I'm naked beneath it.

"It is time I shared my power with you, *Regina*. Once pride is flowing inside you, you will no longer have these lies filtering through your pretty head, these traitorous self-doubts."

He stalks behind me and leans down, his face nestled in the crook of my neck as he inhales. "I can wash away your fears, give you the confidence you deserve. Years under the wicked hand of the evil queen have brainwashed you into thinking you are not adequate for us, undeserving of our gifts. And yet, that is the exact reason why you are more worthy than anyone else."

"What do you mean?" I choke out, my breath hitching when his lips run across my neck.

King Strix's hands cover mine and he unclenches my fingers, allowing the sheet to pool at my feet. My heart thrashes as his hands glide up and down my sides, causing goosebumps to rise on my skin and my nipples to pebble.

"Because a queen earns her devotion, she does not take it. And you have persevered, *Regina*." His hands cup my breasts, squeezing gently, and I moan softly at how good it feels. "Because a queen is born, not acquired." His fingers pluck my nipples, making my breath hitch and my pussy ignite.

"Because a queen puts her people before herself." One large hand slides down my body, running over my stomach, causing it to lurch in desire. "Because we chose you. Out of all the souls in the world, you were born for us. Because a true queen uses her power for good and not evil." He cups my cunt and rubs my outer lips gently and my body heats, desperately wanting more.

"But the one true test is something the evil queen could never learn."

My head is dizzy with desire. "What's that?" I rasp out.

The king rumbles, lightly spanking my pussy, the sting fueling my desire. "That in submission lies power. That in the giving of yourself, you will receive. That in dying, there is life."

With a soft kiss to my neck, the vampire king twists around me and slips out the door, gazing at me through the slight opening. "Someone will come for you soon. I expect you to be ready. Only in complete submission will you find your pride."

With that, the door clicks shut, and I'm left alone with a throbbing pussy and a mind filled with desperate thoughts. I don't know what King Strix has in store for me, but I'll be prepared when he does.

Ready, willing, and waiting.

CHAPTER 30

I don't wait long.

A knock sounds on my door just as I'm wrapping the discarded sheet around my body. "Come in." The smiling face of Katie and the scowling face of Renee enter.

Katie looks quite content with a new set of bite marks on her neck. "Hey, Snow."

"Hi. So, how are things going with Julian?"

Her face heats. "Sooo goooood."

I laugh at her evident feelings for this new vampire. Renee scoffs as she hauls the hot water through my room and into my bath.

"Glad things are going well," I whisper when Renee is out of earshot.

"Definitely. I'm hoping he'll be allowed to turn me soon. If not a full-blown vampire, then at least a drone."

Drone? I haven't heard this term before.

The foreign term is quickly forgotten as I step into the hot water and lower myself into the bathtub. Oils scented with lilac soothe me. I almost fall asleep in the warm liquid, but I'm quickly riled by the women wanting to *prepare* me.

Like usual, my skin is scrubbed and my hair is washed. After drying me, the women bustle around to get my hair and makeup done.

This time, all of my hair is pulled back and twisted into a messy bun, secured by a long, pointed hairpin with a rose on the end. Random strands of curls are pulled out to hang around my face as a crimson stain is applied to my lips.

Dangling earrings are fixed to my ears, and a dainty gold necklace is linked around my neck. The snowflake pendant hangs just above my breasts.

Katie presents me with a deep purple gown and slips it over my head. Renee secures the ties around my neck and swings to my front to adjust it.

There are no words for its beauty, its seduction. Parts of the dress are sheer purple fabric, allowing my pale skin to shine through. Other sections are decorated in purple swirls of glittering amethyst gems. Tiny triangles barely cover my breasts and cut deep, coming together a few inches below my chest. The rest of the bodice is tight, hugging around my hips and thighs. The fabric loosens below my knees and flares out into bunches of gathered lengths that swirl around my legs when I spin.

Sexy shoes the same color as the dress are slipped onto my feet, the heels giving me an extra few inches. Let's just pray I don't slip and fall while wearing them.

"You look beautiful," Katie compliments in awe.

Renee scowls. "Eh. She's okay. I don't know if I'd go with beautiful. More like acceptable."

I make a mental note to ask the kings about the vampire woman, because she clearly doesn't like me. I take a breath to ask her what she has against me when the door in my bedroom creaks open.

Katie and I glance at each other before hurrying from the bathroom to see who rudely intruded without so much as even knocking. When we cross the threshold into my room, my breath hitches.

It's King Strix and he looks like a fucking god.

Dressed in a smart purple suit, the man makes my panties fucking melt, if I was wearing any that is. The dark satin shirt hugs him in all the right places, and the fabric mimics the pattern of my dress at the collar and cuffs. The shirt cuffs protrude out of the arms of his jacket, falling over the backs of his hands. He literally fucking sparkles when he moves. The jacket and pants are a shade lighter than the shirt and show off his broad chest and tapered waist.

His spiked, platinum crown sits proudly on his head, his long blond hair looking like strands of woven gold. The king's deep set, bright green eyes bore into mine. As his gaze moves down my body, fire ignites on my skin as if his eyes are caressing me.

He bites his pouty lower lip, showing off his dimples and strong jaw. The scent of freshly washed sheets wafts over me and I inhale deeply.

"You look magnificent," he compliments, taking a step closer. "Like a true queen should."

I can feel the blush creeping up my cheeks and return the compliment. "And you look..." My words fail me. Because what could I say? That he's the most handsome man I've ever laid eyes on? That I love the suit, but I'd prefer it tossed on the floor? That any woman would kill to walk on the arm of someone as gorgeous as King Strix?

A knowing grin cleaves his face and he prowls closer, rubbing his hands together. "Any of those would work, *Regina.*"

Oh fuck. The mind reading. I'll never remember that.

King Strix stops in front of me and grabs my hands, strumming his thumbs along the tops. "I've been alive for well over a century, and never have I seen someone as stunning as you, princess. Flowers would weep at your beauty, and the sunset couldn't hold a candle to your elegance. It is I who would kill to have you on my arm."

With that, he lowers his head and presses his lips to mine. His kiss is gentle, a caress, a promise of more to come. I almost pout when it doesn't go any further, and he pulls away with a chuckle. "So impatient, aren't we? Well, I wouldn't want to keep you waiting. I have plans, and I have high expectations of you accomplishing everything I have in store."

I gulp and lick my lips. How can I possibly hope to exceed or even reach his expectations? He's a fucking creature of magic, practiced in his art for over a hundred years. I'm a mere mortal with a bruised sense of self-worth and an affinity for punishment.

"Stop worrying, *Regina*. You were born for this. It's time you see yourself as we do. Pride will help you achieve that."

The king pulls me toward my door and I look over my shoulder, fluttering my fingers at an excited Katie, who is raising her hands in victory for me while mouthing, "He's so fucking hot!"

His grip tightens when we exit my room and turn down the hall. I expected guards to flank us again, but find we are alone, save for the random coven member strolling along. All who come across us either bow at the waist or at least incline their heads. My guess is their response depends on their station, and the show of respect changes accordingly. It's so vastly different than how the evil bitch does things. Basically, she expects us all to prostrate ourselves flat on the ground no matter if it's freshly cleaned tile or saturated earth.

"Don't think about her, *Regina*. Tonight, there is only us. Nothing more. Understand?"

"Yes," I respond breathlessly.

"Good. Because in order to receive pride, you must throw it away."

My face scrunches in confusion, and I glance up at him as we turn a corner and head toward a flight of stairs. "What do you mean?"

He smiles down at me, causing my heart to race with just his look. God, he's so beautiful. "Well, one can look at pride in two ways. For example, I could order you to strip and walk through the halls naked—"

"Order me?" I interrupt.

"Yes, *Regina*. Order you. Don't make me prove it." I slam my lips shut and wait for him to continue.

"As I was saying, one person might be so prideful that they know there is nothing to be ashamed of, that their body is perfect, so strutting around nude would be empowering. Then there are those who scoff at the idea of baring themselves, thinking they have too much pride to do such a thing. Does that make sense?"

"So…both people have pride, just the second person has a skewed version of it."

"Exactly. The first person had the pride I do, the pride you will soon. You are perfection, princess, as am I. Why hide what you truly are? People will bow to your beauty, yearn for just a taste of you. There's so much power in that."

He makes a good point.

Dammit.

I definitely relate to the second person more, but something tells me that's exactly my problem. I can only imagine what he has in store for me. If his little example is anything to go by, then I suspect that I'll be *ordered* to shed my clothes soon. The prospect makes my chest feel heavy and sets my nerves on fire.

I've never really been confident with my body. Years of being told how ugly I am has definitely done something to me. Even though I see the want and desire in the king's unnerving yet mesmerizing eyes, I still doubt. I still wonder if this is a ruse from the queen and they are just playing their parts, lugging me along until I feel safe, only to pull the rug out from under my feet.

King Strix jerks and a slap—no, a *spank* lands on my ass. "I thought I told you not to think about her." He grips my chin tightly in his hand, forcing me to hold his gaze. "We've barely started our night together, and already you disobey me?"

"I-I..." My eyes flicker between his until his anger softens.

He drops my chin. "Don't let it happen again," he growls slowly.

Once again, his hand surrounds mine and he pulls me along beside him. My heels click on the floor, but I keep my mind blank, even though the sound makes me shiver. After descending a flight of stairs, we turn down a hallway lit with candles then enter through a wooden door.

I gasp at the sight before me. We appear to be in a foyer of another castle. Everything here is meticulous. Every picture matches, and every couch and chair is strategically placed. The fur rugs are white and unmarred, the tapestries bright and vibrant. Whoever lives here cares about what he presents to others.

Then it dawns on me, this must be King Strix's castle. I look up, wide-eyed, and he just smiles and lifts one blond eyebrow. "Shall we?"

I nod and allow him to escort me through an archway on the right wall. We stride down another corridor, then stop at a closed door.

The king turns me to face him, his large hands cupping my face. "Your test is about to begin. I want you to open your eyes, listen hard, and pay attention. If I tell you to do something, you do it. In gaining your pride, you must also throw

SEVEN SINS OF SNOW

away the poor excuse for it that you hold so dear. Are we clear?"

"Yes."

"Good." The king leans down and plants a soft kiss on my lips. "Then let's begin."

King Strix pushes open the door and I'm immediately bombarded with a plethora of floral scents. As my eyes adjust to the lighting, I see I'm in an odd room. Around the brightly lit perimeter are small, raised stages, just large enough to hold the female standing on top of each of them. Every woman is dressed elegantly, her hair perfectly coiffed, her dress accentuating each body in all the right places. The women move from pose to pose like they are performing for the crowd.

Down the center of the room is an elevated aisle that extends out between darkened tables filled with people. The sounds of glasses clinking and boisterous laughter ring out. Savory smells of fresh beef and baked potatoes make my mouth water.

Looking around, I'm more confused than ever. "I don't understand."

"You will, *Regina*." The king moves to stand behind me since no one has noticed him yet. "See the women on the pedestals? They are nobles—"

"Nobles?" I interrupt. "I don't recognize a single person."

He kneads my bare shoulders and I have to stifle a moan. "That's because they are from other kingdoms far from here."

"And the guests?"

"They are from a town not too dissimilar to Riverwood. They were asked to come here for a special event and do not know where they are or who they are about to meet. They were whisked away in horse-drawn carriages, glamoured, and brought inside. All they know is that whomever the crowd chooses will win a night with the king."

"Y-You mean, you?" I stutter out.

"Yes, me." His finger trails up and down my bare spine, causing shivers to run through me. "You want me, princess? Then show me. Show everyone why you're most deserving of a night with the king. Make them want you. Do whatever you must to win."

I feel the moment when his fingers leave my skin and I turn back to find him gone.

CHAPTER 31

"*H*ello, miss! Are you here for the competition?" I turn back as a short, portly woman comes bustling toward me.

"Uhh, yes?"

"Good, good. It's just about to start. Take a stand on that empty space over there." She points to a vacant stage on the right wall. I hurry over, climb a few stairs, and stand on top. I can almost feel the many eyes roaming over me. I know my dress is revealing, showing off more skin than it covers. But I don't know if that's a good thing for me or not. The people of Riverwood would find my attire whore-ish...though I've never seen a whore in a ballgown laced with jewels before.

I scan the other women vying for a night. There must be twenty women in here, each more gorgeous than the last. There are blondes and brunettes, and a woman with hair that looks like an orange sunset. Another is exotic, with dark skin that looks soft, like velvet, and braided hair.

I feel over and underdressed at the same time. Self-consciousness threatens to make me want to hide, to not be seen. So many years of trying to remain invisible are hard to get over. But I keep my face poised, clench my fingers to keep them from wanting to hug myself, and maintain perfect posture.

Head up, shoulders back, chest out...just like my father taught me.

My eyes widen when none other than Vincent struts down the aisle, looking quite dapper in his black and white suit. His dark hair is slicked back and he holds a filled goblet in his hand as he walks to the end. Even without speaking, he garners attention, and within moments, the crowd has silenced.

Vincent eats this shit up, and I can't help but grin at him. If there's one thing I know Vincent likes, it's attention, and a lot of it. His lips curl into a smirk and he cocks his head before speaking.

"Welcome, everyone, to the first ever Night with a King event. You all were specifically chosen to attend. We scoured the kingdoms to find the most rational and levelheaded people to judge this event, and discover beautiful women to woo our king. You'll find them standing on the pedestals before you. Aren't they gorgeous?"

The crowd claps politely as the women choose their favorite pose and hold still like a statue. Me? I look like an idiot. I don't have a fucking pose. I just keep my posture, and try to keep my hands loose at my sides. The women look like fools with their weird poses. Vincent catches my eye and subtly throws a wink my way.

"Now, to meet the man of the hour, the king responsible for showing us a good time. Please welcome, King Strixious!"

Who the fuck is Strixious?

My question is soon answered when King Strix emerges from the shadows and saunters down the aisle to a mix of responses. He's added a robe to his ensemble, and it billows behind him when he walks. I can appreciate his purple suit and the way his crown sits perfectly on his golden hair even more now. He is absolutely dashing.

The women in the crowd gasp in awe of his beauty, while the men raise glasses to toast to the king. The posed women shift positions, pursing their lips and pressing their best attributes forward. Some push out their chests, others hike up their skirts, showing off long legs, while others cock their hips, displaying enticing curves. Me? I just stand here in the same pose. It's not even a pose really.

The gorgeous king presses a hand to his chest and slightly inclines his head. I'm pretty sure half of the women are visibly swooning. I see flushed faces and eyes glazed in desire. I can't blame them one bit.

"Thank you, noble king. If you'd please take your position, we can get started." King Strix squeezes Vincent's shoulder and turns back, heading to an elegant, polished throne. His blond hair whips about him as he turns and sits down, crossing his legs, one ankle resting on the opposite knee. The king leans back in his throne, relaxed, twirling a strand of golden hair with one hand, while the other runs up and down the polished wooden armrest. The movement reminds me how, only moments ago, those same fingers traveled along my spine. Something stirs low within me, and I glance up to his eyes, finding the King of Pride staring hard back at me.

"Let's get this party started!" Vincent shouts, arms raised in the air. After the guests' cheering dies down, he continues, "This is how it's going to work. Each lady will enter the main stage where I am now and do whatever she must to prove that she's the woman who deserves a night with the king. After each lady has…performed…you, our honorable guests, will vote by applause. Whichever lady receives the loudest, wins. It's that simple."

Vincent turns to the girl opposite me and gestures to her

with his hand. "Up first is a woman from Valgary Rock. She has a collection of dead butterflies and loves to drink excessive amounts of wine. Please welcome, Angelica!" The woman's lips twitch, and she turns off her pedestal and saunters slowly toward Vincent. Blonde curls hang down past her shoulders, bouncing as she walks. Her eyebrows are perfectly arched and her red lip stain is the same color as her dress.

Red and tight, the dress is all lacework. Similar to mine, it ties around her neck, hugs her torso and thighs tight, and flares out at the bottom. The lower hem is covered in red feathers and the section covering her breasts is missing, leaving the swell of her cleavage bare. She drips sex appeal, much like King Lucian does.

The woman stops in front of King Strix and reaches out a delicate hand, tracing her fingers down his jaw. Jealousy flares inside me. I want to scream out, *let go of him, you fucking bitch, he's mine*, but I chew on my tongue and stay silent. This is a test, one I have no intention of failing. Sometimes we need reminding of what we want in life, and seeing her touching him sets off a series of alarms blaring inside my head.

I want him.

No.

I *need* him.

King Strix's face remains passive, even when she sinks to the ground and slides up his legs. I want to bash in her pretty little fucking head. When the king pulls his gaze away from her to look elsewhere, I relax a little. But the crowd is still eating it up. Women are very reserved, so to see a woman flaunting her body and being sexually forward is quite startling. In the Coven of Sin, though I haven't been here long, sexuality is embraced, if not exploited. Vampires can be found fucking in public often, or so I'm told. Stuck in my room, I'm not privy to the public fornication sessions, but something excites me at the thought of watching someone fucking. Naked bodies slick with perspiration sliding against each other, the crescendo of moans as they come close to a climax...

Visions swim across my mind of my night with King Ramsey, the feeling of his cock sliding inside me for my first time. My beliefs of what pleasure should be like had been so skewed. Before him, something as simple as not sleeping in the dungeons or a warm meal brought me pleasure. Here, I've been spoiled, learning a whole new meaning of the word.

By the time I come out of my daydreaming, the woman is back on her pedestal and Vincent has taken center stage again. "Magnificent, wasn't she?" he beams, clapping furiously. "Up next is a woman from Vermillion Heights. She is proficient in the many uses of the word fuck, and is allergic to beans. Please welcome, Sarafina!"

Sarafina rolls her eyes as if Vincent is bothering her by calling her forward. She's uniquely beautiful with high cheekbones, straight, sandy blonde hair that sits just above her shoulders, and deep-set blue eyes. She doesn't wear her dress, her dress wears her. Clinging to her body like a second skin, the black dress sparkles when she moves. It's long-sleeved, tight around the bodice, and flares out at the hips, hitting just above her knees.

You can tell by this woman's resting bitch face that she doesn't put up with anyone's shit. This is a woman who doesn't have a submissive bone in her body. When she stops before the king, she sneers down at him, almost as if she's above his status.

I'm shocked by her boldness.

She seems disinterested in the king, as if she's performing to guarantee she won't win. Unlike Angelica, who gave King Strix complete adoration and attention, when Sarafina reaches him, she looks away from him, flicks her hair over one shoulder, and struts down the aisle.

What a dick. A supreme dick.

A dick supreme?

Yeah, that sounds better.

She walks rather nonchalantly to the end of the aisle, flips off the audience, then heads back to her stand.

Vincent runs out, recovering quickly. "Well, that was an interesting way to show you care! Thank you, Sarafina!" He claps, but only a few join in, laughing the whole time.

"Our next participant is a woman from Muller Lake. She is an avid reader and loves mozzarella sticks! Please welcome, Alyssah!"

Just like the other two women, this one is also blonde, but her hair hits just below her chin, accentuating her beauty. Her blue eyes are so light, they remind me of King Lucian's. Hell, she could pass for a vampire. With pale skin similar to mine, she could be some weird crossbreed between my relative and a vamp.

Her dress is patterned with bright flowers scattered across a thin, willowy fabric. The dress hangs off her shoulders, covering her upper arms in a wispy way. Cut low to reveal modest cleavage, the dress is simple yet elegant. The woman is shy, her cheeks flaming as she approaches the king. She turns to him and does this awkward curtsy. The poor thing ends up losing her balance and falls into his lap with a shriek.

She struggles to get up, her heels catching in the hem of her dress until Vincent charges forward to help her. She must have felt up the king's cock like six hundred times while she tried to claw her way up his body to stand.

As Vincent assists her to her feet and she walks to the end of the aisle, she looks at me, winks, and whispers, "That's how you get Alyssah'd." My jaw drops open in shock. The little minx. She meant to fall on him, to grope his junk, feeling him up like she was fluffing her pillow. Sneaky little thing. I'll be keeping my eyes on her.

She flashes a very proud smile to the audience, carefully turns around, and heads back to her space. Vincent looks at her in astonishment. I'm sure he caught her little ploy, likely hearing what she whispered to me. Looks like the master has been taught a lesson.

I smile to myself. While I might not like that she hand fucked my king's cock, I have to hand it to her—that girl had a plan and executed it flawlessly.

Vincent waits until after Alyssah's applause dies down to introduce the fourth girl, the woman with the onyx skin. Out of all the women here today, she is my biggest competition. She's virtually flawless. Her skin is so dark it almost looks like it glows. Her hair is long and styled in tight braids that hang low down her back. Her face is narrow with soft curves, plump lips, and exotic, deep brown eyes.

Her dress is yellow and so very sexy. The sides of it are nonexistent. In place of fabric are crisscrossing ribbons that weave their way up her sides, showing off all her beautiful skin. The ribbons connect a thin piece of fabric covering her ass in the back and her private area in the front. The woven section ends at the bustline, where the yellow fabric stretches across her perky chest. Her nipples are hard and poke at the material, giving her even more sex appeal.

This girl is on fire.

"Our next contestant is a woman from Clear Water. She is an avid archer and loves riding her stallion. Please welcome, Navarrah!"

Cheers erupt and she hasn't even moved yet. Holding herself with poise and grace, Navarrah glides off her pedestal and saunters her way to the king. She reaches an elegant hand out to him, and I see each finger has a gold ring around it. King Strix is taken aback a bit I think, but remembers himself quickly, gripping her hand and planting a chaste kiss on the back. She remains poised, like a queen, even as the king's lips taste her flesh.

Navarrah then spins in a quick movement, snatching her hand back, her braids flying around her head, and struts to the end of the aisle. She poses hard, hip cocked, legs spread, with one hand on her waist and the other slowly trailing down her front as the men in the audience gasp. I'm in awe of her. She's proud and confident, so full of...pride.

That's it.

She's perfect for King Strix. That's why he was stunned by her, because she gave him a dose of his own medicine.

How can I possibly beat her?

My mind whirls as she blows a kiss to the guests, then heads back to her spot. The king's eyes follow her the whole way. Envy roars inside me, my powers swirling around, ready to burst out and shower everyone in here. But I refuse to use it. If I'm going to win, it's because I earned it, not because I cheated.

The remainder of the women perform for the audience. A girl with brown hair in tight curls wearing an orange dress is even so bold as to plant a kiss on his cheek before two guards, whom I recognize as Cerino and Jovie, have to rush onto the stage and pull her off of him. Her cries pleading for him to choose her echo through the room before she's removed from the party altogether.

Another with black hair pulled away from her face actually dances down the aisle and does a unique twirl on her toes, holding one leg up to her ear. A beautiful woman with tanned skin and light brown hair does little to be remembered by. In fact, I can't even recall her name.

My feet begin to ache as I shift uncomfortably while Vincent announces yet another woman. "And finally, from the quaint village of River...stantanopolus, a woman who loves dancing and spending time with family, please welcome, Sofi!"

Sofi?

I look up and see Vincent smiling at me, his arm gesturing toward where I stand.

Sofi. That's right. The fake name I gave him the first time I met him. Vincent winks at me as I step off the pedestal and slowly walk toward King Strix. I keep my pace measured and controlled, making sure my posture is intact and that my dress doesn't slip to reveal a rogue rosy nipple.

Whispers pick up as I move, my purple dress hugging me. I can feel the intense stares of the crowd sizzling down my skin, the malicious eyes of the other women willing me to fall or fuck up in any way. But I won't allow that to happen.

The king is mine.

And it's time I prove it.

When I get to the king, I can see he's already sporting an erection, judging by the bulge in his pants. I can only hope that was not from the previous women.

"Hello, King Strix. I'm Sofi, and I have a very talented tongue. May I show you?"

The king nods, a grin stretching across his face. Reaching down, I prop my hands on his armrests and lean in to capture his mouth. I take charge of the kiss, softly tasting him, my tongue poking his lips for entrance. He opens for me, and I massage his tongue with practiced slowness in an agonizingly teasing pace. He tries to speed it up, but I won't let him, and I continue to kiss him languidly as if I have all fucking day.

I can feel his growl of impatience vibrate my chest and I smile to myself, knowing I've got him. I pull back, his lower lip clenched between my teeth until it slides out. Then I turn and head down the aisle. The audience is silent from my brazen actions, from the fact a woman who has not yet won took the king's mouth for her own.

But I'm not fucking done yet.

Stopping at the end, I reach up and pull the hairpin from my black hair, letting the soft curls cascade down my back. Then, after taking a deep breath, thinking about the king's earlier pep talk about different kinds of pride, I begin to strip.

I stare at the men and women watching, making eye contact with as many as I can while peeling my dress down my body. The tie behind my neck offers me no resistance as I pull it free and let the bodice drop to my waist, baring my breasts to everyone.

I can hear the sharp intakes of breath as my nipples peak, the rosy buds protruding from my pale skin. But I don't stop there. I sink my thumbs below my dress where it hugs my hips and shimmy it down my legs. Once pooled at my feet, I kick the dress into the audience and watch as the guests become feral, fighting for a piece.

I think about Navarrah and pose like she would. I space my legs apart, cock my hip to the side, and lock one hand on my waist while trailing the other down my body. I cup my breast and tweak my nipple before splaying my fingers down my stomach all the way to my wet cunt. I cup my pussy before sliding one finger up and down my slit. I evaluate the guests, expecting revulsion as force of habit, but that's not what I see.

It's desire. Every man and woman looks like they want to be me or fuck me. It's empowering. Feeling wonton, I slide my dampened finger back up my body and slip it inside my mouth, moaning as I do.

I can hear several people groan as I pull my finger out with a pop. I smile to the guests then turn and head back toward the king. His eyes devour me with each step, my tits bouncing and swaying as I walk. I wink at the king as I strut past him and back around to my pedestal. I keep my poise, my posture perfect, holding my chest out proudly and hands loose at my sides, chin raised.

Fuck these people and fuck these women.

The king will be mine tonight.

I guaran-fucking-tee it.

Vincent stalks back to the front, his eyes glazed over as he looks at me. I know he's fighting for control and I pray that he manages to hold himself back, considering King Thorin isn't here to persuade him otherwise.

Though his gaze instills fear, I don't dare cover myself. There is something freeing about being naked when it's my choice to do so.

Vincent shakes his head as if clearing his thoughts before he speaks. "Well, isn't Sofi just full of surprises tonight! Wow!" He runs his hand through his black hair and slaps himself in the face. "Okay. Let's vote, shall we?"

He gestures toward Angelica. "Anyone who wishes to vote for a particular female, make as much noise as you can when I point to her. Please, to keep this fair, do not vote—or cheer—for more than one woman. Any questions?" When the crowd doesn't respond, he takes it as his cue to start.

"Angelica!" he shouts, pointing to the touchy girl. The bitch pouts when she doesn't get even one vote. "Sarafina!" The woman who I'd actually love to get to know flips off the crowd, yet still earns a few claps. "Alyssah!" The trickster has several people applauding for her and smiles happily. "Navarrah!" The dark beauty inclines her head slightly as the loudest response I've heard from the crowd so far rings out. Claps and cheers, resound. She smiles big, showing a perfect set of bright teeth. Vincent continues down, each girl barely getting a response until it's my turn.

All eyes are on me, and you know what? I fucking love it.

Let them fucking look. Let them watch as I fuck the king and make him mine. The mirror said I'm the fairest of them all. It's time I believed it.

"Sofi!" Vincent shouts, and the response is deafening. I even cover my ears as the cheers and yells for me intensify. Every guest is standing, jumping, and clapping for me. I can't suppress the huge smile that crosses my face. I did it. I fucking did it.

I look across the room to Navarrah and she nods her head in respect, a smirk on her face.

"And the winner is...Sofi!" My chest swells as I prance in excitement. "Go claim your prize," Vincent says, laughing. I don't fucking wait. Turning, I run toward my vampire king, who is standing and waiting for me. Feeling a surge of energy, I leap up into his arms, wrapping my legs around him as he takes my mouth.

"Fuck, you looked so beautiful up there, *Regina*," he purrs, pulling away. "Naked and proud. All eyes devouring you. It took everything I had in me not to claim you right there on the aisle."

"What's stopping you now?"

His grip tightens on my ass and he growls, nuzzling my neck. "You want me to fuck you in front of the guests, princess? You want them to watch as my hard cock pounds your sweet pussy?"

His dirty talk only fuels my desire. I feel dizzy with it. "Yes," I rasp.

I can feel his smile against my skin. "Then so be it."

I shriek as the king tosses me over his shoulder, spanks my ass, and struts down the aisle. "The party is over," King Strix announces. "You are free to go, the carriages await your departure. But for any who'd like to stay for dessert, you are invited to remain as I fuck this woman right here, right now."

The king sets me down in front of him, his fingers

trailing up and down my arms as the guests watch. The other women who were my competition leave, all except Navarrah, who watches excitedly.

"Just look at them, princess. Every man desires you. Craves you. Each of them wants a taste of your supple body." His hands slide forward, cupping my breasts, kneading them as his thumbs glide over my pebbled nipples. "Every woman wants to be you, each one jealous of your perfect body, wishing they had as much confidence as you, desperate for a night with the king. Hell, they might want to fuck you too."

One hand skims lower, sinking between my pussy lips to tease my clit. "Fuck, so wet for me already, aren't you, *Regina*? Does the thought of my hard cock thrusting inside you make your pussy clench in desire?"

"Fuck yes," I groan, closing my eyes as he strums my clit slowly. I'm so sensitive, so pent-up, that it won't take me long to come. With one hand, I reach up and grip the king's neck, and I slip the other behind myself, rubbing his length on the outside of his pants.

"Touch me, princess. Taste me. I'm all fucking yours." Then he bites my neck and I explode on his hand. I can feel King Strix sucking my blood as he strokes my clit, my spine arching, my toes curling into the floor.

His hands leave me and I open my eyes, glancing over my shoulder to see him licking my cum off his fingers. "Mmm, so fucking good. I could eat you for days and never tire."

The king reaches for his cape and unhooks it, letting it fall to the floor. Then he works on his belt, pulling the length from around his hips. I twist to face him, unfastening the buttons on his jacket and shirt, desperate to touch his skin.

When I finally get through the last button, I tug his shirt wide open and lick his skin. I run my tongue over each and every one of his abs, tasting him as I make my way lower.

"Yes, princess," he croons when I drop to my knees. I

make quick work of his pants and free his perfect cock. It's long and lean and oh so perfect. The head is a shade darker than the rest. So flawless and enticing. My mouth waters before I wrap my lips around him. He moans, his fingers snaking into my hair, tugging on the roots.

He guides himself deeper into my mouth, almost choking me. His actions are possessive as he thrusts hard and I fucking love it. I slide my tongue all around him, hollowing out my cheeks, feasting on this vampire king. I keep one hand on his thigh to steady myself, and with the other, I fondle his balls.

"Oh fuck, *Regina*. Suck that big cock. Such a good girl."

If I were a peacock, I'd be preening. His praise only makes me want to work harder, please him better. I hear his breath quicken, but he pulls out before he comes. I look up at him, pouting.

"Don't you look at me like that. The first time I come with you, I will be filling your pussy, not your mouth." The King of Pride drops to his knees and kisses me again. Desire and desperation come through his lips, his fierce need for me growing like a potent storm. I kiss him back eagerly, feverish with my thirst for him.

King Strix pulls away from my lips and kisses down my neck. He supports my back with a strong hand and leans me down so my head is at the edge of the aisle. I don't even know if anyone is watching as he sucks my nipple into his mouth, making my clit come to life once more.

He nibbles and sucks, moving from one side to the other, licking and biting until I almost come again just from that. "Are you ready for me?" he whispers into my ear before licking the shell.

"Yes, my king. Take me. I'm yours."

He growls in excitement, his green eyes flashing, his dimples prominent as he bites his lower lip and lines up his cock with my entrance. We both groan when he sinks inside me, inching his way forward.

"So hot. So wet. So perfect." His hands grip onto my knees and he pushes them wide, his eyes focused on where we are joined. I look down my body, watching his length sink in and out of me, my pussy clenching around him at the sight.

"Fuck, that feels so good," I moan, as he quickens his pace. I'm getting so close, the heat building low inside, almost incinerating me. Then he pulls me up so I'm sitting on top of him as he fucks me from below, and again, our lips crush together. I move my hips in pace with his, fucking him as much as he's fucking me as our tongues duel for dominance.

"Come for me, princess. Come all over your king's cock. I want to see what you look like when your body ignites around mine."

"Oh God." I bounce on his dick, chasing my orgasm. The king licks my neck, his fingers twisting my nipples, and I fucking unravel.

The orgasm takes me by surprise and I shriek, my head falling back as my fangs descend. With a surge of power, I rip the king's jacket and shirt from his body and sink my teeth into his neck, drinking through my climax. The king comes as soon as I bite him, his hot cum filling me.

I can feel his power flowing through me as I slow my pace. His blood is crisp and fresh, much like his scent. It reminds me of fresh strawberries plucked from my father's garden as a child. I curl my hands around him, one fisting his long, blond hair and the other holding his back firmly as I drink my fill. He tastes so good that I don't ever want to stop.

"Enough, *Regina*," he growls, tugging on my hair. "Don't be greedy."

"But I am greedy," I respond when he succeeds in removing me.

The king laughs. "That may be true, but there is something you must remember. Until you complete the bonds, you must still obey. You have no choice not to."

I frown and he takes my mouth once more. Our tongues slide together, tasting our blood, igniting a fire inside me once again.

"Come, princess. It's time we rest. We can play again soon."

With that, the king stands, naked and proud, and lifts me into his arms. I snuggle into his chest as he carries me away, exhaustion beginning to take its toll. "What does *Regina* mean?" I ask through a yawn.

Softly, he responds, "It means queen," before the consistent sway of his gait lulls me into a deep and restful sleep.

CHAPTER 32

$\mathcal{O}$nce again, I wake up alone on the comfy bed in the mundane room. Stretching, I wonder why the kings don't just allow me to sleep with them. What happens to them overnight that they don't want me to see? The old me would've considered that maybe they were embarrassed of me.

But after last night?

After sucking up my own pride to be rewarded with King Strix's version...I highly doubt that's the case. His power flows through me like a summer's breeze. I feel it coursing through my veins, my body growing stronger with his addition.

I'm hyperaware of the glorious ache between my legs, a reminder of the night we had together.

And what a night it was.

Never in my wildest dreams would I ever consider myself brazen or forward, but last night? Last night, I went for it. I took what I wanted and then some, and it was sublime.

Glancing around my room, I see nothing has changed. The soft gray walls are still stark and barren, the room almost empty save for a few vases filled with roses. Would it kill the kings to leave me a fucking wardrobe? I mean, seriously.

I have no intention of staying in my room today. I feel powerful, like I could take on the fucking world. Hell, maybe I will. I slip out of bed and begin to pace, noticing the cold air doesn't make me shiver like it once did. Even naked, I don't feel the urge to pull covers from the bed and wrap them around me.

Is that pride taking over? Or am I becoming more like them?

My stomach growls in hunger, but it's not food I want today. I feel desperate for more of the warm liquid flowing through the veins of my kings. I've had the pleasure of drinking from two of them already and want to know what the others taste like.

A growl emanates from my throat and my fangs descend from my gums. Power and energy surge through me. I feel like I could run for days and never tire. Like maybe I'd be quick enough to infiltrate my stolen castle and fuck with the evil bitch.

Hmm.

Could I do that? Am I fast enough? Strong enough?

Yes.

But I can't infiltrate the castle naked. I'll just have to grab something along the way.

Ripping open my door, I stride past the baffled guards, who don't even attempt to stop me, and jog down the hall-way. I try to remember the way out of here as I pass vampire after vampire staring hard at my bouncing tits as I move down the stairs. Let them fucking stare. Pride consumes me, knowing they want me.

After descending the staircase, I spot my chance at an outfit as two vampires go at it in a dark corner. Stepping near them, I pluck a discarded outfit off the floor and rush from the room. Once far enough away, I slip it over my head.

The female I took it from must be a servant, as the item is more or less a frock. The main part of the dress is a muted brown, except for a piece of white fabric across my chest. The dress covers my upper arms and hits just below my knees. Modest and inconspicuous, I should have no problem achieving my goals.

A sweet scent permeates the air and I recognize it as my envious King Ramsey. I need to get the fuck out of here. I'm sure by now he has caught onto my plan. I rush away from his fragrance and, using my nose, smell my way out of the castle. It's such an odd ability. Or maybe I've just never paid much attention to scents in my castle as they were often nauseating.

Keeping to the shadows, I let my long hair hang over my face and will myself to become invisible. The vampires of the coven are too busy drinking, fucking, and carrying on to notice me in absence of the kings. I grab a discarded cloak from a nearby bench and pull it on, lowering the hood down over my eyes.

The guards flanking the tall staircase sniff at me curiously, as if my own scent mixed with the one permeating off the hood don't quite mix, but they allow me to leave. I take a deep breath once I pass through the final door and into the party room.

The intense beat of the music has my head bobbing along with all the vampires dancing in here. Above the dance floor, three cages are filled with what I now know are donors, two women and one man, in various stages of dress.

I tear my eyes away from the sins of the flesh and focus on the door—my way out of here. Pulling my hood down, I reach the door when I hear a concerned voice call, "Sofi?"

I know I shouldn't look, I should just exit and not look

back. But I don't. Glancing over my shoulder, my eyes connect with Vincent's. He raises his hands in a "what the fuck are you doing" fashion. I shrug and walk out the door.

By the time I'm outside, I'm happy to see that it's almost nightfall. It will be much easier for me to sneak inside once the sun goes down behind the gray clouds.

Stepping out into the muted sun, my skin tingles, but not in a good way. It's almost as if I stepped too close to a fire and the heat licks at my skin. It doesn't quite burn, but almost does. I shift into the shadows, realizing it's not as bad there.

Keeping under awnings, I scurry down the narrow alleyway leading to the village square. I lurk near the exit, watching for villagers. I don't want to draw attention to myself.

The smell of a freshly burst raincloud fills my nose a moment before the raindrops kiss my skin. Still lurking in the alley, I tear off my cloak and throw my arms up in the air, dancing in the rain like I did as a little kid. The cold drops no longer chill me, instead, I find them refreshing.

My stolen dress is soon soaked, the fabric clinging to my skin as I jump and splash in the newly formed puddles. Lightning crackles and thunder booms, the electricity from the storm rolling through me, reminding me that I'm not here to dance in the rain. The sky darkens and I grab my cloak, swirling it around my shoulders before rushing around the perimeter of the vacant square. I keep my hood pulled low, my hair tucked inside the cloak.

Flashes of lightning surge across the sky as I run toward the newly built wall surrounding the village of Riverwood, looming up ahead. This was an obstacle I had forgotten I would come across. Guards are perched on raised platforms looking out toward my castle. But how do I get around them without being seen?

Think, Snow, think.

Then it dawns on me, I need a distraction.

Looking around, I see my out. I crouch down below a shrubbery, waiting until the guards aren't looking, then rush forward, tearing a torch from the wall before running around the side of the closest house, completely out of breath.

I wait for the sounds of alarm to ring out among the men, but with the thunder crashing and lightning streaking across the darkening sky, they don't even notice. Let's hope they are more alert to what I'm about to do next. I keep low, running between the houses, but stay close to the wall. The old, decrepit hut peeks its head up and I grin, knowing this is my chance. With its walls half fallen in, and its thatched roofing mostly blown off, it's the perfect place to burn to the ground.

Praying there's enough dry roofing material left to ignite, I creep through the gaping front door and set my torch down on a pile of dried thatching.

"Yes!" I whisper-shout when it kindles with ease. I toss a few more pieces of nearby lumber onto the flames then run back out. The broken-down hut is covered by a canopy of mature trees that have worked to keep the old house relatively dry. Back across the street, huddled between two houses, I watch and wait.

Smoke billows from the open spaces, and before too long, flames follow suit. In an extreme contrast, the once moisture rich air smelling of fresh rain now stinks of burning wood.

Perfect.

The alarm bell starts to ring and men begin to shout. I need to be careful. The town's male volunteers will be exiting their homes to see who needs assistance.

"Fire! Fire at the abandoned hut!" a voice shouts. "Quick! Quick! Get the buckets!"

I know by now that pails of water are being collected.

Some are scattered around the ground to catch rainwater, while others are being filled from the well.

Feeling enough time has passed, I sneak back around to the wall, hiding against the side of the nearest home and watching with a smile as the two men manning the gate disperse to help.

I hover for a minute, making sure my path is clear, before running forward and unlocking the gate. As quickly as I can, I scurry through and shut it behind me, then take off at a full run toward my castle.

It's such an odd feeling as I near it. The place is filled with a mix of emotions. On one hand, I lived there with my father, which makes me love it. But that was only the first four years of my life. Then the evil cunt bitch came along and destroyed everything. The past two decades have been murder. I love and hate this place.

Aware what fucking pussies the queen's guards are, I know they will be inside shivering from the cold rain. The queen has been stupid, ignorant even, thinking she's fucking untouchable. Most of the entrances aren't even locked or guarded, because who in their right fucking mind would want to enter this castle of doom?

Me, that's who.

Maybe I've lost my mind.

Maybe I've become drunk on pride and envy over the past few days.

Or maybe I just want my fucking castle back.

It's time for some payback, bitch.

This time of day is when the queen dines alone, sitting at the short end of a long table filled with fresh cuisine. She picks through each one, making sure she's at least touched every item, before choosing to fill her belly with her precious wine.

After grabbing an apple from the orchard, I enter through

the last door I escaped from, the one that leads up a flight of stairs to the second floor where my room is. My legs used to tremble climbing these steps, but now, even as I reach the top, I feel like I could climb them over and over again.

I crouch by the door leading into the hallway and listen for sounds, sniff for smells, and extend my senses for any iota of another's proximity, but perceive nothing. I curl my fingers around the handle and pull the door inward, peeking through. The halls are dark and vacant.

Fucking perfect.

I hurry inside and pass the empty rooms before coming to mine. I hadn't intended on visiting it, but now that I'm near I can't help but enter. The space looks just as it did the day I left it, sparse and untouched. The same bedding lies tossed around the bed from when I got out at the servants' request. The same vanity stands with all my perfume bottles, but dust coats the top now.

How long have I been gone?

I shiver at the thought. I've had no sense of time down in the cavern castles. With no change in light from day to night, it's impossible to tell how much time has passed. I couldn't even guess how long it's been, but by the dust, I'd say at least two weeks. Maybe more.

With no time to dwell on the length of time passed, standing inside my old prison, I leave my room and patter down the hallway on bare feet. I come to the double set of stairs that lead down to the first floor and start my descent slowly, listening for guards, smelling for their foul scents as I go.

Again, this space is unguarded. Ahead of me lies the throne room and beyond that the queen's dining area. Veering a sharp left, I hurry down the once grand hallway lined with my elders' portraits and come to a door.

Her door.

The room, once occupied by my mother, is now infected with the evil from the current cunt bitch. My fingers twitch at my sides as I reach for the handle and turn it with ease. I'm surprised she doesn't have this room, her private quarters, protected by at least one guard.

But then it dawns on me—every single person in this fucking castle is bespelled by her. Yellow eyes have replaced the soft browns, gentle greens, and bright blues of the staff. No one would dare enter.

I take a step inside, having no plan, no idea what I'm about to do. My breath hitches as I look around, finding it almost exactly the same as it was when I snuck in here as a child. The massive table is still in the middle, the ancient cauldron sitting atop in the center. Shelves of glass jars filled with ingredients still line the walls.

And then I see it.

The braided, tasseled rope that, once pulled, will slide open the purple velvet curtains hiding the queen's mirror.

A malicious grin cleaves my face. This is my moment. My chance to get back at her before I'm strong enough to take on her magic.

With a trembling hand, I pull the rope. I gasp when the curtains retract, and I'm face to face with the gilded mirror. Even though I hate what it stands for, I can appreciate its beauty. Whomever made this was a true craftsman, an artist. Shame I have to destroy it.

Looking around the room for something to bash it in with, I almost jump out of my skin when a voice speaks to me.

"I had wondered if we would meet again someday.

But that day never came, much to my dismay."

My chest heaves as I turn back around and confront the mirror. "I have nothing to say to you. After today, you'll be nothing but a pile of rubble." I watch in half awe, half horror as the glass becomes a swirling, dark mist and a male face forms. But he doesn't look mean like I remember, instead he looks sad.

"Your threat is more of a blessing, my dear.

You were not the only prisoner here."

Suddenly, my throat runs dry and I take a step closer. "Y-You mean, you don't want to be here either?" I don't know why I had never considered that. This mirror can't pick itself up and move, it doesn't have legs to run away. Instead, it's been stuck behind the curtains of a mad woman for God knows how long.

"I do not wish to serve the queen.

I have been forced, while remaining unseen."

I inch forward another step. "How long have you been stuck in there, may I ask?"

The smoke face's brows furrow, its lips turning down in a frown.

"It is hard to tell time from within this prison.

But I've seen several queens murdered while another has risen."

The evil bitch.

My fists clench at my sides, recalling what the kings told me, that this fucking cunt killed my own mother, the previous queen. "She will pay for what she's done. I won't allow it to stand much longer. I'll be strong enough to fight her soon." I don't know why I'm telling him this. He could easily turn around and tell the evil bitch what I've done, though my instincts say that's not true.

He nods his head.

"Soon, I agree, you will transform.

This is the calm before the storm."

How very fucking true.

"I'm so sorry, mirror, but I have to destroy you. I can't allow her to abuse your power any longer.

He nods his head slowly, understanding written all over his smoky face.

"I've yearned for death for years and years.

It's living, now, that causes my fears.

So do what you must, but remember this.

When the time is right, you must succumb to the bliss.

For in life there is death, and in death there is life.

You can't have your victory without heartache and strife.

So take heed of my words as I wish you farewell.

The others will follow, once freed of her spell."

His final word spoken, the man in the mirror inclines his head in respect, and I'm completely overwhelmed. Tears trickle down my face in anger, in absolute fury, as his eyes close, accepting his fate. My chest squeezes painfully. How could someone imprison a sentient being inside a pane of glass for years with no end, with no change in scenery, and no one to talk to? It's torture. It's heartbreaking to think he's been alone except for the insanity of the queen.

I startle when his eyes fly open, the vacant black orbs staring right through me, but seeing something else entirely.

"She's coming, move quickly, not a second to waste.

Put aside your emotion, do it now, make haste!"

I become frantic, looking for a weapon. I head over to the table and grab the handles of the cauldron, seeing if I can lift the massive item. With my new muscles I'm able to hoist it from the table.

"May you rest in peace," I say, before heaving the heavy cauldron into the glass.

The man in the mirror mutters, "Fairest of them all," his smoky face at total peace as it smashes into thousands of shards that fly across the room.

I did it. I fucking did it. The mirror is no more.

Realizing my time is almost up, I add one final touch. Reaching into my pocket, I pull out the stolen apple.

A green apple.

I take one, juicy bite and set it down in front of the broken mirror then jog toward the door.

I fling it open and run into the hallway just as the queen is turning the corner.

"You!" she seethes, pointing a long finger at me.

"Fuck you, cunt bitch," I shout, before dashing up the stairs. She roars, her magic crashing into the wall behind me. I'm too quick for her to catch.

I run down the empty hall, looking through the rooms for one without bars on the windows. I start to panic when I realize they are all boarded up. But I don't quit, I push myself down past my room, rip the door guarding the stairs off its hinges, and practically fly down the steps.

At the bottom, I tear the door open and startle when a crowd of yellow-eyed guards stands waiting for me.

Shit.

I cry out as hands grip me, as rope is bound around my wrists and secured around my neck. I growl as a hand slaps the side of my face while another pulls my hair, all the while taunting me with their vile words. Then realization settles in and tears mist my vision.

I've been caught.

Captured.

I'll be the queen's prisoner once again.

I tug and pull with all my might, but even with my new strength I can't get them off of me. My sins, envy and pride, do me no good here with bespelled guards restraining me.

"Come on, beast, back to the dungeons for you. I've got a nice, comfy spot already chosen for you." I recognize the nauseating voice as Gerard's.

"Fuck you, Gerard," I sneer.

"Soon, beast, but I'll wait until the queen is done with you. It's not as fun when you're always fighting back."

His words threaten to break me. "No!" I cry out, tugging harder as they drag me around the castle.

"You hear something?" another guard asks the others, looking around the castle grounds. Everyone stops and listens. Through the rumbles of thunder, a new sound emerges.

Howls.

They sound haunted, sad, and angry all at the same time. I narrow my eyes, looking through the darkness that's settled over the land.

"Oh shit, wolves!" another guard shouts. "Hurry! Get this bitch inside!"

At first, I think he's full of shit. We haven't had wolves in these parts for as long as I can remember. But sure enough around a hundred wolves are barreling toward us.

But they aren't just normal wolves. They're enormous. Black, gray, and white with spikes protruding from their backs, the wolves charge forward, snarling and growling. Drool and foam drip from their maws as their teeth gnash at us. I can't say why, but I have absolutely no fear of them and find them terrifyingly beautiful.

Maybe it's because I've made peace with myself and have already accepted death.

Or maybe it's something more profound.

Snarling rips through the air as a huge beast descends on a guard holding me. Its gaping maw clenches over the guard's neck, ripping it out of his body. Another wolf attacks Gerard. I smile ferally as he meets the same fate. One by one the guards drop like flies until I'm standing alone, surrounded by massive wolves, with blood dripping from their mouths.

"You won't hurt me," I whisper, reaching out a hand to the nearest and largest one. I jump back when it...*changes.*

The long snout and ears retract into its head. The fur melts from its body as skin takes its place.

"What the…" I mumble as the large animal shifts into a vampire, a very naked vampire. Tall and handsome, with a broad chest, stern jaw, and a body filled with powerful muscles, King Thorin towers above me. His gray eyes pierce through mine, anger flashing in his gaze. He grinds his teeth and looks down his nose at me. He stands with one hand crossed under his opposite arm, stroking his thick beard with his free hand. He looks menacing. He looks pissed. Feral even. I tremble in fear.

"You are in big trouble, little one." His deep voice rumbles through me and I shiver at his dark promise. He takes a step closer to me and I crane my neck to keep eye contact with the large man. His hand reaches out, his fingers slithering around my neck. "Your ass is mine. It's time you learned what it means to be the harbinger of wrath."

CHAPTER 33

The trip back to the castle was nothing but a blur. I'm not even sure if I was carried in someone's arms or the gaping jaws of a massive wolf. The thunder raged overhead, lightning fissuring across the sky. But I couldn't focus on anything else but my racing heart.

His dark threat taunted me.

You're in big trouble, little one...

Your ass is mine...

Harbinger of wrath...

Even now, hanging by my wrists from a darkened ceiling, my toes just grazing the ground, I still don't know what to expect. I don't know if I've been here a few minutes or hours already. I can't see much, just the wall several feet in front of me made with layers of stone. Shadows flicker on the wall and a warmth heats my back, telling me that there is a fire behind me.

My damp dress clings to me, my hair sticking to my face. But it's my wrists that are driving me nuts. They ache. I flex my fingers, trying to keep them from going numb, while also trying to keep my breathing under control.

I've tried to use my new strength to pull myself down from the rafters, to force my hands through the shackles, but nothing has worked. And I'm so very tired. My escape from the coven and sneaking into my old castle has taken a toll on me. All I want is food—or blood—and my big, comfy bed. But something tells me I won't be getting either for quite some time.

The longer I hang here, the more I wonder if I imagined King Thorin rescuing me. Hell, maybe the queen has me in her dungeons and I'm fucked up on some type of drug. Maybe that was all a hallucination.

Looking deep inside myself, I can sense Kings Ramsey and Strix. Both feel anxious, angry, and perturbed. No doubt I'm the cause of their turmoil. I'm not sorry about it. The trip ended better than I could have ever expected. I went to the castle with no plan in mind, just wanting to fuck with the queen. And I left having destroyed her precious mirror and watching her cock sucking guards die horrifically.

It was so fucking worth it.

So I'll hang here as long as I have to, accepting the pain, allowing it to make me feel alive.

A shift in the air has me stilling. The masculine scent of leather accompanied by blood filters to my nose, the token scent of King Thorin.

"Tsk, tsk, tsk. You are indeed in trouble, little one." His deep voice is relaxed, his composure more frightening than if he were screaming at me. The calm before the storm...

"How dare you leave the coven and not tell a single king. What the fuck were you thinking?" he growls, his voice escalating up a notch. "You alone are the future of my kingdom and yours. You are the last vessel, our final chance for changing the fate of not only our people, but potentially the future of the entire world!" I hear his footsteps pacing behind me, his anger rolling off him in waves. "And what did you do with that knowledge? Did you submit to your kings as promised and keep yourself safe? No! You fucking fled, alone and virtually defenseless, without one fucking weapon to arm yourself, and nothing to protect you but skin and bone and a stolen fucking dress!"

Shit. I never thought of it that way. I was so consumed by hurting the queen that I never even considered the ramifications if I was caught or killed in the process. "I-I'm—"

"What? Sorry? Too little too late, princess."

"But nothing happened," I retort quietly.

A rush of cool air hits me a second before his muscled body presses against my back, his large hand reaching around to cup my throat. "Nothing happened? Are you blind? Did you not find yourself in the clutches of the queen's guard? Did you not see the huntsmen coming to her aid? Did you fall asleep when I had to reveal the existence of my wrath vampires to save your fucking ass?"

The huntsmen were coming? I hang my head in defeat. Of course they would have been. And I had no idea that his wolf people, vampire things were a secret, but why didn't I just ask? It makes so much sense now why wolves aren't seen in Riverwood, it's because King Thorin made it so.

"I'm such a fool." My voice is but a whisper.

His fingers tighten around my neck and he shakes me a little bit. "Not a fool, little one, but a person who has done something foolish. And for that, you must suffer." His hands leave me and I gasp when I'm spun to face him. His gray eyes have a glint of malice and excitement in them.

The wrath king smiles with intent and grips my dress in his hands. His smile widens a moment before he tears it from my body in one quick motion, baring my nakedness underneath.

"Much better. Now there is nothing between me and you

302

but the heated air." His fingers trail up and down my sides before rubbing the under sides of my breasts. Just his gentle touch has my insides clenching, my skin blazing under his fingertips. But I'm also guarded. If there's one thing I've sensed about this king, it's that he'd like a little pain with his pleasure.

"What are you going to do to me?" I ask, breathlessly.

He bites his lower lip and twists my nipples, making me cry out. "Whatever I want, little one."

He takes a few steps back and gestures behind him. Only now do I see the many devices lurking in the dark corners of the room, the whips, collars, and chains hanging from the walls. This isn't a dungeon.

It's a torture chamber.

"A-Are you going to hurt me?" I fucking hate how weak I sound.

He chuckles deeply and walks to the wall, plucking off a short whip with dozens of tassels on the end measuring around a foot long. "Yes, princess, but you will enjoy the pain I give you." He walks back over to me, raises the whip, and drags the leather strands across my breasts. The leather is supple, worn, and feels soft against my skin. But I know better. When lashed across me, it will sting fiercely. "Your skin is so pale, so flawless. I am very much looking forward to seeing how stunning you look with my whip marks striped across your body."

King Thorin begins to pace, his heavy footsteps echoing off the close walls. "Now where to begin…here, perhaps?" The whip rubs along my ass. "Here?" He drags it up my spine. "Or should I give your perfect breasts attention first? I do love to watch how they bounce when you walk. What movements will the whip elicit from them, I wonder…"

I shiver at the thought of his whip, wondering if it will

slice into me like the duke has so many times. I shriek when the weapon's tassels slash across my breasts, stinging my nipples. "I am nothing like her. Never compare me with the one, true evil in this world." Another lash strikes, and I jerk my head to the side, making sure it doesn't reach my face. I'm surprised when I enjoy his ministrations. The whip hurts, yes, but it also feels good.

That arousing sensation deep inside me starts to warm. "You like it, don't you? Are you a pain slut like Marcel? Do you enjoy this feeling I can give you? One of pain mixed with utter pleasure?"

Wah-pshhh!

"Answer me!"

"Yes!" I cry out. I want to be angry with him for subjecting me to this, but I can't. The years of torture, of suffering the kiss of the duke, must have fucked me up, because this…this feels good.

"I watched you once, suffering under the hands of that evil bitch, strung up naked, just like now. That woman tortured you, blood was dripping down your pale skin, but you didn't let it beat you. Instead, you beat her by finding your euphoria. You can do it again."

"But that was—"

"Silence!" He prowls behind me and lays half a dozen lashes across my ass. "Do not speak unless spoken to. The only sounds that should be erupting from your plump lips are grunts of pain or moans of pleasure. Nod if you understand."

I do as ordered.

"Good girl." The king moves, placing himself in front of me once more. "You have no idea how hard it's been, little one," he purrs, tucking the whip into his belt and caressing my breasts with his large hands. "How challenging it's been to know what you are, see you stripped naked, to watch you be beaten yet unable to intervene..."

"W-What am I?"

"Mine," he growls, before descending on my nipple. His mouth feels warm on the hardened bud. I moan as his tongue flicks over it, up and down, over and over. Licking and sucking, nipping with his teeth. My pussy clenches, wetness already leaking from my core.

"These nipples. These perfect fucking nipples. Always rosy. Always hard and plump and oh so sexy. You taunt me with these, my tongue desperate to lick them, my teeth aching to pierce them with my fangs..." He trails off as he moves to my other side, giving that nipple the same treatment. My chest tightens from this one simple action, my cunt ready to fucking explode.

I moan loudly, my head thrown back in pleasure, my legs wrapped around him as I shamelessly grind my pussy against him. Just before I come, he skims down my erect bud with his teeth, grazing the sensitive skin. Then, in a flash, he's moved. One of my legs is yanked up toward my ear and the whip crashes against my pussy.

"Oh God!" I cry out, the sting feeling amazing on my lower lips. Again, the leather kisses me. I moan, my heart races, and another gush of wetness leaks from inside me.

"Just look at this wet fucking pussy, little one." Keeping my leg raised, my cunt spread before him, he dips a finger inside me then swirls it around my clit. "So needy, and I've barely fucking touched you yet." He tosses the whip behind him and sinks to his knees in front of me, throwing my legs over his broad shoulders before his lips smash into my pussy.

"Fuck yes," I moan, wrapping my legs around him and thrusting my hips against his face. The king is skilled with his tongue, diving it deep inside me only to draw it out and circle my clit. He moans into my pussy, the vibrations making my clit fucking throb with arousal. I'm so close. So fucking close.

Again he leaves me just before I come, and I cry out in despair. "Please, King Thorin. Please. I can't take it anymore."

"You can and you will." The vampire king spanks my wet pussy, the sting making me howl with delight before he drops my legs. Using his vamp speed, he unhooks me from the ceiling and tosses me onto a high but small table. Before I can even sit up, my arms are secured above my head and my ankles are bound to the table's legs, my ass perched just on the end.

"Actually," he mutters, his eyes trailing down my body while he strokes his beard. In the blink of an eye, he's moved my legs, securing them behind my knees and up to the table's legs under my head, leaving my thighs spread open. I can't fucking move.

"There. Now I can play with this juicy cunt properly. Can you feel that, little one? Your cunt is pulsing with need. So fucking sexy."

The gorgeous king's muscles ripple as he reaches for the hem of his shirt and rips it up over his head, showing off rows of defined abdominal muscles, and chiseled pecs. The hulking vampire king looks like he's been carved from a fucking rock. He's so huge compared to me. My protector.

A wolf.

I lick my lips, watching him. He removes his belt next. He looks so fucking hot. The bulge in his pants makes my mouth water. He laughs when he catches me staring. His gray eyes bore into mine as he folds the leather strap in half, then snaps it against the table. "Would you like to feel my belt on your cunt, princess? You want to feel the sting on your spread pussy lips, on your swollen clit?"

Fuck, his dirty words make me so hot. I can feel my pussy clenching, pulsing with desire. "Yes," I rasp out.

The king bites his lip as he trails the belt over my lower lips and up my belly to my tits. "Here?" he inquires, rubbing the leather over my nipples.

"Please," I beg. I don't care what he needs to do. Beat me, hurt me, just give me what I need.

He palms my breast, kneading it roughly before tugging on my nipple. "You want to see my cock, princess? You will soon. I'm going to stuff your greedy cunt so fucking full, you won't be able to walk right for days."

Before I can respond, he rears back and slashes the belt down across my breast, right on my nipple. My back arches off the table, a scream leaving my lips. Before I can dwell on the pain, my nipple is in his mouth, alleviating the burn.

It falls out of his lips with a pop. His eyes glance to my other breast. "No!" I cry out a second too late. The folded belt smacks hard into my chest, my breast jiggling from the impact. Again he sucks my nipple into his mouth, soothing the pain.

"Just one more place, little one, and I'll let you see the monster inside my pants. Can you handle it just one more time? I have to spank this cunt of yours before I lose my mind."

He walks back down between my legs, his finger sliding inside me with ease. "Your cunt wraps around me so beautifully. Let's add another finger." I feel the change when a second digit begins fucking me alongside the first. If anything, it feels better than before, and I close my eyes and moan in response.

Just when I think he's going to give me my release, his fingers pull out and the belt smacks my pussy.

My clit burns, my pussy lips sting, and my nipples peak from the pain. His warm mouth quickly replaces the burn, licking and sucking on my clit as his fingers enter me again.

I groan when another digit joins the first two, stretching

me more than ever before. It hurts but feels glorious. I watch, panting, as the vampire king puckers his lips and sucks on my throbbing clit before turning his pale gray eyes up to meet my gaze.

The orgasm takes me by force, exploding through me. My spine bows, my toes curl, and my fingers clench into fists. My eyes seal closed as a high-pitched scream exits my lips, my cunt squeezing on the king's fingers.

King Thorin laps at my clit until the orgasm runs its course. I lie pliant and limp on the table, no longer fighting the restraints.

"Just look at you. So exposed and perfect. Pale skin marked with red from my hand, nipples hard and rosy, cunt glistening. You've done well, princess. It's time to take your king."

My lids slide open as he drops his pants to the floor. His mammoth cock bobs in the air, thicker and longer than the first two kings. I don't know if it will fit inside me.

The king must see the worry on my face. "It will fit, princess, and it will feel so good. Every time I give you pain, you can expect immense pleasure."

The king slides his veined cock up and down my slit, coating it in my own climax before lining it up. His hands curl around my thighs as he inches inside me.

"Oh fuck," I rasp out, having never felt so full before.

"I can't fuck you yet, little one, you're only halfway there."

I lick my lips and tear my gaze away, trying to focus on anything else as I stare at the rafters. A spank lands across my breast and I jolt at the sensation.

"Don't you dare delve into the dark corners of your mind while I fuck you. Stay here with me. Watch my cock as it sinks into you. See how good your cunt takes your king."

My eyes once again focus on where we are joined. The

king inches in, then slides out a bit before thrusting in deeper. Farther and farther inside me he pushes.

"Your cunt stretches so beautifully, princess. You're about to swallow me whole. You should be so fucking proud right now."

Just when I think I can't take any more, when I'm about to beg for him to stop, I realize he's not moving. I look up to his face and see a victorious grin. "It's all the way in. I'll give you a moment to adjust." Still buried inside me, the king leans down and takes my mouth.

His tongue is larger than the others', just like his cock, but his movements don't feel sloppy or uncontrolled. King Thorin kisses me with authority, licking and tasting as he pleases. I moan into his mouth as one hand grips my breast before rolling and tugging on my nipple.

With our mouths still connected, he begins to move. He starts off slow as our kiss grows deeper, needier. My cunt is deliciously filled as he slips out and slides back in. The motion of his tongue matches his cock, fucking me with both at the same time.

His fingers pinch harder on my nipple as his hips work faster, his tongue plunging deeper into my mouth. I curse the fact that I'm bound, as I would like to claw my nails down his back, thread my fingers into his hair, and pull him tight against me. The king growls into my mouth, and a moment later my binds are released.

It happened so fast I didn't even see it.

He sits up and holds my thighs open as I lower my arms from above my head. He slaps one breast, then the other, his pace quickening. My spine arches into his touch, my nipples hard, begging for another sting from his hand. He grants me my wish, slapping both tits at the same time, until I'm crying out, "Yes! Fuck yes!"

The king leans down, running his nose along my neck

309

before he whispers in my ear, "You want to hurt me, little one? Fucking do it. I want you to." Then he bites me, his fangs sinking deep into my skin, and I come instantly. My fingers weave through his hair, forcing him to stay latched onto me.

I keep coming and coming as he drinks, my cunt clenching on his length buried inside me.

"My turn," I whisper, pulling on his hair. The king lifts his lips reluctantly, blood dripping from his fangs.

So.

Fucking.

Hot.

Reaching back, I slap King Thorin right across his cheek. His face whips to the side, blood flying from his lips.

His eyes roll back into his head with desire before he fixes his glazed eyes on me, a grin pulling at his lips. "Take my sin, princess. It is yours." The bearded king turns his head to the side, offering me his neck as he pumps harder and deeper inside of me. I feel my fangs descend, my eyes fixed on his pulsing vein before I strike. I growl into his skin, my nails digging into his back for grip, my legs wrapping around him, wanting his huge cock buried inside me.

I feel his anger, his wrath, pouring from him and into me. I feel bigger, stronger, like I could take on any opponent and kill them with one hand. He tastes like wine, tart and a little bitter with a tang of sweetness. I clench him harder and he moans then growls as he reaches his climax, his cum shooting inside me.

"Enough, little one," he rumbles, when he finally stops fucking me. But I don't stop until his fingers curl around my throat and he forces me to.

Blood drips down my lips and over my chin as my eyes get heavy.

"You were perfect. A true submissive. A perfect queen."

My heart warms at his praise, and I snuggle into his chest as he picks me up and carries me off. I know I'll be asleep long before we reach my room. But one thing I know for sure, I'll be sleeping with an ache between my legs and a huge smile on my face.

CHAPTER 34

*I*t's so nice waking up and not having to worry about who might be watching, which guards are standing sentry at the door to my room, or if the evil bitch is on her way to punish or humiliate me. Here, in the castles of the vampire kings, everything is so different.

Reaching high over my head, I stretch my arms, twisting by body to crack my hips, then flex and point my toes. The sheet covering me slips to my waist and I look down, appreciating the faint red streaks crossing my pale skin. If I thought my healing was accelerated before, that was nothing compared to this.

King Thorin's whip felt so different from the duke, even though the wielder in both cases was looking to inflict pain. The wrath king's whip did sting, but it also felt good. I can't explain it. It's like my mind was able to twist the sensation of pain and make it pleasurable. It was euphoric. It was *hot*. It was nothing like anything I could have imagined.

Yes, King Thorin had me bound, my body splayed before him, but unlike when the evil bitch had done it, this time I *wanted* it. I wanted to feel his wrath. I wanted the bite of the

312

ropes holding me down. The pain made me feel alive, my muscles relaxing in anticipation of the next strike instead of tensing to thwart it.

I wonder what the other four have planned for me...

So many ideas filter through my mind. I did love being tied up, and I also loved fucking while others watched. Maybe I could get into voyeurism more? I got a taste of it with the envy king, but I had no idea what was going on other than the immense jealousy raging through me.

A knock on the door has my head jerking toward it. Hoping it's one of the kings, I sit up in bed, leaning back against the plush pillows with my arms stretched out to my sides and my tits out, and I raise my gaze toward the door.

"Come in," I call in a singsong voice. My excitement recedes when Vincent enters. Not that I don't love seeing him, but I was hoping to fuck something again soon. I think I'm quickly becoming an addict to it. Vincent's gaze immediately focuses on my exposed breasts, not that I blame him. Who doesn't love a gorgeous pair of tits, am I right?

"Avert your eyes, Vincent," I scold, not making any move to cover up. I watch his head almost quiver, like unseen hands are urging it to move, before he turns away. Then it dawns on me. "Did...did you just obey a command from me?"

Vincent growls, still focused on the wall ahead of me. "Not by choice. I take it you are now the proud owner of either Wrath or Greed?"

"King Thorin and I—"

"Yeah, yeah," Vincent interrupts, folding his arms across the chest of his crisp, white shirt. "Save me from the gory details."

"It wasn't gory," I defend. "I mean, maybe it was a little bit but—"

His hands shoot to his ears. "Stop it, please, princess. I can't handle the temptation. I'm barely hanging on as it is."

Realizing I've been a complete asshole, I apologize. "I'm so sorry, Vincent." I cover myself up, pulling the covers back over my chest. "You may look now." His head swivels toward me, his eyes landing on my covered chest with a mixture of relief and disappointment. "Why did you ask if either King Thorin or King Marcel gave me their sin?"

"Because," Vincent starts, walking toward me, "I drank from both kings. Therefore, I respond to commands from either of them."

"But you don't have their sin to command?"

He shakes his head. "No. Not like you do. They have to offer that freely. And, my dear, that is something they hold sacred. Other than with you, their gifts have never been shared."

I chew on my lip. "And since I have drunk from King Thorin, I am, by default, able to control you."

He nods. "It's more like you can compel me to obey, I don't want to misbehave. None of us like disappointing our kings. I imagine the same notion will go even further with you once you become queen."

Queen.

I shake my head and rub my eyes. The notion is still so unbelievable. My whole life, I thought I'd die by the hands of the evil bitch before I had the opportunity to kill her or escape. Now things are so different. Not only do I have the opportunity to become a vampire queen, but potentially Queen of Riverwood again too.

Vincent perches on the end of my bed, a concerned look on his face. "What's going through your mind, princess?"

I sigh. "Where do I begin? This life, this chance I've been given, it's just so unbelievable."

"Well, start believing it. Because the ramifications of your choices are upon you. It has already begun. The winds of change are blowing across your lands. The vampires can sense it. Your people can sense it. The evil queen—"

"Bitch. Evil bitch," I interrupt.

Vincent grins. "Yes, my dear. Even she can tell a force is mounting against her."

"I destroyed her magic mirror, Vincent. It has to have weakened her."

He reaches for my foot and gives it a squeeze. "I was there, you know, one of the wolves with King Thorin. The queen—"

"Evil bitch," I correct.

"Evil bitch... She was completely manic. Her powers were wild and uncontrolled. She was spewing dark magic everywhere, hitting nothing and everything. We didn't lose a single vampire that night. That should never have happened."

"Really?" Hope fills my voice. "I can feel my powers growing. I just pray that once I finish my transformation, as the kings call it, that I'll be strong enough to defeat her."

"You will be stronger, but most of all, you will fight smarter. The evil bitch is crass. She's drunk on power, blinded by her hatred for you. She will make mistakes, and by her reaction to her magic mirror, she's already begun to show signs of stupidity, of weakness."

I nod my head. "You are right. I was shocked when she didn't have a single guard protecting her room and her precious fucking mirror. She's too pompous to think another would possibly cross her to even think of having a sentry by her most prized possession."

"Don't you see, Princess Snow? That is because of you."

I scrunch my face in confusion. "What do you mean?"

He smiles. "It's obvious, isn't it? After you were rescued, she felt humiliated. Nothing the likes of that has ever happened to her before. But instead of learning from her errors, she chose to ignore it, acting as if it never happened. Her nonchalance cost the evil bitch her cherished mirror. And now, she will have to fight at the weakest she's ever been."

Excitement brews inside me. "I want to go now! Fuck it. Why wait for the transformation? Let's attack her while she's still reeling from my invasion."

Vincent laughs and puts his hands up in a placating fashion. "Whoa! Hold on there a minute. We definitely should wait until you've become queen. But even if we didn't, you can't go there now. It's still daytime."

"So?"

Vincent scoffs, "So? Don't you know anything about being a vampire yet?" I glare at him and cross my arms. "Lesson number one—we can't fucking go outside in the daytime. Even through the thick clouds, our skin burns."

I think back on the legends I've grown up learning, the stories passed down through generations. None of them mention the lurkers being unable to walk in daylight.

"I can see the wheels turning in your mind. But for a moment, reflect on every time you saw a vampire, one of your famed lurkers... Were they in the shadows? Under cover of a tree's canopy? Were they always hooded and cloaked, most if not all of their skin covered and protected?"

"They were," I agree. "I never thought there could be a reason behind it. I just thought they wanted to remain mysterious, unseen from the public eye."

"Well, that is also true. They did not wish to be found by just anyone, princess, only by one, very special person."

"Me." He nods, clasping his hands on his lap. "So how is it that I'm still able to walk in the light? I remember a slight tingling on my skin, but not burning."

"You are not a vampire," he says matter-of-factly. "Just because you've earned a sin does not make you one of us."

"I guess it doesn't," I deflate.

"Don't be upset. Your transformation has already begun. It's only a matter of time now."

I sigh. "I know." I think about all he's told me and an idea forms in my head, something Katie once mentioned about a drone. "Vincent?"

"Hmm?"

"Can I use my powers, once I have them, to strengthen the people of Riverwood? Can they, too, drink blood without becoming vampires?"

Vince slides from the bed, tugging his black jacket closed. "That, my dear, is a question for the kings."

"Then that's who I shall ask." I throw the covers from my body and slip from the bed, no longer afraid or wanting to hide my body, and ignore the way Vincent looks at me. Let him fucking look. "Thank you for visiting, Vincent. I always enjoy our talks. But if you'll excuse me, I have some kings to summon."

Lying in the hot water Renee has just brought in, I drip some lilac scented oils into the bathtub and bask in the heat. It feels so good on my skin, cleansing and healing me from the outside. I have my hair twisted on top of my head, held together with the rose tipped hairpin.

I let out a groan as I sink deeper, taking a drink of the wine on the small table next to me. I let my eyes close and think about the three vampires who have given me their sin.

Ramsey.

Strix.

Thorin.

I need to learn how to invade their mind as they have mine. Allowing every muscle I have to ease in the water, my body relaxes as well as my mind. Inhaling the lilac scented mist calms me, and soon I'm almost falling asleep.

No, Snow. You've slept enough.

The mind is a funny thing, providing you with useless information at the drop of a hat. But when there is something you need to find in there, it becomes more difficult than finding a needle in a haystack.

I try and imagine my mind as a long hallway dotted with doors along its walls. Each wall contains a new mystery to discover. I squeeze my eyes shut, trying to picture each door as one of the kings. Four remain shrouded in black and gray tones, while three shine brightly before me.

I go for the green one first, pushing it open with my thoughts. I almost growl when I see behind it. I'm inside King Ramsey's head, seeing what he sees. My envy king is eating, but not the way humans do. His lips are wrapped around the neck of a donor, his crimson hair falling over her face. I don't need to see her reaction to know what his bite is doing to her, because I have felt it before. Even though, rationally, I know he has to eat just like I do, I'm still insanely jealous. The only person who should ever get the pleasure of having those lips upon their body is me.

Come to me, King Ramsey.

I watch him still, release the girl, and toss her aside, his eyes searching the feeding room he's in.

Leave her and come to me at once. Bring King Lucian with you.

The king pulls out a hanky from his pocket and wipes his mouth before saying, *I am coming, flower,* in his mind.

Satisfied, I pull out of his head and search the hallway for the next door. I come to the red one next and shove it open. My wrath king is naked and looking in an ornate mirror. I can only see down to his abdomen before his reflection is lost by the mirror's edge, but his body is dripping with water, making me want to lick every hill and valley along his chiseled abdomen.

He glances to his left, looking into another mirror, but this one reflects the image of King Marcel. The greed king is manicuring his short beard, notching the harsh angles with the blade of a razor. His dark eyes flash when they meet King Thorin's in the mirror and a smug grin crosses his lips.

The wrath king pulls his gaze from King Marcel's reflection and looks back at himself. A razor is in his hand and he's rinsing it in a bowl of water, having freshly trimmed his thick beard. His gray eyes almost see into my soul as he looks at his reflection.

Come to me, King Thorin, and bring King Marcel with you.

In the mirror, I see his eyes widen before becoming stern once more. He nods. *I will be there soon, little one.*

Confident he will do what he says, I pull from his mind and enter the corridor once more. King Strix's purple door is easy to find, bright and shining even in my mind.

I ease it open and find myself looking at King Killian and another absolutely gorgeous man whom I've not yet met. The stranger almost glows with beauty. Lush ringlets of long black hair cascade past his shoulders. Arctic blue eyes, the same shade as the bluest sky, are deeply set in the man's face. But when he smiles, flashing bright teeth behind full lips, I almost melt, and I'm not even with him.

King Strix's eyes flutter between the two vampires sitting opposite him, a view I could watch for days. Too bad I can't see the King of Pride as well. The three of them would be magnificent to watch together. King Killian speaks, though I can't hear what he says, and the other two vampires laugh, my vision bobbing as King Strix joins in.

Come to me, King Strix. Find me, and bring Kings Killian and Dante with you.

Through King Strix's eyes, I see his fist clench on the

319

armrest of his chair and feel his head nod. *We are coming, Regina.*

Content that my king is coming, I pull from his mind and backtrack through the hallway. I look longingly at the darkened doors on the opposite side of the hall. Soon they will be open to me too, and I can explore them at my every whim.

Opening my eyes, I reach for my glass and take another sip of wine before closing them again and burying myself deep in the water. A sudden shift in the air has my body stilling, my heart racing. A week ago, I might not have noticed the change, but everything I am is becoming more and more aware, my senses heightened.

Their scents assault me, sweet and spicy, fresh honey…

A soft hand grabs my foot and begins to rub it as another set kneads my shoulders.

"This is a pleasant surprise, pet," King Lucian coos. "Already naked and ready for us. Simply stunning, isn't she, Ramsey?"

"Delectable," the king behind me purrs, his nose running along my neck. "To what do we owe this pleasure?"

Uhh. Did I have a reason for bringing them here?

My mind is feeling a bit foggy as desire swirls around me like a wind tunnel. I open my eyes to see King Lucian pulling my leg from the water before dotting soft kisses from my ankle toward my knee, while King Ramsey sucks on the tender skin in the crook of my neck.

Fuck, this is so hot.

Loud footfalls announce the others have arrived. Kings Thorin and Marcel march in. The wrath king folds his arms across his broad chest, his hungry eyes devouring me.

"Nice work, Thorin," Marcel compliments, his golden jewelry gleaming on his tanned skin while his eyes rake down my body, no doubt appreciating the way my skin is marked from my night with King Thorin. "How did our princess take to the whip?"

"Like a fucking queen," King Thorin growls proudly.

I smile at the giant vampire when I hear the others enter my room. I look around him to see Kings Killian and Strix walk in. I'm about to ask where King Dante is, but the sloth king enters a few steps behind them, looking as disinterested as possible. Gaunt and unshaven, the sloth king appears more disheveled than I've ever seen him. His eyes are heavy, as if he's been recently woken.

"Oooh, a party," King Killian jokes. "Should we all go and summon our baths so we can soak together? Or better yet, maybe Lucian will let us all play around in his hot spring pool."

"Fine with me," King Lucian murmurs between kisses along my skin. Every place his and King Ramsey's lips touch turns molten. I squirm in the bath as the ache between my legs surfaces, needing more than this. But I have a reason for asking them to come here. I can't let desire distract me.

Unhappily, I pull my leg from King Lucian and push King Ramsey's face away. The vampire kings crowd around my small bathtub, making me feel so little and insignificant. I need to get up and move.

I reach for my glass and down the rest of my wine before gripping the sides of the tub and pulling myself up. Wanting to make a show of it, I stretch my arms high over my head, pressing my chest forward, and lean my head back as the water drips down my body. I can feel their eyes running along my skin. Knowing I have the complete attention of the seven kings—well, at least six—is empowering to say the least.

I let out a soft groan and lower my hands, accepting King Ramsey's assistance to exit the tub. I walk around to the front, push through Kings Thorin and Marcel, and walk back into the bedroom portion of the suite.

After reaching the far wall, I spin and turn back. I smile when I see they've all followed me. Time to get what I summoned them for.

Not bothering with clothes, I fold my arms under my chest, cock my hip, and get started. "I'll get right to the point. I want to make the people of Riverwood stronger. I believe there is a way to use vampire blood to assist in that. I heard mention of the term 'drone.' Can you explain this to me?"

"I can't think clearly with you standing naked like that, little one," King Thorin growls. "All my thoughts are of draping you over my lap and spanking that perfect ass of yours until you're moaning and squirming on my cock."

"That does sound pleasant," King Marcel agrees, a smile pulling at his lips.

King Lucian steps forward, untying his cape from around his neck. "Here, pet, you can borrow this." The dark blue fabric even smells like him and I just want to bury my nose in the softness. Instead, I allow him to cover me without faltering at his touch.

I can't wait to fuck that man—uhh...vampire.

A smug grin crosses his face as he walks backwards to the others.

"I'm serious," I continue. "The evil queen's wrath will be great now that I've destroyed her magic mirror. I must protect my people." Murmurs go up among the kings. Seems not all of them had been made aware of my recent stunt.

"There is a way it can be done," King Marcel informs me. "But in order to create drones, you need my sin first. There is much to be said for greed. It can be cumbersome, but it also has its uses. If it's strength in numbers you seek, then my sin can help you." His smooth baritone washes over me like a soft lullaby.

"Excellent. Also, King Thorin? Will I be able to shift into a wolf now?"

The wrath king's gray eyes flash with excitement. "More than likely, little one. With a little practice, you will be a skilled hunter. I look forward to seeing what your wolf looks like."

I blush at the thought. Feeling a set of eyes boring into me, I flick my gaze toward King Strix. *You are doing so well, Regina, commanding this room. Standing naked and exuding pride before very powerful kings. You make me proud.*

I incline my head toward him.

"Anyone else feeling really horny right now? It can't just be me," King Killian jests. "The way she's telling us what she wants instead of asking for permission, the way she holds herself, the way she speaks… A true fucking queen. Such a turn on."

"Can't you ever be serious?" King Ramsey scolds. King Killian holds up his hands in defeat and takes a step back. I can't help but smile at him. It's nice to find laughter even in dire situations. Sometimes all we have is laughter to keep us from falling apart. Tears of joy versus tears of sorrow. I'd choose joy every time.

I look around for King Dante to see if he wants to weigh in, but the fucker is actually asleep in my bed. I have half a mind to walk over there and punch him right in his snoozing fucking face.

"Well, if there are no objections to our little queen earning my sin, then I invite you, Princess Snow, to come to my suite in exactly two hours, and I will give it to you." The way King Marcel speaks oozes seduction. Just what does the King of Greed have in store for me?

"Let's leave them to it then. Our princess will need to prepare for this." King Strix ushers the others through the door. I look back to my bed and find King Dante is already gone.

How the fuck did that happen?

"See you soon, precious girl," King Marcel croons before shutting my door behind him.

Two fucking hours.

One hundred and twenty minutes.

Let's hope they don't trickle by, because I'm ready for whatever King Marcel has in store for me, and I want it now.

$\mathcal{M}$y heart hammers inside my chest, and my fingers are clammy with anticipation. I'm not scared of what I'm about to experience, just really fucking excited. King Marcel confirmed what I was previously told, that with his sin, I'll be able to give my people an opportunity to become a drone. I still don't really understand what that means, but I plan on finding out right now.

Unlike the previous times when Katie and Renee prepared me for the kings, this time I do it alone. As infuriating as it can be to have others messing with my hair, dressing my body, and painting makeup on my face, I find that I rather miss their company. Having them with me gave me someone to talk to, a friend to calm my nerves or keep my mind preoccupied with other things. But now that's gone and all I have to accompany me are my wild thoughts about what is going to happen.

The leather outfit provided for me clings to my skin. I don't understand why I was asked to wear it. I might as well not have anything on. A black leather strip is strapped around my breasts, only covering them halfway and leaving all my cleavage exposed. Thin straps hold the top up, wrapping over my shoulders, leaving me wondering if it's just going to fall down my body as I walk.

A black, leather skirt rides low on my hips. The short scrap of leather barely covers my ass. I can feel where the hem hits just above the bottom of my cheeks as I walk. More leather surrounds my neck, wrists, and ankles, and high, black boots cover my feet up to my knees.

I almost feel foolish in this getup. In Riverwood, one would not be caught dead in something like this. Yet as I look down at my body, I can't help but feel sexy. I laugh to myself, knowing this is something King Thorin would love to see me in. Perhaps I'll have to wear it again for him some time.

Outside the castles, I look for the one with the yellow flag, knowing I'll find King Marcel inside. The vampires in the coven still stare longingly at me, but now, since I've acquired more sins, they no longer lunge at me.

Several couples are fucking in the courtyard, the sight of their naked bodies glistening with sweat turning me on. Peeling my gaze from the erotic sight, I find what I'm looking for. Nestled between King Thorin's and King Killian's castle, is Greed Castle.

Turning right, I head toward it. The sounds of the churning, underground river echoes on my left. I still marvel at the enormity of this project—carving the seven castles right out of the stone while underground. I make a note to ask the kings how it was done once this is all over.

If I survive.

No. I can't think like that. I *will* survive. I have to. For the kings. For my people. For the entire world.

No pressure.

Like with all the castles, guards flank the doors. I open my mouth to tell them King Marcel is expecting me, but my words are unnecessary. They swing them open before I can even ask them to. Even though they are trained soldiers, their eyes still wander over my body, filling me with pride.

King Marcel's castle reminds me a lot of King Killian's. Its vast halls are filled to the brim with art and trinkets. Excessive numbers of seating and tables are dotted around, while copious amounts of servants roam about, waiting on their next order to fill. Weaving my way through the foyer, around plush chairs and hordes of vampires drinking red liquid, I feel myself being pulled in the correct direction, though I haven't been here before.

A door in the back of the foyer is my destination, and I push it open and walk down a darkened hall. Unlike the previous room, this hall is sparse. Only a few lit candles flicker in the blackness, changing the once happy atmosphere to one of secrets and dark promises.

As the door behind me closes, I hear a lock engage, causing my heart to stutter. I ignore the racing muscle and force my legs to continue forward. Another door morphs from the shadows, this one with no handle with which to open. I raise my hand to knock, knowing this is the place I'm supposed to be, when I hear a series of noises. They sound like the sliding of chains, clinking of metal, and turning of locks.

A moment later, I'm met with the towering form of King Thorin. I startle and take a step back, mad at myself for trusting my instincts. King Marcel is going to be pissed when he finds out I've accidentally searched for Thorin and not him.

"Just in time." The wrath king's deep voice rolls through me like a caress. "We've been waiting for you."

"We?" I squeak out.

"Yes. Come in, little one, and see what your greed king is up to." As King Thorin steps into the light, I see he is dressed similarly to myself. His broad chest is bare, his muscles flexing. He wears leather around his neck and biceps, and tight, leather pants hug his legs. My king is aroused, if the giant bulge is anything to go by.

What the fuck are they doing in there?

The large king steps to the side and allows me entrance. I'm shocked when I look behind him. The room is set up much like the one King Thorin had me in when he gave me his sin, with a few exceptions.

The walls here are not dark stone, instead, they are painted an off-white color. A large bed is situated in the far left corner, and huge armature surrounds it with various hooks and ropes hanging from above. On the right wall, like in King Thorin's room, are profuse amounts of weapons that inflict pain—long and short knives, whips of all shapes and sizes, lengths of leather and rope, candles, cages, blindfolds… I could look for an hour and not spot everything.

But in spite of all that, the most curious thing of all is the King of Greed himself. He's standing in the center of the room, dressed to the nines in a gorgeous crimson and black suit. Gold necklaces hang from his neck and his rings shine on his fingers.

He looks every bit the gentleman, from the way he holds himself to the expression on his face. "Hello, precious girl. We are just getting started." His dark eyes latch onto me, flashing with excitement. "Greed comes in many forms, which constantly duel inside me. Like now, my desire to receive and inflict pain wars within me. I can't choose just one because I'm desperate for both." He takes a few steps toward King Thorin, and tugs at the collar surrounding the much larger king's neck, pulling his face down toward him. My breath catches. Are they going to…

King Marcel's lips crash into King Thorin's. The large vampire growls, tugging at the clothing covering King Marcel. I've never seen a sight so arousing. To watch two extremely powerful vampire kings kiss each other has my pussy clenching with desire.

"You've experienced what it is like to be on the receiving end of Thorin's wrath," King Marcel states, pulling himself away from King Thorin. "It's arousing and exciting, isn't it?"

"Yes, but—"

"I, too, like the big vampire to dominate me. But I also like to be the one in charge. Don't you see? I need it all or I'm never satisfied. I want to fuck and be fucked, I want to hurt and be hurt. I'm greedy, precious girl, and tonight, you shall be too."

Before I can ask him what he means, he saunters closer to me, running a finger along my jaw. "Have you ever really been in control of a male before, princess?"

Have I? "I-I'm not sure—"

"I thought that might be the answer. Thorin, come closer." The wrath king prowls toward us, stroking his dark beard. "Now, I want you to give him an order." I look at the huge king and my throat runs dry. He's so big and powerful, a king like him would never submit to one of my orders. "Do it!"

"Umm. Will you...umm..." I look around, trying to figure out what the hell to ask him.

"It's not that hard," King Marcel gripes, running his fingers through his short, dark hair. "Let's start simple. Tell him to remove my jacket."

I turn to King Thorin. "Will you remove King Marcel's jacket for him...please?"

King Marcel strokes his chin. "Better, but without the niceties. Give the king a fucking order, as a proper queen would."

I turn to King Thorin and narrow my eyes. "Remove his jacket, now!"

"There we go. Well fucking done." King Marcel opens his arms as King Thorin steps in front of him and unbuttons his jacket before slipping it from his shoulders. The large vampire then hangs it on a hook on the wall. "Now I'll have Thorin give you an order."

King Marcel nods at King Thorin, whose face becomes mischievous. "Little one," he begins, moving over to the bed before sitting upon it. "Come to your master and lie across my lap. I wish to spank that perfect ass of yours."

King Marcel's eyebrows rise when I don't obey right away. "Go on, princess."

I flutter my fingers and lick my lips before forcing my legs to move. I'm simultaneously a little scared and totally turned on. King Thorin pats his lap with his big hands. Shakily, I lay my torso on them.

I can only imagine their view with my ass up in the air like this. The kinky fuckers have never provided me with underwear, so my ass is bare before them. King Thorin growls as he rubs his hand up and down my ass. "I'm going to spank you now, little one. Are you ready?"

I nod and bite my lip, squeezing my eyes closed.

Smack!

The sound of his hand bouncing off my ass echoes through the room, and I shriek at the contact. He's rubbing my abused cheek again before I can even register the burning sensation.

"You may stand, precious girl." Lifting myself from King Thorin's lap, I take a few steps back and rub my sore cheek. "This is exactly what I mean. I need to be dominant and submissive, I need to be brutal and sweet. I can't choose between my options, or I'll never be content. I can't stop. I won't stop, until every need is fulfilled."

"Sounds kind of arrogant to me." The words slip from my lips before I can stop them, and I cup my hands over my mouth, my eyes flaring wide at the audacity of my proclamation.

"I guess it is," King Marcel replies, chuckling. "But the fact still remains that this is what it is to be greedy." He smiles and takes a step closer to me as King Thorin watches from the bed. "My turn to give an order. Now, which one of you do I want to boss around?" His eyes flicker between me and the wrath king and finally land on me. "Princess Snow, remove your top and free those perfect breasts. I like to watch them bounce."

I cross my arms over my chest. "First, I have a question to ask you. A few, actually."

King Marcel smiles. "How about we strike a deal? For every order you obey, I will answer a question. Do we have an accord?"

"Yes." I don't even think twice. I'll pay whatever price he wants to learn what I wish to know.

"Then, by all means, take off your top. Or better yet, let Thorin do it for you."

The wrath king grins and saunters over to me, his footsteps pounding under his large frame. Positioned behind me, I can feel his body close to mine. The vampires who once felt so cold against my skin now feel heated. Fingers trail up and down my arms, causing goosebumps to form on my flesh.

I can feel his fingers working the knot tying my top closed. I almost groan in relief when the leather strap is removed from my body, my breasts freed from their prison. "Now for my question." I'm struggling with concentration and want to get it out before I forget. With King Marcel's eyes devouring me, and King Thorin's hands touching me, all I can think about is how badly I want them at the same time.

King Marcel inclines his head. "Proceed."

King Thorin's hands engulf my breasts, kneading them to the point of exquisite pain. "Umm…" I relax my head back against his chest and soak up the feeling of his hands on me. Then, remembering myself, I throw his hands off and take a step toward King Marcel. "How do I make a drone and what does being a drone mean?"

"That's two questions, precious girl. So I'll start with the second until you've earned the first."

He moves closer to me, a swagger in his step, his dark eyes gleaming. "A drone is a human who has been given a controlled amount of vampire blood to consume, thus giving them superior strength and healing, similar to what you felt when you drank the nectar."

So that's how it's done.

"So, in essence, I was a drone then," I mumble to myself.

King Marcel doesn't answer, instead he nods to King Thorin behind me. "Thorin, restrain her."

"Wait, what?" Before I can move, the wrath king has my arms pulled behind me, surrounding them with one of his, his other hand curling around my neck.

King Marcel licks his perfect lips and reaches for me, his fingers tracing circles around my nipples, driving me absolutely wild.

"Do you like this, little one? Do you like how it feels to have two of your vampire kings restraining you, touching you?" King Thorin rumbles in my ear. I moan when King Marcel finally touches my nipples, giving them both a glorious pinch.

"Marcel, take her fucking skirt off. I need her to be bare before I lose control."

"I never conceded to this!" I shout, wriggling in King Thorin's grasp while his erection prods my back.

King Marcel chuckles while trailing his fingers below the hem of my skirt. "That, precious girl, is greed for you. Between the three of us, someone must always be the one to give orders while another submits. It is not our choice which role we must perform. All we can do is accept that sometimes we are in charge, and other times we are not. If you can learn to accept that, to love both sides of the coin, then you will have a spectacular night. If you fight it, greed is not the sin for you."

He's right. This is the test. His test. I must submit to be obeyed. I must be dominant to force my control. Both sides of the coin.

Deflating in King Thorin's grasp, I don't fight it when my skirt is slipped down my legs. "You are remarkable, princess," King Marcel compliments, his eyes roving over me. "I thought you were the most gorgeous specimen I had ever seen that first night you were presented to us. But with vampire blood running through your veins, you're becoming even more stunning. I didn't think it was possible."

He reaches for my hair, tugging the hairpin out, allowing my curls to fall across my shoulders. "Your hair is so soft and shiny, your once blue eyes, darkening." His eyes dip lower. "Your breasts perky, nipples plump, a gorgeous rosy color." His fingers trace a line between my breasts down to my pussy. "And this fucking pussy, perfect lips, slightly swollen, blossoming before me as they glisten with arousal. Because whether you choose to believe it or not, you like what we're doing to you. You like the bite of pain, though you crave sweetness. You thrive on being watched, while you get off on watching others. You are happy to give away control, even though you flourish in commanding it. That, princess, is greed at its finest."

His words make my core flood with heat, my desire for this king escalating to levels beyond my control. I fucking want him, but first I need more information. "How do you turn a human into a drone?" I rasp out, my voice restricted by King Thorin's large hand.

King Marcel chuckles. "I've already answered this, but I shall repeat myself since I'm so distracted by your body." He tears his gaze from my pussy, meeting my eyes, the dark orbs burning into mine. "You create a drone by giving a human a precise amount of my blood. It must not be drunk directly from me, rather dispersed in a small dose."

"How long does it last?"

"Give me an order and I shall tell you."

So many ideas flit through my mind. I have this gorgeous vampire king at my mercy, but only one thing comes to mind. "Taste me, King Marcel. Drop to your knees and fuck me with your tongue."

His eyes darken. "Tsk, tsk, tsk. So very greedy. I will obey your command with pleasure."

King Thorin's grip tightens on my neck, pulling my head back toward him. As the wrath king takes my lips for his own, his tongue invading my mouth, I feel another tongue sliding along my slit.

I moan into King Thorin's mouth as King Marcel holds true to his word. The King of Greed tosses one of my legs over his shoulder and devours me. His tongue swirls around my clit, lapping at the sensitive bundle of nerves, while his finger delves in and out of my opening.

I tug at King Thorin's grasp, even as I deepen our kiss, wanting my hands free to thread into King Marcel's hair. But when King Marcel's finger travels even further backward, tracing the unmentionable hole, I really begin to struggle.

"Relax, little one. It only hurts when you fight it. I promise, Marcel will make you feel good," King Thorin whispers between kisses.

With his tongue flicking my clit over and over again, King Marcel has me on the brink of coming. But the fear of his finger penetrating my ass has me unable to get there. "Allow me to enter you, and I will answer all your questions," he murmurs, before sucking on my hardened nub.

My nostrils flare as my breathing escalates, and King Thorin forces me to keep kissing him. The familiar deep heat pools between my legs, and my chest feels heavy as the orgasm grows in force. I concentrate on how good it feels to have King Thorin holding me, how erotic it is to have King Marcel bringing me to climax with only his tongue.

My breaths become shallower, and then it hits me. I come hard as King Marcel's finger enters my ass, slowly fucking me, while his soft lips suck on my clit. King Thorin's grip on my neck tightens, restricting my air as he plunges his tongue deeper down my throat.

It's too much.

With his finger still fucking me, King Marcel doesn't let up, his lips surrounding my over sensitive clit. My hips buck, wanting him off, the sensation becoming too much.

"You will come again, little one. Give in to your kings. Come for us," King Thorin orders. His hand leaves my throat to play with my nipples, tugging and plucking one then the other. The sensitivity falters, and soon King Marcel's lips feel so fucking good again.

"Oh God, yes," I groan, my head falling back onto Thorin's massive chest. The finger in my ass even starts to feel pleasurable as it slowly pumps in and out of me. The heat builds quicker this time, my arousal literally dripping from me.

I can feel my cunt pulsing and I desperately want one of their cocks inside me. "Soon, little one," King Thorin promises. "For now, come for us."

I cry out when King Thorin sinks his teeth into my neck, pinching my nipple, while King Marcel's lips bring me to climax once again.

My leg becomes too weak to hold me and I collapse in King Thorin's grasp. The large vampire scoops me up and carries me over to the bed where he places me down before lying next to me.

"That was incredible," I say breathlessly.

"You are incredible, precious girl," King Marcel praises, slipping beside me. "Rest for a minute, but don't think for a moment that we're done with you yet."

I can't even contemplate doing that again, just basking in the sensation of the soft bed under me and the feeling of their hands casually touching my skin.

King Thorin toys with my nipple while King Marcel trails his finger up and down my side. "To answer your earlier question, every human reacts differently to my blood," King Marcel informs me, responding to the query I'd forgotten I'd asked. "Some are able to sustain the effects for days, but larger people with more mass tend to burn through it faster."

"And—wh-when I have your s-sin, can I m-make drones?" I ask between pants.

"No. You must be a vampire to have that kind of power."

"Okay," I reply, not really able to form rational thoughts just yet. The kings still, and I can feel electricity flowing through the air. When I finally open my eyes, I see the kings kissing.

I moan as I watch two of the most gorgeous vampires I've ever seen tasting each other's mouths. And they are doing it right over me.

So.

Fucking.

Hot.

"Wow," I whisper, my eyes wide with excitement. I don't even blink, not wanting to miss a second of this.

As if they've only just remembered that I'm here, the kings turn to me. Both pairs of eyes gaze at me with as much hunger as I have for them.

"I need you both, precious girl," King Marcel admits, cupping my cheek in his hand. "I'm too greedy to settle for one."

"Take me then," I breathe. "Take me while King Thorin

takes you." The two vampires share a glance and another soft kiss before moving. King Marcel, still clothed, slips from the bed, and King Thorin joins him. I prop myself up on my elbows and watch voraciously as they undress each other. The wrath king moves first, using brute strength to tear King Marcel's clothes from his body in a mere second.

Standing bare, cock bobbing proudly, King Marcel makes quick work of the tight leather pants encasing King Thorin.

It's so incredibly arousing to watch them reveal each other's bodies.

Two vampire kings, two cocks, two tongues, four hands...

The possibilities are endless.

The kings kiss again, one hand running through the other's hair while their free hand pumps their lover's cock. I've never seen anything so erotic in my life and my hand dives between my legs, easing the ache forming there.

"Seems our princess likes to watch, Thorin, but I'd rather have her participate. What do you think?"

King Thorin growls, "I think you need to fuck our future queen while I sheathe myself inside you."

I only have a moment to wonder if he means in his ass or his mouth before King Marcel grins and prowls toward me. I desperately want to slip his cock between my lips, but that will have to wait for another time, because my pussy is much greedier.

The greed king climbs on top of me, his legs on the outsides of mine, his arms caging my head. "You are everything I've ever dreamed of, princess," he says, his dark eyes searching my gaze. "You will be the most radiant queen alive." Then, gently, the King of Greed kisses me. His lips are soft and careful, cherishing me, his tongue tracing the seam of my lips.

I open for him as I feel a finger sliding along my pussy, swirling in my arousal. It leaves as soon as it came, and my kiss with King Marcel grows more heated. His tongue slides sensually along mine, like an erotic dance. I can taste myself in his mouth, which only makes me hotter.

The bed dips and I look up as King Marcel groans. King Thorin kneels behind him, the wrath king lubricating his cock with my arousal, his gray eyes fixed on King Marcel's ass. Then King Thorin shifts and grips King Marcel's hips, confirming what I already knew...

King Thorin is about to fuck King Marcel's ass.

King Marcel's eyes roll back in pleasure as his head dips into my neck, a deep groan escaping him. I can see King Thorin easing back and forth, knowing that's his way of acclimating us to his huge cock. The thought turns me on in the worst way, and I'm desperate for more. Rolling my head to the side, I offer my neck to King Marcel.

With no preamble, he sinks his fangs into me, and I cry out in pleasure, coming instantly. Marcel uses the distraction to bury his cock inside me. We both groan when he's fully seated, filling me. Then he starts to move, well, more like King Thorin is moving for him. The wrath king is in complete control of this trio. When he draws out of King Marcel, he pulls the greed king with him, removing King Marcel's cock from my channel. Then when he enters King Marcel again, the force of his fucking pushes King Marcel's cock inside me.

It's so sexy.

So erotic.

King Marcel pins my arms above my head and takes my nipple into his mouth, nipping and sucking while King Thorin fucks us both. It doesn't take long for their pace to quicken. My cunt squeezes King Marcel's cock as the vampire kings groan above me.

"I'm going to come in your tight little hole, Marcel," King Thorin growls. "Take all of me, like a good little king."

King Marcel groans then fixes his eyes on me. "And I am going to come in this hot wet cunt of yours, princess. Take me like a good girl would."

Now it's my turn to groan.

Faster and faster the kings move, my breasts bouncing with their thrusts. My orgasm is fueled by watching them work above me. All those tense muscles flexing with every movement. Their stern faces, thick beards. It's all too much.

My back arches, and I scream as my orgasm takes me. I hear King Thorin roar then King Marcel shout as they both come too. Marcel collapses on top of me, still fucking me through our releases, and offers me his neck. "Take my sin, precious girl. It is yours."

My fangs descend rapidly, and I raise my head and bite. I feel King Marcel come again as I suck him down. His blood is delicious, a mixture of decadent chocolate and salted caramel. I can feel greed surging inside me, the desire to want more of everything, the need to have as much as possible, and feeling like I might die if I don't get it.

"Enough, princess," King Marcel whispers, and I wonder how long I've been drinking for.

"She's insatiable," King Thorin remarks proudly.

"Very much so." King Marcel gently pulls my hair, and I reluctantly remove my fangs from his neck. Suddenly, my eyes feel very heavy, and the deep sleep that accompanies earning a sin begins to engulf me in its warm embrace.

"Sleep now, my precious girl. You've earned your rest." As King Marcel plays with my hair, I fall to sleep, sore, aching, and completely satisfied...

For now...

CHAPTER 36

"Snow! Snow, wake up!" I jerk awake as a frantic Katie comes plowing through my door.

I sit up, rubbing my eyes. "I'm up. I'm up. What is it?"

She perches on my bed, a desperate look on her face. "I have news. And it's not the good sort."

My heart races, wondering what could be wrong. Has something happened to one of the kings? Have they decided I'm not who they thought I was? Has the coven been compromised?

My fingers fumble with my sheets, twisting them as she takes a deep breath. "It's Riverwood. The queen...she's...she's invaded your town," she stutters out.

"What?" Frantic, I throw off my sheets and race around my room, unsure what I'm even doing or searching for. "I need to get to them. We need to help them!"

Katie runs to my side, her warm hands holding my bare shoulders firmly. "She's already gone. There's nothing you can do. I'm sorry."

Tears well in my eyes. "Surely there must be something." I

cup my face in my hands and let the tears flow. I've failed them.

Katie wraps me in her arms. "I know. It's okay."

"The fuck it is," I growl, pushing her off. "It's my job to protect them. Mine! They trusted me and look what happened to them." My sadness quickly converts to potent rage. I can feel it brewing inside me, a gargantuan storm. "I thought the vampires were helping me," I fume. "Was that just a ruse? A lie to make me believe my people were safe?"

Katie gasps in shock. "No. Of course it wasn't. After all they've given you, you can't really believe that."

My fingers clench and unclench, my teeth gritting in anger. "I don't know what to believe anymore."

Katie folds her arms across her chest. "You must know by now that vampires cannot survive in daylight. The evil queen waited until the sky began to brighten to attack. She must have had someone spying on the village. The vampires are forced to retreat into the coven during the day. She used that to her advantage, striking the town when it was at its weakest."

Rage surges inside me, almost tingeing my vision in a shade of red. "Of course she fucking did. She's a fucking coward." I'm surprised I'm not wearing holes in the floor with my pacing as I chew on my lip, deciding what to do. "I have to go to them. I have to try and salvage their trust, help them in any way I can."

"The kings won't like that," Katie retorts.

"Fuck the kings," I growl just as my door bursts open and King Thorin charges through.

"Watch your mouth, little one, or I'll be forced to shut it for you."

I level him with a glare. "Just try and stop me." His mouth drops open as I look to Katie. "What time is it?"

341

"Umm. It was nearing midday when I came to tell you the news."

I grin. "Perfect time to go and visit them, don't you think?"

Squaring my shoulders, I stomp forward and push through Katie and King Thorin, reaching for my door. The king's hand bands around my upper arm and tightens to the point of pain. But the pain only fuels my anger, my wrath, which he gave me so recently. I freeze and close my eyes, diving within my mind, searching for my wrath. Just like when I looked for the minds of the kings, each of my sins has a door I can enter.

I hear the noise coming from behind it before I even see it. Scratching. Pawing. *Howling.*

Excited, I push open the door and see a wolf.

My wolf.

She's as black as the night with bright, red eyes. She lowers her torso, getting ready to pounce, and I allow it. I splay my arms wide in my mind, tipping my head up, and embrace her wholeheartedly.

My eyes fly open as pain consumes me. My body feels like it's being ripped apart and thrown back together. My teeth flex in and out of my mouth, every bone in my body breaking and regrowing.

I fall to the floor with a cry, King Thorin's grip slipping from my arm. Paws grow from my hands and feet, and fur sprouts out of my skin until I'm Snow no more.

A thousand scents overwhelm me, my new nose twitching nonstop to learn them all. "How is this possible?" My ear turns to the sound of King Thorin, who has fallen to his knees beside me. "I've never seen someone learn to turn that fast, and you're not even a vampire yet. I wonder what other surprises you'll have in store for us, little one."

He reaches out to touch me, and I back away growling. I

do not wish to be petted or stroked. What I want is to get the fuck out of here. Snarling, I leap at him, taking him by surprise, my paws connecting with his chest as he falls back.

I turn to Katie who backs away with her hands up before I run from my room. The castle looks so different from this angle. Not that I'm small for a wolf. Those in the coven don't pay me much attention, as if it's normal to see wolves prowling around. Perhaps it is.

The stairs are no match for my four new legs, and I fly down them with ease, sniffing the air to find the exit. I push myself hard, running faster, taking sharp corners as if I've been a wolf my whole life.

Quickly, I depart the castle and surge for the stairs leading out. No one tries to stop me. Not the people. Not the guards. They simply allow me passage.

And for that, I'm grateful. My control feels weak, and I'm worried about what I may do to someone who chooses this moment to test me. The stairs melt away before me as I push my legs to their limits. I soar down the corridor at the top and leap through the door, landing on the dais in the party room.

The place is jumping with activity, my nose smelling everything from arousal and cum to wine and blood. Humans and vampires alike are dancing and fucking, enjoying every moment. But I can't linger here. I need to get outside before one of the kings tries to stop me.

I bound down from the dais, keeping to the shadows, and paw at the exit door until it opens. I trot down the candlelit hallway and finally see my destination—the egress to River-wood. The door swings out when I spring at it, and I roll to the ground before picking myself back up.

My claws dig into the stone and dirt as I make a dash for the town square. Above me, the sun attempts to shine through the dense clouds, making me want to howl in frustration. That's one thing I can't wait to return to my people, the warmth of the sun.

I can smell the gathering of my people, but I also scent burnt wood, the coppery aroma of fresh blood, decay, and rot—the fragrance of battle. My ears twitch as a child cries for its father, as a husband mourns the loss of his wife. Grief strikes me through the heart so hard I almost trip.

As the narrow alley ends, I pause. Now that I'm here, I don't know what the hell I'm going to do. For one, I'm a fucking wolf, and it's likely the people will be scared of me. And two, what if they're mad at me? What if they blame me for what's happened to them? I didn't directly cause it by inviting the evil queen to attack. But she besieged them because of me, to get back at me, to weaken me by hurting the village I love so much.

Sitting on my haunches next to the corner of the building, I hang my head and encourage the grief to consume me. I wish to mourn with my people, not as an outcast.

Sorrow and anguish rage inside me, causing my wrath to retreat. Tears well in my eyes as I cry for my people. My howls turn to sobs as tears roll down my cheeks. I don't know how long I mourn before a gentle hand grips my shoulders and a warm cloak surrounds me.

I glance up, realizing I've shifted back, into the face of a woman who is no more than a few years older than me. Judging by the lines on her face, and the bags under her eyes, her life has almost been as hard as my own.

"Princess?" she whispers, startled that it's me.

I nod my head then bury my face in my hands. "I'm so sorry this happened to you. I'm so damn sorry."

She kneels beside me, sharing my grief, her own sniffles indicating her sorrow. "This is not your fault, princess. Don't you dare take the blame for what she has done."

Her kindness moves me and I cry even harder, letting my

frustration, years of helplessness, and the heartache of so many lost lives devour me. The woman holds me, sharing this burden with me until all my tears have dried and a fierce resolve replaces my despair.

"What is your name?" I ask her, wiping the final tears from my cheeks.

The woman smiles at me, her bright blue eyes shining, her dark brown hair reaching just past her shoulders. She's naturally beautiful with a small nose and full lips. Kindness rolls off this woman, and I can't help but want to get to know her. "Rosie. My name is Rosie." A perfect name for such a sweet woman.

"Hello, Rosie. It's nice to meet you." I pull myself up and wrap the cloak tightly around me. "What do you say we take a walk to the square? I need to see our people," I request, offering her my hand.

Her smile grows as she allows me to help her up. "With pleasure, princess."

I return her smile, then turn to face the square where I know I'm going to see some terrible things. Taking a deep breath, using Rosie to give me strength, I walk around the corner.

Devastation sums up the sight before me. Under the canopy of gray clouds, the townspeople mope about looking lost. A man is carrying pails of water from the well before handing it off to another who tosses it on the embers burning in the remains of a thatched roof.

Several small children surround a man whose chest no longer rises to breathe, while their mother holds them tight, tears streaming down her red cheeks. Houses are demolished, others mottled with gaping holes. Blood covers the streets as the corpses of fallen fighters are carried away.

Survivors are already hard at work creating a pyre to burn the dead before animals and other scavengers come into the town, searching for their next meal. Men haul debris of the destroyed homes into the wood pile, preparing for the blazing inferno to come while others heave the dead on top.

Another woman's cries of the deepest anguish imaginable echo through the square as she holds the bloodied corpse of a man to her chest, rocking him back and forth while begging for him to come back to her.

It's all too much and I find myself retreating back to the alley.

"Go on, princess. They need you right now," Rosie encourages me, placing a firm hand on my back.

She's right. I'd be as cowardly as the evil bitch if I run when they need me most. Licking my lips, I force my legs to move toward the square. Saddened eyes gaze at me, but I see no hate there. If anything, they seem encouraged by my presence. I hold the cloak snugly and climb upon the stone table once used to secure Sherry and Enid's wrists for branding.

"People of Riverwood, I'm saddened to learn of your plight with the evil bitch living in my castle. You've lost your homes, your loved ones, your guarded sense of peace. There are no words I can say that will make this any easier, because nothing can change what has happened. I grieve with you as you rebuild your homes and mourn your dead. My heart breaks just as yours does..."

I take a moment to really look at my people. Let them see that I see them, that they're not just a number to me, but a person with a face and a name. "I can't change the past, but I can alter our future. Today, right here and now, I am here to promise you this... Every day I'm absent, I'm working hard. Every day I grow stronger, tougher, sharper. I'm dedicating my life to destroying her. I aim to give you back the community you deserve and a leader who makes her people stronger, instead of finding its weaknesses and exploiting them." I growl the last bit as anger surges inside me at the injustice done to these good people.

I scour those gathered around, looking at their bloodied and torn clothes, their disheveled hair, their tired eyes. I know that vacant look, because it's been on my own face for so long.

"Every night since I've been gone, since you rescued me from the evil bitch, I've been healing, growing more powerful with the help of the lurkers. And now they've come to guard you and keep you safe. But being what they are comes with a price, one the evil queen is all too aware of. They cannot survive in the light of day."

"What are they, princess?" a young man with a slash across his face inquires.

I take a deep breath. They deserve the truth. "They are vampires."

Conversation picks up among those gathered. Whispers of what they know of the monsters flitting through the air. I hear fear, mistrust, and terror in their voices.

"Please, everyone, calm down. There is no need to fear them. They suffer at the hands of the evil queen like you and me. Her magic has banished them to a life in the dark, just like she took our sun from us. Together, with our forces joined, we will destroy her for good."

"But how do we know we can trust them?" an older woman shouts, holding the hands of two very small children.

The answer races through my mind, the words I haven't yet had the courage to say out loud. "Because I'm becoming one." Gasps ring out, sharp intakes of breath as the shock settles in. "They aren't just monsters, as you were warned of. Those are lies used by the evil queen to invoke fear, to take the focus off her weaknesses and place it somewhere else. They are kings, seven to be exact, and they have magic of their own, magic they are sharing with me. I've already received power from four kings. Once I obtain the final three, I will have enough of my own magic to stop the queen once and for all."

I let that sink in, then carry on, "I've already used it to help us. Two nights ago, I destroyed the evil queen's magic mirror with my own hands." Murmurs of shock and awe resound. The feat has always felt impossible. "She's weakened now, her every move made in haste because of her own reservations. It won't be long until she makes her last mistake, and we'll take advantage of it, eradicating her evil from this world for the rest of time."

"Even if that's true," a man speaks, "it still doesn't change the fact that they can't help us in the daylight. That means we're unprotected half the day. We can't fight magic without any of our own."

"Here, here!" Shouts of agreement reverberate, voices escalating.

A smile pulls at my lips, because I know something they don't. "Please. Everyone, listen!" I shout, cupping my hands around my mouth. "I have a solution for that too. There is a way for you to share in the strength of the vampire race without becoming one."

"No thanks!" a stern-looking man yells back. "I don't want those- those vampires to put magic in my eyes!"

Anger wells inside me as my frustration grows. I know they're upset and I'm trying to be empathetic, but they just won't fucking pay attention. "Just fucking listen!" I shout, my voice carrying across the crowd. One by one, they all look at me with wide eyes. "Now," I begin, lowering my voice, "no one speaks until I have finished. I know you're upset and you have every right to be. But arguing will get us nowhere. If you could please just hear me out, listen to my solution, you will come to realize what I have to offer will only strengthen you."

I currently have the attention of everyone, they watch me with suspicion, but also wonder. I know how I felt when I knew for certain the legends surrounding the seven, powerful, vampire kings were real. It was overwhelming, to say the least. "You know me, each and every one of you, many since I was a little girl. Would I ever do anything to steer you wrong or put you in danger? In the nights when they've been here, patrolling your city, have they ever once threatened you? Hurt you? Or have they only ensured your safety?"

The citizens glance at each other with deflated expressions, realizing I've got them. They know who I am, what I stand for, and that I'd never do anything to jeopardize their lives. "The magic of the vampires resides in their blood. In order to benefit from their magic, you must consume a small amount of vampire blood. In doing so, you will gain their strength and enhanced speed, all while maintaining who you are inside."

"Will it hurt?" a little boy asks, hiding slightly behind his mother.

I smile at him and crouch down to get more on his level. "No, sweet boy. It doesn't hurt a bit. I've done it myself. Do I look hurt?"

He shakes his full head of messy brown hair. "There's another benefit," I add, as I stand back up. "Though the length each person will reap the benefit of the vampire blood varies, while it flows within you, the king it came from will be able to sense you. He will know if you're hurt, if you need help, and he can come to your aid. And as soon as your body has metabolized his blood, you will be just as you are now, with no lasting effects."

Silence blankets us as everyone thinks about what I've said. "Do any of you have any questions?"

"I do." With her thin arm raised, a teenage girl steps forward. "How does a person become a vampire?"

Whispers rise as the question many of them have likely been asking themselves is voiced. My people have been through a lot, and I don't want to sugarcoat my answer. "The truth is, I don't know. I have my suspicions, but I don't want to tell you a mistruth based on my assumptions."

"But that's what you're going to do, right?" she presses.

I can feel their eyes on me, wondering what I'm going to say, so I choose my words carefully before speaking. "Sometimes in life, you have to trust your gut, follow your instincts. I feel strongly that whatever the kings have planned for me is what I'm meant to do, who I'm meant to become. Call it fate. Call it destiny. Call it what you will. My intuition is telling me to trust the kings. They've vowed to share their magic with me, and the exchange has already begun. As payment for their power, I've pledged my life. If that means transforming into one of them, then so be it."

CHAPTER 37

*A*fter Rosie gave me one of her demure dresses to wear, I spent the rest of the day helping my people clean up the overwhelming amount of destruction. With my newfound strength, I was able to lift heavy logs and remnants of their destroyed homes. I could carry pails of water across my back and aid in restoring burnt thatching. I watched young children so their parents could get much needed rest, and tended to the frightened livestock.

The strongest men and women worked hard to repair the wall surrounding the perimeter, reinforcing areas believed to be weak, such as the gate. It was laborious, and even my newly grown muscles felt fatigued as sweat dripped down my body.

But the work was satisfying. By the time darkness was creeping across the town, we had all the dead gathered and lit the pyre, saying a prayer for our lost loved ones just as the lurkers were starting to emerge from the shadows. My people still eyed them wearily, but also with curiosity. I saw several humans strike up conversations with the vampires.

Some were able to share a laugh, while others were deep in serious conversation. The sight warmed my heart.

Now, after a long, hard day as I say my goodbyes to the villagers, I think for the first time that, yes, our two vastly different communities can come together.

We can do this.

The evil queen doesn't stand a chance.

Turning back to wave one last time, I feel a sense of peace. Though I don't know what the final installment of this epic battle will be, I'm finally feeling confident that we will be victorious.

I spin back and head toward the narrow alley when I notice someone very conspicuous. The tall, lanky vampire with a gaunt face, unkempt hair, and an impassive expression leans against the side of a building. His arms are crossed, one leg is bent with his foot resting on the wall, and his posture renders him completely unapproachable.

I think mosquitoes would even avoid him, forgoing their next meal. For the life of me, I can't figure out what he's doing here. The sloth king hasn't said a single word to me since I've arrived, and has shown no interest in the fate of his coven or my people, so why show up here now?

Maybe he's not here for me. Maybe he has other plans in mind.

Not giving a fuck what he's up to, I cast my gaze away, intent on walking right past him. If he can't give me the time of day, then why should he expect any different from me?

My stomach flutters as I approach where he stands, but I ignore the sensation and raise my chin, keeping my pace steady. That's when I feel a hand encircle my upper arm.

With a force I didn't think he had, King Dante jerks me toward him, pulling me into his chest. "And just where do you think you're going?" His tone is condescending, like he's accosting me just for fucking walking.

"With any luck, far away from you," I retort, twisting my arm free.

"Unfortunately for me, your statement couldn't be more untrue. Like it or not, we have a duty to perform. Let's just get this over with so we can move on with our lives."

"Duty?" I seethe, my hands clenched into fists. "You call what I'm doing, what your fellow kings are doing, your *fucking duty?*"

His brown eyes remain expressionless. "Yes. No more, no less. Nothing matters to me, not you, not them, not anyone or anything."

My anger quickly melts, concern replacing my wrath. "Why?" I can't understand how someone given so much could not care about a single thing in the entire world. It doesn't make sense.

He shrugs, pushing off the wall. "Can we please ignore the formalities, the niceties, and just get this over with? You give me your blood, I'll give you mine, and we'll call it a day."

"Fine." I don't like this, but what else can I do? I need his sin. If this is the only way I can acquire it, then I have to accept his terms. I have to admit, I'm slightly disappointed. I thought for sure if he just gave me a chance, I could reach him, that we could bond as I have with the others. Sharing something as intimate as your blood is a moment I have cherished with the other kings. Knowing this experience won't be even remotely close to that saddens me.

"Follow me." The sloth king heads toward the coven, his pace slow and steady, as if he's prolonging this exchange for as long as humanly—uhh…*vampirely?*—possible. It's maddening. A newborn baby could walk faster than this. Growling in annoyance, I stay about ten feet behind him, following like a good little servant would.

I kick at the loose stones on the ground, hoping one rogue rock might crack him in the back of the head. Every-

353

thing about him is unbecoming, from his stature, to the way he walks like a potato has been shoved up his ass, to the way he wears his crown cocked on his head. Nothing about him is special, everything unmemorable. I wonder how the hell he even became a king. Surely there must be a better choice than Dante. What a fucking joke.

Trying to pass the time, which is trickling by, I watch the faces of the vampires we pass on their way to Riverwood. They also almost completely ignore the king. Usually, when one of the kings is passing a member of their coven, the vampires will bow or incline their heads, show a sign of respect, but these offer nothing, as if he wasn't even there.

Even as we enter the party room, no one glances his way. I look toward Vincent, who's stifling a laugh at my disposition and flip him the fuck off.

Little fucker.

We amble slowly through the entrance, like he has no fucking care in the world—so very much like a real sloth—until we finally make it to the stairs. Even the needy donor men and women don't give a fuck about him. No women bare their breasts to entice him, no men offer their necks...

Serves him right.

Why would anyone want to show respect to someone who's not earned it? In fact, I wonder if he even has his own subjects—sloth vampires. I know the others do, I've seen them roaming their castles, exploiting their sins in the courtyards.

But how does one indulge in sloth? What would I even be looking for? Vampires who don't interact with one another? How fucking boring is that? No one would choose that life, not willingly.

Grumbling like a child, I think about the other kings whom I've not received a sin from yet—Kings Lucian and Killian. I'd much rather be spending my time with them.

They are so handsome it hurts to look at them. King Killian is funny, always wearing a smile on his face, while King Lucian makes me feel like I'm the most gorgeous woman who ever lived.

King Dante? He isn't even remotely good-looking. His face is unremarkable, lost among the crowd, while the others are beacons of attraction. When I first met the kings, I thought being gorgeous was a requirement. Now, I'm not so sure.

I guess even all vampire kings can't be stunners.

Sighing to myself as we finally get to the bottom of the stairs, I putter behind him as he veers right and heads for a castle with light blue banners. Usually, I'm excited to enter a new castle, but this time, all I feel is gloom. I don't want to be here any more than he wants me here.

Not wanting him to think I'm even slightly happy to be at his castle, I keep my eyes to the ground and don't look at anything, just mindlessly follow him like a lost puppy. And you know what else pisses me off? Not once has he looked over his shoulder to see if I'm still here.

Not. Fucking. Once.

So, as we climb a flight of stairs, walk down a long hallway, and enter through a door, I don't pay attention. I just stand awkwardly as the door shuts behind me.

I don't notice right away how good it smells in here, earthy, with a burning fire and bouquets of flowers. I don't observe how the tiled floor has been replaced with soft rugs or even that the atmosphere feels less oppressive, not until I raise my gaze and find myself completely alone.

I take a step back toward the door when I hear his indifferent tone. "Come and take a bath. You smell awful. The least you could do is clean yourself before the exchange."

Cock sucking little fuck...

I bite my tongue, holding in my retort, knowing it won't

do me any good, and make a beeline toward the only door in the room other than the one behind me. I ignore the large bed to my right, the bureau to my left, and head straight through.

Gauging by the state of the king, I must have been standing at that doorway for some time, because he's already clean, and buttoning up a fresh shirt in front of his misted mirror. "The water has been exchanged. But do make haste, I have no desire to linger here any longer than necessary."

With that asshole response, he leaves the room, and I'm left alone with my jaw gaping open. The audacity of him is mind-boggling. Even if he didn't want to be here, which is so very obvious, at least he could be nice about it.

Growling, I remove my borrowed dress, and slip into his bathtub. Only once I'm completely submerged do I look around. The bathroom is meager, which is surprising for a vampire king.

The walls are worn planks of wood, the tub a tin basin. There isn't even a splash of color. If it was a little colder in here, I'd be suspicious that I was in one of the evil queen's dungeons.

Closing my eyes, I lie back and allow myself a moment to relax. It's been a long fucking day—a long fucking week actually. Or two weeks. However long it's been since I've been here in the Coven of Sin. I empty my mind of the sorrows of today and dip my hair back, wetting the sweaty, black strands.

Glancing around, I find a bottle of soap and dispense a generous amount into my hand before scrubbing my scalp with it. After soaping up my hair, I stand and clean my body with my hands, massaging my sore muscles as I move.

I look down my body, and I'm surprised to note I haven't regrown any body hair. Usually, servants would have to wax me every week or two, but as I feel down my legs, there's nothing but smooth skin. Come to think of it, none of the kings had body hair either, even the burly King Thorin.

Not that I mind.

Body hair grosses me out.

This must be a side effect of all the vampire blood I've been consuming, a much welcomed one.

Using the pitcher resting on a small stool next to the tub, I rinse my hair and body with the remaining hot water before stepping out. A white towel hangs on an antiqued bronze bar, and I pull it off, first drying my hair then my body. I'm just finishing wrapping the towel around myself when I hear a deep groan behind me.

I still, my blood freezing, and slowly look over my shoulder. Standing in the doorway is King Dante, but something about him is off. His hair is a shade darker, and his face is cleanly shaven, but it's his eyes that catch me off guard. The usual nonchalance in his bland brown orbs has shifted to a deep hunger, which is beaming from eyes that are now a soft blue.

"What the fuck?" I say, taking a step back. Even the room itself is changing. The wooden walls are being replaced with soft gray, the tin tub morphing into a gorgeous porcelain one. Everything around me is shimmering, and I wonder if I'm stuck in some illusion or if I've been given drugs.

"It's okay, princess," the glimmering king coos, as his face comes in and out of focus. "Don't be afraid."

"Like fuck I won't be," I growl, retreating farther from him. "Tell me what the hell is going on."

"I've tried so hard to keep you from knowing what I am, hiding in plain sight, as you've said. I don't like the attention, the thousands of eyes lusting after me, vampires constantly wanting recognition from me. It's exhausting."

"I-I don't understand," I stammer, as a white light surrounds him.

"I know, but you will soon. I can't conceal it any longer." The light grows brighter and I shield my eyes as the room is engulfed in a blinding shade of white.

A moment later, everything has changed. The room, the bathtub, and even the king. "I recognize you..." I start, as I scan this new man. I've seen him once before, through the eyes of King Killian. With dark hair as black as my own that hangs past his shoulders in soft waves, and bright blue eyes that a woman could get lost in for days, the vampire I saw through eyes that were not mine steps closer. "You were here, yesterday, with Kings Lucian and Killian. Who...Who are you?"

"I am King Dante, princess. This is my true form."

CHAPTER 38

$\mathcal{M}$y heart races as he moves even closer, the most gorgeous king of them all. He oozes power and grace, making my mouth run dry, and for a moment, I can't even speak. His magnificence is so breathtaking it makes my chest squeeze. The kind of beauty people compare to flawless flowers in nature, to the sky as the sun goes to rest beyond the horizon. He's the epitome of attraction, someone so sexy, so ravishing and seductive, it should be a crime.

And he's walking right toward me.

My breath hitches and I grip my towel tighter, completely frozen to the spot. I can't even move under his gaze that completely consumes me. "How?" I manage to whisper.

This new king stops before me, reaches up to my face, and runs the backs of his fingers gently across my cheek. "Glamour. I hide what I am so I can be left alone. As King of Sloth, I don't often make time for others' needs, only caring about what I want, what I desire. And right now, I'm consumed with thoughts of you."

Even his voice has changed, his once annoying pitch now smooth and melodic. "Me? But I-I thought—"

"Shhhh," he hushes, placing a finger along my lips before sliding the digit into my mouth. I don't know why, but I gently suck on it. "You thought what I wanted you to think. It's all an act. Don't you see?" He pulls his finger from my mouth with a pop and licks my saliva off with a moan. "I only have so much to give, and you deserve the world and beyond, so I hide what I am from everyone but the kings, keeping the facade so I might be left alone. Look at me. Everyone wants a piece of me, princess, and it's exhausting trying to keep them at bay."

"But then why—"

"Why what? Why am I an utter ass toward you? Because I knew if I let you see me for what I am, the other kings wouldn't stand a chance. Because I knew once I had a taste of you, I wouldn't be able to stop myself from constantly wanting more. Because I'm scared of how you make me feel."

"And-and how do I make you feel?" I question, reaching up to run my fingers through his soft hair.

He turns and catches my hand, kissing my wrist. "Alive. For years, centuries, I've hidden, and suppressed my emotions to protect myself and the others from obsession. But you, princess, you make me want to feel, and for that, you will pay the price."

I gulp, wondering what he has in mind.

"I heard about that little stunt you played with Thorin, shifting and running off on your own. Such a naughty little thing, unable to be patient for what she wants. No. You just take it with no thought for others, no care for your own life. As King of Sloth, there is no one better to teach you how to wait. I'll have you begging by the end of the night."

"Begging for what?" Dark thoughts run through my head.

Usually when I'm begging, it's only in my mind—begging to be let out of the queen's dungeons, begging for a scrap of food, begging for the beatings to stop…

"For my lips." He places a soft kiss on my mouth. "For my tongue." He lowers his head and flicks his tongue along the crook of my neck. "For my fingers." He covers my hands with his and forces them open, allowing the towel I'm wearing to pool at my feet. Then, he tilts my head up with the tips of his fingers, forcing my gaze to meet his. "For my cock."

At that I groan as he leans down and languidly begins to kiss me, taking his time to taste my lips until he's satisfied. One of his hands squeezes my ass while the other trails up my spine and threads into my hair.

When his tongue finally prods at the seam of my lips for them to open, I'm already molten. This kiss is everything. It's sweet and sensual as he takes his time, learning my lips and tongue before moving on to the next thing. He's in absolutely no rush, even though my body is already on fire and ready for his touch.

His hand leaves my ass and slides over my hip before gently grazing my slit. "So wet already, princess, so impatient." His fingers leave me and I mewl in protest, pouting like a kid who's been scolded for eating too much dessert.

He chuckles deeply, the smile on his face making my heart flutter and my belly fill with butterflies. His smile would part the clouds and battle the sunshine for beauty. "You sound like a baby kitten. Maybe that's what I shall call you…my little kitten."

I almost fucking swoon before standing on my tiptoes to reach his mouth. His kiss is savory and delicious, a flavor you want to bottle up and pour over your nighttime meal. I groan as his tongue tastes mine, sliding lazily around my mouth.

"Why am I naked and you are not?" I ask, pulling away

from his lips for just a moment. He grins against my mouth, my heart almost bursting just from seeing him smile.

"That can easily be remedied if you can be patient for it, kitten," he purrs. I stifle another mewl. This king is so different from the others. "Let's get out of the bathroom and play somewhere more comfortable."

Play?

Yes, fucking please.

I shriek as he scoops me up, holding me tightly against him before spinning and walking out. His bedroom takes me by surprise. Pure indulgence. The bed is massive, certainly large enough to sleep four or five people. Layers of plush covers and a dozen pillows in soft grays, light blues, and whites make this bed the most inviting one I've ever seen. The only thing that would make it better is a naked King Dante lying in the middle of it.

Gently, he places me down in the center of the opulence, the soft blankets curling around me in a cherished caress. Taking a step back, he roams his eyes over my nakedness as he begins to unbutton his shirt. My mouth salivates when his skin is revealed beneath. Lightly toned, and pale like myself, he's not as built as King Thorin, not bulky and overpowering. He's more like King Lucian. Every inch of him is toned muscle, from his broad chest to his tapered waist. His body is flawless, not a freckle or scar to be found.

He shrugs out of the shirt and steps toward me, not giving in to what I so desperately want to see. "Better?" he inquires with the quirk of one dark eyebrow, running the backs of his fingers along his washboard abs. My insides turn molten, heat pooling between my legs.

"Fucking hell," I blurt, my mouth betraying my answer.

He smiles, causing my chest to tighten. He's right, he is completely irresistible. No wonder he parades around in disguise. Looking like this, he'd never be left alone. Especially here, in the Coven of Sin, where everyone is fucking or thinking about fucking.

If I were him, I'd probably masturbate fifty times a day because I wouldn't be able to resist myself.

"Now where to taste you first..." The sloth king runs a hand through his black hair, pulling it away from his face, showing off prominent cheekbones and a sharp jawline.

He's everything I never knew I wanted.

Resting on the bed next to me, he presses a hand to my chest and pushes me back down to the bed. Funny thing is, I hadn't realized I'd sat up.

"Here perhaps?" Leaning down, his silky hair falling over his handsome face, the king licks the tip of my nipple with the end of his tongue. The touch is but a graze, a tease, yet has me moaning, my spine arching, needing more of his touch.

"Patience, kitten, all good things come to those who wait."

Kitten.

Such an innocent nickname, yet it has my cheeks heating in delight.

"Perhaps another taste is in order." This time he sucks the whole nipple between his soft, full lips and kisses it over and over, swirling his tongue around my areola, tracing the line where the rosy and pale skin meet.

It's driving me wild.

My pussy throbs, my clit ignites, and my nipples bead into hardened tips, reaching for more contact, more pressure. Just more.

I need his lips devouring me, his cock invading me, his hands around my throat, or his fangs penetrating my skin.

Instead, he antagonizes me, caressing me on the very edge of where I want him to. "Don't fucking move," he commands, before gliding to my other breast. He teases me in the same manner, until I'm soaking the bed beneath me, arousal leaking between my thighs. Unable to contain myself, I thread my fingers through his hair and press his lips harder against me.

But the king isn't having it and lifts his head, fire blazing in his bright blue eyes. "This is my show, kitten. If you can't contain yourself, then I will be forced to restrain you. You don't earn sloth by rushing into things. You must ease your way in, take your time, relish every moment, every touch, every whisper of a kiss. I will invade your mind, tantalize your body until you're shaking with need, aching with desire, your every thought consumed by what I'm doing to you."

He goes back to my breast, cupping one while licking the other. I mewl. I just can't help it. He makes me so desperate, so fucking distraught. My fingers clench into fists, my toes digging into the covers as I try not to move. "Please, let me touch you," I beg, not caring how it sounds. "I need to touch you, to feel your body in my hands."

He lifts his head, his black hair surrounding his perfect face, lips wet with saliva. "No."

Groaning, I grip the blankets in my fists to keep myself from moving as he switches back to my other breast. He flattens his tongue and laps my nipple, then blows cold air on the wet trail he left behind. The sensation is delicious torture and it's driving me insane.

My nipples are so fucking hard they hurt, urgently needing his lips to suckle harder or his fingers to pinch them, hell, I'd even take a bite at this point. I can feel him smile against my breast before kissing his way up my chest. The muscles in his arms flex as he sucks on the tender skin in the crook of my neck.

I lick my lips, my whole body heating to the point of

explosion, my pussy fucking throbbing. I can't take this much longer, I really can't.

"You can and you will," he responds, making me feel completely mortified. If he heard that thought, then it's likely he's heard every fucking thing I said as I walked behind him from Riverwood back to his castle.

Every.

Horrible.

Word.

I push that thought from my mind and try to keep my body from twitching. My breathing is ragged, and my thighs rub together ever so slightly to ease the ache. The king unlatches from my neck and rolls his body on top of mine, pressing his fabric-clad cock against me.

"Fuck," I moan, looking down my body to his. King Dante smiles, biting his lower lip, then leans down again to take my nipple into his mouth. This time, he gives me what I want, his teeth grazing the nub. Before I realize I'm doing it, my hand snakes between our bodies, my finger slipping between my pussy lips.

"No!" he growls, snatching my hand and pressing it firmly into the bed beside my head. "I told you not to move. You leave me no other option." Using his vampire speed, King Dante rushes around the bed in a blur. Next thing I know, my hands are tied to the bedposts with a length of silk fabric.

"Now you will have no choice but to suffer my whims," he purrs, prowling around the bed. "You are so beautiful, kitten. So tempting and perfect. Every inch of you begs for my mouth... Supple breasts, smooth skin, and that wet pussy of yours..."

I grip the silk in my hands as the king kisses my mouth again, but not as casually as before. There's an increase in urgency, an eagerness that wasn't there before. Maybe it's because I'm tied down, an act I'm realizing turns me on as much as it does them. Our kiss deepens, his tongue thrusting against mine while one of his hands fondles my breast, pinching the hardened tip. I moan into his mouth before he pulls away, kissing down my neck, between my breasts, licking around my belly button.

Yes, please. Keep going lower.

His soft lips kiss each of my hip bones before he plants another just above my slit. Fuck, this is pure and utter torture. I lift my head, watching with rapt attention as he flattens his tongue, stares up at me with those sparkling blue eyes, and licks me.

"Fuck yes," I rasp, as he wraps his hands under my thighs, pulling them apart.

"So fucking erotic, kitten. Just look at you. Bound to my bed, lips red from kissing me, nipples tight, pussy spread, all just for me." Then, he lowers his mouth, extends his tongue, and lashes my clit, but only for a moment. He knows I'm close. All this torment is keeping me right on the edge of the waterfall.

Swirling his tongue around the place I want him to touch most, the king spreads my legs farther, his fingers holding my pussy open. "So wet, so fucking hot. Just look at what you make me do, kitten. You're irresistible." He dips back down, lips puckered as he gives me what I want, sucking my clit as he hums, but just as I'm about to come, he pulls off.

Tears well in my eyes. "Please," I beg.

"Please what, kitten? Tell me what you need."

I mewl again. "Please let me come."

"Since you asked so nicely…"

King Dante drops back down, attacking my clit, his tongue flicking it back and forth so fast that my legs begin to tremble.

I'm fucking done.

Gripping the silken straps, my thighs clenching his head, I come.

Hard.

My back bows, spine bending, toes curling into the bedding. My vision goes white and I close my eyes, my hips bucking into the king's mouth. I ride his face through the waves of elation until I'm nothing but a twitching mess.

"That...was...incredible..." I praise between pants.

"And to think you haven't even received my sin yet." He's right. Holy hell, he's right.

"You are everything I've ever wanted, kitten. For the first time in over a hundred years, I feel happy."

I open my eyes and peer up at him as he finishes untying me. King Dante tosses the fabric off the bed and looks down at me like I'm the most cherished thing he's ever owned, his hand cupping my face so sweetly.

I feel a blush creeping up my face as I gaze up at him with a smile. "And that, my king, is the best compliment I could ever receive."

Lifting myself up on my elbows, I kiss his lips, tasting myself. I don't know why, but that always turns me on. And before I know it, I've pushed the king down on the bed and worked my way on top of him.

"Now it's your turn, my king. Let me return the favor, make you feel good. I need you in my mouth and I need it now."

His blue eyes flash and he inclines his head slightly. Little does he know that two can play his little game. He wants to terrorize me, keep me from coming until I'm almost insane with desire, then so will he.

I start slow, kissing down his neck, flicking his throbbing vein with my tongue. Then I kiss down his chest, biting his nipple before sitting up and starting on his pants.

His cock strains against the fabric, the shaft and head

perfectly outlined, making my mouth water as I wonder how he will taste. I rub him gently with my hand, sliding my finger around the edge of his head. His cock twitches in his pants, and I can't wait to see what he looks like any longer.

Bending down, my nipples grazing his legs, I use my mouth and untie his pants. He groans when I grip the hem with my teeth and tug them down, my hands helping me slip them over his hips. I sit up once his cock is freed, bobbing happily at me.

It's perfect and beautiful, just like he is. A shade darker than his skin, and a slightly darker head. He's ethereal in his beauty. If I wasn't filled with pride, I'd shy away and feel inferior. But with the other sins guiding me, I lower my face and rub my lips over the head, loving the way it grows harder against my skin.

Smiling to myself, I lean back and pull his pants the rest of the way off before crawling up him. In a bold move, I push my breasts together and fuck his dick with my tits. I watch proudly as his gaze becomes hooded, his muscles tense, and his legs twitch with his impending climax. But I stop before we get too far.

Fucker wants to tease me. It's time to give him a dose of his own medicine. I hold his cock gently and slowly slide my hand up and down, loving how he can be hard and soft at the same time. His cock thickens in my hand, and I have to will myself not to sink my mouth or my pussy down on it.

No. I have to do this his way.

Abandoning his cock, I glide up his body, grinding my wetness against him.

"Little fucking tease, aren't you, kitten?" he purrs.

"All good things come to those who wait," I retort with a wink, using his own words against him. He smiles and bites his lip, pulling my head down to his mouth.

I kiss him languorously, like he did me, taking my time to

taste his lips, learn the flavor of his tongue as my legs straddle his, my core sliding along him.

Then I work my way down his body again, taking my time to taste every inch of his chest, to nibble on his nipples, and purposely taunt him. I lick my way lower, rolling my tongue over each hill and valley of his abs, tasting his skin. I feel his hand snake into my hair and push me lower, but I swat him away.

"Tsk, tsk, tsk. One must learn patience. Don't make me tie you up," I tease.

"Kitten," he growls, his deep tone making the simple word sound like a warning.

Sitting up, I grab my tits and give them a squeeze, rolling my nipples and moaning while I grind on his cock.

"Fuck, you're so sexy, kitten. I could watch you for hours and come a thousand times and never tire of looking at you."

Interesting. The other kings have said something similar.

Smiling, I scoot back and take his cock in my hands again, trailing my palms softly up and down his shaft. His hips thrust, and I have the urge to smack his cock for being bad, but I resist.

When I finally grip him firmly, he groans, the noise so hot, so sexy, that I want to make him do it again. A bead of precum forms on his slit and I can't hold out any longer. I need to taste this king of mine. Lowering my mouth, I grip his base with my hand and suck the head into my mouth. I slide my tongue across the slit, savoring his sweet and salty flavor that I quickly become desperate for more of.

When his cock pulses in my mouth, I know I've got him. Hollowing out my cheeks, I release my hand from the base and sink all the way down, swallowing him whole. He moans again, legs twitching, fingers gently weaving into my hair.

I let him but maintain control. I take him slowly, working my tongue around the head before sucking down the rest of him.

Over and over again, I repeat this at what I know is an agonizing pace for him, until his breaths become shallow, until I can feel his thighs shaking, until his fingers grip my hair so hard it hurts.

Then I pull off, just as his moans were increasing, with a smile on my face.

He growls, his eyes flashing. "That's it, I can't fucking take this." In one quick move, he's flipped us, his arms pinning mine down, his knees spreading my legs open.

He leans down, whispering in my ear, "This pussy? It's mine." Then he plunges inside me. I cry out in ecstasy, his cock filling me so gloriously. "Mine. Forever. Say it," he growls as he begins to move.

"I'm yours."

"Louder!"

"I'm yours!"

"Damn fucking right you are. This hot fucking body—" Thrust. "These perfect breasts—" Thrust. "And this tight fucking pussy."

The king grips my shoulders and fucks me with abandon, pounding in and out of me. My breasts bounce and his eyes get hazy, sweat coating his brow.

My pussy clenches when he changes angles, smacking into a spot inside me that makes me wild. Another orgasm brews within me, a sizzling heat heavy inside me.

My breathing becomes shallow and the king leans down. "I have to taste you," he whispers into my ear before sinking his fangs in my neck. I cry out, my pussy pulsing, and come while screaming his name.

With my cunt milking him, my blood flowing through him, I know he's close. King Dante pulls off my neck and sits up. The sight of him with my blood dripping down his chin to his chest, his abs tightening and cock thrusting inside me, will go down as one of the most erotic things I've ever seen.

Gripping my breasts in his hands, he pounds my pussy until his moans grow louder. "Take my sin, kitten. It's yours," he rasps, voice deepening.

He rolls us again and holds my hips up as he fucks me from below. He arches his neck, and I feel my fangs descend, my eyes fixed on his throbbing pulse. Then I lunge, sinking my fangs deep into his neck. We cry out together as he reaches his climax, hot cum spurting inside me as I drink him down. His sloth surges into my veins, contradicting the greed inside me. I want more of his blood, it's savory, the flavor changing the more I drink.

"Enough, princess." His voice has my eyes flying open, my mouth still attached to his neck. Grudgingly, I disconnect from him and retract my fangs, but lick at his wounds to get every last drop of his blood until it's gone.

I collapse onto his chest, our bodies still connected. His arm cradles me as I trace his skin absentmindedly with the tip of my finger.

"King Dante?" I murmur through a yawn.

"Hmm?"

"Will you still use glamour around me after this?" I'm wary of his answer. Never again do I want to see that shell of a king he used to wear, not when I know the glory of his true self.

"Never. Now that we've bonded, I don't have to pretend anymore, the desire to hide from you has vanished. I never knew how good it could feel to let someone in, and now that I know, I'm never letting go."

"Good," I say, as another yawn overtakes me.

"Sleep, kitten. The changes in our world grow more and more evident each passing day. Rest while you can, because when the lightning crashes and thunder rolls, we need you to weather the storm." With that thought churning in the back of my head, I nestle into him and enjoy this fleeting moment, knowing when I wake up, I'll be alone.

But not for much longer.

Two kings to go and my solitude will end. Never again will I wake up alone. At least that's my plan once they claim me as theirs. That thought leaves a smile on my face as I fall into a deep sleep in the arms of King Dante. Just before sleep takes me, he mutters, "It is I who hopes you don't use your glamour on me."

CHAPTER 39

The smell of fresh bacon wakes me. My eyes flit open to see Katie standing at the foot of my bed, holding a tray. Sitting up, my sheet clutched to my chest, I inhale deeply. "Good morning, Snow. I thought you might be hungry after sleeping for three days."

"Three days!" I shout, jaw dropping as I run my hands through my tangled curls.

"Yep. Must have been a good fucking."

"Katie!" I gripe, tossing a pillow at her. She laughs, swatting it out of the way just before it crashes onto the tray.

"Don't deny it! Tell me, who was it this time? Killian? Dante? Lucian? A king sandwich perhaps? I need details."

I laugh at her fierce interest in my sex life. But I have to admit, it is nice to have a friend to share things like this with. She's my inner circle, the only member actually. I don't know what I'd do without her. She gives me advice, cheers me up, calms me down. I can rely on her for everything, and for that, I'll be forever grateful.

"It was Dante."

"Ugh," she grumbles. "That had to be awful."

Not wanting to give up the details of the king's life lived in a haze of glamour, I just shrug and grab a piece of bacon, shoving the whole slice in my mouth. "How're things with Julian?" I ask around a mouthful of food.

A dreamy look plasters itself on her face. "My sweet Julian," she coos on a sigh. "I can't get enough of that vampire."

"By the looks of the bites all over your body, he can't get enough of you either."

Her smile is huge. "Yeah. I just wish we could stay the night together. I hate when he kicks me out during dead time, but I totally get why."

I scrunch my nose in confusion. "What the hell is dead time?"

"You know…dead time?" When I shake my head, her eyes go wide. "You mean to tell me that you've slept with five vampire kings and you don't know about dead time? Haven't you ever wondered why you always wake up in your bed, Snow?"

"Well, I just kinda assumed it was some weird thing they decided on doing before I sleep with them all."

Katie slaps her hand to her forehead. "Sometimes, Snow, you can be so naïve." She scrubs her hands down her face, then folds them in her lap. "Dead time is what I call the time…when the vampires die."

"They die?" I shout, mortified. "What do you mean they die?"

"Well, they aren't exactly alive, now are they?"

I drop my head in my hands, rubbing my temples. "Katie, I have no idea what you're talking about. The kings are alive. I've fucked them, drank from them. I've felt their pulses flitter under my tongue—"

"I know, Snow," Katie interrupts. "But have you ever spent an entire day with them?"

"How the fuck should I know? I can't fucking tell time down here. There are no windows or doors—"

"And for good reason. Not only do they burn in the sun... you do know about that, right?"

"Yes," I grumble.

"Okay, just checking. Because you seem to be quite misinformed, so I want to make sure—"

"Katie!"

"Okay, okay!" She holds up her hands in a placating fashion. "Well, I hate to be the one to tell you this but, vampires? Well...they aren't exactly alive. And because of that, they have what I call dead time. When the sun climbs over the horizon, they feel a sort of pull, as Julian describes it. It guides them into the darkest corners of the coven where they literally die until after the sun sets again. Some of the older vampires can resist the pull, but most of them can't. That's why you don't get to sleep with them. Because they don't want you to see them during dead time."

"Wow," I whisper, cupping my cheeks. "I had no idea."

"Could you even imagine your horror, waking up next to the seven and their bodies being lifeless and cold? You would have freaked the fuck out," she exclaims and giggles.

"And then some." I nod, agreeing with her. "I wonder why they didn't tell me."

"Probably didn't want to scare you, is my guess. They are awfully protective of you, and you tend to be a little reckless at times."

My cheeks heat. There's no denying that.

"Yeah, and the main reason I'm reckless is because they sometimes try to control me. I've grown up under the tyrannical nonsense of the evil cunt bitch. I will not be told what to do ever again."

"They're not like that," she soothes in a calming tone. "You need to get over yourself."

I jerk my head toward her. "Excuse me?"

"Oh, come on, Snow! Don't be so thick! The kings only 'give you orders' if that's what you want to call it, because they want to keep you safe, not because they wish to control you. You can't even compare them to the evil queen. They are nothing like her."

My shoulders sag. "You're right. I don't know what's gotten into me."

Katie starts counting on her fingers. "Ramsey, Strix, Thorin, Marcel—"

"Shut up!" I laugh, pushing her shoulder. She falls back to the bed snickering.

Katie wipes the tears from her eyes. "I have to admit, though, watching you change into a wolf was really fucking cool."

I laugh. "Thanks. But now I can't use that as a disguise to slip away again." My thoughts drift through that day. Turning into my wolf, seeing the people of Riverwood, helping them through their devastation. Then my night with King Dante...

My night with King Dante.

That's it!

I should have glamour now, right?

I look at Katie, who narrows her eyes, raising herself up on her elbows. "What are you planning, Snow? I recognize that look in your eyes."

A huge grin creeps across my face. "Come here." Katie takes my offered hand and I pull her up, tucking my sheet under my arms so I'm not flashing my tits all over the place.

Concentrating on her face, I memorize every freckle, every smile line, the shade of her eyes, the color of her hair. Focusing on exactly what Katie looks like, I close my eyes and search for my door. They are coming to me easier now. My wolf paws at hers, dying to be let out. I almost say fuck it and rip hers open. It felt so good to be inside her lithe, canine body.

But today is not that day.

King Marcel and King Dante now have a door in my hallway, leaving only two remaining in shadow.

But not for much longer...

Using my senses, I gravitate toward the door across from King Dante's light blue one, knowing my glamour is inside it. I throw it open, eager to step through. Inside is a mass of color, swirling in a colossal, mesmerizing tornado of every shade of blue, yellow, green, orange, purple, and pink. Blacks and whites shift in and out too. It's as if a giant art set is at my fingertips, and I just have to choose the right colors.

I step inside the vortex, my hair swirling about my head. Concentrating on my memory of Katie, I recall every nuance about her. When my skin begins to tingle, I know I'm doing something right.

Katie's muffled voice echoes in my mind. "Snow! What's happening to you?" I ignore her, the sensations in my body heightening.

Then it stops abruptly, and I open my eyes. "Katie, what do you see?" Right away, I know my voice doesn't change because I sound the same as before. I look down at our joined hands and recognize mine as unchanged. I frown, thinking I've fucked this up somehow.

"You-you're...you're me," she whispers, her hand covering her mouth in shock.

"Am I?" Forgetting I'm naked, I slip out of bed and pad into my bathroom. Looking in the mirror, I see my own reflection. I stare back at myself, my hair disheveled, ever darkening eyes, dried blood crusted to my skin, and remnants of my time with King Dante all over me. "So when you look at me, Katie, you see yourself?"

"Yes. It's fucking weird," she whispers, creeping up behind me.

"Am I wearing your clothes too?" Katie nods. "I look like myself to me," I tell her. "So I wonder how I'll be able to tell if my glamour falters."

"I don't know, Snow, but one thing's for sure…"

"What's that?" I question.

"This is fucking cool." She smiles at me in the mirror, catching my eye.

I turn toward her. "Time to create some mischief."

Her smile falters. "Oh no. No, you don't. Not disguised as me, little lady."

"Try and stop me," I tease, ducking out of the way as she lunges to grab me. Using my enhanced speed, I rip open my door and rush out.

"Snow, wait!" Katie calls, her voice growing softer as I run farther away. "I have something important to tell you…"

Eh. It can wait until later.

Once I think I'm far enough away, ensuring I won't run into the real Katie, I slow my pace and realize I'm just about to exit a door leading from the castles. By the orange banners hanging from the ceiling, I know I'm in King Killian's foyer. I ignore the stares from other servants, likely wondering why I'm not holding a tray filled with wine or blood, or why I'm not straightening up the hundreds of pillows spread over the many chairs.

But I don't care.

Today, I'm Katie, not Snow, and I intend to take advantage of it. Raising my chin, I march toward the doors and let the guards open them for me. But when I exit the castle, I startle, completely unprepared for what my eyes are seeing.

It's my people.

They're here, in the coven.

At least some of them are.

I see more walking down the steep staircase, their eyes darting around at the magnificence of this place. Some look worried, others excited. I spot Rosie holding the hand of an elderly woman, as two strong men carry her slowly down the stairs. Excited to see her again, I raise my hand to wave but quickly tuck my arm back down. I'm Katie right now. She'd have no idea who I am.

Tearing my gaze from her, I walk through the droves of people. King Marcel is standing on a raised platform. He looks gorgeous. His hair and beard are neatly trimmed, his gold crown sparkling on his head. He wears a loose-fitting, off-white shirt that leaves his chest bare, showing off the many necklaces he likes to wear.

King Thorin stands behind him and off to one side, his chest puffed, eyes watchful. A black cape is tied around his thick neck, and he strokes his beard thoughtfully.

Next to King Thorin is King Lucian, who's looking very dapper. He has on a dark blue suit, reminding me of the one King Strix wore the night I received his sin. King Lucian wears his crown proudly, his messy black hair sticking out from under it. He smiles at a group of whispering women, whose faces immediately redden from his attention. I can't blame them. He is so beautiful it hurts.

King Marcel raises his hands to command everyone's attention and begins speaking to a large group of Riverwood people about what it means to be a drone. "Any citizens interested will receive a small dose of my blood, which is ingested by drinking a mixture with mead. The effect will happen immediately, meaning once you drink my blood, you cannot undrink it, therefore, you've made a commitment to become a drone. With my blood flowing through your veins, I will be able to sense you and feel your emotions if I wish. This will prove helpful when we make our stand against the evil queen.

379

"Attributes you will notice changing include, but are not limited to, increased speed, strength, agility, and healing. It is unknown how long you will retain vampire benefits, as each individual will process my blood differently. Are there any questions?"

As individuals raise their hands, voicing concerns and excitement, I turn from them and eavesdrop on a group of rather battle worn looking men. One of them squeezes the shoulder of another, telling him how sorry he was that he couldn't save his brother.

"What happened to you?" I inquire, unable to help myself. A man I recognize from Riverwood, with a large gash running across his cheek, glances up at me with sad, tired eyes.

"The evil queen attacked again, just as dawn was beginning to break earlier today. We held out for a good part of the day, but eventually, without the help from the kings and other vampires, we didn't stand a chance and her huntsmen broke through." Tears glisten in his eyes and he shakes his head, trying to stop the flow of emotion. He clears his throat, his voice breaking. "We lost a dozen more people. That number would have increased tenfold if the kings hadn't shown up again at dusk. They defended us in spite of our apprehension toward them, then invited us into the safety of their castles. We will forever be in their debt."

No words I could say will ease his pain. I leave him in the hands of his friends and walk aimlessly. So many thoughts are filtering through my head. The evil queen attacked again? My time, our time, is running out. I need to get these final two sins and become whatever it is that the kings seem to think I will become once I have all seven sins inside me.

Before I know it, I've walked all the way over to the underground stream and I sit down on a stone bench, my elbows on my knees, head in my hands, watching the water flowing. It's an odd sensation, because when I look down, I'm sitting here completely naked, but with my glamour in effect, I look like a clothed Katie. That slight tingle still licks my skin, letting me know I've managed to maintain it.

Picking up a small rock, I toss it into the river and watch it sink. I can't believe the evil queen attacked again. My poor people. My heart breaks for them.

Wallowing in my sorrows, I don't even realize when a handsome, young vampire sits down next to me. "Hey, Katie. Want to head up to my place? I'm feeling very parched..." The vampire lowers his head and sniffs my neck as I freeze like a statue. "Mmm. You smell good. New soap?"

"Uhh."

"What? Cat got your tongue? If I remember correctly, that tongue was all over me last night."

Oh shit. This must be Julian. What the fuck am I going to do?

"I...uhh. I have to go. Yeah. I need to tend to her. Uhh... Snow... Uhh... Princess Snow. Yeah." Quickly, I stand up and back away. "I'll... I'll see you later! Okay!" Then I wave awkwardly and run away.

"Katie!" he yells, as I weave through the crowd, hoping he doesn't catch up to me. I make it all the way back to where King Marcel is deliberating with a new group of people when the older woman Rosie was helping raises her hand from the chair she's resting on.

"I'll do it," she proclaims firmly, her voice quivering with age.

"You? But, Grandma—"

"No buts, Rosie Posie. I said I'm going to do it and I intend to."

"Good woman," King Marcel says with a smile. "What is your name?

"Marie. My name is Marie."

"And how long has it been since you've had the use of your legs?" King Marcel inquires.

Marie exchanges a glance with Rosie. "Oh, I don't know. Five or six years at least."

The greed king grins. "How about we see what those legs will do with a bit of my blood helping them?"

Marie smiles warmly. She oozes kindness, just like her granddaughter Rosie does. "I'd like that very much, Mr. King."

"Marcel. King Marcel," he corrects, jumping down from his pedestal and holding out his hand, golden rings on each finger. "Pleased to meet you, Marie. Welcome to our home."

"Pleasure is all mine, King Marcel."

He smiles, beckoning a servant standing nearby who's holding a tray of goblets. "Don't be frightened by what you are about to see," he warns, as he brings his wrist to his lips and bites. I see a hint of fang before he retracts them which, for some odd reason, I find completely arousing. King Marcel then holds his arm over the glasses and allows a single drop to enter each drink before grabbing one and handing it to Marie. "My lady. If you please…"

Marie licks her lips, her eyes never leaving his. "I come from a long line of strong women. It's going to take a lot more than a couple of sharp teeth to scare me." Then she swipes the glass from him and places it to her lips, drinking it down without hesitation. "It's good," she proclaims, wiping her mouth with the back of her hand. "I taste the mead but also a hint of chocolate maybe? Dear Lord. Do you have chocolate blood?"

I stifle a laugh, because I tasted the same thing when I drank from the king.

"How do you feel?" King Marcel asks quietly, his dark eyebrow arched.

"Good," she answers, her voice stronger, not as shaky.

"Great even. In fact. I'd like to try and stand. Rosie, help me up."

Concern is etched into Rosie's face, but she doesn't argue, instead she helps the old woman. Their hands joined, Marie grunts, her legs shaking, and with the crowd around her gasping in awe, Marie stands.

She fucking stands.

I'm almost moved to tears.

"Grandma!" Rosie cries out, throwing her arms around Marie. My heart warms at the sight.

"I can't believe it," Marie weeps, tears of happiness streaming down her cheeks. Releasing Rosie, she takes a tentative step, then another, until she's walked over to King Marcel and inclines her head. "Thank you, my king."

"No need to thank me, Marie. It is I who should thank you, for showing your people how to be brave. You have made a difference, and I feel very fortunate to have you here with me on this night."

Marie takes her time turning back to the crowd. "I can walk!" she shouts, arms raised in the air.

The people swarm her. Hugs are exchanged and tears are shared as a line of people forms in front of King Marcel—a line of people waiting for their chance to become drones.

Yes.

This is it.

We can fucking do this.

My heart swells at the encouraging sight. Seeing my people down here in the coven, intermixing with the vampires...I couldn't be any happier. They are safe, at least for now, protected by the vampires and our secret lair until I can finish my transformation and take on the evil cunt bitch.

I can see the tension leaving their faces, relief replacing worry as they realize the monsters they grew up learning about are not monsters, simply different.

So often people mistreat what they do not understand. Those who are different in a way that makes them stick out in a crowd are often ostracized from the community. Not because they are bad, but because they are unknown. They are misunderstood, judged, just for being who and what they are. Now, the vampires are getting a chance to prove they are not the monsters the legends speak of, but quite possibly our salvation.

Funny how the world works, its ways mysterious. We may not always know the path we are to take, but fate does. And she has a method of getting us to our destiny in ways we may not expect. The experiences taking us there, the journey, makes us who we are. If we didn't know pain, we could not really understand joy. If we did not feel despair, we could not appreciate happiness. It's a constant battle of give and take. And if you're not paying attention, your opportunity to grow could fly right past you.

Me? I'm ready to grab it by the balls and make it my bitch.

"Well, well, well, what do we have here?" I freeze as King Lucian's sweet and spicy scent rolls around me. "A stowaway. Shouldn't you be tending to the princess?" His voice is mocking. He knows I'm not Katie.

"How?" I whisper, as his chest presses into my back.

"Well, for starters, you're the only one standing completely naked in the crowd. Hard to miss you."

"Oh fuck." My arms shoot up to cover myself as I realize I can't feel the tingling anymore. My glamour wore off and I didn't even notice.

King Lucian laughs, covering me with his jacket. "Don't worry, pet, I much prefer you naked."

"How long could you see me?" I ask, spinning to look at him.

"Not long. I followed your scent first. You still smell like blood and sex from your night with King Dante. Tell me, was he a good lover?"

I bite my lip, my cheeks heating.

"That good, huh? Well, I can't let the King of Sloth top the vampire who wields lust, now can I? Looks like you have a long night ahead of you, Princess Snow. Because what I have planned for you, will take me hours to complete."

CHAPTER 40

My insides flutter in anticipation. King Lucian was the first vampire king I ever talked to. He's the one who invaded my dreams, the one who risked his life coming to the castle to try and steal me from the queen. He's the first one I saw naked, the king I shared my first kiss with.

And I want him so fucking badly I can taste it.

"Soon, pet," he purrs. Gripping my shoulders with his hands, King Lucian steers me from the crowd, away from my people and the other kings, and straight to his castle which is dead center between them all.

The guards open the doors for us when we get close, inclining their heads in respect. But as soon as the doors shut, my chest begins to feel heavy with anticipation. The huge corridor is just as I remember, lined with life-sized statues of men and women carved from white stone, performing sexual acts or exploiting themselves. You can't walk through here and not become completely turned on by all the nudity, even if the subjects are static.

As we exit through the corridor and into a sitting room,

the smell of incense grows, heightening the senses. King Lucian tugs at the jacket covering me and pulls it from my body, leaving me naked before all. Even though the castle is crowded with people, no one is paying me any mind. Why? Because they are all fucking.

The pairings are endless. Men with men, women with women, several men with one woman. Sweat covered bodies glisten, the melodic sounds of moaning in every pitch causing heat to pool between my legs. His soft hands knead my shoulders as he guides me through the lovers and up the swirling stairs to the gilded, ivory doors at the top—the entrance to his suite.

We pass through the sitting area with oversized couches and chairs perched under the arched ceiling, which is painted to mimic a gorgeous sunset, and into his bedroom. It's just as I remember it.

Luxurious silks in blue and black drape over his decadent bed, carved in the likeness of a tree complete with branches and leaves. You'd think the silks would be out of place, but they complement the bed perfectly.

The bedding is purposely messy, displaying the many layers of sheets, blankets, and throws creating the plush sleeping area. Even the walls here are lined with fabric, making it warm and inviting, though every inch of wall space displays an erotic piece of art.

I have a sense of déjà vu as King Lucian removes his crown, and runs his fingers through his messy, black hair. He turns and sets the crown on his bureau before unbuttoning his shirt. Just like the first time I saw King Lucian naked, I feel a mixture of excitement and anxiety.

What if I'm not good enough for the lust king? Sure, I could please greed, wrath, and even sloth...much to my surprise. But I'm fairly new at this whole seduction thing.

What if I can't be what he needs me to be? My pride flutters, giving me a boost of confidence. I can do this.

"You are gorgeous, pet, but filthy. Why don't you head into the hot spring and I'll join you in a moment," he suggests, before he finishes unbuttoning his shirt.

He's right. I'm still covered in blood and cum from however long ago my night with King Dante was. Nodding, I walk past him as his eyes assess me.

The pool room is just as I remember it, which surprises me. Maybe it's because I was so spooked, scared, and nervous the first time I came here that I thought perhaps I'd imagined it all.

But that couldn't be farther from the truth.

The dark, stone spring is surrounded by candles of varying heights. Some bundles of wax pillars sit in pools of their melted predecessors, their sweet fragrance invading my nose as the wax heats. Mist rises from the hot spring, coating my skin.

I dip my toe into the warm liquid and almost groan, having forgotten just how glorious this is compared to a tub. Dropping to my butt, I slip my legs in then lower my body down. "Ahhh," I moan, as the warmth consumes me. I even duck under, scrubbing the sweat from my face, soaking my long, black hair.

"You mustn't make those noises yet, pet, we've only just begun."

I startle, glancing over my shoulder. I see King Lucian standing naked and perfect, his arms folded, as he leans against the entrance to the room.

Fuck, I forgot how beautiful this king is. Every inch of him is perfection, from his broad chest to his tapered waist, to the long, straight cock bobbing between his legs.

My mouth waters at the sight of him, and I have to chew on my lip to keep from drooling. King Lucian flashes me a knowing smile, because he's aware of exactly how he makes me feel.

Unfolding his arms, he strides past me, his tight ass so fucking sexy, and enters the pool, settling in the same spot as last time. "Feeling better?" he asks, before submerging himself. When he stands back up, droplets of water cascade down his body, delineating every hill and valley of his skin. He runs his fingers through his wet hair, his blue eyes ablaze, knowing he's torturing me.

"Uhhh..." What the fuck did he ask me? I'm at a total loss for words. My mind can't seem to focus on anything but him. Not on my hunger. Not on my excitement from seeing the people of Riverwood safe. Nothing. Except him.

King Lucian lowers himself back into the pool and snaps his fingers. Like before, servants seem to melt from the black walls. The king and I are each given a goblet. By the smell, mine, at least, contains red wine. I'm hoping the same is true for him, unable to bear the thought of another's blood filling his mouth.

He takes a sip of his, eyes sparkling, his tongue darting out to lick his lips. I take a moment to appreciate how gorgeous he is. His messy black hair hangs in front of his eyes and he whips his head to move the rogue strands. His face is clean-shaven with an angular jaw and dimpled chin. Sharp, dark eyebrows arch perfectly above his piercing, blue gaze surrounded by thick, black lashes.

He is pure seduction.

A wave of warmth that has nothing to do with the hot spring surrounds me. I can't tell if I'm just aroused, or if the king is pushing his lust at me. The cause doesn't really matter, because the sensation is pleasing. I let it roll through me, resting my head back against the brim of the pool, my body soaking under the warm water below.

With his eyes shimmering, a smile tugging at his lips, the

king stands and offers me his hand. Smiling, I slip mine into his and allow him to pull me to my feet. His eyes roam my body with a fierce hunger that makes me want to both cower and display myself in front of him.

His hands come up, reaching for my breasts, but holding back, he merely traces the outsides of them with his fingertips. Even from just that small touch, I shiver, my nipples tightening.

I want to be touched.

Tasted.

Fucked.

The king slides behind me, pulling my wet hair off one shoulder, and places soft kisses along the plains of my neck, his fingers digging into my hips. I moan, reaching back to run my fingers through his hair.

"You have no idea what you do to me, do you, pet?" he murmurs against my skin. "I have a surprise for you. Sit down and let me show you."

With me in his lap, we submerge ourselves again, water cresting just above my chest. He lifts my legs, placing them on the outsides of his, leaving my pussy spread below the water. His hardness presses against my ass, taunting me. If I just moved a little bit, I would be at the perfect angle to fuck him.

"Not yet," he whispers, his hand slowly grazing my pussy lips. "You may enter." Confused by what he means, I take a breath to ask when a couple emerges from the darkness. The woman is wearing a dark blue dress that reveals her form without clinging to her skin. The man is in a matching colored suit. Both people are beautiful in a human way. They don't have the grace and elegance of the kings, but before meeting the seven, I would have considered this couple to be a handsome pairing.

The man has short, blond hair and dark brown eyes, while the woman has green eyes and light brown hair pinned to the top of her head. They eye us with excitement, but also a little trepidation. I wonder if King Lucian means for them to join us tonight, which leaves me a little disappointed. Though I didn't mind sharing Kings Thorin and Marcel together, the idea of having a couple of strangers touching him makes me angry.

"Settle yourself, pet, and watch. This couple is here to entertain us. They wish to please their king and future queen by putting on a show. My lust has invaded their senses. Just look at them and you'll see."

Looking at them with a different set of eyes, I see how hooded their gazes are, how shallow their breathing is. The woman's nipples poke excitedly at the fabric of her dress, while the man's cock prods at his pants.

I recognize the slack looks on their faces—they are aroused.

King Lucian adds slight pressure where he rubs between my legs, and a soft, needy moan escapes me. "So responsive, pet. Now give them an order. You want to see him strip first or her? Your choice."

I don't know how to feel. Knowing they are under the influence of the king's lust makes me wonder if they would actually choose to be here in absence of it. But then I remember dancing in the cage above the party, lust swirling around inside me. I took my clothes off because I wanted to. I bared myself because it felt empowering.

"Do you both wish to be here?" I question, needing to hear their responses for myself. I've suffered far too long under the control of another to ever wish that upon someone else.

"Yes," the woman responds first.

"Yes," the man says next.

Their admission relaxes me, and I settle back into King Lucian's chest, not even realizing how tense I'd gotten.

"Better?" King Lucian asks in my ear. I nod, my eyes focused on the couple. "Good. Then let's allow them to share their gift with us." He plants a kiss on my shoulder, then rubs up and down my arms. "Let's start off slowly. What are your names?"

I take a drink of my wine. "I'm Jordan, and this is my wife, Tess," the man I now know as Jordan answers.

"Nice to meet you both," I respond, not wanting to forget my niceties, but totally feeling awkward.

I feel another surge of lust. It licks across my skin, grazing my nipples and pinching my clit, and my body comes to life. Tess and Jordan suck in a gasp, the same wave rolling through them. "Now, Jordan," King Lucian purrs behind me, "why don't you take off your wife's dress for her? She's looking very heated."

Jordan inclines his head before slipping behind his wife. Eyes focused on her back, he loosens her dress, then slips it from her shoulders, allowing the garment to pool at her feet. Tess is left wearing underclothes, the likes of which I haven't seen before. A dark blue lace bra covers her breasts, and a matching pair of panties sit high over her hips.

It's so erotic.

My eyes turn to him, an order blurting from my lips. "Take off your jacket, Jordan, and have your wife remove your shirt."

"There you go," King Lucian whispers in my ear. "See how much fun this is?"

I nod, my eyes focused on Jordan as he shrugs from the suit coat. His wife spins, her back to us now. I'm startled to see her panties are absent from her ass cheeks, just a thin strip of fabric stuck between them. So. Fucking. Hot.

Her hands shake as she unbuttons his shirt. Jordan keeps

his eyes trained on us, his dark brown gaze flitting from me to the king. Tess finishes, then steps behind her husband, pulling the shirt from his body. Jordan's thinner than the vampire kings, but still displays a muscled frame.

"Take off your top, Tess," I command. After my first encounter with a woman in King Ramsey's suite, I have come to realize I really enjoy a woman's breasts. Something about how they move, the slight jiggle when they walk, I find it completely arousing. I love discovering what color each woman's nipples might be, how big or how small they are.

Tess steps out from behind her husband and reaches behind her back. The top loosens and then falls from her shoulders. Her breasts are spectacular. Not as big as mine, but perky and soft-looking with small, pink areolas and pert nipples.

"Play with her breasts, Jordan," King Lucian orders, as if he could sense my desires. Jordan steps behind Tess, desire flashing in his gaze, and cups his wife's chest. He's slow at first, then kneads them harder, eliciting a moan from Tess. Jordan moves to her nipples, circling them with a single finger. I watch, fascinated, as her pink buds harden before my eyes. So fucking hot, so erotic. My own nipples tighten in response, as if Jordan was touching me.

"Both of you, take off the rest of your clothes," I demand. They oblige, Jordan lowering his pants while Tess slips the panties off her hips. Though they are both stunning naked, I have no desire to touch them myself, but find myself desperate to feel my king thrusting inside me.

"Soon," King Lucian croons. "For now, we watch. But if you are a good girl, you shall be rewarded."

Good girl.

Those words turn me molten.

Jordan's cock bobs, his hands clenching at his sides. "Now," King Lucian begins, "I wish for you both to sit as we are, with Tess on top of Jordan." They sit on the edge of the pool, facing us but a little unsure of their positioning. "Tess, keep your arms locked behind you. Jordan, spread her legs for us."

Tess's breath hitches as Jordan moves her thighs apart, displaying her pussy lips. My core heats, wanting those lips spread wide to see what lies inside.

I shriek when I'm jerked from the pool. King Lucian pulls us both out using his vampire speed and perches us outside the pool, opposite the husband and wife. He settles me into his lap, then spreads my legs apart, mimicking Tess's position.

"Now, pet, whatever command we give them to perform, we will mimic. Does the thought of them watching us, watching me touch you while they touch each other, fill you with desire?"

"Fuck yes," I moan, my voice wanton. I've watched others fuck, and had others watch me, but never when it's this intimate, this close. Tess's and Jordan's gazes are heated as they await our next command.

"Jordan, play with your wife's cunt," King Lucian orders. "Tess, play with your breasts." The couple moves, Jordan's hands sliding up Tess's thighs, rubbing her outer lips. My breath hitches as King Lucian does the same to me, spreading my legs, hands working my pussy. "Play with your breasts, pet. Do as Tess does."

I moan as my hands come up and squeeze my chest, mimicking Tess as she kneads her breasts before pulling on her nipples. It's like my eyes don't know where to look. I want to watch her hands manipulate herself, but I also want to see Jordan's actions. His finger delves between her lower lips, circling around that nub at the top. I lick my lips, pressure growing low inside me, and King Lucian slips a finger inside my pussy before tracing circles around my own clit.

Tess's eyes close, her thighs spreading wider to allow her husband better access. A gush of arousal leaks from inside me as Jordan spreads her cunt open with one hand, then fucks her with his finger. I've never watched something like this before, seeing her cunt stretching to accept him when he adds a second finger, listening to her seductive moans.

King Lucian slips his finger inside me, then adds a second, fucking me while Jordan fucks his wife. Tess's eyes fly open, both hers and her husband's narrowing on my pussy. Fuck, I'm so hot from watching them observing King Lucian touch me, play with me, while we watch them.

Jordan slides his fingers back out and strums her clit as the king moves to play with mine. Before I know it, Tess and I are panting, chests rising and falling, moans growing higher and higher.

"That's it, Tess. Come for us. Come all over your husband's fingers."

"Fuck yes," she moans. King Lucian's fingers move faster over my clit, my pulse racing, legs shaking.

Tess cries out, her pussy actually clenching, cum leaking from her channel.

I'm fucking done.

With one more stroke to my clit, I scream, my hips thrusting as I come too. King Lucian eases me through it, his pace slowing until my orgasm is over.

Tess collapses into Jordan's chest, eyes closed.

"Thank you, Jordan, Tess. That will be all." Jordan looks disappointed, his face in a firm scowl as he makes no move to leave. King Lucian growls. I look over my shoulder to see his reaction and gasp. His eyes are glowing as he stares at the man. Jordan's face goes slack, his eyelids lowered. "Jordan, Tess, you will leave this place and tell none what transpired here." Jordan nods, then scoops up his pliant wife, snatches their clothes from the floor, and disappears into the darkness in the back of the room.

"What was that?" I manage to whisper.

"I had to compel him. A power given to those that wield lust, because so many are drawn to us, wanting a piece of us. It allows me to make them forget they saw me, disremember where to find me. But enough of that. What did you think of the show, pet? Did you like it?" King Lucian purrs, his lips caressing the shell of my ear.

"It was amazing," I say breathily, still reeling from the orgasm.

"Good. Because I'm not done with you yet. That was just an appetizer."

My eyes shoot open as he scoops me up, then walks us back into his room. He places me down in the middle of the plush bedding and just stares at me.

I don't cover up. I don't cower. The old me still lingers inside my mind, but the new me is beginning to overpower her. In fact, I like it when the king stares at me, it drives me wild. Each place his gaze lands on my body ignites as if he were touching me.

"Now there's more to lust than using your eyes, pet." King Lucian slides open a drawer in his bureau and pulls out a length of black fabric. "Your other senses heighten when others are taken away. Your eyes, for example." The king walks toward me, cock proudly erect, and bends down, placing a kiss on each of my eyelids before sliding the cloth around them, tying it tight behind my head. "Can you see me?"

"No," I respond. Even with my eyes open, I'm still in utter darkness.

"Good." I hear footsteps, he rummages around in something, more than likely his bureau again, then his steps draw near. I gasp when something tickles my belly, the soft item moving up to graze my nipples.

It's subtle but feels very good. Curious, I ask, "What is that?"

"A single feather." He moves from breast to breast, tracing each one before teasing my nipples. The sensation is nice, but not enough, leaving me desperate for a harder, firmer touch. "So responsive," he praises, trailing it down between my breasts to my stomach and lower.

I feel his fingers surround my ankles and pull them, moving my legs slightly apart. Then he resumes touching me with the feather, tickling it over my pussy lips before moving it up and down each leg.

"Raise your arms above your head, pet," he orders. I happily comply, wondering what's coming next. The feather glides along my sides, its touch but a whisper, making my skin erupt in goosebumps. "See how touch can be enhanced without being able to see?"

"I need more," I whisper.

He chuckles deeply, and I feel the bed sink on either side of my legs as he climbs on. The bedding depresses near the sides of my head, and a heat builds between us as he leans down. His mouth descends on my neck, gently licking and sucking the tender skin. I lift my hands and run them up and down his back, feeling his muscles flex as he moves. King Lucian shifts lower, his hands grasping my breasts, fingers toying with my nipples before his mouth sucks one between his perfect lips.

"Yes," I groan out, one hand pulling on his hair while I press him firmer to my breast. I cry out when his fangs sink into me, so close to my nipple that I'm both terrified and completely aroused. He drinks me in, sucking on my nipple at the same time, while his free hand snakes between us and slides over my pussy. I try to spread my thighs, wanting him to touch me deeper, but his legs are on the outside of mine and stop me from moving.

He pulls away and moves to my other side, the tip of his fang grazing my hardened bud. "No!" I cry out, as he presses his fang into it. Fuck, it hurts so good. My body shakes with the sensations. I desperately want to see him, watch what he's doing to me. He sucks it into his mouth, moaning as he does. The vibrations from his groans tickle my nipple further.

The king releases me and climbs up my body, whispering as he does. "Feel my mouth on you, my tongue tasting you, my fingers playing with your body. Hear how happy you make me and smell the copper tang of your sweet blood. Let the sensations overwhelm you, let them seduce you." Then, with a growl, he crushes his lips to mine. I moan into his mouth, opening for his prodding tongue. I let my fangs descend and nick his tongue, tasting the sweet spiciness of his blood in our kiss. He growls, his hands pinning my arms by my head. I become dizzy with lust as his blood trickles through me, desperate for more of him.

I pull one of my wrists from his grasp and reach between us, sliding my fingers around his length, giving his cock a firm squeeze. The king moans, his tongue thrusting deeper into my mouth, his cock jerking in my hand. I slip my fingers up and down his hardness, loving how smooth he feels, completely aroused by the deep moans coming from his mouth.

"Touch me, pet," he purrs. "Squeeze me, make me feel good."

"Mmmm," I hum into his lips, as he kisses me again, moving my hand faster, sliding my thumb gently over his slit and wetting it with precum. "I want to taste you, my king."

"Yes," he groans, flipping me so I sit above him. I pull the blindfold off and look down at the king I'm so enthralled to be with. His hands squeeze my hips, his blue eyes hooded with need and hair messy from me pulling on the black strands. "Turn around, princess," he rasps, twirling his finger in a spinning motion. Confusion eats at me. Why wouldn't he want to look at me?

"I don't understand—"

"Shh, pet. No questions. Just fucking do it before I go crazy with my desire for you. I need to taste you as much as you do me." Nodding, recognizing the sincerity blazing in his eyes, I stand and turn so he's looking at my ass and his cock is in front of me. His fingers dig into my hips and he pulls my ass back toward his face. At first I'm mortified, thinking of the king looking at my asshole, but then a firm hand presses between my shoulder blades, forcing me to lean down.

His perfect cock tantalizes me, precum dripping from the tip. I just have to taste him. Lowering myself the rest of the way, I take the king's cock into my mouth and hum around the head, swirling my tongue over his softness. He tastes sweet and spicy, just like his scent, making me want to work hard for more. I pull off when I feel his tongue slide along my pussy and moan loudly.

A spank lands on my ass and I shriek as King Lucian growls. "Put my cock back in that pretty little mouth of yours, pet. Don't let it slip out again."

I groan at his demands, gliding my mouth back over him, pumping my lips up and down his length. He's well-endowed and I struggle to take him all, my mind spinning as he laps at my clit.

Fuck, this feels amazing. The king moves from my clit to my pussy, hardening his tongue as he dips it inside. Knowing the king's tongue is inside me, tasting my arousal as it leaks from me, has my pussy clenching. He moans against me, the vibrations igniting my clit.

"Keep sucking," he growls, and I realize I'm just lying

here, unmoving. I can't help it. What he's doing feels too good, and I can't concentrate on anything else. "Suck my cock, pet. Take all of me in that hot mouth. I want to hear you gag."

Fuck, his words make me so hot. Wanting to please the king, I concentrate on what I'm doing, saliva leaking from my mouth as I take him deeper. He rewards me for my actions, attacking my clit with his tongue. I feel my orgasm brewing, my second one of the night. But I still suck the king's hard cock. Using one hand, I fondle his balls. He growls against me, hips jerking, forcing his cock deeper into my throat

The king gets his wish as I choke on him, which only makes him lick me faster, his moans making me want to swallow him down farther. I begin panting, struggling to breathe with all of him inside my mouth. The whole thing is throwing me over the edge.

His legs tremble, his breaths are ragged, and his moans are growing more and more frequent. The sights and sounds, the tastes and smells, they overwhelm me. The lack of air, the king's tongue spearing and licking me, his precum igniting my taste buds, the smell of our blood while his legs tremble beneath my fingertips, it's too much.

Then he does the unthinkable, grazing his fang on my clit before sucking the pain away. I shriek, pulling off his cock, my orgasm engulfing me like a tidal wave. My vision goes white, I thrust against his face through it, grinding my clit on him, my pussy clenching on air.

Then I'm flipped again and he bites, his fangs sinking into my inner thigh. I come again instantly. My spine bows, toes curling, fingers clenched into fists. My nipples tighten to the point of pain, my skin sizzling with lust.

It's fucking incredible.

My voice grows hoarse from my cries until King Lucian

finally removes his fangs from my thigh and climbs up my body, laying kisses as he goes. "You are magnificent, pet. I could feast on you every hour for the rest of my life and never grow bored of how delicious you taste, never tire of watching how gorgeous you are when you come, never fail to find new ways I can make you scream."

I want to respond, but I fucking can't. I can only lie here, catching my breath, my body completely spent. "We're not done, pet. I still need more of you. I need to own you completely and utterly, fuck you until the only word you know is my name. I need to see your body writhe under mine, and tears stream down your face from the enormity of the pleasure you are experiencing. I. Need. More."

"I-I can't," I whisper.

"That's where you couldn't be more wrong." The king grips my chin firmly and I open my exhausted lids, finding his bright blue eyes boring into my soul as he forces me to hold his gaze. "You are a princess. Our future queen. The first queen of our coven since our inception centuries ago. You are fated to the seven, born to good and decent people. You come from a line of royalty beloved by those who were ruled by them. You've suffered torture, yet still remain sweet and innocent. You've been starved, you've been beaten, yet the light inside you still burns bright. No one can break you, nothing can stop you, you've proven that time and time again. So, Princess Snow, don't ever let me hear the words 'I can't' fall from your lips again."

Whoa.

I've never thought of it that way.

"Now, spread your legs so that I may fuck what's mine. I need to sink my cock deep inside you and fill you with my cum. I need to taste your blood on my lips again, then feel your fangs pierce my flesh as I give you my sin. I need you, pet."

"Take me," I whisper.

King Lucian brings his wrist up to his mouth and bites, then holds it over my mouth. I extend my tongue and eagerly receive the droplets of his blood. I immediately feel better, less tired, and oh so fucking ready to fuck my king.

The king's eyes flash when he sees my resolve kick in. "I'm going to fuck you so hard, pet, for making me so depraved, so desperate for you."

Growling, he grabs my bruised hips and flips me onto my stomach, then pulls my ass up, forcing me to my hands and knees.

He spanks my ass before saying, "You ready to take this cock like a good girl, pet?"

I glance over my shoulder, locking eyes with him. "Fuck me, my king."

He groans, "With pleasure," then spanks me again and I moan loudly as the head of his cock prods my opening. Without warning, he grabs my hips and plunges inside me. I cry out at the sudden fullness, my pussy stretching around him. "Your cunt is more perfect than I could have possibly imagined. So tight and wet, so hot. I can feel you squeezing me, your pussy milking my cock."

He starts moving and we both shudder in utter bliss. King Lucian does as promised and fucks me hard. My moans are disrupted as he thrusts in and out, his groin smacking into my ass. The king changes angles, lowering himself to hit that glorious spot inside me.

I see the waterfall in my mind again, and I wonder how the fuck I can come four times in a single night. But as my orgasm brews, my core heats, and my blood turns molten, I know I can.

I can, and I will.

I firmly grip the sheets and fuck the king back, bouncing off of him hard. He growls, snaking his hand under me until he cups my throat and pulls my torso up. It's only now when I realize part of the tree behind his bed holds a giant mirror. I don't even recognize the woman looking back at me.

She's not the meek, scared thing I used to be. Instead, she's powerful...proud. Her previously thin frame is now lined with lean muscle. Even my eyes are changing, growing darker, blacker, my gaze once filled with suppressed anger now blazing with fervent desire. "See how magnificent you are, pet."

My eyes catch his in the mirror, his fingers tightening around my throat as I reach up to hold his arm. "See how beautiful." His free hand moves to my breast, squeezing hard before working my nipple. "See how supple, how responsive." His movements grow harder, faster, my climax erupting like a violent volcano. "So majestic. Breathtaking. Exquisite."

Our bodies are slick with sweat as his head towers over mine, making me look small and vulnerable, but I couldn't feel any stronger. Bringing this king to his knees, being the reason for his pleasure, for his slackened face and lust filled gaze, empowers me.

"And the best part of all? You're mine." With that, he bites me again in the crook of my neck, his eyes still fixed on mine. I watch myself come before my eyes close in ecstasy. Seeing the king drink from me is one of the most erotic things I've ever seen. My orgasm roars as my spine bows, the king's grip on my neck tightening. He growls against me as my eyes open, watching the flush of arousal spread across my skin. The king fucks me through it, and the force of his thrusting has my tits bouncing wildly. Then he pulls off my neck, my blood trailing down my breast.

Growling, the king slips out of me then spins me again, shoving my back up against the headboard. I shriek when he pins my arms above my head with one hand, his other throwing my legs wide as he plunges inside me again. With his free hand gripping the headboard, he impales me over and over. His blue eyes full with desire as he chases his own release. A trail of my blood leaks from his mouth, dripping to his chest, his white fangs still elongated, making me so fucking hot.

I need to feel him come inside me, I'm desperate for it. Locking eyes with him, I growl, "Fuck me. Take me. I'm yours."

That's all he needed. King Lucian tosses his head back and roars, his fingers digging into my wrists, his hot cum spurting inside me. "Fuck yes," I moan.

The king leans over me, brushing his lips over mine. "Take my sin, Princess Snow. It's yours." He bares his neck. My fangs descend and I lunge for him, our bodies still joined, and pierce his flesh. His blood invades my senses, consuming me. It tastes like honey infused with hot spices. My taste buds erupt and I bite harder, making the king come again, his cock pulsing inside me. He groans, eyes closed, his hot cum filling me. He threads his fingers through my hair, pulling on my scalp.

And I drink.

I suck that sweet nectar from his veins until all I know is him, until all my thoughts are consumed by everything that is King Lucian. His scent invades me, his body is inside me, and his blood ravages mine.

King Lucian.

"Enough, pet." My eyes fly open and I swipe at the face nearing mine, trying to keep me from what I want. "I said enough." This time the words are said in a different tone, one I must obey. With a growl, I withdraw my fangs. King Lucian falls to his back, his chest rising and falling, his muscles flexing as he sucks in air. His cock glistens with our combined releases.

I move to sit up and my vision instantly goes black. I feel myself falling when strong arms catch me. Warm blood drips from my lips, my head hanging limply over his arm.

King Lucian cradles me against him, gently petting my hair and stroking my face as the darkness of slumber pulls at my mind. "You did so well, pet. Performed so beautifully. My ability to compel is yours now, along with my sin. Almost nothing can stop you now. So sleep. Rejuvenate. The final phase is nearing. Soon, your old life will be but a whisper in the wind as you start anew, taking this world by storm."

With those final words, I crash into the darkness, one step closer to my beginning and my end.

CHAPTER 41

The time for my transformation is almost here, although I'm still not exactly sure what that means. I've just awoken from what I'm sure was a several days long slumber, and an unquenchable thirst gnaws at my throat. But this time, it's not food nor water that I yearn for.

I'm not sure how to feel about this. After so many years held prisoner under the queen's rule, I became indifferent to food, purely because what she allowed me to eat were scraps from her own plate or worse. More often than not, my meals were skipped, whether the evil cunt bitch chose to have me starve or no one cared enough to remember to feed me, I can't be sure.

But, eventually, food lost its luster. Yes, I craved sustenance to soothe my aching belly, to make my muscles stop trembling, to allow my tongue to unstick from the roof of my mouth. However, I never desired decadent cakes or salted bacon, probably because I'd forgotten what such things tasted like.

Pathetic.

Now, with freedom in my grasp, my desire for a hot plate

filled with roast covered in gravy or potatoes nestled in a pool of melted butter wanes. I've said before that the ways of the world are mysterious, and this is a perfect example. It's ironic, to say the least.

Padding through the castle, staying close to the shadows, I wait. I listen. As more and more vampires retire to wherever it is they go to sleep, and the castles steadily grow quieter, I wait for my chance.

I don't even know why I'm doing this. It's stupid really. If the seven wish to keep me from knowing about dead time, then I should respect their desires and shut the fuck up about it.

But I can't.

The desire for their blood is consuming me.

Plus, I need to know what happens during dead time. Why do they die? Are they really dead as she proclaimed? If they are dead, then how can they speak? How can they breathe, drink, fuck...? It makes no sense.

I've used my glamour again, becoming the gorgeous brunette, Tess, that King Lucian brought into his suite for us to play with. Looking down at myself, I still can't believe I'm wearing someone else's skin when all I see is my own naked flesh. It's quite an odd sensation.

I've come to learn in my escapade as Tess, that not just lust vampires are horny. Fuck no. Almost all of them are. Granted, Tess is a gorgeous woman, but I'm being propositioned left and right.

"Want to fuck?"

"You smell good enough to eat."

"What is a pretty little human like you doing wandering the castles all alone?"

Luckily, after my time with King Lucian, I now have the ability to compel in my arsenal. I thought it would be harder to use than it is. Hell, the first time I used it, only a few minutes ago, it just came to me. I didn't even have to find the door it lies behind in my mind. I just willed it to happen and it did.

The vampire didn't know what hit him. One moment he's flashing his fangs at me, trying to be seductive—which he failed miserably at—and the next, I have him asking the man across the room if he'd like to go skinny dipping in the river.

I had to stifle my laughter at the vampire's stunned face as he pulled his fangs out of the girl next to him. It was fucking hilarious.

As I exit into the courtyard, I head to said river and perch on the bank, looking back at the castles. The need for blood is overwhelming my thoughts, clouding my judgement.

Blood.

Dead time.

Blood.

Dead time.

I can't shake the obsession, thirsting for crimson liquid, desperate for answers.

Which castle should I sneak into?

Who would be the king most likely to indulge in sleep?

Which king is more likely to forgive me for leaving my room and give me their blood that I so urgently desire?

My gut says it's King Dante. The sloth king would sleep every hour of every day if he could, and since he can, he does. He also has said that he's obsessed with me. He won't deny me. But as I gaze around the vast expanse of open cavern in front of the Coven of Sin, I feel pulled to mingle with my people.

Tucking my desires in the back of my mind, I abandon my disguise as Tess and search for clothes, a discarded dress or shirt I could wear. Usually, there are always vampires fucking each other, or donors stripping down to offer vampires their choice of location to drink from, but there's no one here.

Fuck.

Why the fuck have I not been given a wardrobe? I mean, seriously… I don't require anything fancy. Hell, I'd walk around with borrowed clothes, not needing anything new. But to actually be deprived of clothing is starting to bother me. I think it's a way the kings underhandedly try to protect me. If I can't have clothes, then I won't leave my room, which is logical thinking to be honest. But how quickly they have forgotten that I will not be caged any longer.

I hide behind a nearby rock and conjure up a dress inside the glamour room in my mind. I make it brown and nondescript, something any of the women in Riverwood might have in their homes. One might think that their future queen should wear more elegant things, but I do not wish to make my people feel like I'm flaunting anything in front of them. I just wish to make them feel equal after being treated as much less for the last two decades.

My skin tingles and I know I've succeeded.

Stepping out from behind the rock, I run my fingers through my curls, hopelessly trying to tame them, and march toward my people. The kings have graciously set up a camp for them out here. Rows and rows of makeshift beds line the far right corner, running all the way from King Strix's castle, past King Dante's, and halfway across King Ramsey's.

It must be morning by the state of everyone. Small children still sleep bundled up in tattered blankets on the ground. Women hover over little firepits, cooking warm oats to feed their families. The men are working with the town's blacksmith, learning how to forge swords and armor.

A line of people stand ready to get measured for chest plates. Even sweet Marie is asking for arms, though I hope someone will be able to talk her down. Against the opposite side of the cavern, in front of King Thorin's castle, is all the livestock my people were able to save and coerce into entering the dark cave and descending the long flight of stairs.

There are cows, pigs, chickens, goats, and even some donkeys. The evil cunt bitch didn't allow them to own horses, ensuring her control, making it almost impossible for people to flee.

My fingers curl into fists, and I envision pummeling the evil bitch's face into mincemeat.

Knowing I need to calm myself before meeting with them, I take a deep breath and think about the incredible time I had with King Lucian. Memories of his body hovering over mine, his lips tasting me, and his cock filling me help to calm me down. Then I remember the taste of his hot blood and how it ravaged my body…

Blood. I need blood.

"Princess Snow!"

Startled, I turn to see Rosie waving at me. Not wanting to scare her, I makes sure my fangs are retracted, then smile and change course to head her way. "How are you?" I ask, walking into her open arms. We hug, and I can't help but sniff her neck before pulling apart, my hands still on her shoulders. "It's so good to see you again."

She does an awkward curtsy. "And you as well."

"How are the people faring?" I question, dropping my arms and taking a step back. Her nearness is too tempting.

"Quite well, considering the circumstances."

"I'm so sorry," I say on a sigh. "I wish I could've been there."

"Well, I, for one, am glad you weren't." When I give her a confused look, she continues, "It was horrible, princess. The evil queen was wild, her huntsmen feral. Nothing would stand in her way. She didn't care what she destroyed, whom she killed, as long as devastation was left in her wake. I'm glad you were here, safe, preparing to take her on. And so is everyone else."

To say I'm relieved would be an understatement.

"Princess Snow, it's such an honor to meet you." I turn toward the speaker and smile.

"Pleasure is all mine, Marie." Marie startles at my use of her name. "Your bravery was so moving. Tell me, how are you feeling after drinking the king's blood?"

Blood.

I suppress a shudder, my mouth watering for the liquid.

Marie's eyelids flutter closed, and she inhales deeply. "It makes me feel young again." Her muted brown eyes open, sparkling with delight. "I can smell things I couldn't before, hear things my old ears have long forgotten. My body is stronger, my legs are working again. And my bent fingers have straightened." She shows off her old hands, dancing her fingers in the air. "I can't thank you enough. I heard your speech and know you've pledged your life in exchange for whatever the kings are giving you. So let me be the first to say thank you for your sacrifice."

I press my hand to my heart and incline my head. "You are most welcome, but it is I who should thank you for sticking by my side through all of this."

She smiles warmly. "I knew your parents before they were slain. You are so very much like them."

My blood freezes. "You-you knew them? What were they like?" I pull her to a bench, sit down beside her, and she wraps her spotted hand over mine, gently squeezing.

"They were the most wonderful leaders. Fair and just. Your father's smile would light up any home, and his laughter was so contagious that you couldn't help joining in with him, even if you had no idea what he found so funny. And your mother...she was a gentle soul. She was compas-

411

sionate and giving. She'd be the first to help a new mother with her baby, and calm a nervous bride as she prepared for her marriage. She'd mend torn clothing and knit blankets for those who needed them." Marie considers me, her eyes roaming my face. "You look very much like your mother, you know. But you have your father's eyes, though they're a shade darker than I remember."

I'm at a loss for words, tears misting my vision. "Thank you for sharing this. No one has ever told me anything about my parents before."

Marie's hand squeezes mine. "Happy to share. It's nice to remember the good times when we've been surrounded by so much bad for so long."

Filled with happy feelings, I bid Marie and Rosie goodbye. I speak to a few more people, encouraging those forging weapons and sharing advice for the strategists. After engaging with any who wished to do so, I say goodbye and head into King Dante's castle.

The guards allow me in with no preamble, and soon, I'm making my way through the corridors leading to his room. The struggle to hold my glamour battles with the need to consume king's blood. It seems like the more I use my glamour and my ability to compel, the deeper the desire for blood becomes.

Growling, I shake my head, trying to rid myself of the cravings, worried they will make me do something I'll regret, and try to focus on something else.

I remember Katie recently told me that all the guards are wrath vampires. Something about their ability to shift into wolves and their relationship with the moon allows them to avoid the compulsion for dead time.

Along the way, I open Dante's door in my head and find it completely black inside. I don't know if this means he's sleeping, dreaming, or something more insidious.

Unsure if I'd be admitted into his personal suite, I decide to glamour myself into looking like him and conjure the king's face in my mind.

First, I picture his long, curly, dark hair, then his pale blue eyes deeply set in his face. I picture the angles of his jaw, his full lips, his bright teeth flashing me a panty melting smile...

Inside the doors in my mind, I step through the one holding my glamour and build myself a King Dante. My skin tingles, and I know my transformation is complete, but fuck, I wish I could verify it.

With thoughts of his blood consuming me and the desire to learn about dead time now long forgotten, I try not to look sneaky and I keep my posture steady, my head lifted, and saunter up to his suite. When I try to enter, the guards there draw their weapons and push me back, their gazes trained on me, searching my body for areas of weakness. "Stand back, intruder!" one of them shouts.

My jaw drops. I'm so close. Please don't let them stop me now. "Intruder?" I gasp, trying to lower my voice and sound offended. "This is my room. How dare you keep me from it!"

A guard scoffs, "This is no more your room than the evil queen is my mother. Get the fuck out of here, and don't try this shit again. Next time, we won't be so gracious."

Now I'm just mad. I've disguised myself to look like him, I can feel my skin tingling. "You will let me in. I don't know what the fuck crawled up your asses, or what drugs you've taken that you've become so bold as to not allow me into my own rooms! Look at me! I'm King Dante!"

They look at me, then back to each other as I think about how careful I was when creating my glamour.

"That's it, we're taking you to the kings. Hold out your wrists." A guard pulls off a pair of handcuffs from his belt, holding them with gloved hands, when it dawns on me... In the haze of bloodlust, I made a grave mistake. I've been parading around as King Dante's true form, and no one but the other kings know what that looks like.

"Shit," I mutter before backing away, my hands up in surrender, looking longingly at King Dante's door. "There's been a misunderstanding. I-I can't explain it right now. But—"

"No buts! Who the fuck are you anyway? Clearly you're not a citizen of Riverwood. Your crown would indicate royalty, and I already know King Dante is inside his suite." He stalks closer, his nostrils flaring and eyes narrowing in suspicion. "Are you a spy for the queen perhaps?"

Before I can respond, one of them lunges for me and I totally freak out, turning and running as fast as I can, my ability to use compulsion lost somewhere in my torrid need for blood. One guard charges after me, sword drawn, his lips pulled back into a feral snarl.

I squeak and book it for the stairs, taking the sharp turn of the hallway as fast as I can. I must look hilarious, this noble king running from the guards, shrieking like a scared child. Looking around, I realize I don't even know where I am in the castle. The only other time I came here, I hung my head, pouting, following behind the false facade of the sloth king. Even today, I didn't pay attention to my path, I just followed my instincts.

So when the guard behind me slices at me with a set of extended claws, I fucking run even harder. I crash through a rather messy looking sitting room, each corner stuffed with blankets, pillows, and cushions, and sprint through a dark hallway.

"Stop that false king!" the guard shouts, as I smash into someone's hard chest. I take a step back, eyes wide, and look up into the face of Jovie, one of the twin guards. I want to tell him who I am, tell him that I mean no harm, but really, what could I say? I'm not willing to break my

SEVEN SINS OF SNOW

glamour, although that might be the only way of getting out of this.

But that means the kings would find out what I was up to and I don't want that to happen.

Staring into Jovie's eyes, I focus on my compulsion ability and call it forward. I see his face go slack, eyes unseeing, and command, "Let me go and tell no one you saw me. Oh, and stall that guard."

Jovie releases my arms and walks past me as I take off down the hall, causing the candles to flicker as I run past. Finally, I come to a door that very much reminds me of the one barring the entrance from the town of Riverwood into the secret party room.

Instinct kicks in, and I extend my fangs, bite my wrist, then rub my blood on the cracked wood. I let out a breath when it swings open and I tumble inside, slamming it shut behind me. Leaning against it, I catch my breath, trying to breathe as quietly as possible. The guard shouts as he runs past, and by the sounds of it, several others are with him, but they never even stop by the door.

Knowing I've made it, that I'm safe at least for now, I search this new room to get my bearings, but in my haste to enter, I caused the only light in here to flicker out. I'm in utter darkness.

"Well, this isn't good," I mumble to myself, as I stretch my arms in front of me, making sure I don't crash into anything. Inching my way along the cold floor, I realize I can't do this all night, so I look inside my mind and find the kings' doors. Pushing open King Lucian's, I see only darkness and quickly retreat. Kings Ramsey, Marcel, and Dante offer the same bleakness. It's not until I enter King Strix's that I see something.

He's standing with his arms crossed, looking down at a long white box. King Thorin is with him, and King Killian is

415

there too. They all seem to be arguing about the box, pointing to it, then speaking to a fourth person I don't recognize. The stranger is obviously human by his pot belly, pink skin, and balding head, and is wearing a belt with various hooks and loops holding a collection of tools.

Before King Strix realizes I'm in his head, I pull out and seek him like I sought King Dante. With my hands out in front of me, eyes wide open in the dark, I follow the gravitational draw I have to the King of Pride.

I don't know how long I travel through this darkened tunnel. It feels like hours. The thirst for a drop of a king's hot, decadent blood claws at my throat. It's all I can think about as I trudge through the shadows. Why the pull to the king couldn't have taken me back outside the castles is beyond me.

When the string tying us together finally grows shorter, the line taut with his closeness, my course veers, and I crash into another door. I fumble for the handle, but before I open it, I need to decide who I want to be. Should I stay as King Dante? Surely they wouldn't expect me to take on this form. He uses it so rarely they'd have to believe it was him.

I enter my glamour room and check to make sure all his parts are in place, then I push the door open. Funny how all these castles can be so vastly different, yet have obvious similarities. For instance, the hall I've just left could be the twin of the one I entered inside Sloth Castle.

Its darkened walls are highlighted only by sparsely placed candles. Voices draw near and I take a deep breath, refreshing myself with King Dante's gait. I do not wish to be discovered again. I push open the door at the end of the corridor and find myself entering the indulgent sitting room of King Killian's castle.

A few donors are scattered here and there, most eating early breakfast and drinking tea from hand painted cups. A group of women laugh at something, and show off their recent bite marks, still red and healing from a vampire's fangs while recounting exactly how they received them. I can just picture Katie sitting with them, eager to pull her dress open and reveal Julian's newest additions to her body.

I have to refrain from smiling. Perhaps, if my life would have had a different path, I might have joined them. As the faux bookcase closes behind me, the women turn to me, their jaws dropping open. At first, I can't figure out why they're gawking at me, then I remember—I'm King fucking Dante, and I'm a sexy bitch.

Lowering my voice, I say, "Hello, ladies." Their reactions are surprising. I've never been sure if a woman could actually swoon, though I think I've come close a few times, but fuck if one isn't doing that right now. She's beautiful and gawking at me, mouth gaping, eyes wide. She's thin, with shoulder-length blonde hair and bright blue eyes. As she stares at me, I can hear her heart rate quicken, see the flush creeping across her chest to her neck, her face turning pale.

"Oh shit, Dani!" one of them shouts.

The woman I now know as Dani keels over, falling face first off her couch. Her girlfriends shriek, kneeling on the floor next to her. One fans her face while the other pours water from a nearby glass on her forehead. "Dani, Dani, wake up," a brown-haired girl urges, patting poor Dani's pale cheek. I smile at them, tossing the gaggle of women a wink before passing by.

I bite my knuckle, in total fucking shock that this just happened. No wonder King Dante parades around with a false face all the time. If I had people swooning over me left and right everywhere I went, I could see how exhausting that would be.

I head through the arched doorway in the far back of the room and recognize the deep voice of King Thorin coming from behind a closed door, scenting his decadent blood in the air.

"We have to make sure it has the integrity to contain a newborn in case she wakes up early. We've never done anything like this before. We can't be sure of the outcome and need it to be reinforced."

"I'm not having it made out of fucking brick, Thorin," the dulcet tones of King Stix's voice chimes in. "It should be gorgeous, like she is."

Wondering what the fuck they are talking about, I push the door open and walk in. King Killian startles, jumping back. "Shit, Dante. Could've told us you were coming. Thought your ass would have been sleeping hours ago when the pull started."

I shrug and cross my arms, not wanting to use my voice since I still sound like me. "Let's have Dante weigh in," Thorin growls, gesturing at me. "Our pretty boy, Killian, seems to think the queen's casket should be more beautiful than strong. I've been trying to tell him what a fool he is. She won't care if it's beautiful, not if she beats her way out of it too early."

Queen's casket? Is this a coffin they are having prepared for the evil cunt bitch? And if so, why? Why have anything special created for someone so cruel? For all I care, the bitch's corpse can rot in the dirt while worms and maggots invade her body, that is, after I tear her into shreds first.

Looking down, I can admire the craftsmanship of the box. It's composed of white marble, lined with glittering silver streaks and ornate carved filigree, making the stone look like a piece of art. Inlays composed of gold roses surround a beautiful script. But I won't fucking read it. Anything created for the evil cunt bitch is something I don't fucking have a care to see, hear, or know.

When I don't answer, King Strix gives his opinion. "I

agree with both of you. I think she deserves something beautiful, but that doesn't mean it can't still withstand a newborn."

Newborn? Now they are talking about babies?

"Strix is right." Killian turns to the human man who's been busy jotting down notes on a piece of parchment. "Let her have both. Give us something strong but elegant, just like our future queen."

I have a moment of nausea thinking that perhaps I've been wrong all along. There's no way in hell they'd be making some fucking box for me, which means it *has* to be for the evil cunt bitch, which means they *have* been betraying me all along. My head spins and I grip my temples to try and steady it.

"Dante? Dante, what's wrong?" Killian marches over, concern on his face. I try to wave him off, but he won't have it, firmly gripping my shoulder. "Shoulda stayed in bed, eh?" he jokes, slapping me on the back. I grunt something unintelligible and try to calm my breathing.

This isn't happening. It can't be happening. Everything they've said has come from the heart. I can feel their sincerity. They are mine as much as I'm theirs.

As my eyes come back into focus and I try to think my way out of here, my gaze narrows on the box. Inscribed in the white stone is a name.

My name.

> *Here lies Queen Snow, first of her name.*
> *Queen of the Coven of Sin.*
> *Ruler of Riverwood.*
> *Mate to the seven.*
> *May she rest in peace.*

CHAPTER 42

*T*hey mean to kill me.

Holy fuck, they want to kill me.

Gripping the sides of my face with my hands, I stare at my name engraved on the casket—*my casket*—seeing it run through my mind over and over again.

I feel my glamour fade, my intense reaction to seeing my own fucking coffin destroying my concentration.

"What the fuck? *Regina*, what the hell do you think you're doing?" King Strix rushes to me, engulfing me in his arms.

"Little one," King Thorin growls, hurrying over. "You shouldn't be here."

"But she is here," King Killian says calmly. "So let's forget about the fact that she shouldn't be and deal with the reality that she is."

"Don't fucking touch me," I snarl, throwing their arms off me as I take a step back. "I thought I could trust you. And the whole time, you've kept up this-this facade? This lie? All so you could kill me and put my corpse in a pretty fucking box?" Tears fall from my eyes.

"Princess—" King Killian begins, but I cut him off.

"No! No more lies. I won't believe a fucking word you say anymore. I won't let you kill me, not when I'm this close to saving my people from the evil bitch controlling them. I-I thought you were different."

"We are different," King Strix soothes, his hands up in submission. "This isn't what you think it is."

I scoff, "Oh really? This isn't a fucking casket with my fucking name on it?" Now, I'm irate. How dare they insult my intelligence. I can feel my wrath brewing inside me, churning within my belly, red misting my vision. "I am not a fool. Nor will I linger here while you-you lure me with your good looks, your seductive voices, your-your delicious fucking blood. No more. I'm done. And I'm taking my people with me."

I turn to charge out of here when I run face first into the broad chest of King Ramsey. "Just where do you think you're going, flower?" he growls.

I take a step back. "I-I'm leaving." My shaking voice betrays my lack of confidence.

"Like hell you are," he croons. "This isn't over yet. You will listen to what we have to say, even if we have to strap you down and force you to hear us."

"That's the best idea you've ever had, Ramsey," King Thorin agrees, excitement flashing in his gray eyes.

"Killian, is the throne room prepared?" King Strix asks.

King Killian nods. "It is."

King Strix grins. "Then let's take our little princess there. Let's finish this, once and for all."

"No!" I shriek, when they descend upon me. I snarl, kicking and screaming, shouting profanities as they restrain me.

"You're so cute when you're mad, flower," King Ramsey coos, holding me with ease.

"And so sexy," King Killian adds. "Of course you had to

traipse in here naked, forcing our hands to restrain your supple body while you writhe between us. That's not how I planned our first time together, but with the situation being as it is…"

"W-What would you have me do, m-my kings?" an unfamiliar voice asks. I jerk my head toward the sound and see the portly human standing there, his eyes darting from me to the kings and back to me. In my rage, I'd forgotten he was here.

"The time has come," King Killian declares. "What you've made will have to do. See to it that my coven moves it safely to its final place. And thank you for your service."

The man nods, swallowing hard, and turns to leave.

Gripping my body, the kings move, taking me up to the throne room. I try compel them, screaming at them to let me go, but their grip only tightens. I look inside my mind, searching to find my wolf, but my thoughts are too jumbled to see her.

"Let me go!" I scream, trying to twist my body, doing anything to free myself.

"We can't do that, little one," King Thorin retorts. "We've claimed you as our own, we started your transformation. This can only end one way. Our way. And if you would just listen—"

"I won't hear more of your lies!" I shout.

"Thorin, save your words until we have her prepared," King Ramsey suggests. "She can't refuse to listen then."

The journey to the throne room is a blur. The kings carry me like a battering ram through darkened tunnels similar to the one I traveled to get here. The kings remain silent as I growl, scream, and fight until my voice grows scratchy and my muscles tire, while the insatiable thirst for their blood festers.

Finally, I deflate, yet they still don't acknowledge me or

even try to talk to me. Hanging between them, I feel so defeated. How could I have not seen this coming? Even King Lucian alluded to my death, yet I chose to ignore it. How did he put it?

The end to your beginning, and the start of your transformation.

In the dark corners of my mind, I feel the other kings stir. A flash of King Dante's arctic eyes, a whisper of King Marcel's greed, the sweet and spicy scent of King Lucian.

We are coming.

I hear them in my mind, unsure if their words are meant to comfort me or if I should take them as a potent threat. I don't think they mean to help me. Maybe their message was meant for the other kings.

My heart breaks at the thought of their betrayal. I trusted them. I gave them my body, my mind, my devotion. I submitted to them in every possible way, did everything they asked and then some. I've given myself, my blood, my very being, my fucking soul...

How could one person's life be so tragic? I couldn't write a story as awful as this. How can someone survive utter despair time and time again?

When a door creaks open and flickering light finally illuminates my surroundings, I see that we are back inside the cathedral room where I first met the kings. We pass behind their seven thrones, down the five stairs, and over to a stone table perched in the middle. Kings Lucian, Marcel, and Dante stand stoic behind it, their arms clasped behind their backs, in full king garb.

Too bad for me, I can no longer appreciate their beauty, it hurts too much to acknowledge it.

As they lay me down on the table, the cool stone frigid along my back, I close my eyes and enter the darkened corners of my mind where I like to hide from the world.

Here, I can shut off sensations from my body to try and cope. I've hidden inside these shadows so many times during the merciless torture sessions the evil cunt bitch inflicted upon me.

So as the kings strap my arms into binds above my head and tighten another set over my ankles, I draw away from reality and pretend that I'm somewhere far away.

In the recesses of my mind, I can hear them speaking to me. I catch words like, *princess*, *please*, *ours*, and *yours*. Then I feel their hands descend on my body, cleaning my skin with warm water. I smell the softly scented lilac soap as their fingers caress every inch of me.

Their touch is gentle, washing me as if I was a precious heirloom they want to preserve.

"Come back to us, Princess Snow."

I don't know who is speaking, their voices joining in a soothing chorus as they cleanse me. Their touch is not sexual in any way, more orderly, ritualistic almost, like preparing a lamb for slaughter.

The thought throws me deeper into despair.

As the kings finish with their ministrations, heated water is poured all over me, rinsing the soap before soft towels pat me dry. Still, they chant, using a language I've never heard, but one that sounds so beautifully spoken with their thick accents.

"Princess Snow, we need you. Come back."

"Come back to us."

"Please, hear us. We are nothing without you."

My chest clenches. I want to believe them so badly, but the tendrils of doubt have dug their claws into me. After the life I've lived, one fraught with deceit and disappointment, it's become hard to forgive, to forget.

"Open your eyes, little one." The command from King Thorin pulls me from my hiding spot, forcing me to be present with them. I lock gazes with the King of Wrath. His handsome face is pulled into a frown, his gray eyes considering me with frustration and sadness as he strokes his dark beard. "You will hear us. You will listen. Then you can make your final choice—doing this the easy way, or the hard way."

I nod once, unable to speak without my voice stuttering in sadness. The kings hover above me, their faces illuminated by the braziers and flickering candle chandeliers. Each one wears his crown proudly. I want to shrink under the gazes of the seven. There is fury in their eyes, and desire, anger, and need.

"We didn't know how to tell you," King Marcel begins. "How could we put into words a reality so terrible, you might have rejected us?"

"We couldn't allow that," King Ramsey agrees. "We haven't lied to you, flower, merely omitted part of the truth."

"You're right to be concerned, pet," King Lucian adds. "Seeing one's own casket is not an easy sight to behold. But I've always warned you that there would be an end to this life in order to begin another. You chose to ignore that warning, chalking it up to something darkly poetic instead of a blatant foreshadow."

He's right, of course. They have all alluded to a grim end for me, a conclusion that must be finalized before I can commence as something new.

"You offered yourself to us, *Regina*, in exchange for our gifts," King Strix reminds me. "You struck a deal and confirmed your commitment, knowing what we are. You've already taken six of us, there is no turning back now. Killian will complete the transfer of sins, then we will finish what we started."

King Killian grabs a platinum tray filled with seven tiny glass vials. Each king grabs one and bites their wrist, dripping their blood into the clear mixture. One by one they pour the concoction all over my body. It smells like their blood mixed with oils. Fourteen hands then descend on me, massaging it into my skin. Everywhere they touch comes alive, and not a spot on me is missed.

The crimson mixture is massaged into my hair, down my neck, over my breasts, and across my belly. It's rubbed between my legs, and down my thighs to my feet, their soft caresses igniting my body.

"You must accept your fate, precious girl." King Marcel's smooth tones wash over me as he rubs the mixture across my right breast.

"In life, there is death, and in death, there is life," King Lucian intones, the words sounding eerily familiar. His hand slides down my belly before diving between my pussy lips. "You know this to be true. As your old existence ends, you will be reborn. Transformed. A more powerful version of yourself. One who can wield the sins for her own and take back her stolen throne."

"Accept us, Princess Snow," King Killian pleads. "Accept me, take my sin, and become who you were born to be." He stands between my feet, his hands rubbing up and down my legs, thumbs sliding across my inner thighs. "Save yourself. Save your people. Save us all."

"You were born to lead," King Dante asserts. "Give yourself to us, and in return, we will become yours, together for all time."

"We care so much for you, flower," King Ramsey murmurs. "You've crept into the vacant pieces of our hearts we thought no longer existed.

"You make us better kings," King Thorin continues. "You are the strength that keeps us together."

"The heart that makes us beat as one," King Strix adds.

"You are the fire that keeps us alive," King Lucian coos.

"The reason we fight so hard each day," King Marcel concurs.

"You, Princess Snow, have enriched our lives so fully, we no longer wish to exist without you," King Strix discloses, his voice laced with emotion.

"We need you, kitten," King Dante implores. "Please, allow us to give you the deepest parts of ourselves so that, together, we can banish the evil from this world and create a better place for us all."

"We know what we're asking is almost impossible to comprehend," King Killian explains. "But in your sacrifice, there are monumental rewards."

"Please, pet. Be with us. Give us yourself. Let us worship you every day for the rest of our lives," King Lucian pleads. "We no longer wish to be your kings, but rather, have you as our queen."

My chest tightens, my heart fluttering with a plethora of emotions. Somewhere, deep inside me, I think I always knew I would have to pay the ultimate price to achieve my goal of ridding the evil cunt bitch from the world. But I never really allowed myself to wrap my head around it. Hearing the kings' words, their heartfelt pleas, and seeing the sincerity and affection written across their handsome faces, there is no way I could possibly say no. Yes, the kings have to kill me, but my life isn't ending, not truly.

I can do this.

I *will* do this.

Nothing can be more painful than a life lived alone, trudging through an existence filled with fear and oppression. All my life, I haven't truly lived, merely existed. I refuse to do it any longer.

I gaze up at the kings, one lone tear trickling down my face. Killian's bright green eyes stare down at me with such devotion. Lucian's blue gaze looks right into my soul.

Ramsey's sly smile clenches my heart. Thorin's stern face beseeches me to give myself freely. Strix's eyes sparkle, expressing a thousand silent words too profound to be spoken. Marcel's dark gaze considers me with deep affection. Dante's full lips are turned in a hopeful smile.

How could I ever disappoint them?

How could I ever even consider leaving them?

Whether they know it or not, they've given me something I never thought I'd ever find again—pure and unadulterated love.

"Will it hurt?" My voice breaks when I ask.

"Yes," Lucian admits, "but you will survive it, and we will be with you the entire time."

I swallow the lump in my throat, blinking the tears from my eyes, knowing what I'm about to do.

"Okay. Do it." My tone is firm and clear. "I'm ready."

CHAPTER 43

$\mathcal{T}$he kings visibly relax, their eyes flashing with desire and excitement. Killian removes the straps from my ankles as Marcel and Dante pull my legs apart.

"So beautiful, so perfect," the king of gluttony praises. "I had much more planned for our first time together, but those plans will have to wait for another day. Because right now, I can't stand another second not being inside you, not tasting your flesh, not drinking your blood. I need your cunt wrapped around me, milking me," he rumbles seductively. "Tell me you want me, sweetheart. I need to hear it from your lips."

"I want you, Killian. I need you. Take me," I respond without hesitation. Killian growls and reaches for his crown, pulling it off his sandy blond hair before running a hand through it. He puts the crown down and begins to disrobe. I tug at the restraints surrounding my wrists, wanting to run my fingers over this glorious king.

"I'm so sorry, little one, but the restraints must stay," Thorin tells me. "Once we begin the process of completing your transformation, we cannot stop it. The side effects of what we are about to do are virtually unknown. We can't risk you overpowering us or running away. It is for your safety as well as our own."

I nod in acceptance. I'll feel better knowing I can't hurt anyone.

Killian wets his lips. "I've been waiting a long time for this," he purrs, as he slides between my legs, pulling his shirt off as he goes. His body is spectacular. He has more color than some of the other kings, giving him a sun-kissed glow that pairs well with his sandy hair. I bite my lip as he pulls down his pants, revealing his thick cock.

The King of Gluttony fists up and down his length a few times before climbing onto the table and lining up with my entrance. We groan in tandem as the head of his cock breaches my pussy. "So hot, so tight, so perfect," Killian praises as he inches his way in, his fingers digging into my hips. Next to him, Dante's and Marcel's gazes are fixed on where Killian and I are joined, heightening the sensation.

"Take your king, precious girl," Marcel murmurs, his eyes focused between my legs. "Feel how he stretches your cunt, feel his thickness as he slides inside you."

Dante groans as he watches, his hand cupping his groin. I must be a kinky shit, because I really do get off on being watched. The other six pour more of their oils on my skin, the ritualistic feeling to their actions shifting to one of sensuality. Lucian and Thorin play with my breasts, while Ramsey licks down my neck.

Killian moves in and out of me at a slow pace, taking his time to stuff me full before pulling out. "Your cunt blossoms so beautifully around Killian, kitten," Dante growls. "I could watch your body writhe for days and still need more."

Marcel runs his hands up and down my leg, massaging the oils deep into my skin. I moan when Killian leans down over me, putting my ankles up over his shoulders, hitting that spot inside me that drives me wild.

"I need you, princess," he groans, before taking my lips, his cock sliding in and out of me. Our tongues dance together sensually, slowly. He tastes sweet, as if he just drank a goblet of mead. I moan as he folds me in half, angling himself inside me.

Killian ends the kiss, his eyes blazing into mine. "I had intended to tie you to my wall and learn every dip and valley of your body with my tongue. I wanted to taste you as you came, bringing you to climax over and over again. But this will have to do, sweetheart."

Killian sits back up, his hands on my ankles as the mouths of the other kings descend on me. His gluttony wars within him, his need to have as much of me as he can battling with how much he loves having all of us together at the same time.

My climax brews, creating a low heat in my belly. I can no longer tell who is touching me where, all I know is unbelievable sensations. Lips and teeth graze me, and tongues taste me as Killian fucks me into oblivion.

My breathing grows shallow as Killian licks my inner ankle. I can sense the bloodlust pouring from the kings, their need to drink from me driving them crazy with desire. "Now," he growls, and the other six kings sink their fangs into me. I scream as pain and pleasure slams into me. Then Killian roars, his muscles flexing as he comes inside me before he sinks his fangs into my leg.

I shriek, my vision going white as I come hard, my pussy clenching around the gluttony king as the seven drink from me.

My mouth waters as I fantasize about Killian's blood filling my mouth, coating my tongue. Killian fixes his green stare on me, a trickle of my blood leaking from the corner of his mouth where he's attached to my ankle.

431

I'm fucking done.

I need him.

And I need him now.

The kings pull off me, roaring, my blood surging inside them as Killian crawls up my body, our lower halves still connected. "Take my sin, sweetheart, it's yours." The gluttony king arches his neck, and I pull hard on my restraints, my fangs descending, until they finally sink into his skin. I moan, finally getting the drink I've been chasing for hours. His sin courses through me at a burning pace. My body sizzles as if struck by lightning. It's like time stops, the world watching for this crucial moment, the change in the winds, the shifting of momentum.

My blood becomes heated as I'm pulled from Killian's neck, still desperate for more to drink. I growl as my legs are tugged back down into the restraints. Glancing around, I see that all the kings have stripped. Crowns and clothes are set aside. Now nothing exists between me and their naked flesh.

"So fucking gorgeous."

"Stunning."

"Perfection."

They all praise me as they lower their heads and bite me again. Two kings are on my neck, two on my wrists, two more drink from my inner thighs, and one from my breast.

"Ahhhh!" I scream as they drink from me, my vision going fuzzy.

Then, they pull off, my blood seeping from the wounds as they smear it all over my body, covering my skin like a painting. They work in unison, and no one speaks, every movement a graceful dance. Then they descend again, this time licking me. A mouth flicks my clit while two more suckle my nipples. A pair of soft lips kiss down my neck, licking as they go, while others taste my legs. They work, licking and sucking all over my body until my cunt is leaking, my body is shaking, and an orgasm of immense proportions is escalating inside me.

My heart thrashes, my clit throbs, and a huge weight is pressed on my chest.

"We need you, princess, we all do," Lucian croons. When I nod, he slides between my legs, lining himself up. I turn my head to find Marcel standing beside me, and I open my mouth to take him.

Marcel groans greedily as I wrap my lips around him, just as Lucian sinks inside me and waves of lust caress me like another pair of hands. Two more cocks are slipped into my palms and I cup them as they fuck themselves into my fists. Marcels fucks my mouth hard, holding my face so I can't move, forcing me to take all he has to give. Another king has climbed on top of me, perched between my chest and Lucian, his thick cock fucking my tits.

I can't see who it is, but I get a flash from the king's mind, seeing his mammoth cock sliding between my breasts, so I know it's Thorin. I hear Lucian's groans grow louder, deeper, his fingers digging into me as he orgasms hard. The King of Lust's hot cum fills me as his roars echo around me.

"Keep sucking, precious girl," Marcel growls when my lips grow slack. A fist wraps in my hair, tugging on it, giving me that ounce of pain that drives me wild. So I suck on Marcel as another king plays with my pussy. I can feel a finger swirling around inside me before sinking down to my other hole.

I can't fucking move. Can't cry out. Can't say that I'm scared of this, that I don't want them to touch my ass. With Marcel's cock thrust down my throat, with my arms and legs bound, I'm totally helpless.

"Don't worry, kitten, I'll make it feel good." Dante's soothing voice washes over me as he sinks his finger inside my ass, slowly fucking me with it. "Relax, let me fuck you. Let me take your ass, kitten."

I moan as Marcel's thrusting grows more rapid, my jaws aching from being forced open. Dante adds a second finger, taking his time to stretch my ass just when Marcel comes down my throat. I choke on his cum, even though it tastes just like his blood—sweet and salty.

Dante swirls his fingers around in my ass as Marcel pulls out of my mouth. Thorin has climbed off me and is playing with my breast while he watches Dante. Lucian is licking circles around my other nipple, his lips caressing gently, keeping me on edge. Killian is hovering over my pussy, his fingers dancing around my clit. Behind me, Ramsey is licking up and down my neck while my hand pumps his cock.

The sensations are insane.

My body trembles when my head is wrenched back again, where Strix waits with his cock in his hands. "Open, *Regina*," he orders. I widen my lips to take him as Thorin spanks my breast, tugging on my nipple. I moan around Strix, feeling Dante remove his fingers from my ass.

My breathing becomes hurried and my body tenses when I feel his head breach my asshole. I scream with Strix's cock in my mouth. Thorin bites my nipple, Ramsey sucks on my neck, and Killian's mouth descends on my clit.

It's too much.

I come again just as Dante sheathes himself inside my ass. It's an odd, full feeling, one I can't describe. It burns yet feels good. "Such a good girl," Dante croons, as he gives me a moment to adjust before he begins moving in and out. Strix runs his fingers through my hair, forcing my head back as he stuffs his cock farther down my throat.

Someone is playing with my pussy, their fingers entering me so I'm being fucked in both holes as another set of digits dances over my sensitive clit. I try to move away from the sensation. I'm far too sensitive to be touched there again, but the firm straps won't let me move, so I'm forced to endure it.

Thorin has switched places with Ramsey, allowing the King of Envy access to my breast, while Thorin's huge cock pumps in my hand, my fingers unable to touch around its girth. Ramsey and Lucian continue playing with my breasts, kneading them gently before lashing light spanks on my nipples. Strix tugs my hair firmly, his cock smacking into the back of my throat as Dante's thrusts grow quicker in my ass.

A pair of lips surround my clit and hum, the sensitivity once making me flinch now gone. The mouth between my legs grows fierce with desire, the sensation becoming more desperate as their lips suck the nub harder. The fingers inside me move faster, hitting my sweet spot with each thrust while Dante moves against them in my ass.

"So perfect for us," Killian coos. "A true queen, taking her king's so beautifully."

"She's magnificent," Thorin agrees. "She's everything we wanted and more, offering her flawless body to us, so vulnerable, so hot and wet and needy."

"Oh fuck," Dante roars, a second before his cum fills my ass. The lips on my clit suck hard, and I come again, my vision darkening, my eyes closing in ecstasy.

A moment later, as a tongue is gently lapping at my clit, Strix groans. "Take all of my cum like a good girl, *Regina*. Drink it all down. Don't let a drop escape your lips." I moan, humming around him as he shouts and comes in my mouth. I drink him down, moaning around his fresh, citrusy flavor.

I pant for breath as both Dante and Strix pull their cocks from my body. I'm fucking spent, gasping and twitching from exertion.

"You're not done yet, little one." I slide open one exhausted eyelid and peer up at Thorin, his large hand pumping his massive cock. "You have two more kings to take."

I can't form words.

As my wrists are loosened and my legs are unbound, I can't find my voice to pose the question. Why are they untying me?

A moment later, I'm flipped and lifted as Thorin slides under my body. "Take your king like a good girl," he croons as my torso is raised, Kings Marcel and Lucian lining me up with Thorin's mammoth cock.

I sink onto it slowly, sweat coating my skin. We groan together as I take him deep inside me, keeping my pace steady on shaky legs. It's when I reach up to run my fingers through my hair that I realize Lucian and Marcel are in control of my wrists, holding the length of leather bound to them.

Thorin cups my neck with his hand, wrath winding its way between us, and pulls me down to him. He takes my mouth, his tongue searching mine, dominating me, his need to give me pain surging as his other hand wraps around my hair, pulling hard, and forcing my body to drape on top of his.

And now I understand why...

Another cock is prodding at my back entrance, and I know it can only be one king, the only one left.

Ramsey.

"Take my cock in your ass, flower, while Thorin fills your cunt. Take us both at once. Let us fill you so completely, you'll never be satiated without us again."

I moan into Thorin's mouth. Lucian and Marcel force my arms behind my back as Ramsey lines up with my ass. I scream against Thorin's muscled chest as Ramsey enters me, my body trembling as Thorin's cock rubs against Ramsey's. I feel as though I might burst if they try to move.

But they do.

Thorin releases his grip on my neck and hair as Ramsey pulls out of me. I turn back to watch as Thorin grips my hips, drawing out of me as Ramsey plunges back in. There is no reprieve, just sensation. Lucian and Marcel tug at my wrists, pulling my torso up.

Strix and Dante descend on my breasts, licking and biting, sucking on my nipples as Thorin and Ramsey fuck me from below.

My breaths grow ragged as the kings take my body and use it for their own pleasure. My breasts feel heavy in the kings' mouths, bouncing as Thorin's and Ramsey's movements grow faster with need.

Killian fists my hair, making me gasp, and pulls my head back and to the side. "You are so beautiful," he groans, as his lips crash into mine. I moan as the kings use me and another orgasm builds. My pussy clenches around the massive wrath king's cock, my clit tingling as my nipples are sucked and bit. Ramsey spanks my ass as he thrusts in and out, smacking each cheek back and forth.

The sting of Ramsey's hand has me moaning into Killian's mouth. Then all the mouths leave my body, my arms lifting over my head as Lucian and Marcel raise me slightly from Thorin's body. Thorin scoots down to the end of the table, with Ramsey now standing behind me as I dangle by my wrists. Thorin and Ramsey have full access to my body, thrusting in and out of me, their cocks sliding against each other. My tits bounce in time with their movements. Thorin's grip on my thighs tightens and Ramsey digs his fingers into my hips.

"Tell me, how does it feel to have seven vampire kings at your beck and call, ready to please you, to serve you in any way you desire?" Thorin groans before he roars, his eyes rolling into the back of his head as he finds his release. A

437

second later, Ramsey plunges into my ass, his shouts of pleasure fueling me as his hot cum spurts deep inside me.

Killian steps in front of Lucian and cups my pussy before sliding a finger rapidly over my clit. I'm done for and come again.

Everything goes dark as I float in euphoria. Here, I no longer feel my body. Sensation dissipates, sounds grow muffled, my vision is black, and even where the kings touch me is numb.

I don't know how long I float in the clouds, reveling in the ecstasy of this one glorious moment, but the next thing I know, I come to and find myself looking up through hazy vision, strapped down to the table. Every inch of me hurts. My nipples are hard and aching, my ass used and throbbing, my exploited cunt pulsing.

I can feel the stickiness of their cum between my legs, coating my pussy and ass.

"Please understand, pet, how difficult it is for us to do this, to take your life," Lucian murmurs with utter sincerity. "In order for the transformation to be complete, we must drain you, all of you."

"We need every drop of blood in your body," Killian explains.

"Every ounce of your energy to become ours," Marcel continues.

"Say it, flower. Say that this is what you want. Say that you give yourself to us, that you are ours for all of time," Ramsey implores.

My response is paramount. I can either choose to change, to become one of them, to take my place on their throne as well as mine, or I can walk away from this. But the decision isn't even mine to make, fate decided long ago who I'm to become. I can't back down now. I won't. As much as it scares me, I want this. "I'm yours. Use me, my kings. My life is in your hands."

I can feel the mood in the room change. What was pure bloodlust driving the kings to tease me, to fuck me, morphs into something more, something greater.

A profound change is upon us. The electricity in the room buzzes, as the building of something monumental grows thick in the air.

The seven begin chanting again as I pant to catch my breath.

"For one."

"For all."

"For the seven."

"For the coven."

"For the people."

"For the world."

"For our queen."

Then, they bite. My screams fall silent as the seven siphon the blood from within me to the point of pain. I feel them growl against my skin. Two on my neck. Two on my wrists. Two on my breasts, and one on my inner thigh.

I feel their emotions pouring off of them and know this is the final act. Thorin's wrath rages, his need to protect me warring with the fact that they have to kill me. Killian's mind is turbulent, he needs all of me, more blood, more of my body, yet knowing he's hurting me is destroying him. Lucian's lust washes over me. He's desperate to make this feel good for me, although he's equally unable to stop drinking. Marcel sucks greedily, as only the King of Greed can. His fangs sink deep, drinking hard, though he struggles with the need to also feel my pain as much as he's giving it.

Dante is torn. On one hand, he wants to take his time consuming me, but on the other, he doesn't want to prolong my pain. Ramsey's need to have more of me than the others peaks. He drinks harder, taking more of my blood as waves of envy pour off of him, but he also wishes to console me, to be the one I run to for comfort. Strix is bursting with pride as he consumes my blood. I can feel how proud he is of me for giving them everything I am, though his pride tugs at the fact that it's in his nature to save me.

As the flurry of their rapidly changing emotions, needs, and desires war within them, they seep inside me, causing my brain to spin out of control. My heart pounds painfully as it tries to produce more lifeblood. Liquid lava replaces my blood, searing my veins as if lightning was surging within me. I can no longer see, can no longer hear, and my voice is completely gone.

All I know is pain, a despondent agony from which there is no reprieve. My head pounds, and my brain is desperate for oxygen. My skin burns as if fire is blazing upon it. So I scream silently, my mouth gaping in a soundless cry as the life is drained from me.

I have no tears to cry, no regrets as my life flashes before me. I see my father, his caring expression, telling me what a beautiful princess I am and how much my mother loved me. I see the faces of the seven rush past. A smirk from Ramsey. A stern expression from Thorin. Lucian biting his lip. Killian running his hand through his hair. Marcel's dark and knowing eyes. Strix's handsome smile. Dante's heated gaze.

Everyone I ever cared for...

As I choke for air, my body growing more and more weak, I succumb to the feelings. I close my eyes, my body deflating, submitting to the kings, giving them everything I have to give.

The pain slips away and my thoughts grow fuzzy as life leaves my body. I don't fight death, because I no longer fear it. Instead, I embrace it, knowing this is not the end for me.

Soon, I will be reborn, no longer a meek princess, but a formidable queen.

As the last ounce of life is sucked from my veins, my lungs devoid of air, the world goes black. Time stops, and all sound is silenced as I fall through the dark abyss into the blackness of the beyond, never more depleted, never more fulfilled.

CHAPTER 44

*S*wirling through the darkness, I feel like I'm floating. Nothingness spreads out as far as I can see. My arms and legs rise and fall, as if a soft wind is blowing them, and my hair billows around my head, obscuring my vision. I narrow my eyes, looking into the vastness of oblivion, wondering where I am...how I got here...

I try to recount what last happened to me, but my memory fails. As I twist my body to look around, I feel the space between my legs throbbing, feel a dozen places on my body aching as if I've been bruised or bitten.

What happened to me?

Contemplating how I arrived here, I glance around, trying to take in my surroundings. Around me, the dark vortex I'm in churns with dazzling colors. Streaks of stars fly past, and purple and pink mists swirl in a smoky dance.

To my right, a bright flash of light catches my eye and I turn to see a spotlight shining in the distance. A hidden door opens in the light, and out steps a man and a woman. I don't recognize either of them, but I instantly know who they are.

"Mother? Father?" I move to reach them, desperate to see them, to receive my first hug from my mom, and whiskery kisses from my dad. But my limbs just flail around, my body remaining where it is. Another flash of light has me turning the other direction. Tearing my gaze from my parents, I watch as another door opens. Behind it sits a platform of sorts with seven thrones perched on it.

The seven.

My heart stirs at the sight as memories bombard me of my last moments. The bites and the blood, the drinking and fucking, the way they used me completely, bringing me to heights of exquisite pleasure over and over again...

I turn back to my parents, longing squeezing my chest, knowing I have a choice to make. I could take the easy way out and go with my parents, end my old life, starting the next with them. Or I could take the path less traveled, one filled with danger and uncertainty, and dare I say love.

My gaze flickers between the two choices as I float between them.

"Go, my child. Be with them. They are your destiny." I turn to my parents, my heart clenching as I hear my mother's voice for the first time.

"Listen to your mother, Snow. We will meet again in the next life." Father's words pull a sob from my lips. Why did it have to be this way? Why do I have to choose?

"We love you, Snow. We will meet again," Mother shouts, as my body begins to move toward the door containing the seven. I hadn't even realized I'd made my choice, but as I hurtle toward them, the figures of my parents growing smaller and smaller in the distance, I know this is the right decision. Because, sometimes, the hardest choices are the correct ones. Because I don't want to look back at this moment and wonder, if I went with them, how different would things be.

Accepting my fate, my destiny, I toss my head back and throw my arms open wide, letting the invisible force pull me to where I'm meant to go. Just as I breach the threshold of the doorway, a bright light flashes, blinding me, and as I fall through the white chasm into the next chapter of my life, I hold onto the memory of my parents' voices. "We love you, Snow. We will meet again."

I WAKE WITH A START, GASPING FOR AIR. MY EYES FLY OPEN, seeing nothing but blackness around me, wondering if it didn't work. Fear threatens to weave its icy tendrils around my spine as I search the darkness for something, anything.

Maybe I'm still dead, the promises made to me broken by some unknown force. Maybe there was a third door I didn't see, the choice of where to go never really mine to make.

My nostrils flare, smelling the blood of the seven still coating me, the sticky residue of their cum between my legs. I pat my hands down my body, feeling that I'm real, that I'm not dead.

But then where the fuck am I?

A gnawing thirst rages in my throat, making me claw at my neck. The desire to feed is all-consuming as my fangs drop, desperate for fresh, hot blood. I need to feed, and I need to do it soon.

Propping myself up on my elbows, my forehead smacks into something hard. I reach up and feel a low roof over top of me and extend my arms out, feeling down the length of whatever I'm in, realizing it's small, barely large enough to encase my body.

I push at the ceiling and find total resistance. It doesn't move a fucking inch. Wrath surges within me, deep-seated anger at my imprisonment.

No.

I will not be held captive ever again.

Growling, I lie back down, losing control. My snarls echo in the small space as I rip down the cloth sides with my claws. I punch at the obstruction restraining me, kicking out as I try to escape the madness.

A feral cry escapes me as I lash out, throwing my body up against the top when finally, it budges a bit. Excitement fills me and I growl in anticipation. I crash into it again and hear the distinct sound of rock breaking.

Then the scents invade my nose and completely overwhelm me. Sweet and spicy, citrus, leather, fresh falling rain, honey, chocolate, and wine.

The seven.

My mouth waters as images of their blood pouring into my mouth like crimson honey threaten to drive me to madness. The thirst burns my throat, making me growl in frustration. I feel them calling for me, desperate for me as much as I am for them, their thirst rivaling my own.

My actions become wild as instinct takes over. I scream and howl, thrusting any part of my body against anything it can reach. The smell of my blood permeates the space from my wounds, but I don't even feel the pain. This is not pain, this is my plight for freedom.

Another crack sounds and a morsel of light shines down on me. The aromas of many assault me. There must be hundreds of beings out there just watching, waiting.

The notion that it could be the evil queen flits through my mind, but I quickly squash it. I know she's not here, not because I can't sense her, but because I can feel *them*.

The seven.

My kings.

With a ferociousness I didn't know I was capable of, I flip onto my belly, forcing myself up on hands and knees, roaring as I shove the low ceiling above me with my back. I growl and scream, my limbs shaking and teeth gnashing, as I push with all my might, the rock digging into my spine.

I'm desperate to get out of here and flatten myself to the floor, then, with a burst of energy, I shoot my body up like a vertical battering ram. The resounding crack signals my success as pieces of stone fall onto my body. I brush them off with ease, my muscles feeling stronger, more powerful than ever before.

My body hums with magic as I raise myself up to stand, shaking pieces of stone from my hair. Blood trickles down my naked form, some seeping from the wounds I suffered bashing out of my stone prison. Before me sit the seven in their regal thrones, surrounding the coffin—my coffin.

I made it.

Crowns of gold and platinum decorated in jewels sparkle on their heads. Their eyes are narrowed on me, watching, waiting to see what I will do.

"Snow," Lucian purrs, as he rises and steps forward. Damn, he looks good. He has on his full king regalia, from the suit to the cape. His arctic eyes flash with an emotion I cannot name as he walks toward me. My fingers twitch, throat burning, fangs descending to take a fucking bite of him—of what's mine. "You gave yourself to the seven, and in return we gave to you. We watched you grow from a beaten girl to a ferocious woman. You blessed us with your body, shared your mind, and gave us your heart. You allowed us to consume you in every way possible, submitting beautifully while maintaining complete control. You have never broken a word spoken or a promise whispered, confirming what we always knew. You were born for us, destined to rule alongside the seven, reborn as something greater than this world has ever known." He stops before me, his sweet and spicy scent making my mouth water. My heart races and my eyes

446

roll into the back of my head as I bask in his seduction. "Three days ago, you died a princess. Now, you rise as our queen."

As I ponder the fact that I've been dead for three days, the King of Lust lifts a crown off a velvet pillow perched on a nearby stool. It's beautiful, elegant, and regal. Swirls of silver intertwine with gold to construct the sharp tips. Gemstones of every color are seated within it, creating a mosaic of hues.

Thorin rises from his chair with a white cape folded across his muscled arm. He says not a word, but stands behind me, then drapes it over my shoulders. Lucian smiles as he places the crown on my head. The other five kings stand, rushing over to me, relief clear on their faces as they reach out to touch me as if to confirm I'm really here.

Happiness threatens to overwhelm me. I'm here. I did it. I survived.

Lucian wraps his arm around my shoulders and gently urges me to turn around. When I do, my mouth drops open in shock. Every man, woman, and child of Riverwood watches with hopeful eyes. Every vampire in the entire Coven of Sin stands before me.

I recognize the space we are in as the huge cathedral room I was in when I was first introduced to the seven.

"Ladies, gentlemen, and vampires alike," Lucian shouts, "may I present to you the ruler of the coven, leader of River-wood, mate to the seven, Queen Snow!"

The resounding cheers almost knock me over, so loud that mothers cover the ears of their little ones. Tears run down the faces of so many of my people. There's relief and happiness and excitement, families hugging each other with joy, knowing our oppression may finally come to an end, that we might now have the power to fight off the evil suffocating us. The vampires celebrate too, shouting and cheering, their glasses raised in a toast.

I know I should speak, but my words are lodged in my throat. I'm so moved by the sight that I can't form thought, completely unable to find the right words. But as their cheers die down and the seven flank me, my new power brewing inside me, I know just what to say.

"My people! The time has come for us to fight." The cheering rises once more, the energy in the room sizzling through the air. I turn to the vampires. "No longer will you be forced underground, hidden from existence and treated like monsters." I look to the people of Riverwood. "No longer will you live afraid and scared of a tyrannical, evil queen. No longer will your homes be destroyed, your children live in fear, or your families starve or worse."

I walk to the end of the stage, closing the ends of my cape around me. I spot Katie holding hands with Julian and Rosie with her arm linked with Marie's. Marie gazes up at me with affection, then winks, encouraging me to continue. I take a deep breath and let it out slowly. "The time has come for our oppression to end, for our worlds to join together and fight for our future. The evil queen sits on a stolen throne, her magic waning even as we speak. She will rue the day she killed my parents, used her magic for evil, persecuting those who didn't deserve it, subjugating us with her power."

I take a deep breath, shaking my head at the years of misery and affliction we've endured. "For too long we've suffered. And now the final battle is about to begin. The fight ahead of us will be long and hard. There will be anguish and pain, destruction and death. But we will prevail. We will be victorious. And when I vanquish the evil queen once and for all, I'll rip her beating heart out of her chest and bathe in her blood."

Shouts of agreement resound, fists pumping in the air in celebration.

"Together, we will create a new life, where our two societies can live in harmony. To the people of Riverwood, I promise you I will see your homes rebuilt, your farms bountiful, your children running free as their laughter flits through the air. To my coven, I promise you a way of life where you can come out of hiding and be proud of what you've chosen to become. Follow me, stand with me, fight with me, pledge your life to me as I have given mine for you."

The room falls silent, and I wonder if I've failed to say the right thing. Glances are exchanged, wide eyes watching with a courage I've not seen in all my years.

Then, one by one, they fall to their knees. Every man, woman, and child, every vampire, everyone.

My throat burns for a whole new reason. Though the hunger is still gnawing at me, I now swallow the lump in my throat, trying to hold back my tears.

"You've done it, my queen," King Strix whispers beside me as the kings form a line in front of me. Then, to my total disbelief, they all take a knee before me, their crowns removed, hands on their hearts, and heads bowed.

The kings kneel for me.

A flurry of emotion brews inside me, one so strong it makes me wonder if my chest might explode. Seeing their devotion, their respect for me, changes something inside me.

Fierce resolve brews within my heart as I glance at all those before me.

I know we can win.

I know I can defeat the evil queen.

A smile breaks out on my face as the kings rise, surrounding me in a giant king circle. "How are you feeling, little one?" Thorin asks, his large hand cupping my chin.

I look up, gazing into his gray eyes, and answer as honestly as I can. "Thirsty."

CHAPTER 45

The kings swarm me with my admission, and I squeal as they lift me up and carry me off the stage. Thorin grabs me from the others. I wrap my legs around his waist, his hands cupping my ass. "If my queen is thirsty, then she needs to drink." Thorin arches his neck to me and I lunge.

I don't need to think about my fangs elongating, don't consider who else might be watching. I just drink.

I drink and drink and drink.

His molten blood coats my mouth, tangy but slightly sweet, and I moan happily against his skin. Thorin spanks my ass lightly. "There, there, little one. You keep making noises like that and my blood won't be the only thing inside you."

My pussy clenches at the thought.

"Relax, Thorin," Marcel scolds. "Our queen has just awakened from her three-day hiatus, and all you can think about is your cock. Shame on you."

My borrowed cape is torn away as new hands wrap around me, pulling me from Thorin. Marcel's handsome face appears above me, a smile playing on his lips as he considers me with his dark eyes. "Still thirsty, precious girl?" I answer by flashing him my fangs. "You were so perfect out there, you know. A true queen." He kisses my forehead then offers me his neck.

My fangs pierce his skin, and this time, he's moaning right there with me. His salted chocolate blood flows from him and down my throat, helping to ease my thirst, but it's still not enough.

I need more.

I need them all.

"My turn." Ramsey's dulcet tone warms me as he lifts me from Marcel. "I can't take it any longer, my queen. I need your lips on me. Drink, flower. Take as much as you need." Ramsey cradles me against his chest, raising me so I can access that plump vein in his neck. And I do.

He jolts when my fangs plunge inside him, his breath coming out in pants. His long, crimson hair tickles my face as his honey blood consumes me as much as I'm consuming it. "Yes, flower. Take it. Take it all."

"Why would she want you when she could have me? Come here, sweetheart." Killian's lighthearted taunting makes me grin as he pulls me from Ramsey. I love that he can always find humor in things, always keeping the mood surrounding him on the happier side. "First, I need to taste your lips before I burst from wanting you so desperately."

Killian takes my mouth, tangling his tongue with mine, and I wrap my legs tightly around his waist. He holds my ass with one hand and kneads my breast with the other. "Drink from me, my queen, before I abandon all pretense and fuck you right here on the floor."

I laugh as he smiles, presenting his neck. Licking my lips, I latch onto my gluttony king, knowing how much he needs more of everything. I drink from him while threading my fingers through his sandy blond hair, tugging on the strands. "Yes, my queen. Drink from me. Take what you need from your kings."

I suck hard, his blood so delicious I fear one day I might drain him dry in my greed for it. Killian stumbles, almost falling, both of us almost crashing into the ground as another king grabs me.

"Killian can't have all the fun, pet." Lucian's blue eyes flash with mischief as he tugs me to him. "I need to feel you, my queen. I need to taste your flesh, I need to exist inside you as you drink from me."

"Fuck yes," I respond, my voice shaking with desire.

"Such a good girl," he praises, as I wrap my legs around him and sink down onto his cock, not remembering when he took his pants off. "Ride your king, take what you need."

Lucian lowers us onto a chair, and I realize now we're back in the throne room where it all began. Gripping the armrests, I begin to move, his perfect cock buried inside me.

The smell of citrus and fresh strawberries assaults me as I bounce on top of the King of Lust. Strix sidles up behind me, his wrist already pierced and bleeding. "Drink from me, *Regina*. Drink while you fuck your king."

Growling, I latch onto his wrist with my mouth, my fangs sinking in. His blood pours through me as Lucian's hands grip my hips, grinding me along his length. I take from them both, fucking and drinking, having never been happier in my whole entire life.

Lucian moves me faster, my tits bouncing with each roll of my hips. And soon we're both coming. I pull off Strix's wrist, tossing my head back as I cry out in ecstasy.

"You're not done yet, kitten." Dante's gorgeous face comes into view as he pulls me off of Lucian and swaddles me up in his cape. One large, muscular arm holds me tight against his broad chest. With the other hand, he traces my cheeks and jaw, as if memorizing my face.

His black hair sweeps in front of his face, hiding his masculine jawline while exploiting his full lips. Dante brings his finger to his mouth and pierces it with his fang, then offers it to me.

"Drink, kitten. Drink, then rest. We have much planning to do. There's a battle to prepare for, an evil queen to slaughter, and a world to reclaim. So rest. Rejuvenate. Know that we are here. We have you. You are safe."

I suck his finger into my mouth, drawing his blood from it, drinking while his steady gait lulls me. Now that he's mentioned it, I'm quite tired. With his finger in my mouth, his savory blood coating my tongue, I fall asleep, happy, fucked, and satisfied.

Sometime later, I wake up nestled in a bed covered in plush blankets, surrounded by the sleeping bodies of my kings. I smile to myself, knowing that the days of waking up alone are behind me. By the orange color dispersed throughout the lavish bedroom, I can only surmise that this is Killian's suite.

Next to me, on my left, Ramsey lies curled, facing me, with his red hair cascading over his face. Beyond him I can see Dante's black locks and the gold necklaces of Marcel. On my other side is Killian, one arm draped across me, sheets resting low, exposing the sexy dip below his hips. I have the urge to try and tug it lower using my toes. Next to him is Strix, and Lucian is sleeping on the very edge.

One of them is missing...

"Good evening, little one." I push myself up on my elbows

and look toward the origin of Thorin's deep voice. "Feeling rested?"

I consider his words and take note of my body. No aches or pains plague me, my muscles feel stronger than ever, and even my mind feels bright and alert. "I feel incredible," I answer with a smile. "Never better."

Thorin pushes himself up from an oversized chair, which barely housed his large frame, crossing his arms over his broad chest. "Good. Because there is much work to do. Come with me."

Thorin stalks to the end of the bed and tugs the covers from my body. His gaze heats as he takes in my nakedness. Reaching for me, he grips my ankle and pulls me toward him. I take a quick glance at Killian's cock as my legs fall open, inviting Thorin to either take a peek, touch me, or taste me.

"Why do you tempt me, my queen?" Thorin growls. "My mouth waters for another taste of your cunt, and my hands tingle to mark your pale skin red again. But that must wait for another time. Your subjects await you."

Smirking, my shoulders scrunch up innocently before I scoot down to the end of the bed and wrap my fingers around Thorin's shirt. It doesn't take much coercion to pull him toward me. Our lips collide as a guttural growl erupts from his throat. Thorin grabs my face in his hands and kisses me hard, his tongue brutally lashing against mine.

I pout when he pulls away and picks me up, setting me on my feet before grabbing my hand. I trot next to him as we enter a sitting room. Before me, on a grand sofa large enough to seat all eight of us and then some, is an outfit.

Not just any outfit, but one made for battle.

Thorin walks over and picks it up, holding it in front of him for me to see. "I designed this just for you."

My eyes go wide, jaw gaping. Such elegance and detail

have been put into it. I walk toward Thorin, reaching out a finger and dragging it down the ornate chest plate. "Did you get this in Riverwood?" I ask breathlessly.

"Yes and no." I turn back to see Lucian standing in the doorway, admiring my ass. "Thorin commissioned it, your human blacksmiths work much too slowly. So we had them teach some of his wrath vampires who took to the art quite well."

I turn back, nodding. "Can-can I put it on?" I request, looking up at Thorin. His nostrils flare, his gray eyes assaulting me.

"It would give me great pleasure to see you wear it, my queen."

My queen.

Those two little words make my chest hurt with emotion. Lucian moves closer to help me don the attire. A small, leather top is laced up my chest before the large metal piece is placed over it. Thorin adjusts it while Lucian straps me in.

Surrounding my neck is a high collar, loose enough so I can move my head, but tight enough to protect. The chest piece is gorgeous. Above my breasts is an intricately woven pattern with soft curves and languid tendrils made of platinum and gold. So elegant and feminine that it could only be worn by a woman. Expanding to encompass my breasts, the metal has been molded around them as if the artist had memorized my body before creating it. The metal narrows along the waist, giving way to thick leather. Several buckles hold the sides together, covering my waist.

"Step in, pet." I look down and see Lucian kneeling at my feet, holding the rest of the outfit in his hands. Biting my lip, I slide my legs in and he pulls the pants up over my hips. Made of leather and metal, the pants fit me like a second skin. Supple leather covers me all the way to my ankles, but a metal skirt-like piece rests lower over my hips, made up of three layers of armor.

Lucian offers me boots next. I accept his help as he guides the first boot up my leg. It weighs nothing, as if I were walking on bare feet. But then Thorin grabs metal coverlets and slips them over my boots. The metal has been pounded into sharp points at the front of my shins, providing a great weapon should I be close enough to kick an enemy.

A belt is fixed across my hips, and a pair of daggers are slid into matching sheaths on either side.

"You forgot this." I spin back and see Killian walking in with my crown in his hands. "Every queen needs her crown. Especially in battle." With a smirk, he places it on my head. "There. Now no one will question who the true queen is. I can't wait to see the look on the evil cunt's face when you kill her once and for all."

"Here, here," Marcel cheers, walking in behind him. "My, my, my. You look stunning, precious girl. I almost don't recognize you with clothing on." I narrow my eyes at him, shaking my head, but I can't hold in my smile. Because he's right. Most of the time, I'm not given clothing. I've pretty much become accustomed to walking around naked wherever I go.

"Pity she needs them at all, isn't it?" Lucian muses.

Thorin strokes his beard, his chest rising and falling rapidly as his anger festers. "The time for joking is over. Wipe those smiles from your faces and get your heads out of the clouds. We will engage in battle soon. The evil queen will not be laughing, and neither should you."

"Geez, Thorin, lighten up a little bit," Ramsey scolds amidst a yawn, his red hair wild around his head. "Looking good, flower."

I can feel my cheeks heating. "Thanks."

He shrugs and moves farther into the room. "Now we just need to do something with all this luscious hair…"

"Katie will know what to do with it."

"I sure do!" I turn toward the sound of her voice then bolt toward my friend.

"Katie! You're here!" I engulf her in a huge hug as her arms wrap around me.

She pulls away, her hands squeezing my shoulders. "I couldn't just let you run off defending the realm from evil without having your hair done, now could I?"

We laugh and she pulls me over to a chair, encouraging me to sit as she tugs a comb from her apron and puts the handle in her mouth.

"Hard to fucking sit in this thing," I complain as I lower myself onto a chair.

"It is not made for sitting, little one," Thorin growls.

Katie and I exchange a look, trying not to laugh as she removes my crown and begins tugging on my matted hair. As she works out the curls, I realize it's probably been days since I've showered, not since the night of my death when the kings washed me.

Fuck, I probably smell something fierce.

I move to lift my arm, intent on smelling my armpit, but the armor on my shoulders prevents such movements.

"So—many—fucking—curls," Katie grunts, tugging the snarls out. After dousing my black locks in oil, she begins pulling my hair away from my face. Soon, she's managed to corral the whole mop into a tight, intricate series of braids. I stand to look in the mirror after she pins my crown to my head and appreciate her work.

Navarrah would love these, I think to myself, wondering if I'll ever see the woman who inspired me so much ever again.

This is the first time I've looked in a mirror since my transformation—since I've become a vampire. I look like myself, but also so vastly different. For starters, my eyes, once blue like my father's, have turned black with a hint of red in the iris. My once pale skin would look tan in comparison to how white I've become.

Snow White.

It could be a new color.

The contours of my face have even changed, the angles becoming sharper, cheekbones higher, and nose more pointed than round. My eyebrows have a high arch, making me look sensual but serious. Even my lips are fuller, plumper. Now, I wish I didn't have all this armor on so I could see what the rest of me looks like.

"That makes two of us," Strix purrs, sidling up next to me. "I much prefer you naked and spread out before me like a grand feast."

I smile at him in the mirror as he hugs me from behind, placing a kiss on my cheek.

A crash booms, and I pull from Strix to look at the door to the suite. Jovie and Cerino have barged in, their chests heaving as they spot Thorin.

"King Thorin. We have news. The evil queen is gathering her armies. Huntsmen are saddling their horses, and her guards are arming themselves. If she chooses to invade, she could be inside the coven within two hours."

My mouth runs dry.

This is it.

The moment I have envisioned so many times during my life.

Excitement ripples through me, my heart racing in anticipation. In her hunger for war, her blinding hatred for me, she's once again made a grave mistake. Instead of waiting to strike during daylight, when the coven must seek shelter from the sun, she decides to attack now, at night.

A malicious smile graces my face. "Then let's meet her

head-on," I growl. "I'm done waiting for her, wondering what her next move will be. I'm done with her controlling everything from the clouds to the people. Her reign is about to end, and I can't wait to see the light fade from her eyes when it does."

CHAPTER 46

*A*fter bidding Katie goodbye, and telling Jovie and Cerino to ready the people, I turn to my kings. "I need you all to drink from me. And don't fucking ask questions." Bringing my wrists to my mouth, I pierce my veins and hold them out. One by one they come to me, taking my wrists, and drinking my blood.

I can't explain why this is so important, only that I know it is. Call it instinct. Call it what you will. But I need this to happen as much as I once needed food to survive.

As they drink, my blood mingling with theirs, an awareness of them grows within me. I've been able to sense my kings on some level ever since we exchanged blood. But this is different.

"It's your version of a drone," Marcel informs me, after passing my wrist to Strix. "You giving your blood will allow you to feel us as if we were your own body. You'll have a sixth sense now, a new power, one we only surmised might happen once you became the Queen of the Vampires."

"What else can I do?" I question, curious and excited.

Marcel shrugs. "We simply do not know. Most covens are

ruled by kings, whether several like us or just a single king. Queens are fairly unknown. And fated queens even less."

"So...there might be powers I have that you're unaware of?"

Marcel nods. "You are a wonder, my queen. Unique and gorgeous, a mighty force. None will stand in your way should you choose to remove them. You just have to trust in yourself, the rest will fall into place."

Marcel kisses my forehead then rushes off to prepare for battle. As the final king—Dante, of course—pulls from my wrist, kisses my cheek, and leaves my room, a new visitor arrives.

"Vincent!" I can't help but be excited to see my vampire friend.

"Hello, my queen. Might I say how dashing you look tonight." Vincent grabs my hand and kisses the back of it, then wiggles his eyebrows.

I laugh and pull my hand away from him, wiping his kiss off in exaggerated movements and pretending to act like it was gross. He smiles and tugs on his outfit. Only now do I realize he's also in battle attire. That realization has my smile falling from my face.

Thorin's right.

The time for joking is over.

People's lives are at stake.

My life is at stake.

Vincent's mood turns somber, as if he can sense my thoughts. "Please, my queen, allow me to escort you down to the courtyard. Everyone has gathered there."

I nod and move toward the door, allowing Vincent to guide me. My feet step forward on autopilot. I don't even remember the walk down to the courtyard, my mind completely consumed with the imminent meeting of the queens, wondering who will prevail.

It has to be me.
It has to be me.
It has to be me.

I can't even consider the ramifications of defeat, the losses too grand to really comprehend. My death would be the catalyst to what might be the fall of my people, and maybe the coven too.

Vincent leads me out of the Gluttony Castle doors, where I pause at the sight, my eyes finally taking in my surroundings.

The people of Riverwood are intermixed with members of the coven. Humans and vampires alike are adorned with armor across their chests and heads, with long swords hanging from their belts. The vampires' battle attire is less cumbersome, allowing them to move more freely, using their speed to their advantage.

Rows and rows of the newly forged army stand proud and ready. The smell of molten metal still lingers in the air, and the heat from the blazing fires has created a smokiness in the vast space.

I can feel my kings coming to me, longing to be near me for this epic moment. I can sense excitement, worry, and another emotion I can't quite discern. But it's deep and dark, emerging from a place they keep secret inside themselves.

Thorin arrives first, then Ramsey. The others soon join us. Once my kings have flanked behind me, I begin to move. A makeshift platform has been erected from timber brought down from above. I climb the three stairs leading up and walk to the center, my kings fanning out behind me.

Columns of fighters stand before us in organized lines, spreading out the length of all seven castles. There must be hundreds gathered.

An army.

All eyes are on me as side conversations silence. The only

sound besides my rapidly beating heart is the clanking of metal as my soldiers shift on unsure feet.

"You can do this, my queen," Strix whispers in my ear.

He's right.

I take a deep breath and focus on my pride, letting it consume me as I find the right words to say.

"My people, members of the coven, the day has come to take a stand against the evil invading our lands and our lives. The imposter queen has controlled us, manipulated us, threatened us, and murdered us. That stops today."

The army cheers, shouting words of agreement. I hold up my hand to silence them. "Today we take back what is rightfully ours. Today we vanquish the evil suffocating us and begin a new life together. The battle will not be easy, as nothing worth doing ever is. Our path is riddled with pain and uncertainty. We will suffer. We will know hurt. We will not all survive."

Worried glances and quiet murmurs are exchanged among them. "But in the face of adversity, we will emerge victorious. The evil queen is desperate, her powers waning. She will do anything and say anything in order to get what she wants. Do. Not. Trust. Her. Close your ears to her lies. Shield your eyes from her infectious gaze. Ignore her attempts to lure you, to draw you in, because once she sinks her claws into you, you're as good as dead."

I begin to pace back and forth across the platform, needing to expend some of this pent-up energy.

"My people, my kin, my coven. Fight with me on this day. Let us wage such a war that history books will tell of our tale, that children will pretend to be us, that our story goes down as the new legend in Riverwood, passed down through generations to come."

I pause and face the soldiers standing before me, the brave souls willing to give up their lives for the future of another. My heart swells with pride as I glance from face to face.

"Over the years, the evil queen has won many of the battles fought against us, but today, together, we will win the war. Because we have something she doesn't have—the will to survive, the desire to start living where we once only existed. Let your anger fuel you, let your sadness incite your rage. Take no mercy on her or her huntsmen, for she will have none for you."

Unsheathing my daggers, I lift them into the air and raise my voice, shouting as loud as I can. "Today, you are an army to be feared. You are soldiers, warriors, defenders of our lands. It is up to us to take back what was stolen. Fight with me. Fight for our world. Fight for yourselves. Fight for our future. Search within yourselves and find that inner strength I know you all have. Let it be your guide. Today, under the watchful eyes of our ancestors, let us end this tyranny and suffocating oppression. Right here. Right now. Once and for all."

The army erupts in a cacophony of sounds—cheers and shouts, howls and roars. Every soldier has unsheathed their weapon, and they brandish them in the air. The wrath vampires snarl and dig their claws into the ground, having shifted into their wolf forms.

Pride swells within me as I watch the fight flicker in the eyes of those gathered. Lust also rages within me, but this time it's not sexual gratification that lures me, it's the desire for spilled blood.

Observing the army, I realize many of them have waited their whole lives for this moment, and now it has come. They are ready.

The kings move closer, touching me, letting me know they stand behind me. I can feel their devotion for me, their fear of seeing me in battle, but also their willingness to let me fight, though it pains them.

Thorin moves first, shouting orders to those he's appointed as commanding officers. The soldiers fall into formation and march toward the stairs leading out of our underground safe haven.

Ramsey and Marcel step up next to me, and I glance over at them, only now seeing my kings.

Decked out in shining armor, crowns flashing on their heads, capes billowing around their ankles, my kings look fucking fierce. The usual lust and desire in their eyes has been replaced with anger and violence. The need to cause pain oozes off of them.

I've forgotten too soon that the queen has cost them so much as well. It was because of her that their kind—my kind —had to go into hiding. It was because of her that they were unable to stand in the light without a painful death. It's because of her that they were forced to live in underground cities where their very existence was shrouded in secrets.

Ramsey lays a possessive hand on my lower back as we ascend the stairs. My heart pounds louder than the largest drum, my blood coursing through my veins faster than a rushing river. I can feel the change in the air, the static so thick it's like walking through fog. The very world is on edge, waiting for the one final moment, a moment that will change the course of the world forever.

Memories of fighting my way out of my own coffin rise in my mind. This moment is very much like that. The box that once surrounded us is breaking, my people are escaping their binds and tasting freedom for the first time.

As we emerge through the vacant party room, down the long, candlelit hallway, and out into the back alleys of the town, a sense of urgency burns within me. The night is newly fallen. We must defeat her before the sun rises or be faced with battling without half of our army.

Thorin leads the militia through the town and over to the gate in the wall, which once offered the citizens protection, but now hangs ominously off its rusted hinge.

Beyond the remains of the dismantled fence lies our enemy, spread out among the hills leading to my stolen castle. Sitting atop her largest stallion, wearing a pointed crown gleaming from the light of surrounding torches, is the evil cunt bitch. The urge to lower my eyes wars within me, but I remember how Lucian was able to suffer her stare and not fall under her spell. She no longer has that power over me.

Point for Snow.

The huntsmen ride on massive horses, their hunting dogs yipping at their hooves. The ominous wailing of their trumpets sends a chill down my spine. Every time I've heard it, I was on the run with the huntsmen on my tail, waiting with rusted chains to bind me and drag me back to the evil cunt bitch.

Things are so different now. I'm different. For once, I'm able to look at her and not cower, not consider the different ways in which she might torture me.

As my army spreads out behind me, I realize we have the numbers to defeat her. Though my soldiers lack training, they make up for it in heart. They want to win, and they will kill to do it.

It's such a different fight for the huntsmen. They have nothing to gain by defeating us. Nothing changes for them. But for us, everything changes if we dethrone the evil queen. And that will make all the difference.

The evil queen, my loathsome stepmother, and murderer of my parents and so many others, raises her arms and a black smoke swirls between her hands, a weapon I know far too well.

"People of Riverwood, hear me!" she shouts. "Do not let this beast deceive you. You cannot win this war! And once I've won, slayed your precious princess, anyone who fought beside her will be put to a painful death. I'll sever your bodies limb from fucking limb while your children watch in horror. I'll become the creature who lives in their nightmares, haunting them every time they shut their eyes. This is your only chance, your final decision. Come to my side and your betrayal will be forgotten. Fight beside me and you shall be rewarded. Choosing Princess Beast, means you've chosen death. You have five minutes to decide."

The kings spread out behind me, trying to calm the people who've begun to whisper in the dark.

"Don't listen to her," I shout. "This is what she does, all she knows. She threatens you with your very life to get what she wants. Don't give in to her lies. There will be no reward for you, only years of endless suffering, just as you have already endured. Stand strong. Stand by me. Take back your freedom!"

Thorin calls upon his wolves and they slink to the front lines, eyes set on the huntsmen's horses and dogs. As the wolves snarl, gnashing their teeth, the horses begin to whinny in distress, detecting the predators prowling toward them.

Not waiting for the end of her five-minute bullshit countdown, I raise my dagger and shout, "Soldiers! People of Riverwood! Vampires of the coven! Are you ready?"

The resounding roar is all I need to confirm what I already know.

We are going to win this.

A murderous smile cleaves my face as I stare the evil queen in the eyes and yell, "Attack!"

The armies charge, wolves and humans and vampires screeching, shouting, growling, and snarling as they sprint for the enemy. The huntsmen raise their swords and charge. The kings and I fall back, watching as our armies collide. The cries of agonizing death are already ringing out among the metallic clash of swords.

The giant wrath wolves leap from the ground, knocking huntsmen from their steeds, their strong jaws ripping out the throats of their enemies. The vampires parry their foes, twisting and dancing out of the way of every strike.

My people are not as lucky. Unskilled in battle or use of the sword, the men and women fall easily. Marcel marches toward me, his dark eyes soaking in the fight before us. "It's the people who didn't drink my blood, whether due to their own ignorance, fear, or some other ridiculous reason, who are falling. My drones, they are all thriving in this."

He's right. The drones have a yellow sash around their torsos, and so far, only the normal humans are the ones losing. "Marcel, where are the elderly and the children being kept?"

"Deep in the bowels of Wrath Castle. Thorin has it protected with every possible weapon you could think of."

I nod as a huntsman plows through a group of humans, swinging a flail. The spiked, iron ball crashes into the head of an attacking man, causing it to explode in a blast of bone, blood, and brains. It's hard to stomach. Near the evil bitch, spears are thrown, lodging into their prey. A huntsman goes down as a trio of vampires claws at his throat. A wrath wolf dies as a yellow-eyed guard guts it with a dagger.

So much death and destruction. It makes my heart sad to lose a single life. But this is war. Many lives will be lost on this night.

The evil queen begins to launch her magic into the fight, her targets unclear. Her black smoke wraps around a guard, choking him, then snares a woman holding her own against another guard. They both perish, their choking noises lost under the clamor of battle.

The potent, coppery stench of spilled blood wafts toward us as the winds begin to shift. The static in the air grows thick as the wind picks up around me. I look up and see black clouds swirling above in a formation the likes of which I've never seen.

Even the vultures circling overhead abandon their chance at a meal and head for the trees. Wrath wolves begin to howl at the sky, their animal instinct warning them that something of immense proportions is brewing.

I lock gazes with the queen, her eyes flashing with malice. She holds her hands out to her sides and slowly raises them, her head thrown back in terrifying laughter. A crackling, black ball of magic forms between her palms, and with a roar, she brings her hands down. The magic bursts from her hands like shards of black glass, impaling anyone near her. Huntsmen, guards, humans, and vampires go down like dominos, spreading out before her.

She cackles maniacally, watching the destruction, relishing that she's the cause of it.

Then it hits me, like an arrow through the chest. We are fighting an enemy who fights without a choice to. The huntsmen...the guards...they've all been bespelled by her. Without her influence, they might not choose to fight alongside her. The evil queen has done to them what she's done to us all—taken away our freedom, our choice, our ability to think for ourselves. This war was never between her followers and my people. It's only ever been between two people—her and me.

"My queen, don't do anything rash," Strix pleads beside me.

"It's not rash if it's right. I can't allow this to continue. I

469

can't let innocent people die for a fight that was never really theirs to begin with. This is my fight. My battle. No one else's. It's time I ended what started so long ago."

The kings call after me, but I ignore their appeals. I feel their sins wrapping around me like a blanket, each one possessive, as if their hard bodies were pressed against mine.

Thorin's wrath fills me with anger, Ramsey's envy makes me desperate to take what belongs to the evil queen. Marcel's greed creates a craving for more. More people. More power, more of everything. Lucian's lust ignites my insides, turning my blood molten, ready to burn anyone who dares to spill it. Killian's gluttony causes a ravenous hunger to gnaw inside me. Dante's sloth encourages my patience to let her come to me. But it's Strix's pride that throws me over the edge, swelling within my chest, making me feel all powerful as if nothing can stop me. Nothing and no one.

Fuck this.

"Cease fighting!" I order, my voice carrying on the violent winds.

"Huntsmen, guards, retreat!" the evil queen counters, withdrawing her forces as she dismounts from her horse. Our armies withdraw, leaving a bloody battlefield in their wake. I step over mutilated corpses, beheaded vampires, impaled humans, slaughtered wolves, dogs, and horses.

I can't allow myself to feel sorrow for their deaths.

There will be a time to mourn, a time to grieve, but right now, it's my time to regain control of my life.

The evil cunt bitch prowls toward me as if she hasn't a care in the world. Her face is passive as she considers me. "Hello, beast," she growls, her hands perched on her hips. "Tell me, how does it feel to be the kings' whore? How many monsters did you have to spread your legs for? How many of them did you have to fuck to fool them into believing that you're worthy of a crown?"

"All seven of them," I declare proudly. "I fucked every single one, felt their cocks as they came inside me. They ravaged my body and drank my blood as I consumed theirs, sharing in their power, becoming their sin."

She smiles, looking demented, ruthless, and psychotic. "The seven sins of Snow. How fucking poetic."

I growl, "You can take poetic and shove it up your ass, bitch."

Her smile falters, but she recovers quickly, holding out her hands, palms up. "I've waited too long for this, beast. Since the day you were born, the day I poisoned your stupid bitch of a mother, I've tried to kill you. You were immune to the toxic contaminants I laced in your meals. You healed from your sessions with the duke when each one should have killed you. And for years I couldn't figure out why. Why were you so fucking special? Why did the fates seek to keep you alive when the world would be so much better off if you were dead?"

As she brings her hands together, another swirling black ball of dark magic appears, this one just for me. "And then I realized it was because your heart was too pure, my dark magic couldn't destroy it, poisons couldn't drown it. But things have changed now, beast. You are no longer the pure soul you once were. You have sinned. And now? You're mine!"

The evil queen casts her magic at me. Time slows to a crawl as I watch it hurl toward me. I see every crackle of darkness, every sizzle of magic, and I know exactly what I have to do.

Reaching up, I tear my armor from my torso, baring my chest, leaving nothing but a thin piece of leather between me and the pulsing ball of power. I toss my head back, extend my arms, and embrace her magic. My body jerks as it embeds into my chest, her power curling inside my belly, racing through my veins, and making my nipples tingle. Her power melds with my own, changing, becoming something new, something not seen before.

I open my eyes and meet her gaze. She gasps, and I know she sees her death in my eyes. My body sizzles with power. Bolts of electricity race across my skin, leaping off me in colors of the sins. Red, orange, yellow, green, purple, and light and dark blue tendrils of magic crackle as it streaks up and down my limbs.

"How?" she cries out, her mouth dropping open in despair.

I smile, baring my fangs. "Because," I start, lifting my chin, holding my shoulders back, and puffing out my breasts, "not only have I sinned, but I've become sin itself. I am a vampire, the monster you have always feared, creatures of your own creation, formed from the blackest parts of your demented soul. We take the darkness from others, sucking the sins from their very being, and use it to feed ourselves, just as you forced us to do so long ago. In your madness, you've forgotten what we are, the very essence of the creatures you created. And now, because of your indifference, because you are blind to anything you do not wish to see, I've absorbed your magic and it surges inside me, nourishing me, making me more than you'll ever be."

"No!" she shrieks, her hands shaking as she covers her mouth, her knees buckling as she realizes her mistake.

"Yes," I croon, stalking closer to her. "It is over for you... you evil cunt bitch. Your reign of tyranny is at an end." I stand above her now, towering over her kneeling form as she trembles before me. "You cannot kill me now. You never could. You never will."

Sneering down at the thing I hate most in the entire world, the personification of pure evil, I look inside myself and reach for my new power. I feel it burning within me, buzzing in my veins, as it leaks out of every pore, every inch of skin. I feel it bursting from my eyes and expelling from my fingertips in a myriad of color, lighting up the dark night and growing in strength like the storm above me.

With one hand, I reach out, envisioning her neck within my clenched fingers, and I lift her from the ground. Her hands encircle her neck, scraping and clawing at her skin as she chokes, even though I'm not even touching her. I beckon her closer while her face turns red, until she dangles right in front of me. With my other hand, I reach back, curling my fingers around an emblazoned ball of my own power.

"You killed my parents, imprisoned me, tortured me," I growl, wrath leading the way. "You banished a new group of people to a life of darkness, you captured an entire town, starving its people while you wasted food and water. I feel nothing for you. You are a liar, a coward, a demon of the worst kind. I should torture you as you've done to me, keeping you alive only to bring you to the edge of death over and over again, giving you a taste of the brutality you've inflicted on others. But I'm nothing like you. So tonight, as I watch the light leave your eyes, I'll fulfill the promise I made to my people and bathe in your blood."

With a battle cry screaming from my lips, I thrust my hand forward. My magic explodes when it enters her chest, my hand disappearing inside her. I watch her eyes, eyes that used to instill me with fear, and observe with delight as hers now fill with terror. I smile, fangs descended, as I reach around her heart and pull it from her chest.

Her choked screams sound like music to my ears as I bring her heart to my lips and bite. I drink from her still beating muscle, taking her darkness, feeding myself with all that she is. With my fangs still latched onto her heart, our eyes locked in a stare from which neither of us can break, her body convulses uncontrollably, and I watch with pleasure as the life leaves her eyes.

My chest heaves as I toss her heart behind me and grip the queen's lifeless shoulders, raising her corpse above me with a strength I didn't know I had. I howl, my voice growing hoarse with my cries, and rip her completely in half. Blood bursts from her torn body, showering me in the hot, crimson liquid. I rub it into my skin from my neck to my chest and down my belly.

And then I dance.

I fucking dance in the rain of her blood, bathing in it, smearing it all over my body.

I celebrate her death as thunder booms overhead and lightning races across the sky, as gleeful tears pour down my cheeks with the knowledge that this is finally over.

I look up to the skies as the clouds part, the light of the moon beaming down on me for the first time since my father's death. I'm overcome with emotion and scream to the skies, "I did it, Mother! I did it, Father! The queen is dead!" Then I collapse to my knees as I'm assaulted by overwhelming feelings of happiness, relief, anger, and sorrow. With my head in my hands I sob. I cry for my victory. I cry for the many times she tortured me. I cry for my murdered parents, for the many years of my life I can never get back. I cry for the people of Riverwood, for the vampires in the coven. I cry because it's over. I cry because it happened.

As my screams and sobs rack my body, I feel them come for me.

The seven.

My kings.

The very reason this has come to an end.

They surround me with their bodies, lending me support and comfort. They shower me with praises, telling me how proud they are, how incredible I was, how I saved the world from evil.

It's all too much.

In the safety of their arms, the security of their hard bodies, I succumb to exhaustion and allow myself to fall into the welcoming embrace of darkness. But just before my exerted body renders itself into unconsciousness, I hear the kings shout, "All hail Queen Snow. Forever may she reign!"

The resounding cheers and shouts of, "All hail!" calm my soul, and for the first time ever, my heart smiles.

CHAPTER 47

Two weeks later....

$\mathcal{I}$n the days following the death of the evil queen, many fantastic events have occurred. The first being the discovery of my blood being an elixir of sorts, enabling vampires who drink it to become daywalkers. This find gives our coven an entirely new way of existing. Vampires who have not seen the light of day for a century or longer are all suddenly able to watch the sun rise over the horizon and feel its warm rays caressing their skin.

The shift in the mood is unmeasurable.

And speaking of the sun...

I was told the morning after the war had been won, the most beautiful sunrise painted itself across the sky. Of course, I slept for the better part of the next four days, but I'll take their word for it.

Riverwood is rebuilding, my once stolen castle now back under its rightful owner. The seven have helped me restore it to its former glory. The vacant hearths now roar with fires, and the desolate hallways are now filled with people. I've offered accommodations in the castle to any citizen in River-wood who wanted it. Many have taken me up on my offer, including one of my favorite people—Marie.

We sit for hours and talk over tea and cookies. She's taught me how to bake and crochet. She's become family to me, the mother I never got to meet, and I'm so grateful for the time we spend together.

A week ago, something unbelievable happened. I was sitting with the seven—well, I was fucking the seven in Killian's bed, or rather, they were fucking me—when the walls around us began to tremble, pictures falling onto the floor.

We jumped out of bed, naked as the day we were born, and raced out of the shuddering castle. Once outside the doors, our jaws about fell to the ground. The cave once keeping us hidden in the dark had collapsed, and beams of sunlight lit up the castles for the first time. My kings were the only vampires who didn't instantly start to burn. That's when we realized there must be something in my blood that allows them to become what the seven call daywalkers.

It became imperative that every member of my coven consume my blood. We have a schedule now, allowing ten members a day to enjoy the gift I can give them. Marcel has told me that in a few months' time, I will have bestowed daywalking abilities to every member.

Thorin about lost his shit at the thought of everyone drinking my blood, but after we assured him it would be drunk via a glass, just like when Marcel created the drones, he calmed down. But he insists on standing guard during every handing out of my blood in case the vampires get out of line. His possessiveness warms me, and I encourage him to stay.

While we're on the subject of drinking... I have forbidden my kings to consume blood from anyone other than myself or one of the seven. No more fucking donors. Most of them are quite agreeable to this. Marcel, in particular, loves donating to the other kings, and if I'm being honest, I love watching it.

Katie got her wish. Shortly after our coven emerged into the sun, we gave Julian permission to turn her. It was fascinating to watch. Just like me, she was drained of her blood, buried in a coffin, and had to fight her way out. She's doing well, adjusting to the persistent hankering for blood, but I know Julian keeps my friend well fed. We still find time to enjoy each other's company. Her favorite activity is to sip blood from fancy crystal goblets while exchanging sex stories.

Sherry and Enid were rescued from the dungeons I used to frequent. They have since recovered with generous donations of vampire blood from all of my kings and me. Enid is being courted by a rather handsome, reformed huntsman. She eats the attention up with a spoon. Sherry has decided to join the coven, and will begin her transformation as a sloth vampire in the next few days, purely because she wants to have glamour.

Speaking of glamour... Dante no longer uses his, allowing everyone to see him in all his glory. It's actually kinda funny, because the poor guy has a gaggle of women following him wherever he goes, giggling when he looks at them. He told me that Dani—the girl who fainted when I pretended to be him—has become his most loyal follower, and asks him all the time if she can clean his fangs for him. He hasn't figured out if she's just into teeth or if she's a kinky shit. Only time will tell.

Marcel does as only Marcel can, sticking his nose into everyone's business. He must always be the giver and the receiver, the one who knows all, and the one who needs to be told more secrets. We joke that he runs around like a chicken with its head cut off, not knowing where the action might be, so he tries to be everywhere at once.

Killian, true to his sin, has stayed as gluttonous as possible. The vampire has brought even more furnishings and art into his castle, and extended his already massive bed to accommodate all eight of us. We sleep in his room quite often, as no one really wants to allow just one of the kings to keep me for an entire night.

Strix's favorite pastime is dressing up in his finest attire and meandering around the castles with me on his arm. Every time we go on one of these walks, he hand selects my outfit and matching jewelry, and has Katie come do my hair and makeup. I no longer suffer through Renee's snide remarks. After becoming queen, I forced her to go on a date with Jovie. Of course Cerino wouldn't be left out, and the trio have been inseparable ever since.

Lucian makes love to me almost every day, at least once. Sometimes more often. Our desire for each other is insatiable, and I'd have it no other way. He's made a game of our sessions, finding new ways to torture me, new ways to make me come. Sometimes we strip down and masturbate while watching each other, seeing who can come first. Winner gets to sink their fangs into the loser first. I win a lot and sometimes I lose on purpose.

Thorin continues to drive me wild with his dominating presence. He's bound my body in more ways than I can count, spanked me, whipped me, and made me bleed. Each time I think I can't handle another second, I come so hard that I become euphoric, losing hours of time. Marcel joins us often, sometimes wielding the whip, and other times he is the receiver, occasionally both. Greedy little fuck.

Ramsey is a broody vampire. He tries to brush it off, but

his jealousy has been through the roof since I awoke. He's always trying to get me to himself, his crimson hair giving him away as he lurks in corners, watching me, waiting for his time. The King of Envy takes from me often, filling me with his cum. I think he likes his scent on me. If that calms his jealousy, then I'm all for it.

After killing the evil cunt bitch, many of those under her spell were released from its grasp. Everyone influenced by her magic has no recollection of the time they lost. Some have forfeited years to her, decades of their lives gone forever. It's quite tragic. We've offered them homes in the castle, in the town, or in the coven. Most have stayed, but some have left, wanting to start a new life in another city.

At Thorin's request, those who were not immediately released from her spell, their yellow eyes still betraying their enslavement, are now held in the castle's cells. Unlike the dungeons, the cells have toilets, food, and water. We know eventually the spell will wear off and they will return to who they once were, and we want them healthy when that time comes.

A surprising amount of Riverwood citizens have taken up our offer to turn into vampires, our coven growing in number. From what Marcel tells me, we are one of the largest covens this side of the world. I hope to travel some-day, see other covens, and meet more of our kind.

Vincent has become an ambassador for the Coven of Sin, and has set out to meet with other covens to learn more about vampires from other parts of the world. I wish him well on his journey, although I will miss his company.

The seven and I have discussed the possibility of building a new castle, one created for all eight of us. But the reality is, most of us like to have our own spaces. And with our newly joined communities, there are better things we can be doing with our time and resources than building a ninth castle within the same lands, though Killian and Marcel strongly disagree.

Cupcake and I have bonded. Together, we enjoy long rides through the countryside. I still think he has a sixth sense about me, turning the way I wish in my mind without any guidance. He's a noble and loyal horse and I love spending time with him.

After everything I've been through, I realize that every day is a gift, one that I don't take for granted. I can breathe easier now, living a life without stress, without fear, my only worries being when I'll next get to drink or fuck.

I'd envisioned this so many times, fantasizing what freedom might feel like, but I never thought it would be this good, this happy. That I'd be surrounded by friends and have seven lovers.

Seven!

I still can't wrap my brain around that.

I have something you could wrap your mouth around, pet, Lucian purrs in my mind, as he pulls the strap of my dress down off my shoulder. I've not yet grown used to the fact that we can communicate without speech, and still prefer to vocalize my thoughts.

"Do you?" I jest.

"Me first," Ramsey interjects. "You know I taste the best anyway."

Marcel scoffs, "Better than caramel and chocolate? I don't think so."

"Who cares who goes first as long as we all get a piece of the queen?" Thorin grumbles. "You all keep acting like this and I'll tie her to a wall in my dungeon where you'll never find her."

"Oh, kinky!" Killian laughs. "I've always wanted to tie up our queen, spread her milky thighs apart, and lick her until she screams. Maybe I'll join you in this sex dungeon."

"The more the merrier," Dante rasps, as he takes my nipple into his mouth.

"You heard the queen," Strix growls. "She needs more. Let us give it to her."

They descend like rabid wolves. The rest of my clothes are torn from my body as the kings strip, revealing seven glorious, bobbing cocks, all vying for my attention.

Lying on my back, I relish the seven lips kissing me, seven tongues tasting me, and fourteen hands manipulating my body in ways I could never fathom. This is what it means to live.

As a soft tongue laps between my legs, and another climax brews inside me, I'm still baffled by my ignorance, never realizing how much I was missing. To think an orphan child, imprisoned her whole life, would grow up to mate with seven kings and become the ruler of their coven as well as my own people... I shake my head in wonder at the turn my life has taken.

As the kings bring me to the height of pleasure over and over again, I can't thank the fates enough for giving them to me. If I never saw another person again for the rest of my life, I'd still be satisfied with how my life turned out.

Just me and my seven sins.

THE END

DEAR READER

Hey there! I hope you loved Snow as much as I enjoyed writing it! Thanks so much for picking it up. It was quite an adventure writing it, Snow and her vampire kings consumed me. This book wrote itself during a very difficult time in my personal life and I think that showed in the story.

If you enjoyed this book, please consider leaving me a review! Reviews from readers is what keeps me going and encourages others to try the book for themselves.

Thank you so much again for going on this journey with me. If you like reverse harem books, I have many more for you to enjoy. Just keep scrolling to see them.

XOXOXOXO

Lox

ALSO BY LOXLEY SAVAGE

FEATHERS AND FIRE SERIES

- Bound for Blood
- Cursed to Crave

SINISTER FAIRY TALES

- Seven Sins of Snow

THE FORSAKEN SERIES: CO-WRITTEN WITH K.A KNIGHT

- Capturing Carmen
- Stealing Shiloh
- Harboring Harlow

AFTERWORLD ACADEMY: CO-WRITTEN WITH KATIE MAY

- Dearly Departed

WICKED WAVES: CO-WRITTEN WITH ERIN O'KANE

- Twisted Tides
- Tides That Bind

ABOUT THE AUTHOR

Loxley Savage is from a suburb in northeast Ohio. She loves Harry Potter, games, and dark roast coffee. When she's not chasing after her three, gorgeous daughters, or spanking her naughty husband, she's writing down the stories in her mind as fast as her fingers will fly.

Follow her here...
    Facebook Page
    Facebook group - The Inferno
    Instagram
    Bookbub
    Amazon